Babylon Babies

SEMIOTEXT(E) NATIVE AGENTS SERIES

This work is published with support from the French Ministry of Culture / Centre national du livre.

Ouvrage publié avec le concours du Ministère français chargé de la culture - Centre national du livre.

Published by Semiotext(e)
501 Philosophy Hall, Columbia University, New York, NY 10027
2571 W. Fifth Street, Los Angeles, CA 90057
www.semiotexte.com

Special thanks to Giancarlo Ambrosino, Eric Arlix, Justin Cavin, Robert Dewhurst, Patricia Ferrell, Paul Grimstad, Andrew Lutsky, Filip Marinovic, Andrew Lutsky and Goody-B. Wiseman.

Cover Photo © David Ashley / Hoa-qui / Zefa
Backcover Photo: G. Simoneau / Septembre 2004 © Edition Flammarion
Design by Hedi El Kholti

ISBN: 1584350237
Distributed by The MIT Press, Cambridge, Mass. and London, England
Printed in the United States of America

Babylon Babies

Maurice G. Dantec

Translated by Noura Wedell

<e>

Shout outs:

To Jeremy Narby, for his studies on DNA and shamanic rites (see *The Cosmic Serpent*, New York: Tarcher/Putnam, 1998), to Mary Barnes and Doctor Joseph Berke, for *Mary Barnes: two accounts of a journey through madness* (New York, Harcourt Brace Jovanovich, 1972), to Richard Pinhas, to Gilles Deleuze, to Norman Spinrad and the Heldon group for the Schizosphere Experience, thank you to Pain Teens, Prodigy, Portishead, Björk, Death in Vegas, Headrillaz, Crustation, Primal Scream, NIN, Fluke, Aphex Twin, Massive Attack, Garbage, Fœtus and PJ Harvey, thank you as well to NOII Kmar, Thierry, Spagg and the rest, thank you to Spicy Box, thank you to Nirvanet—Marie France, Christian and Shanti—, thank you to François D., to Martine V., to Myriam, Jacques and Tristan—they know why—, thank you to Lucio for "B-Paradise", thank you to Yannick B, thank you to Antonin, Flo, Mike, Julie, DJ Endless and the residents of 10 Ontario Building, thank you to Donna Haraway for *The Cyborg Manifesto* and to the Cyborg Handbook team, Routledge (NY), thank you to Salomon Resnik for his studies on "psychotic experience," to the team of Doctor Ian Wilmut, to Dolly, to the Princeton Experiment Advanced Laboratory for man-machine quantum interactions, thank you to Perpendiculaires, thank you to Série Noire, thank you to Philip K. Dick, thank you to the Raynal Family, thank you to Michel Goldman for his precious advice, thank you to Thierry B., thank you to Christian M., thank you to Eric L., thank you to the girls: Suzanne R., Adriana, Patricia, thank you to my sister Monique, thank you to Sylvie, thank you to Eva, thank you to Montreal and the whole gang.

To Eva,
to my father, my mother
and the children of the future.

The apparition of consciousness in the animal realm might be just as much a mystery as the origin of life itself. However, one must suppose, although it poses an impenetrable problem, that we find there an effect of evolution, a product of natural selection.

— KARL POPPER

This world is not conclusion.
A species stands beyond—
Invisible, as Music—
But positive, as Sound—

— EMILY DICKINSON

Part 1

He Who Searches and Destroys

And, just as water does not have a stable form, in war, there are no permanent conditions.

— SUN TZU

1

So living was an incredible experience, where the most beautiful day of your entire existence could be your last, where sleeping with death guaranteed seeing the next morning, and where a few golden rules were constant. Never walk in the direction of the wind, never turn your back to a window, never sleep in the same place twice, always stay in the sun's axis, trust in nothing and no one, suspend your breath with the perfection of the living dead on the point of freeing the metal's salvation. Occasionally, a few variables could slip in, the sun's position in the sky, the weather, who you were dealing with.

From where he was crouching at the top of the embankment along the path, Toorop towered over his victim. In the west, the sun was lowering onto the horizon, lacquering the ochre earth of the SinKiang Northern Highlands a volcanic yellow orange. The air was dry, still vibrating with the day's accumulated heat. It had an unreal purity. It was perfect weather for killing.

A cool wind blew in from the east, from the low grounds, the great Taklamakan Desert. The word in Uygur meant, "the place you enter, but from which you do not depart." The air, which was torrid in the plains, at this 2000-meter altitude was as sharp as a bayonet sheath. Once the sun had set behind the eternal snow capped peaks, the air would freeze faster than you could breathe in or release your last breath.

The man was lying on his back. One arm, stretched perpendicular, had been stranded on a little thistle bush. The other was folded beneath him. The man was still alive. It wasn't his lucky day. Each breath produced a reflex shudder of muscles. An exhausted groan intermittently escaped his blood filled mouth. Toorop was giving him a grace period of a few minutes, at most. Minutes that would seem like hours. The 12.7 mm bullet had entered the biological structure diagonally, near the liver. Toorop knew, however, that it could have come to rest in the cerebellum, in the femoral artery, or in an even more sensitive organ.

The young guy's face, like a chemical test, revealed the surprise of a life viciously sliced by a crazy projectile turning back upon itself on impact, before zigzagging in all directions inside the body. This type of ammunition diffuses its energy with such intensity that, in addition to physiological trauma, the shock wave it puts in motion provokes serious nerve damage. A beautiful Manchu face, not more than twenty; the watery eyes endlessly pondering the fragility of existence faced with the metal of pain.

Toorop remembered the *I-Ching* aphorism to which the fourteenth of the *Thirty-Six Stratagems* referred. "It is not I who seek the young fool; the young fool seeks me." The 14th stratagem was curiously entitled "Raise a corpse from the dead," and went like this:

He does not let himself be used who can still act for his own purposes.
He will plead to be used who can do nothing more.
One must use the useless for one's own ends.

In such circumstances, this sermon was no more obscure than another. The agonizing man had served his ends well. Climbing down the embankment, Toorop knew what had to be done.

Three young buzzards had just alighted, croaking, next to the body. Not paying it the slightest attention, they started furrowing into the olive green jacket, boring through the cloth with a single honed stroke, to recover a piece of bloodied meat they'd gulp down with a jerky head gesture. Toorop had a clear vision of the condemned man's ultimate reflex movement, trying to delay his end. The carcass shuddered; a trembling hand attempted in vain to raise itself from the earth and scribbled upon it an illegible message. For an instant, Toorop considered the natural process occurring. His gaze didn't even try to avoid the bloody rosette constellating the soldier's abdomen where the birds were working, or, on the orange-yellow earth around him, the black puddle with crimson contours that the rocky moor drank up avidly.

As he approached, one of the buzzards, flapping his wings, let out a dissatisfied croak and straightened into a posture of aggressive ostentation. The two others continued to feast on the man's stomach, impassively wading in a carpet of blood, spongy tissue, and intestine parts.

A smell of guts and shit tickled his nostrils at the whim of the wind's breath. The dead or dying man's perfume left his mouth with a residue like the after taste of rank beer. Toorop had just extracted the "Schiskov" from the holster on his back. It was an Aurora, a polyvalent weapon equipped to deal with any kind of urgent situation, and quite simply the world's best assault rifle. Toorop cocked the breech with a sharp movement, aimed, and shot a bullet smack into the soldier's head.

The gunshot vibrated for a long time in the natural echo chamber of the high mountains. Toorop heard the man's sigh in it, finally delivered from this world of flesh and steel, finally freed from life, and from the three buzzards.

As the birds of prey fired off toward the raw dusk sky, wings bloodied, and the shot's echo resonated in the immense space before him, Toorop thought a passage from Rumi, or a verse from *Dead Man Walking*, was in order. But he felt a sweet vibration running along his thigh, cutting short his flow of thoughts. His hand plunged into the pocket of his battle-dress and emerged armed with a small Motorola GPS cell phone. The LCD screen flashed a message from General Command, informing him of the presence of Chinese drones in the sector. It was alphanumeric, encrypted by a special CIA program that those PLA number crunching shit faces could keep trying to decode. Even their highly parallel processing Fujitsus developed with Yakuza funds in Sichuan underground factories couldn't touch it. According to the Russian dealers who supplied the program, it was impenetrable. The sum of the planet's computer resources, even with fifty years of uninterrupted work, couldn't crack it. Four-eyes with the British accent, in charge of the demo for the Uygur guerillas, wanly appreciating with a nod of the head, called it Transfinite Re-encoding with Chaotic Modelization. For the Uygurs, it simply meant Allah didn't want the PLA to decode their communications. That was the least He could do.

Toorop turned to the west, where the sky combined azure flashes with milky, napalm hued machines. He knelt down beside the body and started the looting. A local make automatic, an exact replica of a 1911 model Colt. With two full chargers to boot. A French make grenade. In the jacket pocket, he scored a pack of Kools made in Peking. He hated Kools but he could exchange them for Russian Marlboros or Indian Camels.

He flipped the body over with his foot, rolling it along the rocky ground. The AK-47 was strapped across its back, the butt facing up. Intact within was a brand new 30-bullet magazine, fresh out of the assembly lines of the Ministry of Military Planning. Toorop retrieved the booty with an experienced hand. It was the law of the mountain. The transparent secret of nature. The hunting code. The ritual exchange of life and death fetishized through trophy. All that shit, just a habit. That went back to the origins of the world.

With an assured gesture, Toorop lifted the sleeves of the mountain jacket; the GPS biobeeper made a slight, black carbon swell, running just under the skin near the left wrist, above a very pretty gold watch. Copied from US Army technology, the main function of the biobeeper was to send out a digital radio signal on a regular basis indicating the position and metabolic state of its wearer. For now, a small red diode pulsed there in silence, as if saying its wearer wasn't at his best, and that he'd stay at this position for awhile.

With the tip of his knife, Toorop pierced the epidermis, disembedded the small component, threw it into the ravine, and the gold watch into the bottom of a pocket.

He turned the body over again and finished the search by reaching for its magnetic ID tag and a few crumpled bills in different local currencies. The military tag was just to give the PLA bureaucrats some work. The clams would be for later, for Almaty slut dives, a few new-look Es from Kazakh dealers, possibly a Russian version Taiwanese flick shown in a Soviet period movie theater, its heavy constructivism and patched up seats having witnessed the parade of asses of all the generations since Khrushchev. At least.

Toorop emerged from his reverie and walked over to the Kirghiz horse, a beautiful gray mare mottled with black, which he mounted without resistance. His own had succumbed to a bad fall three days earlier. This mare was the pure bounty of Allah, as the Uygurs would have said. She was both robust and slightly wild, young and experienced, a real mountaineer ride. He caressed her muzzle, took her by the reins, climbed onto the PLA regulation saddle, its brass buckles stamped with the red star, and moved down the path towards the body. He gave it a last look, hung the Barrett on the saddle, placed his Aurora in his back holster, slung the Chinese AK-47 across his chest, and with a yap and a kick in the ribs, led the animal towards the sunny bluff, turning his back to the white heights of the Turugart Shankou.

The hoof sounds on the rocks covered the croaking of the buzzards circling over the body behind him. Later, at the bottom of the pass, a sharp gust of cold wind made him realize that the sun had just disappeared behind the mountains. A slate-blue shadow swooped down onto the lunar gray stones. The sky was turning an abyssal violet. The first stars were visible. A crescent moon appeared between two snowy summits, great ashy mounds caught in a shaft of black light and lacquered in mercury. The lunar orb would reach its zenith in the heart of night.

It was breathtakingly beautiful.

Kill two men a week, at least. Live on the prowl, levying arms, munitions, food, drugs, cash money—or plastic, clothes, horses. Endlessly hound enemy communications to predict border-patrol movements. Be constantly on the move, by night. Avoid search and destroy drones. Sometimes wait for days on end before you see a silhouette appear in the viewfinder. Try to have some kind of silent dialogue with the prey before you pull the trigger, and again merge into the dark, melt into it, sleep a bit, wait for a new morning, a new man to kill.

This was his life now, and Toorop had no complaints. As he remarked long ago to a war correspondent in search of "picturesque characters," someone had to do it. A handful of men had to fight for lost causes in the world's last frontiers, and sometimes for much worse. The wheel of history had to go on crushing lives if the rest of the world wanted to continue feeding on their TV screens.

At the time, the girl from the BBC hadn't answered. Her Digital Video Camera locked onto him like the globular black eye of a vampire machine. Toorop knew instinctively that she thought he was crazy and, he wondered how she'd seen through him so fast. Only a freak would spend his time in the steppes and mountains of Central Asia with two or three Chinese strategy books in his pocket, an arctic survival blanket from the Russian Army capable of weathering temperatures lower than -50 degrees centigrade, a US Air Force First Aid Kit complete with emergency supplies, and whole boxes of new-age methamphetamines in all possible forms, each geared to a specific use. Epidermal patches, auto-injectable capsules, pills for sensory or motor activity reinforcement, anti-fatigue bracing, oxygenation, red blood cell count, memory tone, or information processing capacity. Better than a Tour de France cycling peloton, he'd said, smiling. The modern headhunter's pharmacy.

He didn't give the girl the complete list on the spot. He just muttered something like: "the science of war does not allow for error."

Journalists, especially Western ones, constantly had to be reminded of the basics.

Toorop always wondered why the gift had been revealed to him during the last months of the war in Bosnia and Croatia.

True, during the first part of the Bosnian conflict, the government army was incapable of coordinating its reaction to the joint assaults of the Yugoslav Army, and of the Karadzic, Arkan or Seselj militias. In its defense, during the first months of the war, the government army quite simply didn't exist. The state itself had just been created and recognized by the UN. That's why Bosnian combatants, during this period, formed a heteroclite cohort of bandits, adventurers, mercenaries, daredevils, and lost soldiers whose recruits had just traded in their electric guitars for AK-47s.

While participating in the summer of '95 offensive of a Bosnian Special Forces unit, he was swept up in a state of grace. It was neither religious or mystical exaltation, nor the natural cocaine that irrigates the brain when the excitement of danger is at its highest. No, it was just as if an old cantankerous equation that had been resisting for a while had just been beat. War was probably the *easiest* thing to do, but it was the most *difficult* to succeed in. Its only rule was that it had none, or rather, that each war invented its own in the creative chaos of violence; and that those who pronounce the rules win out in the end. In ex-Yugoslavia, as in all the devastated landscapes Toorop had since passed through, these rules were, for the most part, unknown to the belligerents themselves. Those who made them congregated in vast international conference halls and decided upon the outcome in lieu of the men dying on the ground. From now on, this was part of the new laws of war that each period takes along with it when it dies. Toorop thought he'd probably die with it.

At the beginning of August, waiting for the Dayton Accords back in Sarajevo, Toorop stayed in a suburb of the city just below Igman Mountain. For the entire war, Hrasnica had been the strategic bolt, the only umbilical cord tying the Capital of the Bosnian State to the small territory it controlled.

The first thing that hit Toorop when he got out of the big German Mercedes cab was the impression of deja-vu, coupled with an intense sensation of strangeness. It didn't take him long to figure out the chemical synthesis gripping his throat. Saying Hrasnica was like saying La Courneuve, or the names of any of those Parisian ghetto-suburbs that had inherited the same ideologues, and the same architectural concepts.

Strangely enough, the first details you noticed were the windows. They were all camouflaged by tire parts, and plastic sheeting was stretched in lieu of panes. The building surfaces presented the entire munitions catalogue available to the armies of the Warsaw Pact, or close. It leveled out from top to bottom, gnawing at the buildings like urban smallpox. Assault rifle and machine gun impacts on the lower floors. Anti-tank rockets, 30 mm anti-aircraft canons on the next ones. Heavy projectiles such as type 100 mortars, 120 caliber tank munitions, 122 type rockets or 150 type shells on the higher floors, and the roofs like stomachs open to the knife of a demented surgeon.

Toorop thought this image was somehow a good representation of XXIst century Europe. Its future was here, in a wasted pop-art compound, in urban modernism ravaged by the fire of weapons. It was Le Corbusier revisited by Stalin and his cronies.

Toorop had passed through a good bunch of destroyed cities since 1991, certainly. Most often, however, they were traditional Balkan small towns. From Dubrovnik to Vukovar, from Zenica to Donji Vakuf, he'd seen his fill of mosques and churches in ruins. During the autumn of '92, when he was fighting in Sarajevo itself, it was still an old historic city that was being bombarded. Same thing when he passed through Mostar, returning from the attack on Bihac. Here in Hrasnica, there were no museums, no historic bridges, no libraries to save, no symbols for his symbolic chest to protect for the symbol merchants. It could have been Ivry-sur-Seine, Montreuil, La Garenne-Colombes. Small shabby suburban houses, dilapidated malls, concrete columns. BHL hadn't slept there.

It was night, and already very cold. Winter comes fast in Sarajevo.

He found himself on a little deserted square strewn with all types of litter. Thousands of little yellow sparks, shiny cylindrical and 7.62 caliber, glowed like strange, generously dispersed nuggets. The streets, the gardens, the squares of the whole city were thus constellated with AK-47 shells; you walked on them as if on cinders, found them in stairways. It wasn't uncommon that one should lodge itself under your shoe, and end up accompanying you to your bedroom, to the foot of your bed.

Trucks were parked everywhere, and in any which way. Thirty-eight tonners like the German Mercedes that had dropped him off a while ago, freighted by a humanitarian organization. It's crazy how many good, charitable souls there are in this lowly world, attracted like shit flies to the fresh puddle of blood, Toorop thought to himself before the night's silent and still merry-go-round. By daybreak, it would start turning again, with a thousand 350 hp engines, butt-fucking each other in uninterrupted lines that filed out for kilometers to the UNPROFOR checkpoints that guarded the entrances to downtown.

There was a small vendor in a fold-up cart. The only spot of light around. A generator thundering on some cinder blocks set up a bit farther off produced the current. Electricity had returned to Sarajevo; but downtown and strategic zones had priority.

A group of three or four guys, ageless, dressed in a mix of civilian and military garb, were talking to the vendor as they ordered "pivos" and kebabs.

Toorop was hungry. He had twenty-one Deutsch marks and a handful of Croatian kunas. A fortune; he wouldn't have exchanged them for a truckload of Bosnian dinars.

He ordered a lamb sausage sandwich and the donkey piss that people around here called beer, and asked straight out about lodging. He had money for about a month. The vendor understood that he was foreign from his accent. He didn't flinch at the insignia of the 108th Brigade Toorop wore on his battle dress. The guy had been there and back.

The vendor raised his hand and said *"One minute, I'm back"* in rough English. He got out of his fold-up cart, asked Izmet, a dude wearing army camouflage and a blue and white humanitarian windbreaker, to keep shop. He disappeared into the night, towards a large, impact-ridden column that loomed obscure and silent behind the deserted mall a few meters away.

It didn't even take the vendor two minutes to return, accompanied by a slew of kids. One of them stood apart from the group, introduced himself as Kemal Hasanovic, with a room to rent in his family's apartment.

Toorop looked at the kid, twelve or thirteen, Sarayliya. You could negotiate with him, he was already an adult. Toorop got the room for five marks a month. The kid basically gave it away; his eyes lit up at the sight of the Special Forces insignia. Toorop told himself it would help out with the tummies, and that the kid had probably thought so too.

The Hasanovics were a typical Sarayliya family. Irina, the mother, was Serbian, born in Sarajevo. The father, a solid fellow with an impressive black mustache, was a Muslim from Zvornik. They lived on the seventh floor of the tower, in an apartment straight out of a 1950's advertisement, just a few details off: they removed their shoes in the entrance, and when Toorop passed the bathroom, he realized the sink and bathtub were filled to the brim with water.

Full jerry cans and plastic bottles were lined up in the hallway between the rooms and leading to the kitchen. Sarayliyas had a few hours of electricity at night, but they practically had no running water.

First thing, Kemal, even before taking off his humanitarian Adidas, pressed a switch to check if the electricity was back. Nothing. The apartment was bathed in darkness, except for a few candles in the living room. Sometimes the electricity was out during the early hours of the evening, especially in the suburbs, and especially when the historic downtown needed it: when Parisian intellectuals came to sleep at the Holiday Inn, or discuss modern theater.

Kemal introduced Toorop to his parents, and to a paternal sister-in-law. The young woman had been severely mistreated by the Chechen militia, and suffered from epilepsy. Toorop knew Bosnia and Croatia overflowed with warehouses stuffed to the brim with medicine. Enough to compete with the number of cafes per Frenchman. But he also knew everyone looked the other way when it came to trafficking and the black market—an aspirin tablet was worth more than a Kalachnikov cartridge.

He spent the first evening drinking Slibovic with the Hasanovic family. The father, like most men, served in the Bosnian Army. Every day, he'd go to his post near Igman Mountain, and at night, he'd come home. He left his AK-47 leaning against the wall at the entrance of the living room, like a simple umbrella. It was, in fact, a job like any other, thought Toorop. And jobs, in these parts, there were tons of them.

So, he hadn't hidden who he was, or what he'd done. They exchanged war stories downing the Slibo bottle. Toorop pronounced a few magic words: Brcko, Kupres, Donji Vakuf, Jajce, Bihac. The Hasanovics gave him free room and board, but Toorop gently refused. He offered to pay three marks for the month, and they celebrated the deal with a second Slibo bottle opened on the spot. Toorop caught a last image as he collapsed on his bed: the slit tires obstructing the windows, and the familiar silhouette of an AK-47 leaning against the wall, trembling like a mirage.

He spent the next two or three days wandering the city. But very rapidly, something clicked in his tormented brain.

He wanted to see the military maps. He wanted to understand the invisible strategic mechanisms at work while he'd been under fire.

With the help of a few editor buddies from the *Lilian*, the Bosnian armed forces newspaper, he managed to get a complete set of maps together that illustrated the weekly evolution of the different front lines. Then he spent days and nights on end, in his room, on the seventh floor of the tower, reading and rereading the maps. He soaked up the moving graphs, the sudden fluctuations, the stalls, the breaches, like the combat of extremely complex biological entities. It was a sort of abstract comic strip he was desperately trying to link to the experience he'd lived through.

He dreamt of these maps when he finally crashed, his heavy and feverish slumber laced with local hash. They were superimposed on the recurrent images of the war he'd known, terrifying and frighteningly violent syntheses. But sometimes, he'd come upon them at the heart of a banal dream, laying on a flying nightstand of pink sugar, or in the midst of an aquatic and silent world, tattooed in the mouth of a giant fish that was swallowing him.

In November, the Dayton Accords were signed. Sarajevo entered a strange psychological smog. When Toorop received his official demobilization notice, he held the sheet of paper between his fingers for a long time, as if it were a message informing him the dream was over. The Serbs from the Ilidza suburbs and from elsewhere were invited to get the fuck out. The UNPROFOR evacuated, and was replaced by a NATO unit. Toorop told himself it was really the logical summary of this war, from the European viewpoint. First they send peacekeeping forces, while the war is raging. And once the peace treaty is signed, they send in troops from the North Atlantic Military Treaty. It made him want to puke so bad that one night, drunk enough and fucked up on Kemal's dope, he took it out on two fools from the UNPROFOR. They were leaving the city, toasting it in a place near the famous Market Square, breaking open champagne and flooding the bar with wads of Deutschmarks fresh out of the Buba.

In Toorop's head, a strange equation had started to factorize. On average, a head-sergeant at the UNPROFOR made around 25,000 francs a month, and the basic army Joe made the salary of an executive. For the superior officers, it added up to a nice little package. In the Bosnian Army, the basic asshole made one mark a month. Same thing for second classmen and subaltern officers in international outfits. So, in thirty-four months of service, Toorop made about that much. Around twelve hundred francs. It was only thanks to a war correspondent for *Libération* in Mostar that he reached the capital with twenty-one marks, his monthly mark, plus twenty he'd gotten off him in exchange for a few authentic anecdotes.

The two guys belonged to a Supply Corps of the French Army. Toorop recognized their insignias, but hearing them, they'd routed out the Serbs surrounding Sarajevo by themselves. They were complacently hitting on a group of young chicks belonging to some humanitarian organization: Harmony International, Doctors of the Rich World, Artists-Jack-Off-for-Sarajevo, who knows.

After a while, it started to get on his nerves. He turned around on his stool and glared at the group.

"Hey warriors."

The two guys stopped short in the middle of their heroic story and stared at him, vaguely intrigued.

"UNPROFOR?" he asked.

The guys stared him down, trying to understand the Bosnian inscriptions on his insignia. Fucking jack-offs, thought Toorop. He quickly deciphered their appointment. Corps of Engineers. Administrative services. The guys shuffled papers in an office. They weren't even the "peacekeepers" holding a white stick to direct traffic under Serbian sniper fire.

One of the guys tried to pull off the professional warrior type.

"Yeah, we're from the 2nd Rima ."

Toorop widened his smile.

"No kidding," he said, extending his hand. "108th Bosnian Brigade."

The guys froze, but one of them stupidly held out a hand in return. Toorop grabbed it and blurted out:

"Hey Fuckface and Douchebag… I'm sure you guys are fucking pussies."

And he pulled the hand violently towards him, unsettling the guy from his stool while his knee came up ferociously to meet his nuts and his skull projected forward as if to send the ball flying to the back of the net.

After that, his memories were confused. He'd done *them*. But other guys from their unit having a drink in the back of the room, or who came in at that moment, he didn't quite remember. In short, some other French Blue Helmets joined in, before the Bosnian and the French Military Police charged. He woke up in a cell at the local police station. His head was the size of a watermelon, but he knew he'd gotten those two white-collar losers from Engineering, and at least one of the young assholes trying to play Rambo. OK, then it got complicated with the other four.

Thanks to his friends in the 1st Corps, Toorop was let out after the first night, the time it took to patch things up amiably with the unit bosses of the UNPROFOR. Early in the morning, three guys from the Bosnian Army came to get him. They had the certificates in order and the killer faces that silenced in advance any possible question from the local cops. The whole thing had been buried; the UNPROFOR unit was leaving Sarajevo in the coming days. Toorop moved back to Hrasnica.

The next day, when he woke up, it was beautiful out and very cold, and he had a hard-on.

He did a quick calculation and realized, dumbfounded, that he hadn't fucked in almost two years.

Half-heartedly, he unhinged his hand already soldered to the rigid member.

He got up, washed summarily in the bathroom, took care of the different contusions marking his face, his forearms, his back. He contemplated his face for a long time, and concluded he really didn't have anything of the sweetheart in him. The black eye on the left wasn't huge, but a violet bruise covered the cheek on that side, and a slash from a broken bottle zigzagged across the top of his shaved head. A few cuts streaked the other side of his face along with the bayonet scar he'd gotten in one of his only hand-to-hand combats—around Brcko, when their squad attacked a machine gun post. The scar was short. The guy died before finishing his gesture, but still, the blade had run from the right temple to the top of the jaw.

At best, it could pass for the result of an encounter with a tactless windshield; at worst, for the scar left by a disgusting skin disease with an exotic name. He couldn't expect to score with the local Claudia Schiffers in the improbable case that Serbian mercenaries and French writers had left a few in their wake.

Toorop bought a small batch of Italian and Croatian porn magazines. It did the job for a few days, long enough to find another war.

When he found himself in Grozny, early December '95, at the start of the Russian offensive, everything had been adding up real fast. In mid-November, rumors had started in Sarajevo. Dissolved Islamic units were enlisting in Chechnya. Some international volunteers had followed. A network of mercenaries was established. Post-Soviet Azeri and Chechen officers. Turkish Intelligence agents. With numerous contacts at their disposal in the Bosnian capital.

Toorop put off his decision till the day after the American elections. But it had nothing to do with it. On that day, he had five deutschmarks left. One of them went to pay off what was left of the rent, and the others to stock up on basic necessities from the black market: a half-cartridge of Croatian Wolfs, a handful of humanitarian Mars bars sold on cardboard displays in the street, and a stick of hash that he negotiated from the fourteen-year-old dealers that Kemal knew, in exchange for the Bosnian Special Forces insignia. He rapidly said his goodbyes to the Hasanovic family, and went towards downtown Sarajevo. He walked up a long column of thirty-eight tonners stopped at a checkpoint. He knew exactly who to see to get a one-way ticket to Grozny.

The cards were clamoring for their share of blood and truth.

And he didn't even have a measly couple of Bosnian dinars hiding at the bottom of his pocket.

Toorop had been walking for two days without the slightest rest, except for a short twenty minutes every four or five hours to take a piss, recharge his batteries with a disgusting *made in* Russia ration of K, and a gulp of cold tea to accompany the speed tablet. The Kirghiz nag was overloaded with all his equipment and the loot from a good month of hunting in the mountains on the border. He'd wanted to do the last bit of road the tough way: as a true foot soldier, so as not to exhaust the animal and risk a broken leg, like had happened with its unfortunate predecessor. Fatigue was starting to produce the typical effects of drowsiness, those micro-slumbers that lasted a few fractions of a second, more and more often, longer and longer. He dug into a pocket to find the small leather satchel stuffed with a local coca leaf Uygur mountaineers chew to confront the kilometers at high altitude.

For a long time, he masticated the bitter paste forming in his mouth. Its active ingredient soon had him soaring. His legs got their rhythm back, his boots formed a hypnotic, black leather and dark gray Gore-Tex ballet in constant back and forth, a strange tight groove, the stone path like a drum splattered with white light.

He walked the entire day, in one go. Then stopped with the sun, like a heliotropic animal.

When he woke up at dawn, after a couple hours of sleep programmed to the second by a special patch set in the bend of the elbow, it was splendid weather. A blue sky of terrifying purity. The sun wasn't very high, but its unbearable yellow light already scorched the moor.

He took to the road serenely.

Before him rose the snow-capped heights of the Fergansky Mountains he was just starting to scale. Farther down, behind him, in the valley below, he could still discern the long line of a Kirghiz Army patrol. The sixty men of the company spread out in a column a good kilometer long. As Guevara reminds us in *The Bolivian Diary*, a group of foot soldiers only goes as fast as its slowest element.

A bitch of a Kirghiz donkey refused to move, rearing against the rope pulled by two soldiers. Toorop saw a group of men come to the rescue, and hang onto the leash that stretched to the point of breaking. But the old ass wouldn't hear a thing. Toorop started walking again. To each his own.

He was within a two days march of the camp. He'd soon meet the patrols guarding access to it.

He brought the flask to his lips.

He swallowed a long gulp of lukewarm tea to wash away the bitter residue stuck to his teeth and palate. His body moved on its own, a sweat covered robot, drunk with exhaustion.

He felt good.

2

Night was the best time to kill. The Schmidt & Bender viewfinder was equipped with an unsurpassed hi-definition photonic amplifier. The latest Barrett cannon had a muzzle brake with a silencer that concealed both the flash of the firing as well as the noise it made. It was the US Army sniper weapon. A fearsome weapon, rustic and sophisticated, a weapon worth its price. He had to negotiate for weeks before the Uygur guerilla he fought for decided to order a few. The war trophies he'd been bringing back to Prince "Shabazz" Ali Valikhan's general headquarters provided the most edifying of demonstrations.

Night was also the best time to read. When sleep was useless or, for multiple reasons, impossible, Toorop took advantage to feed his brain its favorite dish. Of course, even on the borders of war torn Western China, one could come across some *Playboy* or *Reader's Digest* issues. But Toorop had better to chew on. Sun Tzu's *Art of War*, *The Thirty-Six Stratagems*, *The Bolivian Diary of Ernesto Che Guevara*, *Seven Pillars of Wisdom: A Triumph*, by T.E. Lawrence, and *Battle for Gaul*, by Julius Caesar were the essential elements of his library, along with *The Gay Science* and *Dithyrambs of Dionysus* by Nietzsche, plus a collection of Persian poetry. Reading allows a confrontation between new experiences and ancient knowledge. Toorop knew better than anyone how useless it was to reinvent warm water, most of all during a war, faced with technically superior enemies in higher numbers.

So, after the Chinese victory at Urumqi, Toorop convinced Prince Shabazz to rage a war in accordance to his means, and to those of his adversary. A war of erosion. Never look for the fatal blow, but create a constant hemorrhage, without endangering the bulk of the troops. Dispatch small units along the entire length of the borders between Kyrgyzstan, Kazakhstan and the People's Republic of China, and special force commandoes living self-sufficiently deeply embedded behind enemy lines. Even better, Toorop had convinced the young son of an Uzbek tycoon and Uygur princess, fluent in a few languages and Harvard educated, to read, and most importantly, to have his men read a certain number of books that any professional soldier owes to himself to have read. The officers' tactical command, the subaltern officers' behavior, even that of simple soldiers, improved substantially during this period. The survival rate of the units rose considerably. Average destruction and enemy losses followed suit. Toorop had felt an irrepressible surge of pride.

So much so that one day he took it up directly with Prince Shabazz. He was returning from Almaty, where a secret conference of the National Uygur Movement had taken place. The recent successful campaigns by his Eastern Turkistan Liberation Forces had strengthened his positions within the conference. On the other hand, rumor had it that the local border patrol division was being changed, and replaced by a combat unit from Central Tibet. For Shabazz and the Uygur commanders, it was proof that their activity worried Peking, and that they'd whipped the 27th.

Toorop didn't want to be a bad sport, but he tempered their enthusiasm a bit. The fun was over. It was time to get down to business. It was imperative they not reproduce the Urumqi disaster.

Twenty years of war toughened your hide, and strengthened muscles and personality. But it also used you up, eventually. Especially when your specialty was shouldering lost causes.

Toorop killed himself repeating this to anyone who wanted to hear. It was urgent that they coordinate the efforts of all forces present, both the Tibetan guerillas and the army for the secessionist Southern provinces. They had to extend the conflict to the northwest of Peking by trying to resuscitate a Manchurian independence movement. Same thing in Inner Mongolia. Toorop could tell that the Russian secret service men were real fucking interested, and most of all, that rotten colonel who provided them with weapons.

But Toorop realized, on the other hand, that the National Uygur Conference gave as much a fuck about Tibet or Hong Kong as he did about his first AK-47 bullet. They were too preoccupied with their own power struggles.

That spring night, just before the Tian Shan operations, he said it straight out:

"It's imperative that we make peace with the UNLF. All this political warmongering is useless. It's stopping the process of the conference, and paralyzing any strategic advance of the movement."

Toorop spoke in English. A strange little alarm went off in the back of his head. Give a horse to whomever speaks the truth, says the Afghan proverb, he will need it to' flee.

"Me? Make peace with that pig Hakmad? Never! You hear me, never! Don't count on me, don't ever count on me to betray my father's memory."

The young sheik's eyes drilled into Toorop like those of the Kirghiz hunting falcons he was so fond of. Like the one that had alighted on his fist just a few minutes before to pick at a piece of raw meat on the folded knuckles.

Shabazz's father had been assassinated at the beginning of the century under mysterious circumstances. No one had ever claimed responsibility for the car explosion that killed him, along with his escort, in Tashkent. Yet, Shabazz was sure that Hakmad, and what would become the UNLF, were behind the attack. Maybe they'd even executed the hit themselves.

In these parts, vendettas go back to the time of Tamerlan. There'd be no weakening on his part.

But he needed to loosen his position. Only a preliminary unification of the National Uygur Movement would permit the major advance: operational and strategic cooperation with Tibetan resistance movements and with the Southern Army.

"Prince Shabazz. This is a critical moment. Northern forces have strengthened around Shanghai. It is said that Wuhan will fall any day now, and the Russians inform us that troops are amassing in Dukou along the high banks of the river. The Northerners could cut through towards Kunming, take the democratic forces from behind, and attack Hong Kong through the Guangxi. We need to…"

"Stop right there, Brother Toorop."

Prince Shabazz raised his hand.

"Stop. All this is very interesting, but as you undoubtedly know, we have no way of controlling the flow of events on the Yangtze Jiang!"

His irony had shown through, and the Sheik looked to his officers for backing. They tried to laugh with elegance, according to the image they had of the distinguished chuckle of a Foreign Office diplomat.

Toorop let slip a feeble smile.

"That's precisely the problem, Prince Shabazz, we *still* don't have any means of influencing the flow of eve…"

The young Sheik straightened up, annoyed.

"How do you expect us to have any?! Have we *ever*, even once, gotten close to the source of the river?"

Toorop risked it all. He traced a summary map on the sandy earth with his finger.

"That's why we're losing the war, each of us on their own. The Han militia in Tibet, the border patrol here, and the bulk of the PLA in the middle. If we don't rapidly form a coalition with the other revolutionary forces, the Northerners will win. They froze the front last year and they're stronger now. They'll take care of us one after the other, believe me, once they go on the offensive. Nothing will stop 'em."

"We are stopping them, Toorop."

Toorop tried a bad laugh. His finger drew a few arrows going from North to South. The map of China evoked a monstrous animal.

"No, Prince Shabazz. We're an insect bite on the back of an elephant. The 27th and the other border patrol units, those were just little zakouskis. Just wait for the PLA mobile air divisions to show up…"

"What do you want us to do?" Shabazz said, imploring Allah, palms open towards the sky. "We are in His hands, and so are the Southern Chinese, even though they stubbornly ignore the teachings of His scriptures."

"We must coordinate our efforts," Toorop let out with an annoyed sigh.

"And how do you want us to coordinate our efforts with an army that's five thousand kilometers away?"

"We must first unite all our forces, Prince Shabazz. We must lead the National Conference out of its dead end. We have to unite with the UNLF and its allies, and then we should concentrate our efforts with the Tibetans. It's imperative we relieve the Southern Army, and create a fucking mess in all of Western China, Prince Shabazz. That's how we can coordinate our efforts with the democratic forces."

Shabazz pouted. The arguments were air-tight. They'd hit like a computer assisted round of artillery, with meter-to-meter progression.

"Hakmad won't be a trustworthy ally," the Prince answered with a spiteful pout.

Toorop had to agree. Hakmad was a vulgar gangster. A drug and weapons dealer who'd first gotten rich selling complete arsenals to the different Afghan factions. He was hooked-up hardcore to the Dushanbe and Almaty mafias, and he'd constituted the backbone of his paramilitary formation by digging into the formidable potential for human resources of his gang.

The UNLF had quickly become the principal armed branch of the Uygur movement. At the very beginning, it was practically the only one.

"We must simply get him to understand that the main objective is your country's independence. That's why we're fighting, isn't it?"

Shabazz didn't answer. He looked unflinchingly at Toorop.

"Sheik Shabazz," Toorop almost pleaded, "please understand that the fate of all of China is in your hands... But we can't do a thing without Hong Kong, Shanghai and Lhassa. Our fates are tied. All the books I've gotten you deal with that one thing: isolated minority forces can unhinge the colossus with intelligence and audacity by uniting their efforts, and mostly by forcing the enemy to disunite its own. Remember Julius Caesar at Alesia."

Shabazz ended the discussion with a simple movement.

"I'll see what I can do, Toorop," he said.

He hadn't been able to do a thing, obviously.

Toorop never alluded to it again, and embarked on his long manhunt in the Tian Shan Mountains. The most important was the library. Books. You can't hope to win a war without having certain books on your side.

The funniest thing had been the Russian colonel's mug. He was simultaneously a drug and arms dealer for himself, and an intelligence officer for the Kremlin. On the Kazakhstan border, at the usual meeting place, Toorop ordered the agreed upon material, unloading the ton of hash and the hundred kilos of opium as an advance for the transaction. Then, adding a large additional bag to the scale, he asked negligently if they could get him something a bit special.

"*Chto?*" let out the GRU officer with his robot voice. "*Prostitutok?*"

Toorop lit a spliff of that sublime weed. He looked the officer straight in the eyes and he let out a long dragon of smoke.

"*Niet. Knigi.*" he answered.

The officer observed him silently a few minutes, and then his face sketched an icy smile.

"*Black books?*" he asked.

Toorop shook his head. He already had the guerrilla manuals and the snag repertoires. Even the most obscure fundamentalists who saw in them the Devil's hand put up with them. No, what he needed were a few basic works. He presented the list to the officer.

As he skimmed over the words on the old dot matrix printer sheet, the Ruskie's face grew excessively long.

Toorop never knew how he did it, but when he delivered the merchandise, the cases of books were there, in the middle of a few tons of Russian war material.

The man came towards him, the list in hand. It was the same Toorop had given him, barely crumpled.

"A few Tadjik and Turkish translations are missing, but I can't do more than this," the officer blurted out, sinister.

And so it was that Prince Shabazz's little army found itself endowed with a mobile library consisting of a few venerable books translated into about all the languages of the region. Sun Tzu of course, but also Julius Caesar, Liddell Hart, Guderian, Mao Zedong, Thucydides, Toukhatchevski, Guevara, Lawrence, Napoleon, Machiavelli, Clausewitz, de Gaulle. Everything immediately photocopied, digitalized and distributed from one end to the other of the territory on which said army operated.

A few Uygurs, whose families had been exterminated by the "savage columns" of the communist generals, refused to read the local translations of *The Little Red Book*. They saw in it the bloody image of the despotism they combated, with their fucking Jihad dream as razor sharp as Saladin's own Yatagan.

Toorop and Prince Shabazz had to debate for hours to convince the recalcitrant officers.

"Replace the Despot's words with your own," Toorop said after a while, when night and the discussion were well advanced, and he'd started to have enough. "When Mao says communism, replace it with justice, national independence or the Kingdom of Allah, or whatever you want, I don't care. What matters is that you understand how Mao defeated the Kuomintang, *because he had read this other book here.*"

And Toorop showed them the Turkish language copies of *The Art of War*.

Which meant: you'd better get on with it.

That night, the night that would transform his destiny, he owed his salvation to his horse, the one he'd stolen a few days ago from the man with the buzzards. The beautiful Kirghiz mare had just enough time to rear and neigh before disappearing, along with everything else.

He and his mount were advancing on the shrunken moor of a rocky point overlooking a vast plateau. Tree groves and wild shrubs spread out here and there drew silver structures under the moonlight. Prince Shabazz's camp was below, ensconced in the middle of a crown of rocky crags, less that ten kilometers away according to the GPS module. The bonfires of the guard posts created a highway of red fireflies in the night.

Ten kilometers of night in the mountains; that meant hours. But he had to make it. And mostly to piss. Right away. He stopped the mare and observed it an instant. The animal was close to exhaustion. Toorop decided to give it a few more minutes to breathe. He looked at the heavy charge it had carried unflinchingly for days with compassion. The mare started grazing on the short grass outside the path with no consideration whatsoever for his mood.

Toorop walked to a nearby thicket, a clump of scrawny young conifers overlooking a small rocky cliff and a mass of fallen rocks. He unzipped his fly with a sigh of contentment and set about copiously quenching the thirst of this parched nature.

He raised his eyes to the sky, immense, a million stars thrown there like metallic sand on a jewelry box. They were so sharp, so close, so bright that he could have dipped his hand into them and retrieved it filled with luminous powder.

It was cold, even though it was summer, Toorop said to himself, shivering. A biting breeze was blowing from the Southwest, from where they'd come. He wrapped himself into his Russian Army Arctic Division jacket.

Above him, the stars exuberantly filled the sky. He programmed himself an explosive mix on the biocompatible patch, enough to take on a triathlon, easy, and let himself be invaded by the cosmic hypnosis of the night skies. As he turned back towards the mare, a wolf cry reverberated in the mountain echo.

And the drone sprang out.

It was an old Chinese Army model, but still young enough to accomplish its mission: search, ceaselessly. And destroy. Ceaselessly. Like Toorop. A silicon version. A giant carbon and black refractory metal dragonfly around three meters long, equipped with two miniature wings, a rudder and two micro-rotors. An array of thermal sensors. A 14.5 mm rotating cannon. A few anti-tank rockets. And the cold-bloodedness of machines.

There was simply a white flash. Blinding. The dragonfly had turned on a xenon projector, thought Toorop on his way to the ground. The high-powered ray trapped the mare in a concretion of light; the terrifying noise of the rotating cannon bore through the atmosphere, swallowing the horse's whinny in its wake. Then an anti-tank rocket shot out with an icy whistle. The deflagration made the air, the earth, and even the stars tremble. A gunpowder-smelling sirocco warmed the cold, high mountain air. When Toorop could again discern something, flat on his stomach behind a prickly bush, he observed the black machine that whirled, buzzing, around the exploded and smoldering carcass of the Kirghiz mare. The organic wreckage of an infernal mechoui. The machine's sensors were in action. The characteristic red lights blinked below its bulging hydrocephalic killer head. It emitted the buzz of a mosquito pumped out by a wall of speakers.

Toorop crouched in the peaty soil, trying to become that fucking clump of bushes that was separating him from the machine. Knowing quite well that if the drone's scanner focused in his direction, the thermodynamic analysis would reveal right away the presence of a humanoid animal shape behind the thicket. And the onboard computer would give a detailed list of the nature of the metallic objects lugged by said humanoid. The clump of brush would be reduced to ashes within the second, along with everything within a 10-meter radius. Toorop knew that the volumetric detector rotating in the machine's head could record his every movement. At this distance it was a miracle that it still hadn't detected his breathing.

The drone was settled in stationary flight over the smoldering remains of the mare. The buzzing tone changed. Then Toorop thought he heard something like a digital flow, a pure binary rustling. He raised his eyes slightly from the short grass. The machine was slowly turning around, towards the plateau below; then, with faultless predator style, it took off.

Toorop's eyes followed it a minute, until the entire sky flared up.

Pyrotechnic thunder lit thousands of giant stroboscopes in the mountain night. Reddish arrows flowered like corollas above the plateau.

The camp was under attack, a stupid voice inside his head kept repeating, as he gripped his weapon, trying to analyze the situation. They were firing on the camp. From all the surrounding mountains, including the ones whose crest he was following.

Rays of light flew out of the darkness, breaking on the camp like Greek fires of the atomic age. Following the rockets, mortars and heavier artillery leveled the edge of the encampment, adjusting their fire. Napalm blazed in whirling dervish dances. Glowing clouds, fumes from the blaze, and smoke gas now snaked above the plateau, phantom dragons beneath the frenetic light of flare rockets. In a strange, jumpy cinemascope, he saw the line of defense get chopped to bits by anti-aircraft missiles and mortars. Then anti-tank projectiles finished off the antique Kazakh and Russian T-55s half-buried at the four corners of the plateau.

Toorop quickly faced the facts. A large, well-trained and well-equipped force was attacking, acting in a precise and coordinated matter. Surely that Chinese division that had come from Tibet to relieve the local border patrol unit.

Toorop started to climb towards the summit of the crest when he heard voices shouting something a little above him, about fifty meters to his left, to the North, barely audible under the din of the arsenals in heat.

There was the sound of footsteps on the loose stones, metallic noises, voices again. He saw a few silhouettes pass by and followed them with his eyes to a large, flat boulder beneath him, where they took up position. Two machine-gunners with M-60s, a dozen guys armed with zolias and AK-47s, but also with M-16s, and two guys lugging a pair of mules loaded with ammo. One of them shot a flare rocket into the sky. The scene was lit up a phosphorescent green. They wore the traditional local Mujaheddin cap.

They weren't PLA assholes.

They were Uygurs. In other words, UNLF militiamen.

The plateau where Shabazz had set up his High Command Headquarters was perfectly protected from the Chinese by a long series of mountains in Kirghiz territory. He was protected from the Chinese, *not from an army of competing guerrillas who knew the terrain perfectly*. From where he overlooked the show, the impression was striking. You could have been in Sarajevo, staring from the slopes of Mount Igman, or the Serbian hills surrounding the city. Thousands of orange deflagrations and blazes laughed in the darkness.

Then Toorop heard the sound of the rotors, and saw a swarm of black hornets appear above him. Cobra AH helicopters, US Army stocks, masses of them, and a few French Super-Pumas filled with foot soldiers. The UNLF was throwing all its forces into the battle. It was war for total supremacy. There'd be no mercy.

Toorop slung the Aurora across his back, adjusted the survival kit that never left his side, and started scaling the mountain as quietly as possible.

Behind him, surges lit up the sky into a diabolical Omnimax.

The old mechanism of learning and instinct emerged from the oil of his memory. In a fraction of a second, his brain synthesized some old memories from twenty years before. Back when they'd pierced through Serbian lines North-West of Donji Vanuf, with the Bosnian Army Special Forces and the HVO Croats, and hooked up with the Crni Lubadovi, the "Black Swans" of the Vth Corps that tracked down Arkan militiamen day and night. They'd spent weeks in the forest-covered mountains of the region, feeding off animals and wild fruit.

Toorop breathed in and took on the assault of a sandy ravine, leading to the other side of the peak.

He advanced in the dark night of the Kirghiz Mountains, and disappeared like a ghost, both to the soldiers populating them with barbaric noises, and to his own consciousness, focalized on the austere work of survival.

3

It was fucking hot. The whole region was a mess, and Colonel Romanenko contemplated his new problem. A problem that didn't have the tact to wait for the ashes of Shabazz's army to cool. That very morning, Moscow had let him know dryly of its disappointment in regards to the Uygur situation. And since then, he felt like he was dancing on lava fresh out of a volcano. Any unforeseen circumstance menaced to throw him in it alive.

Romanenko glanced, as icily as possible, towards the sunken mass in an armchair at the back of the room continuously sponging off its forehead. He sighed, and then methodically detailed the problem.

Mechanically, he grabbed a big Cartier pen lying on the spotless desk. He played with it a minute in his hands, both elbows leaning on his leather desk-cover. The platinum cylinder superimposed itself over a shapeless gray sweatshirt covering a slight frame. He sensed the shapes beneath it were agreeably feminine. He calibrated a triangle-shaped face opening onto a large forehead, underlining the deep blue eyes, and their unfathomable depth, with a metallic arrow. Western, thought Romanenko as he put the pen back. But she could have passed for a native Siberian. It was something… strange, like faraway arctic roots.

Romanenko glanced at the man in the back of the room melting like a stick of butter in the sun, and repressed a nasty smile. Perspiration was a quasi-unknown phenomenon to him. The bad Chinese air conditioning had never worked well since it had been installed, back during Hong Kong's retrocession. He was the only one who had never made the slightest remark on the subject.

The situation was disconcertingly simple: Gorsky had him by the balls. It didn't make much difference if he turned this way or that. For a long time, the Siberian Mafioso had been the main dealer he had had to negotiate with in the region. Gorsky paid him cash for the tons of opium and hash that Prince Shabazz exchanged for the weapons, generously provided by the Kremlin. Romanenko was thus winning on both boards. He sold complete arsenals at a high price to the Uygurs in exchange for industrial cargoes of dope. He loaded the stuff onto Gorsky with a generous profit margin, and gave Moscow the impression that he controlled the situation. It had worked well for three years, but the fortunes of war had decided otherwise. For now, Prince Shabazz was hiding somewhere with his Uzbek allies. Commerce with the ETLF wouldn't resume for a while.

Romanenko had bet on the wrong horse. Hakmad and his Kazakh mafia friends were going to control 100% of trans-border trafficking in the region.

It would take months, maybe years, before he could establish lucrative contracts with the new hash, opium and war lords.

And Gorsky had come along.

With a strange contract to boot.

A contract.

And the woman that went with it.

"What's your real identity?" Romanenko asked.

The young woman glanced worriedly towards Gorsky, who encouraged her with a movement of the hand, and with a smile that was meant to be friendly.

"My name is Marie Zorn."

Romanenko didn't lose sight of her for a minute. At the same time, he was trying to intercept the frequency coming from the sweating mass, on the periphery of his vision.

"Marie Zorn" he said, rapidly typing the name on the computer keyboard. "Nationality?"

The young woman stiffened slightly on the mangy, communist era chair.

"Canadian. Well, Quebecker, now. I was born in Rimouski, June 28th 1986."

Romanenko jotted down the information, reprimanding a nasty smile. Happy birthday.

"Do you have the photos and the chip?"

The young woman nodded, shuffling a bit nervously through her bag.

"Relax," Romanenko said, taking the objects from across the table. "Everything's gonna be fine."

Then he turned to Gorsky.

"It's gonna be a few days for the passport. It takes that long to decode the chip and reinject it neatly onto the one from the genetic ID."

"I know," went the Siberian, impassive.

"Is there a nationality you prefer?"

This was addressed to both of them, but he only stealthily glanced at the young Canadian, well, Quebecker.

She herself was looking questioningly at the fifty-year old with the white hair and the opaque black glasses, smiling unperturbed, deep in his armchair, using a white silk handkerchief embroidered with his initials to sponge off his forehead.

"What is it you desire, Marie?" He belched out, cracking up. "Go ahead. You're at the GRU here, the nationality supermarket. Choose, Marie, choose!"

The young woman turned questioningly towards Romanenko.

"Wha... What do you suggest?"

They'd been speaking Russian since the beginning of the conversation. The young woman spoke with a strong accent but perfect grammar.

"Are you an English speaker?"

"Yes. Well, I'm bilingual if that's what you mean. I lived in Vancouver a few years. But I'm mostly a French speaker."

A hint of pride, nothing but a fugitive ghost under the pale mask, a little foam in the eyes blue as a cold autumn sea.

Romanenko started sketching the virtual diagram of the false identity he was going to make her.

"Do you speak other languages? I mean, other than English and ours?"

The young woman thought a few moments.

"I learned Cantonese in the streets of Vancouver. My father taught me a few rudiments of Slovene and German. I learned to speak Russian in the mix!"

A little laugh punctuated the sentence with its brief flash.

Romanenko finished constructing her mental identity.

"Perfect," he said, leaning back on the armchair. "I think I could have you pass for European. Slovene, that's good. Or Swiss. How about that? Swiss passports are pretty, and very well respected almost all over the planet. I'll provide you with Swiss francs and Euromarks. OK?"

The young woman murmured a barely perceptible *Da*, feebly acquiescing with her head.

"Now, I'm going to explain what you have to do, Miss Zorn. First, you're going to go to a hotel on the other side of town. You'll take a taxi, with one of my men. Don't do anything. Don't try to spot it, but a whole team will be providing your protection constantly. Understood?"

The young woman nodded.

"Then all you'll have to do is wait. Don't go out. We'll bring your food to the room. Wait for me to call, or for one of my men to come get you. *Ponimaiete?*"

"*Da*," the young woman articulated weakly. "*Ponimaiu*. How long?"

Romanenko sighed slightly.

"We have a few administrative details to take care of... let's say a few days? Maybe a week... Maybe a bit more..."

The young woman didn't answer. She played nervously with strap of her bag.

Romanenko shot a glance towards Gorsky. He was sprawling in the armchair, with a large smile on his face, wiping the sweat off his forehead. He made an explicit hand gesture.

"Well... I think that'll be all, Miss Zorn."

He picked up the phone and asked his secretary to get Gheorgui Solokhov as fast as possible.

The young second lieutenant showed up right away. Romanenko told him in two words, *Hotel Irkutsk*, what he and his Cossack gorillas had to do.

When the girl had left with Solokhov, he sank deep into his armchair, waited three seconds, and turned towards Gorsky. He observed the vast, pallid, lunar face. His eyes moved from the albino skin marked with brown spots like craters left on the surface of a dead star, to the latest stereoptics that restored life to eyes destroyed by war years ago, and finally settled on the pale thin lips like surgical scissor blades that curled over advertisement white ceramic teeth, setting off the yellow flash of an old canine cast in pure gold. A kind of wild animal with ice sweeping through its veins. The polar bear of the cold lands.

"Why me, Anton?" Romanenko asked.

Gorsky burst out laughing.

"Why you? Come on... there's a huge list of reasons, Pavel. You're the military intelligence officer posted in Almaty. You've got connections in Moscow as well. You can get tons of passports. You know all the little local deals we're interested in. You're from Novosibirsk, like me. And from now on, we know each other well. You're just the perfect guy."

"You didn't understand me, Anton. Why should *I* be the one to execute the transfer?"

"I already told you. Because it's my client's wish, Pavel Vasilievitch. And my client is going to cover us in dollars."

"For what reason? I want to know why."

He didn't want to leave that card unturned.

Gorsky snorted like a buffalo and blurted out:

"'Cause it's out of the question that my activities appear in this operation in any degree whatsoever. That's why I want your men to do the job. And that's why this is an essential item of our contract. If everything works out, you'll be doing transfers like these once a month, then once a week, and maybe even more. I'm an intermediary. But I'm also responsible for the smooth running of the whole operation. So you're gonna be stuck with it, comrade."

Romanenko swallowed his saliva.

One hundred thousand dollars. One hundred thousand dollars per transfer. Twenty-five thousand up front. Cash, straight up. Twenty-five thousand in the middle of the operation, the total if it works out perfectly. And enough to hand out to get the Embassy staff on your side. At that rate, per year, you'd be swinging millionaire zeros, in US dollars.

He didn't even wonder what astronomical fee Gorsky had gotten for himself.

"What's she carrying?"

He'd tried the Lady directly, but had few available munitions.

Gorsky cracked up.

"She's not carrying anything, Pavel, not a thing."

Romanenko scrutinized the opaque black surface of the Ultra Vision Raybans facing him.

"Listen, Anton, you can't ask me to do this blindly. I have to know."

Blindly, he thought, try to grasp the allusion, Siberian.

Gorsky blurted out some kind of laugh.

"Are you joking? That's exactly it. Even I only know a tiny bit of the truth. And that's how I like it. Follow my advice, do the same thing."

Romanenko shut himself up in silence. It seemed to him he could see the ticking countdown float above the invisible chessboard separating them.

"Listen," Gorsky started up, "what I can tell you is that she's not transporting drugs, weapons, smuggled diamonds, microfilms, secret chips, or strategic plans. Nothing like that. OK? Nothing."

"Nothing like that," Romanenko just thought to himself.

That meant she was transporting something else. Something worth at least double, or triple, one hundred thousand dollars, maybe more.

Come on… A lot more.

Infinitely more.

Anton Gorsky sat down heavily on the Lexus Stereolab seat. The real calfskin leather let out a sensual creak as he stretched his legs out with a moan of pleasure.

Kim, his Japanese-Korean chauffeur, was waiting calmly, one hand on the steering joystick. The other was fixing a few applications on the onboard computer. He was wearing a bulletproof composite T-shirt, and was now setting the parameters for the visioning window on the windshield. The intertwining dragons formed an immense fresco, from the knuckles to the shoulder blade, testifying to his membership in the Towa Uai Jigyo Kumiai, a Yakuza branch, originally from Korea, with which the Novosibirsk group had had strong ties for a long time.

The Stereolab Lexus could easily have done without a chauffeur; its onboard artificial intelligence and its sensors replaced the most skillful driver with no competition. But Kim was more than a simple chauffeur. He was simply the best Yakuza bodyguard west of Vladivostok.

The Lexus took the big North road, the one that led to Semi-palatinsk, and to the Russian border. Through the passenger side window, Gorsky didn't pay the slightest attention to the sight of the lake reservoir of Kapchagai, a long comma of approximately one hundred and fifty kilometers by twenty. In the distance, he'd certainly have discerned the intense activity reigning in one of the UNLF fortified camps, and the stormy mass that was approaching.

He turned his cell phone on, tapped a few buttons, and put the hand piece into his right hand. He attached the optical interface tube onto the neurofiber lens of his RayBans, and asked his intelligent desk to open a series of applications. He sent a super-encrypted e-mail to an addressee in the Russian Far-East.

Then he asked Kim to fix the air conditioning. It was like a hammam in here, Jesus Christ, shit, he had to wipe his forehead every ten seconds. The young Yakuza did as he was told quickly but without haste, just like a Zen machine, a simple appendage of the onboard computer.

The car had been driving non-stop for hours. Gorsky had been cold, had asked Kim to lower the fucking air conditioning, it felt like Kolyma, Jesus Christ.

Then he'd snoozed a bit.

When he woke up, they were leaving Bourliou-Tobé. On his left, through the window his head was leaning against, he glanced sleepily at the banks of Lake Balkhach.

The sun was setting in the west. A yellow-tinted orange was slowly dropping down over the waters of the lake. They were halfway there. The last stretch of road, in the Tchinguis Taou, was an old, badly tarred ribbon, with a few kilometers of rock at the end. The digital screen lined up a series of numbers in the right corner of his field of vision. Numbers, precise to the decimal.

He wouldn't be in time for dinner, Gorsky told himself before dozing off again. The Chingiz Mountains stood out like a blue shadow in the Northwest. The sun had just disappeared behind a line of fire.

Romanenko is really the perfect instrument. A dream.

That thought recreated the image of the colonel in his mind. A machine as precise and assured as an English butler, and just slightly less dangerous.

When he'd met him, the Russian officer was carrying out lame little deals with the local guerrillas. Thanks to him, and to the resources of the Siberian mafia, the colonel had amassed an anticipated retirement fund worthy of a cartel leader. In a few years, he'd catapulted from the craft stage to the industrial age. And henceforth, he was going to satellize him into multinational business orbits.

Gorsky had found in Romanenko the perfect man. What he called: a sure rival. A cold bureaucrat, without feeling, as precise and constant as a computer. But a bureaucrat. Which is to say a guy who wouldn't get his feet wet for a friend, even less for his wife. For anyone in fact. A guy who wanted to play on the board of History, but who had nothing of the real player. He didn't have the rage. He didn't have the spirit.

He wasn't a killer.

Once the Siberian had left, Romanenko shook up Ourianev to get the Swiss Passport operation rolling. A treat for any GRU officer posted in a strategic capital of the Russian government. Even an asshole like Ourianev could do it. All he had to do was search the Embassy stocks.

Then Romanenko called the man from technical services posted in Almaty, so he'd be ready to code the girl's genetic program onto a copy of the "secure" UN chip. The chip would be delivered within the hour, by escorted messenger. The two times three billion nucleotide sequence would be patiently re-sequenced into the nano-quantum component, and thus implanted into the heart of the new memory-passport web itself. The "secure" UN chips were, of course, made with the technologies that any minimally active secret service had precisely set out to violate since their appearance ten years before.

Romanenko knew that the service had, at its disposal, a copy of all the writing systems that countries used to draft their passports. It possessed the perfect replica of the special writer with which each country printed the readable data, identities, visas and such. The letters and numbers that made up the ID were a layer of preliminary information, visible to the naked eye. The signs themselves were made up of encrypted micro coding that only the specific and encrypted key of the border service could read to prove the document's validity. The distribution of neuronal memory paper had boomed once it hit the market around 2005. The regulating authorities of the UN adopted it as a standard for the new electronic passports it intended to promote as part of the Unopol program. In less than ten years, the experimental program had become reality for the fifty most developed countries; the others were supposed to catch up within the decade.

The memory paper integrating the neuronal network, with the individual genetic code, led country leaders to believe they finally had infallible protection against fraud. As usual, they created a new separation between the ordinary Joe who, of course, couldn't even think of cracking the slightest code sequence, and the usual winners at that little game: intelligence services, mafias, or hackers who possessed the necessary kit to establish a perfect fake in the name of the US president, or the UN secretary general.

After Ourianev had gone, Romanenko started a new list, a list that would add itself to the thousand other ones stored in databases in his PC's memory.

Romanenko liked lists. They allowed him to quantify a universe that was more and more resistant to prediction. Establishing a list bordered on a little known art, an occult and very particular geomancy. You didn't amass disparate information in any old way, but on the contrary, you had to order it, to proceed to a classification, intertwined *classifications*. You had to make choices, establish secret links, trace invisible diagrams, and, thanks to this high precision mechanism, you could relate two trivial facts separated by many years, or two people distanced by a few thousand kilometers.

Marie Zorn was going to open a new list. She'd rub shoulders with Gorsky, of course, a Mister X (client of Gorsky's), an account number where the money would be deposited for him, and a few questions.

What Romanenko knew added up to nothing, or close: Marie Zorn lived in Kazakhstan under a false identity. They now had to send her to Canada, *to Quebec*, with a real-false passport in her real name, but with a phony nationality.

One hundred thousand dollars for a real-false passport. No, no, no, he thought from the first minute of the meeting with Gorsky, it doesn't make sense.

The girl had a specific worth.

If Gorsky was telling the truth, and she wasn't transporting anything, that meant that *she*, as such, represented all that dough.

That meant she *knew* something worth at least that price.

He typed a few questions off the top of his head:

—Marie Zorn's false Kazakh identity?

—What can she know that's worth at least (100,000 times X) dollars?

—FSB agent? Another service? Mafia spy? Renegade scientist?

Gorsky was a specialist in high-tech trafficking. In the nineties, his numerous contacts with the post-soviet military administration had allowed him, at first, to unload defense technologies all over the world—applications, components, databases by the cartload.

He'd also served as intermediary for a few unemployed ex-USSR scientists and their Iranian, Iraqi, Libyan, Israeli and South-African employers. The flow had gradually run dry at the beginning of the century when the Russian Federation was once again able to pay its researchers decently.

Thus, once the Vladivostok mafia became allies with Novosibirsk, then with a Yakuza branch (to counter the Yekaterinburg families and their new Japanese friends), his mission had been to penetrate the underground markets flourishing in the Muslim Marches of Russia's ex-empire, and in Western China.

In about ten years, he'd greatly diversified. His deals covered pretty much the whole palette of high value-added clandestine activities available on the planet.

The girl was a scientist, or something like that; it was the only serious lead.

In one go, he typed:

—What kind of scientific activities does Marie Zorn specialize in? (Find the trace of Marie Zorn in Canadian and US universities, reconstitute her career path.)

—If Marie Zorn is so important to Siberian mafia, why send her to Canada? (Find connection between Siberian and Russian-American mafias in Canada—what activities.)

And mostly:

—Why have her travel under her real identity, with a passport under another nationality established by a GRU officer?

By instinct, Romanenko smelled something fishy. There was a mix-up, a big mix-up somewhere.

The Irkutsk Hotel was in the northern suburbs of the city, someplace out of the way of the dangerous neighborhoods, and of the big luxurious establishments where the diverse mafias had set up their general headquarters.

Romanenko stationed awhile on the other side of the street to make sure the operation was set up: Solokhov and his Cossacks, guys that could doze on their nags, taking turns sleeping in their crummy old VW Golf.

He recapped once more the few elements in his possession. He had to see the girl.

The Siberian had been relentless in his prior negotiation.

First point: get the girl to Montreal as fast as possible. Second point: ask her no questions, apart from those needed to take care of the small technical details.

Third point:

"Pavel," he'd said, pounding out each syllable. "I want you to charge two or three of your best men with the operation. Invisible guys that have never been to North America, and that are clean. Not your Cossack fools. I want specialists. I want you to build up a team. They'll be paid in diamonds. I want you to introduce them to me as fast as possible. The girl has to be gone within ten days, that's the final deadline."

These were typical conditions for one of Gorsky's contracts.

One hundred thousand dollars was worth getting a bit worked up over.

Solokhov had taken the adjoining room, with a connecting door. When Romanenko joined him on his cell, he asked him to inform Marie of his visit, then call the Cossacks and have them keep an eye out, and finally make sure the entrance and the hallway were perfectly deserted on his arrival.

Solokhov recruited the hotel guard's services, a guy who worked for them every time they used a room to hide a witness, an escapee correspondent, a renegade, a terrorist, a Marie Zorn.

The Kazakh guard, Ulganov, was a thick brute, practically two meters tall. He was built like a brick wall, and could block the front door just by standing there sideways. Romanenko knew that beneath the counter he kept a 12-gauge 00 Buckshot shotgun, and a Desert Eagle chambered as a .44 Magnum, ready for use. Heavy artillery calibers that looked like pathetic toys between his catcher's fists.

For now, he was behind his small portable TV set, streaming the multicolor images from a Pepsi-Cola ad. He gave Romanenko an underhand sign as he passed by towards the old Soviet period elevator with the Social-Realist fresco welded into the stainless steel of the cabin.

Marie Zorn was stretched out on the bed. She was watching an Australian satellite channel on an old Japanese television. Romanenko caught some images of a woman with blown-out hair, and picked up that John, who loved Barbara, had gone off with Cindy.

Marie Zorn lowered the volume as he came in, turned towards him, and timidly got up.

"Hello, Miss Zorn," he said in a playful tone. "How do you feel this morning?"

The young woman didn't answer. She gestured towards the armchairs of the small lounge before preceding him there.

Romanenko sat down in an old thing with no style, just ugly, and waited for her to start. In vain.

"So, how's the room?"

"It'll do. Do you have any news of my departure?"

Romanenko wove his hands together and placed them under his chin, a chess player's attitude.

"Things are moving on their own time. Your passport is being made. How long have you been in Kazakhstan? It's for your entry visa," he added immediately, without any particular intonation.

"My entry visa?"

"Dear Miss Zorn, if you're getting to Montreal from Kazakhstan, you have to have entered at one point."

Either the girl had arrived illegally into Kazakhstan, or she'd come with her tourist visa and her entry had been registered by immigration. It would have taken him two minutes to check on his PC, but he wanted to test her, without knowing anything, so as to maintain an authentic behavior. He'd check later, of course.

"Miss Zorn, Marie… I can call you Marie, can't I? Marie, I just want to know if the way you came into this country was legit."

The girl hesitated a moment, squirmed on her armchair.

"I… I came into Kazakhstan illegally," she whispered.

"Why?"

"I… I think Mister Gorsky wouldn't want it to be known."

"Oh," he said in an even tone. "Can you tell me where you were before? I'm going to have to back up your trail a bit to establish reliable documents."

Romanenko gave her a bit of a breather. He had to be careful to construct the image of the honest good guy, upright, straight, friendly and attentive.

He knew that Gorsky's men spied on their conversation. Solokhov had deployed the standard countering systems in the next room, but of course that didn't cut it, faced with the sophisticated technology that the Siberian Mafioso had at his disposal.

So, he had to walk on a particularly tight rope. Act in the way Gorsky anticipated; get the info out of the lady without crossing the red line, i.e., being too explicit in his interrogation. At the same time, this meeting, one of the rare ones he'd have, should allow him to glean two or three strategic pieces of information.

Already, one thing, she'd entered on the sly.

He needed to probe, gently, as in a minefield.

The young woman still hadn't answered the last question. He had to play it smooth.

"Marie? It's important you understand this; if they gave me the mission to bring you *home*, it's because it's one of our specialties here, the transfer of correspondents (a simple esprit-de-corps boast). And if we're so good at it, it's for one simple reason: we think of everything, Marie, even the unthinkable. That's what they pay us for. To foresee the unforeseeable. We have methods for that."

"I…"

He drove the nail in.

"Let me explain this concretely, Marie. The idea is to anticipate the accident, or, more likely, the possible accidents. You can get sick, break a leg; the plane might have to make a technical stopover in another country, a country where you might have had previous judicial history. The plane could get hijacked, the Third World War could start, we're worse than Lloyd's, you have no clue the number of catastrophic scenarios we're able to imagine. The first thing, of course, is that your passport contain your genetic code. But in case a sanitary, judicial, fiscal or other type of administration decided to check your trail, I have to make sure they don't stop in the middle of nowhere."

He understood he'd broken through defense lines.

She lowered her head, and then raised a pair of resigned eyes towards him.

"I was coming from Russia. I met Mister Gorsky in Novosibirsk. Then he brought me to the Chingiz Mountains. And here."

"*The Chingiz Mountains.*" He refrained a smile. Good hit. And that one, he hadn't even asked her directly. She'd given it up without thinking, without being conscious of delivering small bits of truth with each spoken word.

And without Gorsky being able to do a thing about it.

That evening, in the Embassy office, he sent for Ourianev. They had to constitute this fucking team as fast as possible. It was urgent to go through a new casting.

That afternoon, his artificial intelligence had rapidly synthesized two or three primordial bits of information related to the Chingiz Mountains. First, they'd been sheltering one of the Kazakh mafia branches for a long time.

Second, that branch was a weapons supplier for Hakmad and the UNLF. Third, it was known that the Kazakh branch was linked to the Siberian mafia, particularly to the Novosibirsk boys, to which Anton Gorsky belonged.

Finally, an investment company located in Barbados that he suspected belonged to the network of Gorsky's fronts, had just conducted a series of financial transactions towards a Swiss holding company, a holding that owned a research laboratory in Kazakhstan.

A medical research lab. Where Marie Zorn came from.

He knew instinctively that he'd just moved up a pawn onto a strategic square of the board. If he wanted to accentuate his advantage, there was just one thing left to do: go to the premises. Which meant bear down on Gorsky. And let him know as soon as possible that it was useless for him to hide that part of the truth any longer.

So, that night, he stayed alone in his office, in front of the computer screen, lost in deep, strategic reflections.

He logged onto his favorite programmable Kriespiel. An experimental application from Vancouver, conceived by Canadian, Chinese and French engineers, that functioned with the required dose of artificial intelligence.

The Kriegspiel had centuries of military history in its memory. It was called MARS, of course, Modeler for Advanced Research on Strategy.

For now, he asked it to resume mapping out the course of the civil war as it was happening in China at that very moment. MARS was capable of surfing by itself through the right information networks, and presenting a living map of the conflicts pre-selected by the human user.

China had become a life-size concentrate of all XXth century wars. It had all kinds of terrain: mountains, steppes, deserts, great grassy plains, cultivated prairies, swamps, coastlines, jungles and urban mega-centers. All possible types of combat had left their mark: great tank battles, air-land offensives, guerrilla and counter-guerrilla warfare, naval combats, terrorism and counter-terrorism, cybernetic attacks, large scale civilian massacres, and, recently, inter-militia wars.

MARS showed him the front lines and the troops in action, nearly in real-time. The demarcation line between the secessionist Southern provinces and the Northern armies largely followed the long sinuous curve of the Yangtze Jiang.

The Southerners, after last year's flash victories, especially the capture of Shanghai, hadn't been able to clear the river, except through a few bridges rapidly squashed by the Peking Army. But they held all the big cities south of the mouth of the Yangtze: Shanghai, Nanking, Suzhou, Zhanjiang, Wuhu and Nantong, surrounded by the Northerners.

In the east center of the country, they were losing Wuhan, but with heavy casualties for the assailants. Some were already speaking of a Chinese Verdun, without specifying for whom.

In the western center, combats were raging in Southern Sichuan for control of the river cities of Chongqing and Luzhou. Last year, the Southerners hadn't been able to realize the capture of those cities. Now a few million Northern soldiers amassed in Chengdu, Nanchong and Wutongqiao, on the other side of the river, blocking their passage and shelling their positions night and day.

On the other hand, it was clear that the PLA was preparing something in Yunnan, on the borders of Vietnam and Burma.

Romanenko had been following the Northerner's strategic plan from the beginning. He'd seen it take shape in advance in his own head.

Before the end of the summer, he'd bet his Swiss bank account on it, the Northerners would counter-attack west of Sichuan, along the Indochinese border, where no one was waiting for them.

He asked MARS to generate the histo-processor and to launch the offensive as he had sketched it out, and probably just as the PLA generals had planned it.

According to his own information, for months an uninterrupted flow of material and men had been running between Wutongqiao and Dukou: a city recaptured by the Northerners at the end of winter, situated high up on the course of the river, about three hundred kilometers from the Burmese border. Romanenko knew that the Chinese military leaders, on both sides, were heir to a millennial tradition in the art of war.

The Northerners could close in on Kunming: from Dukou with the bulk of their forces, and from the mountains around Dongchuan, with specialized infantry. Kunming taken, they'd go north/northeast towards Guiyang with a first army whose mission was to take the Southern forces in Sichuan from behind. Then they'd send another army towards the southeast, across Guangxi, to seize Nanning, Zhanjiang, cut through the Hainan Peninsula and advance toward Canton and Hong Kong.

After joining up with combat forces in Sichuan, the Northeast Army would open the floodgates to a few additional armies. One of these would descend towards Guilin, closing in on Liuzhou with the Southeast Guangxi Army. Then, together, they'd surround Canton and Hong Kong.

The others could rip up the Southern Army's belly south of Wuhan.

It would be practically over for the Democratic Army and for the Chinese Secession. Once they'd passed the Yangtze, no one could stop the PLA divisions.

The Kriegspiel sent a message in a window on top of the screen:

PLA OFFENSIVE ON KUNMING.

RUN TIME IN PROCESS.

ARTILLERY AND TACTICAL BOMBING PREPARATION—REAL TIME: 2 DAYS, KRIEGSPIEL TIME: 2 HOURS.

THEATER OF OPERATIONS:

—XVIIth ARMY, GENERAL LI FENG, THROUGH DUKOU TOWARDS CHUXIONG.

—XXIst ARMY, GENERAL SONG, THROUGH DONGCHUAN AND THE WUMENG SHAN TOWARDS QUJING.

—55th AND 80th AIRBORNE DIVISIONS TOWARDS THE DIAN-CHI AND FUXIAN-HU LAKES.

While the computer took on the role of the Peking Armies, Romanenko tried to elaborate a tactical defense that could save the secession's ass.

He remembered the discussion he'd had one night with the western mercenary that advised Shabazz and negotiated the dope. He wondered for a moment what the guy had become, after the UNLF offensive. Probably dead by this time, he thought. They'd exchanged biting remarks on the war conduct of the "National Conference" of the Uygur movement.

Of course, the only solution for the Southern Army was to coordinate its efforts with the independence struggles led by Eastern Turkestan and Tibetan guerrillas. For example, by being able to threaten the western flank of the troops Peking was amassing in Dukou.

But for that, Hakmad's and Shabazz's men would have to make peace. Might as well ask Peking to establish democratic freedom.

So, there was no other way: he had to withdraw before the troops the Kriegspiel was hurling at Kunming. On the one hand, to protect Hong Kong and Canton; on the other, the Sichuan Army. Finally, he had to risk it all and counter-attack by piercing through PLA lines, towards the northern capital on the other end of the front.

He asked his virtual staff headquarters to program the offensive for the next day, at five in the morning, from Nanking and Wuhu in the Far-East, in order to trap the Jiangsu Army north of the river.

Then he went to bed.

4

The Wallabies were roughing up the Springboks on her screen, and Marie Zorn didn't give a fuck. What the other channels were showing didn't interest her any more than this one, so she'd come back to Star TV.

The images served as a reservoir for forgetting: be it Southern Hemisphere rugbymen or young siliconed Californian bougies, *The Charge of the Light Brigade*, or *Three Berlin Babes*, it was all the same.

She needed to forget.

Forget who she was, where she was, how and why she'd come, how and why she was going to leave. Forget what she still remembered, as if through the effect of a bad miracle. Total amnesia would have been a hundred times better.

There was a commercial break. She didn't have anything special to do, she got up and entered the bathroom.

She sat down on the toilet seat and urinated. It was extremely hot in this early July, and she moped all day in the room. She drank liters of Coke or mineral water. She pissed at least once an hour.

Then, she decided to take a shower. Water had been rationned since the beginning of the summer. The great droughts brought on by the greenhouse effect turned the elementary liquid into a commodity about as strategic as uranium, oil, or a well trained brain. Some announced that the current main conflicts were in fact wars for control of drinking water. Others affirmed that humanity would soon tear itself apart over a few rare biotopes. A little while ago, she had seen an ecology documentary, on a private American channel, announcing an iminent climactic disaster for the end of the decade. Global temperatures had risen a good degree centigrade in some fifteen years. In Bangladesh, or in the Pacific, thousands of square kilometers had been engulfed by water, and they were hastily building new dikes in Holland or North Germany, and pretty much everywhere near coastlines and major rivers. The ozone hole now covered all Antarctica, along with a good half of Australia and Southern Patagonia. It menaced the edges of the Southern tip of Africa, a continent already largely devastated by desertification. Its collegue on the North Pole was almost as vast. The statistics weren't good, Marie had easily concurred. But the dramatic information obstinately refused to take form in her mind. It remained suspended like a bubble on the limits of her consciousness, a simple fact, like the temperature, or the shower rationing meter, indicating she had less than thirty liters of water for the next twenty-four hours.

As the aerosol jet of warm water cascaded on her body, Marie felt her hands reach out on their own to meet her lower stomach. They settled there gently as if to test its soft curve.

She lifted her face towards the white plastic shower head and closed her eyes under the stream, her hands crossed just above the pubis.

The image ripped through her, like electronic interference streaking a screen.

She howled in pain.

It was blue.

It was blue and yet it shone with an unbearable white light, pure, sublime and deadly.

There seemed to be two shapes, no, *two energy sources*, she clarified.

It moved, sparkling with that blinding white-blue light, a din of infra-basses echoed in her head. Marie found herself prostrated on the tiles of the shower, while the jet continued to pour down over her, unperturbed.

The two energy sources were both similar and different.

The information had crystallized in a deeply buried strata of her consciousness, but the echo of that revelation managed to rise up to her, that little brain prostrated beneath the shower subject to an unknown radiation.

She felt nauseous, but couldn't throw anything up other than spittle spotted with meager biological residue.

Her consciousness tried to form the normal explanations in her situation, but the two energy sources were piercing her mental field with that cosmic white-blue machine.

So she cowered like a fetus in a placenta, an old impulse, the ultimate and original impulse. She saw the shower pummel a few centimeters from her face, the water movement swirling there evoked a dancer's last salute before his stage exit, the last flash of life before death.

The cosmic machine started speaking to her in a language, the words of which she didn't understand, but whose meaning seeped out to her, almost as osbcure.

She didn't notice that the stream of water had stopped and that the counter flashed a red band showing ZERO.

When she regained consciousness, she assimilated a mass of information at once. She wasn't in the shower, the cosmic machine had disappeared from her consciousness; she was dry, vaguely dressed, and Solokhov, the young Russian subaltern from the Embassy, was leaning over her. He was slapping her, and took on a slightly embarrased look when she opened her eyes.

"Miss Zorn? Miss Zorn? Do you feel allrrite?"

He was speaking to her in English, thought Marie, wondering why. She spoke Russian fluently.

"Ya sebia horosho chuvstvuiu. Mogu li ya vypit' niemnozhko vody?"

"Koniechno."

The man ran towards the small fridge and took out a Siberian mineral water bottle. He poured a large glass and came back towards her, looking worried.

She drank it avidly. Night had fallen, but the heat had been stored up all day over the city, locking it like a caldron cover on high heat.

Solokhov sat down on the side of the bed.

"I called Romanenko. He's coming with a doctor," he whispered in Russian.

Marie felt the blood rush to her face. Gorsky had asked her to make sure to have as few medical examinations as possible. Which meant none.

"*Why did you do that*?!" she started screaming in French, before realizing how ridiculous her attitude was.

The young Russian straightened up, speechless.

Marie didn't want to apologize, so she got up and locked herself in silence in the bathroom.

She stayed there till the doctor and the Russian colonel arrived.

"I'm fine, really, I assure you. I just forgot to drink enough and it's extremely hot today."

Romanenko observed Marie Zorn unblinkingly.

She was pale, and the bags under her eyes were heavy half-moons beneath two shining globes sunk into their orbits. Visibly, she hadn't slept.

On the other hand, the garbage in her room was filled with cans and plastic bottles.

She was lying to him.

The Kazakh doctor was a service contact, he'd keep his mouth shut. He was already ausculting the young woman with a stethoscope. He took her blood pressure, inspected her eyes with a little micro-pocket torch, did the knee reflex thing, checked that her tongue wasn't coated, nor her throat infected, nor her ears. Then he contemplated with a detached stare the number steadying in red LEDs on his MediKit screen.

"I'm noticing a slight tachicardy. Are you under any medication?" he asked, prescibing a few strong aspirin and some light anxiolitics.

"Don't worry," she answered. "The trip does make me slightly anxious. But that's all. I'm fine. *I won't be sick.*"

That, thought Romanenko, squinting, was meant for him.

He decided, however, to write down the incident in his secret file, once he got back to the office. He probably shouldn't give it more importance than it had. It's true, today had been damn hot, and he could understand that the girl was a bit nervous.

But Solokhov had found her in the bathroom, *fainted*.

That must absolutely be jotted down on his list, with the corresponding hour and date, and Doctor Ouissourov's confessions.

Romanenko and the doctor gone, Marie asked Solokhov to leave her. She was fine, really. She didn't understand why they made all this fuss for a little dizzy spell.

She tried to maintain the mask of fragile authenticity that had protected her so well since the beginning. It was a slightly shy sincerity that she knew how to put on in difficult situations.

She had fucked up.

Gorsky would know before dawn that something abnormal had occured.

She lay down on the bed. Before leaving the hotel, Romanenko had announced he'd have her passport tomorrow, as if it were an unimportant detail. They were going to verify a few things with Gorsky, then she'd leave.

And it was just the beginning, she thought, shuddering.

With a mechanical gesture, she swallowed the pills the doctor had left. She turned off the little bedside light, the screen across from her was now airing an old *Beverly Hills 90210* episode. She'd seen it as a kid, and it seemed incredibly insignificant. She wondered what extraterrestrials would think of us, contemplating the scrap of our civilization. She zapped onto one of the Hertzian channels, Russian, and fell asleep in front of the *nth* retransmission of *Swan Lake*.

The offensive on the Jiangsu had worked, thought Romanenko as he observed the image moving on the screen.

He'd closed off an entire army on the island, and annihilated a few large units of the front line, north of the river. Another army, decimated, was retreating towards Henan.

The Kriegspiel seemed to opt for reserve divisions from Jinan for its reinforcement. But it also halted the Wuhan offensive, an announced operation objective.

MARS was still massing its troops in north Yunnan. Kunming taken, it would soon throw its dagger towards Hong Kong, but now, Romanenko had taken back the initiative on the Oriental coast.

He could throw the bulk of his forces into the open breach, according to the plan concocted in the last few days, and charge towards the Yellow River. He would put all his available forces in the great battle that would decide the outcome of the war. Till the last foot soldier standing.

He was at this point in his reflections when two events occurred at the same time, or close.

First, the Kriegspiel processor sent a message onto the screen, and some forms were drawn up and started moving.

DOUBLE OFFENSIVE FROM KUNMING.
RUN TIME IN PROCESS.
—XVIIth ARMY TOWARDS NANNING. THEN HAINAN PENINSULA.
XXIst TOWARDS GUIYANG THEN ZUNYI.
XXXth AS REINFORCEMENT FROM DUKOU:
—1st MANEUVER UNIT TOWARDS GUIYANG (2nd ARMY CORPS).
—2nd MANEUVER UNIT TOWARDS NANNING AND HAINAN (2nd ARMY CORPS).
—3rd MANEUVER UNIT FOR COMBAT SUPPORT AT KUNMING (1st ARMY CORPS + 1st AIR DIVISION).
DEPLOYMENT OF THE XIIIth ARMY TOWARDS DUKOU FROM XICHANG.

"Good Lord," Romanenko had time to say; now the race was on.

Then, on the other side of the room, the door opened and Captain Ourianev entered.

With news.

"I think I have the man for us, Colonel."
He harbored a large smile.

Romanenko gave him a cold look, regretfully turned away from the Kriegspiel, and showed Ourianev the armchair.

The young GRU captain sat down, still smiling, and playing with his mustache. He seemed genuinely relieved, and proud of himself, thought Romanenko.

"So?" he said, detached.

Ourianev settled into his armchair.

"You'll never guess."

Romanenko sighed in annoyance.

"Stop playing riddles. We don't have much time left."

Gorsky's conditions were explicit. No one from the GRU, or from another Russian service. No Mafiosos, no hit men on file with Interpol. No war criminals, the men had to be invisible to the North-American Customs Bureau. A team of three, a simple duo if there was no other way.

Might as well send a man to the moon with guys who'd never sat their asses down on the seat of a plane, even in coach.

Ourianev had selected, however, a small group of possible candidates. Among them, two guys and a girl stood out.

The first was a forty-five year old Russian ex-cop, a sometime bodyguard, who bummed around Almaty. He was a strong guy, knew how to handle a weapon, and knew about security work. But Romanenko smelled his alcoholism right away, and his intelligence was limited.

The second was a Northern Irish protestant from Belfast who had belonged to a radical Orange branch. For the last fifteen years, he was wanted for his participation in a few deadly attacks in Ulster, and he had worked for diverse unappealing employers under multiple identities, in Brazil, in Africa, in the Middle East, and then in central Asia. He went by the name of Dowie. His real name was William Mac-Dowell. It was said that he was a real live classy iceberg number, a specialist in close protection who liked to kill and knew how. However, there was nothing in his file indicating he could direct such a delicate operation. On the other hand, he'd participated in assassinations, and had a Europol warrant on his ass.

There was still the girl. A case. An enigma. Romanenko and Ourianev hadn't been able to disentangle the roots of her personal past.

She was neither ugly nor pretty, just an honorable average. A bit horsy, with big teeth and a good size frame. But it was all muscle and willpower, tanned by the sun of desert treks from her most distant origins, thought Romanenko.

She was as blond as Marie was brunette, as tall as the other was small, as tan as the Quebecker was pale.

She called herself Rebecca Waterman. Supposedly, she'd been sergeant in the Tsahal, was born in Haifa of an American Hassidim father from Brooklyn and a Russian Jew from Odessa. She spoke both parental languages, plus Hebrew and Arabic, of course. She'd done graduate studies; knew the United States perfectly. Yes, she'd already been to Canada; yes, in the new free Province of Quebec as well; yes, she knew Montreal; yes, she possessed some rudiments of French.

Romanenko had tried to see if the girl wasn't an agent of the Mossad or of the Shin Bet. It was really too good to be true, but she wasn't on file anywhere. Even the GRU Muscovite services had nothing. His contact at the FSB had given the same response. In Israel, everyone serves in the army; there was nothing exceptional in her having been sergeant in the Tsahal.

Answering his questions, she said that she was simply a traveler, that she covered the world back and forth; that she'd been bumming around Central Asia and Southern Siberia for close to two years; that she had put a posting in the local newspaper, need job, any kind, urgent; that Ourianev had come upon her in a bar in the city.

It didn't even take Romanenko two minutes to draw the appropriate conclusions: only she could claim to conduct the operation.

Romanenko wasn't more misogynistic than the average man, in general, or than the average Russian Officer, in particular. He accepted the news without any great joy—he'd deal with it, that's all.

And now, he was watching Ourianev. His eyes sparkled with self-contentment, a mix of pure pride and dumb joy, horrifyingly mingled in the same smile.

The moron, he thinks this is a "game," without knowing what all "games" really imply: the absolute surpassing of contingencies.

"So?" he snapped icily.

"So?" Ourianev stupidly repeated, a dramatic scheming air between his brows. "So here it is, Colonel, the jackpot, the bonus prize, straight from the Chinese border."

Romanenko expressed ostentatious boredom, staring at his subordinate with an aloof glare.

"So, I brought you the Uygur mercenary, Colonel Sir," Ourianev quickly added.

"The *what*?"

"The mercenary, Colonel Sir. Shabazz's mercenary, what's his name again, *Zoorpe*?"

Romanenko stiffened.

Cornell Zoorpe. In other words, Hugo Cornelius Toorop.

The old 108th Bosnian Brigade volunteer.

Shit, he got through. He survived.

Romanenko had no fucking clue how, but he got to Almaty, in a region infested with enemy militia, then managed to enter the Embassy.

He bore his stare into Ourianev's. It was a look of pure ice, frozen with liquid nitrogen.

"He's here?"

"Yes, he's waiting in the office next door."

Romanenko's mental computer remembered the Toorop/Zoorpe list.

That young asshole Ourianev was right: he was quite simply the man for the job.

5

Things had gotten worse on the other side of the Tekes River.

First, Toorop had walked for days to the Terskey Mountains in the middle of enemy troops converging towards the Chinese border. He could hear the sound of the fighter planes over the area, and he often caught a glimpse of their trail in the sky. He prayed they hadn't replaced the old UNLF Mig rudimentary avionics by top-notch Russian systems, for no God can hide you from the view of the most efficient radar. Hussein's soldiers had learned it at their own expense, just before dying, two decades ago.

Then he walked for more than a week in the Terskey Alataou, his eyes following the road along the Issyk-Koul Lake from the top of the crest. He ate what he could find: roots, flowers, insects, bird eggs.

During the day, groups of helicopters and troop transport planes flew over the foothills of the mountain chain. Sometimes he'd stay for an hour or two under a boulder, a rock face, in a cavity, face down in a bush, in a hole, or beneath a dead tree trunk. Sometimes he fell asleep.

At night, he walked endlessly, directed by his cell's GPS module tuned to an ArabSat channel like a bat in the dark.

Sometimes he allowed himself a few hours of programmed bio-sleep, in cold and humid caverns, or even simple crevices of rock, barely larger than coin-lockers.

One night, the day before arriving on the banks of the Tekes River, lying in his survival blanket on a mossy nook, Toorop rummaged through his bag and fell upon two pages of newspaper rolled up around some old pieces of humid candles. He started reading under their quivering glow.

Two pages of the same Kazakh daily in Russian from a few months ago. A sports column with commentary on the regional football derby that took place in Almaty between the Kirghiz and Uzbekistan teams. You could also follow the feats of a young Kazakh athlete, training hard for the next Olympic Games in New Delhi. His strategy books had been shredded with the horse downed by the drone. For weeks Toorop hadn't seen a printed page; he would have devoured the Who's Who or the Obituaries till the last line.

The other page dealt essentially with tabloids and criminal matters. A serial killer terrorized the Krasnoyarsk region. In two short years, he'd killed and cut up a good ten young women, each time leaving the bodies close to a police station or an administrative service. A whole page was devoted to his sinister exploits.

On the other side, they commented on the Russian Federal Criminal Bureau investigation of the mysterious explosion of a business plane above the Tartar Straits in February. Obviously, the Russian cops were at a loss.

He devoured the printed text till the last drizzle concerning the burning of an old office building downtown in the Capital, attributed to the local mafia. Then the patch sent its active ingredient. He fell asleep like a log.

As the days and nights went by, the long uninterrupted marches ended up producing their psychotropic effect: that interior rhythm that makes the non-separateness of body and mind palpable, the one and the other like pieces of the same living machine.

He arrived within view of Prjevalsk at dusk on the eighteenth day of trekking since the attack. He hid on the north flank of the mountain and watched the lake waters shimmer beneath the oblique rays of the sun. The city was a bit more to the east, a white spot colored by the orange sun in the ochre desert, arid, a simple surface warmed by the light. The road left the oriental side of the lake to melt into it. A bit farther north, the plateau shouldered towards the Tekes valley.

He saw a Jeep pass by, along with a Toyota pick-up, armed with a machine gun and two old double-barreled anti-aircraft Prahas.

It was already late. Days are long in early July. It was imperative that he pass through before one in the morning.

He was less than fifty kilometers from the border.

And from the two men who were going to block his way.

Day was breaking when he arrived on the north bank of the river.

Before he'd covered three kilometers, he heard the sound of a plane coming from the northeast. He managed to hide under a rocky bluff before the Sukhoi, marked with UNLF insignia, passed slowly, in a deafening roar, above his head. An hour later he knew he had to pass the Kazakhstan border; he found himself on the side of a small road, an unfinished hybrid of forest path and country walkway, with paved sections between rocky stretches. That's where he passed an antique road sign from the soviet era, rusted over, set above the rut it leaned into: *Almaty* (in Cyrillic), *250 kilometers*. It was half eaten by a lacy oxide hole.

After fifteen kilometers north/north-west, and a good three hours of walking, the path opened onto a small outcrop of rock that dominated the great Kazakh Steppes spreading endlessly before him. Far off, a brand-new highway, two lanes, black asphalt and yellow line glowing under the afternoon sun, barred the steppe from east to west.

Over towards the north, clouds shaped like zeppelins, or furious horses, surged in sulfur hordes above the horizon. The cloud linings were a violet black. The sky like a stretched gray-blue cobalt sail, rocked by lighting bolts of electrochemical white. A big summer storm was blasting over the Ili River and the Kapchagai Lake reservoir.

A cold and humid wind started to blow.

To the orient, the sun beamed above the horizon, and the sky evoked the set of a biblical film. Clouds gorged with static electricity now crossed over him like menacing zeppelins. The north was nothing but a dense black cloud with spectral iridescences, but the light of the morning sun spread through a sparkling prism in the vast azure clearing overhanging the horizon, to the east. That light reflected like the ray of a giant projector under the magnetic vault of the black-blue-purple clouds.

Toorop raised his head to the heavens.

There was a sharp flash to the north; the steppe froze in a Polaroid flash of divine dimensions.

The thunder rolled, like the echo of a cannonade.

Then it started raining.

And the voices sounded above him.

He hadn't understood what they were saying, but turning around, surprised, he got the general sense of their words: there was someone there, below.

The two voices came from the summit of the rocky spike close by, flanked by that crumble of rock he'd just passed.

They were on horseback. They were armed. One of them was watching him with binoculars. The other was already shouldering an assault rifle.

At the same moment, a burst exploded, and the rock started crackling around him. In one breath he latched onto the steel of his weapon and threw himself into the rocks.

His brain recorded the specific melody of the enemy gun, and located it in the jukebox of his memory. Armalite M-16, Colt model, recent, a very good weapon.

So they were guys from the UNLF. Probably a special unit charged with patrolling the borders south of the Kapchagai lake reservoir.

He brandished his weapon with both hands above the rocks and inundated the supposed position of the gunmen.

Only the liquid rustle of the elements answered.

A few minutes passed that were as long as hours. He noted with surprise that his breath was a bit short, and that a sledge-hammer had decided to take care of his temples. In his chest a dam pump had started up. Rain was falling by containers, in a succession of giant flashes, under the thunder's cannonade.

He could go neither left nor right, nor backwards. That would mean cross the border again in the other direction. There was no getting around it; he had to kill them.

He charged, without taking the time to think too much.

When he got his breath back, and his wits, he realized two things at once: the rain had stopped, as brutally as it had started, and he was in front of a rock column that a violent explosion had horribly sectioned and carbonized. He recognized the visual signature of his own grenades: the latest Russian defensives, crammed with aerosols inflammable under pressure, and carbon steel micro pellets. The rock was blackened from the explosion in a six-meter area around the point of impact. The surface was studded by thousands of little holes as if hit by a smallpox of fire. The corpse of the first guy lay a few meters away, blown by the thermal wave, partially burnt, amputated of a forearm. A half-torn leg jutted at an ineffable angle. His head, disfigured, half-detached from a spine laid bare under the bloody flesh, seemed at a loss as to what had happened to it. What was left of his horse was smoldering more than ten meters from the point of impact; a sculpture of smoking viscera and strips of blackened flesh on bones coked by the flames.

Toorop caught a glimpse of the silhouette of the second gunman, a bit farther. He was lying in a hole dug in the rock, next to the corpse of his decapitated horse. He moved with difficulty. Each gesture wrenched from him a grimace of pain.

Toorop seized his chance.

The Schiskov trembled in his hand and against his shoulder, like some kind of giant vibrator. He shot without pause, emptying the charger of its mortal swarm. A rumble of thunder burst through the whole mountain. He felt like Zeus sending down a storm of powder and steel, only more fucked-up, more dangerous, more human.

Toorop walked forward a few meters, the gun pointed. He ejected the magazine, immediately shoved another in its place, taped backwards onto the waterproof Chatterton, and froze before the total absence of enemy reaction.

He could see the top of the shattered skull, like a big decayed mouth blackened by a putrescent infection or a carnivorous flower. It was as if a supersonic parasite had dug through the brain and spurted out on the other side. The man was as immobile as the rocks around him, red with his blood.

Toorop stood on the rock a long time, enveloped by the odor of powder and wet stone. Rays of sun sprang from between the clouds. He dropped the weapon to his crotch, still holding it, as if it were soldered to his hands. A north wind was chasing the storm clouds towards Kirghizia and, after a while, the sky became a painfully pure blue. The sun formed a sphere of perfect atomic-yellow light.

He climbed implacably, warming up from one minute to the next. It would soon be noon and the sky itself would become as white as salt under a projector.

The heat of the high desert plateaus. The crystalline luminosity of the air after the rain. The immensity so blue above him and the telluric presence of these desolated mountains. All of this warranted a stop.

He breathed in deeply, cleared his mind of all parasitical images, and started chanting a sura from the Koran. It was the sura of "the folding up":

When the sun is folded up,
When the stars do fall,
When the mountains are set in motion,
When the she camels shall be abandoned,
When the beasts shall be crowded together,
When the seas shall boil,
When souls are restored to their bodies,
When the girl who was buried alive shall be asked
For what sin she was slain,
When the page of the book shall be unrolled,
When the heavens shall be stripped away,
When hell shall be ignited,
When Paradise shall be brought nigh,
Every soul shall know what it has produced!

He branched into an old U2 song, *Mofo*. He remembered listening to it over and over all summer of '97 in the Panshir Valley. It had been gift from a passing friend, that BBC journalist who'd scored him a Philips Discman that ran on LR6 batteries, and the two mixes of the season. It went something like:

Got the swing got the sway got the straw in lemonade
Still looking for the face I had before the world was made…
Mother, Mother, sucking rock'n'roll

His song rose into the mountains. He sent it off, into that sky of great magnitude, and great magnanimity, for it to welcome kindly the souls of those two unknown warriors for whom he'd barred the way.

6

Romanenko's eyes stayed fixed on Toorop whose eyes were fixed on him in return. There was nothing aggressive there, nor ostentatious, just two professionals mutually evaluating each other.

Romanenko was studying the thick black beard, the hollow eyes, the dark rings beneath them, the emaciated traits. Shabazz's mercenary had lost a good ten pounds. His clothes were a painful sight.

"Your survival rate is largely above average, Mister Zoorpe," the colonel finally said before returning his eyes to his screen. "But your suit is simply disgraceful."

He'd contacted Ourianev on his cell about ten kilometers from the city. The captain couldn't believe his ears. Thrilled, he set up a meeting place at a bus stop in the eastern part of the city. Five hundred meters from a Kazakh Army roadblock.

Ourianev had sized him up, head to toe, twisting his mustache, and said:

"How about changing employers?"

Then, he brought him to the Embassy in a big Japanese car with Russian diplomatic plates. The roadblocks were a breeze. Ourianev brought him directly to an office on the top floor. He hung out ten minutes in a little hall where a surly secretary with a big bob and big boobs was typing out reports on an antediluvian PC.

Then, they had him enter this room, where this cold blooded forty-year old was waiting for him: knife blade face, blue-gray steel stare behind little steel-rimmed glasses, black, smoothed back hair. This was the post-Soviet bureaucrat, now reconverted into illegal business, with whom Toorop had traded tons of hashish and opium for war equipment.

Toorop had never been to the Embassy. Transactions were carried out in a commercial storage zone on the Kirghiz border, where the GRU had a warehouse and a phony company.

Romanenko always seemed to him like a cold and bland phantom, without any real weight. He couldn't say why, but here, in this big office, with its austere furniture and closed Venetian blinds, he emitted a new aura. Toorop felt the predator machine behind manners that were too smooth to be only effeminate.

Romanenko scanned his screen with fucking intensity, and then hit a few keys. He tore his gray-blue stare from the machine and drilled it deeply into Toorop's. Then calmly articulating the words:

"Five thousand dollars. Plus expenses."

Toorop didn't blink, opened into a large smile and, just as calmly, answered:

"Who do I have to kill for that?"

The colonel deigned a snarl of kindness.

"No one. We've got specialized personnel for that type of mission."

Toorop took it in without flinching. That was something. When Ourianev had made him the perfect-timing-proposal, he'd prepared for the worst.

"So, what do I do then?"

Romanenko vaguely consulted his file, placed a hand beneath his chin in the position of Rodin's *Thinker*, and raised his eyes to Toorop.

This is too much, he thought. Stop fucking around. You're not king of the world.

"Escort someone to Canada. To Quebec, to be exact. Take care of their security there for the time that's necessary; then come back, or disappear into thin air, or do whatever you think fit."

Toorop barely thought about it.

"Five thousand US dollars?"

"Yes."

"Plus expenses?"

"Yes, plus expenses."

He suspended his answer a second.

"What exactly are we escorting?"

Romanenko granted himself a kind of cold-water shark smile.

"You're escorting a person. I will tell you who and how when the time comes, and on the condition, of course, that we agree."

Now, Toorop leaned back into his armchair. Come on; don't take me for a fool.

"Passing the North American border with drugs is practically life, these days. So, excuse-me Colonel, but you're a joke with your five thousand dollars."

Romanenko closed himself off. His face was as white as a new sink.

"I told you escort a person, Mister Zoorpe. I didn't say anything about drugs. Or about anything *else*."

It was Toorop's turn to shut his face up. But he kept a shadow of irony on the corner of his lips.

"So, OK, what *else* precisely?"

Romanenko looked at him with his spectacle-snake stare without answering.

"Listen, if I'm risking my life for five thousand dollars, I'd like to know *why* at least. I'm a lucid proletarian, let's say."

Exhausted, in any case, he thought. As for lucidity, it was more the delirious intuition of truth, the hallucination of fatigue.

Romanenko still stared at him with the same frozen intensity. Then he looked at Ourianev, in the third armchair.

Turning to Toorop, he said coldly:

"You're gonna have to excuse us, Mister Zoorpe, but it's urgent that Captain Ourianev and myself have a little preliminary conversation before we continue any further in this discussion. Would you mind waiting in the sitting room? Irina will get you coffee."

Toorop didn't really understand what was going on, but he felt he'd scored a point, without meaning to, maybe even by acting against all the rules. What was that GRU spectacle-snake-head plotting, he wondered, leaving the office. The big bob/boobs secretary led him to the sitting room, an austere library full of works of military strategy, and later brought him a cup of Turkish coffee.

He waited almost half an hour, but he came across a work by

General Libbett in English, the American Sun Tzu specialist. He didn't even notice the time.

When Ourianev came back to get him, the Ruskie sported a mysterious smile beneath his Cossack style mustache.

Romanenko was in the same place. He made him sit in the same armchair, with the same gesture. Toorop felt like he was reliving a freshly recorded tape.

"Mister Zoorpe, or rather, should I say Mister Toorop. After our little discussion Captain Ourianev and myself have decided to change the terms of our little proposal."

Toorop settled into the bottom of the armchair to see what was coming.

"I… First, we're gonna double your salary. We're talking ten thousand US dollars, Mister Toorop."

Toorop smiled. The guy thought he was all that 'cause he cracked his false ID. Fine, with the means at the GRU's disposal it wasn't much of a feat.

"To what can I attribute this sudden favor?"

The colonel tried to appear human and fair game; what came out was a cold and mechanical grimace.

"Mister Toorop, we're going to ask you to answer the same question you are asking yourself, just as we are, which is: *what are we escorting exactly?*"

That was a bit harder to take in.

"What are you talking about? You don't know what the smuggler's carrying? That's a new method."

Romanenko sighed at length, resigned.

Toorop was thinking fast. If it wasn't drugs, what the hell could it be?

In the library, thinking about all this, before grabbing Libbett's commentaries on the Warring States Period to fight off sleep, he wondered awhile if the GRU was hiring guys like him to smuggle renegades, or fallen agents. But it seemed too outlandish: the GRU had its own teams, pros.

If Romanenko was asking him to escort someone to Canada, it meant it wasn't for the GRU but for himself, or for one of the Mafioso outfits with which he operated.

There, before the unshakable mug of the intelligence officer who'd just admitted to the unthinkable, Toorop told himself things were going from outlandish to sci-fi.

"Mister Toorop, I'm going to try to explain the situation in a few words. First, we're engaged in an intrusion operation targeting a branch of the Siberian mafia. Got it?"

"Magnificent opening remarks," he let out, sinister.

"What comes next is even better… This branch gave us the mission to escort a certain person to a certain place."

"Right, to Quebec."

"Right. Third, we're supposed to start a subsidiary branch. This is the first operation. We're testing. If we want to be able to continue, this absolutely has to work. Mostly, however, like I was saying, I'm going to pay you double so that you deliver the information: what's the chick transporting?"

And there, Toorop caught the bureaucrat at fault. A serious fault. One second of inattention and pure vanity, and he let Toorop sort out a huge statistic: fifty percent of the population at once.

It was a girl that he was going to have to escort.

He wondered for an instant if he was going to end up in some adolescent smuggling, some white woman trade, or some business like he'd discovered in Europe, twenty years earlier, by the greatest of chances.

He remained stoic, waiting for additional information.

Four-eyes wasn't feeling it. He stared at his subordinate with a distressed look.

"Well… this… *person* isn't transporting drugs, arms, secret chips or microfilms. We had her checked out."

"OK. So, what is it then?"

"It's ten thousand dollars I'm paying you to answer that question. But let me give you the results of our own investigations: first we thought Marie Alpha was a scientist…"

"Marie Alpha?"

"It's the girl's code name," said the officer, resigned.

"All right, go on."

"Well, a scientist. We looked for her trace in the student social security files of all North America: Marie Alpha dropped out before getting the Cegep. That's the equivalent of a high school diploma. She's not worth a thing on that count."

"She's worth at least ten thousand dollars though. Who's paying for this deal, in the end?"

"The other leads concern the Siberian mafia—the less you know about that the better off you'll be, and the longer you'll live."

Toorop burst into a kamikaze laugh.

"No kidding? Colonel, now it's your turn to listen to me. If you want me to discover what kinds of secrets or strategic materials she's packing, you're gonna have to raise your cooperation a level, as they say in diplomatic language. That's without taking into account that the proposed salary would make a Haitian slave laugh."

Romanenko stared at Toorop again with that cold intensity he seemed to cultivate meticulously.

"No one's forcing you to accept the mission, Mister Toorop."

"No one's forcing you to propose it to me. I'm not sure there's a whole truckload of volunteers scrambling at the door, Colonel Sir. But I'm still a conscious being, regardless of what I seem. I know I don't have an unlimited quantity of means of persuasion at my disposal. It would seem that my union delegate is momentarily unavailable."

This only set off a cold smile.

"I make note of this flash of lucidity with satisfaction. Ten thousand dollars and a new passport plus a vacation in America. In your situation, I know some people who'd kill mom and pop without the slightest remorse for that."

"My parents died a long time ago. That shelters me from those kinds of temptations."

"Very well. Can we get back to the main point of our conversation? Here's the general schema: it's pretty complicated, the man… the Siberian Mafioso whose organization we're trying to infiltrate is a specialist in high-tech smuggling of all kinds. He does it all, a clandestine techno-mall: military software, experimental hallucinogens, strategic databases. Of course he also does more conventional trafficking, arms, drugs, miscellaneous racketeering… he also deals in animals."

"Animal?"

"Yes, rare breads, or extinct species reconstituted by neogenesis. He owns a company in Taiwan, a technological consulting firm that has a whole lot of micro-firms on the island. You know how it goes over there… That firm is linked to a network of other firms that function as fronts all over the world and all this is very…"

"Complicated, I know. But don't worry, I'm used to complicated things."

"Well, we're trying to figure out how all this works, how it fits. Yesterday, we were able to find the trace of a branch of the Purple Star here in the capital, as well as in Semipalatinsk."

"Purple Star?"

"It's the name of the Taiwanese firm. It has a branch, under another name of course, with some kind of office in Almaty, but also with warehouses up north, on the Russian border. You get it?"

Toorop vaguely acquiesced in silence. He didn't get much, except that the mafia and the intelligence services shared a pronounced taste for border zones, which seemed so trivially self-evident.

"As your Canadian trip progresses, I'll transmit all the information I'm able to provide. In return, you've got to discover what's up. For ten thousand US dollars."

Toorop mumbled something, then said:

"And what if I don't find out."

"I'll pay you the five thousand for the escort."

Toorop inhaled, knowing full well he was risking his fate on the roll of the dice. He slowly got up from the armchair. He was beat. Canada, that wasn't bad. Ten thousand dollars, or even half, that was unhoped for. And anyway, he had no other joker up his sleeve. So he held out his hand to Romanenko and forced a smile.

"Colonel, you've just hired me."

7

Marie Zorn watched the storm break over the city nestled beneath the window in the metal-framed rocking chair. She finally fell asleep as the television lulled the nocturnal space of the room—an Iranian TV series subtitled in Kazakh that she didn't understand at all.

In the morning, she woke up in the same state as the night before.

The anxyolitics had transformed the ice of despair into a vague misty line floating in an indistinct present.

Of course, what she was doing was bad. Of course, she knew it. But that knowledge was now empty of all emotional charge.

Before her life had fallen for good into darkness, she'd known a few moments of joy, and on the island she even thought she was cured. The medical team assigned to her waited on her hand and foot. She'd been pampered. At the same time she spent hours each day with all those machines of such human consideration. The island itself was ravishing, and the gulf of Siam: an ocean of maternal warmth.

The other doctor, the one Gorsky had introduced to her in the Chingiz Mountains, did not resemble the island people in the least. He was an old and sinister individual, cold, sure of himself, egotistical. On the island they would have labeled him a cold-blooded sociopath.

This man engaged in prohibited practices, abominations. And she, in a moment of loss and pure detachment, had accepted to be an accomplice.

It was too late to back out now.

Much too late. Two weeks to be precise.

Later, Solokhov brought her breakfast. No, he didn't have any news. The colonel had gone up north to take care of some minor details; when he came back, she would certainly be able to leave within forty-eight hours.

Marie knew what "certainly" meant for such men. She knew it meant "maybe" or "maybe not." She felt that there were complications.

She spent the day in front of the television, swallowed a few anti-depressants, and fell asleep at the end of the afternoon, overcome by the heat.

She almost immediately dreamed of one of her recurrent universes.

She found herself above the magic island on her flying umbrella. She landed in the serpent-head jungle to meet the Tree-Indian.

The Tree-Indian was a sacred figure of the island. He was a great sage. He was very ancient, and he knew everything, or almost, about the mysteries of the universe. His roots were so long they ran beneath the entire surface of the island, up to the beaches, and so deep they touched the secrets of the center of the earth.

Near the tree was a phallic-shaped sex-machine mushroom. It was one of the machine-organs of the island. Marie could use it directly: to feed herself, ask for information, establish a connection with another machine-organ, or experience pleasure.

On the dream island, Marie had many machines at her disposal. "Schizomachines," as Doctor Winkler and his collaborators called them. These "machines" allowed her to control production of her dreams. They were directly connected to her unconscious, and they were its specialized organs. Thanks to the "neurapplications" they injected, she'd learned to control the flow of her limitless psychic production. Winkler, the official boss of the vast transdisciplinary program, had told her these "mental machines" and a new neurapplication prototype would allow her to do what no human could dream of doing till now.

That's what the island people had discovered by studying people like her. You're not sick, Winkler told them one day. It's just that humanity doesn't know how to use the potential of brains like yours. They've been made for something that today's humanity is just discovering.

Marie Zorn understood only very partially what Winkler meant. But, like the other patients in the experiment, she quickly grasped the particularity of the laboratory machines: to give their brains a virtual space in which their mental production didn't crowd the real, or rather, only did when they ordered them to.

Later, she learned how to synthesize the neurapplication in her own brain, to make the lab machines work in her dreams and produce what Winkler called by the barbaric name of "neuronection."

None of this meant a thing to Marie. Like all the other patients on the island, what she saw first of all was that they didn't shove neuroleptics down her throat or try to "reduce" the uncontrollable mental flow. Instead they tried to channel it, and above all, to do something with it.

The Tree-Indian had lit up with a fluorescent green phosphorescence, indicating he was in possession of information concerning the *nature* of the event.

The little phallic shaped sex-machine turned the same color, vibrating at exactly the same frequency. A message-organ emerged from it, a flying octopus-heart, one she'd just conceived of. The octopus-heart opened its pinkish mouth to vomit a stream of message-blood that wrote something on the ground.

The message-blood formed a double serpent in the sand.

Marie knew it was a sign of the utmost importance. Winkler said that this type of sign came from the "DNA machine." It was beneath the island, at unsuspected depths, at the tip of the Tree-Indian's rootlets, just at the center of the earth.

Under the shamanistic serpent in two crossing waves, a rudimentary text had formed:

FROM THE MATRIX
LIKE TWO
SOLITARY
MACHINES
COME
FROM NOWHERE

She asked her recording hand machine-organ to jot down the message. The little diodes she had placed on the tips of her fingers were flashing chlorophyll green, so she knew everything had gone well. Her eye organ-machine had perfectly connected to the recording hand.

Then she asked the Tree-Indian to spell out what it meant. But he explained that you couldn't decode the message from the double serpent. It came from a hyper-protected zone of the DNA machine. The Tree-Indian himself was in no position to offer further explanations.

So she left the island on her flying umbrella and asked the mother-program to wake her up. Somewhere in the sleeping depths of her neocortex, a group of neurons fired and sent a long sequence of electro-chemical codes towards the hypothalamus, a program based on the transition of theta wave to waking frequency.

She emerged from REM sleep a few minutes later, passed into baseline sleep, and woke up.

Her right hand was already gripping the pen on the bedside table, the notebook laying on the pillow ended up in her left hand, and the dream message was scribbled on the paper in one stroke.

FROMTHEMATRIXLIKETWOSOLITARYMACHINESCOME-FROMNOWHERE.

It didn't evoke anything in particular, no memory, no referent that she could grasp. The message was coherent but remained cryptic. She couldn't, however, get rid of the impression of already knowing what it meant.

Groggy, she stood up. The day had not yet risen. She took a long gulp of cool water directly from the bottle she got out of the fridge, and posted herself at the window a few minutes.

Then she came back to bed, and to Star TV. An Indian TV movie.

Why not?

The star couple of the moment was singing, embracing right in the middle of a color-saturated prairie. Syrupy music snaked through the space. Solokhov banged on the adjoining room wall.

Gorsky wiped his brow and placed his hand over his eyes to scrutinize the horizon at the end of the long white track, luminous and deserted, stretching out beneath the implacable Kazakh sun.

Romanenko and his mission commander were late.

He'd just called Kim who was waiting over there, at the other end of the track. But Kim still didn't see anything coming.

Romanenko had been up to par, exactly as planned. It had taken him less than two days to find the connection with the Chingiz Mountains. Then he'd been able to set up a team just barely behind schedule. This meant that next time, if he was really under pressure, they could fork over the package in seventy-two hours.

He heard noise behind him and turned around to see Thyssen, the doctor's counselor, that young pretentious prick, that little carnivore yuppie son of a bitch. Thyssen had apparently gotten Doctor Walsh under his control, thanks to a skillful blend of pure voracity and two cent jack-offs on the future of humanity. Roughly the Nobel Prize plus Bill Gates' fortune.

Thyssen had recently been able to place another doctor close to the Mandarin, a forty-something jerk supposedly called Zulganin. He'd been awarded a few State diplomas dating back to the ex-USSR and claimed to be a big shot in genetics. Gorsky had looked into it: Zulganin had been a gynecologist in the hospital of a seedy Krasnoyarsk suburb. He'd done a bit of analytic biology, had a veterinary diploma, but had no known dissertation in genetics.

Gorsky didn't care. He just wanted the lab to run smoothly. And he had to admit that Thyssen's role was essential: while the young megalomaniac took care of the official boss, and quite well in fact, he had the breathing space to expand his traffic and turn the business into a genuine cornucopia. Zulganin's competence was enough to cover ninety percent of operational needs. The old doc and his genetic and advanced cellular biochemistry team at the University of Toronto had done years of research, and that was no joke. He'd found the trace of some old copies of *Nature*, from twelve, thirteen years back, in which Doctor Walsh had published a few great articles that had caused a stir at the time.

Thyssen got close and grimaced:

"They're late, your boys."

Gorsky didn't answer. The one thing he would have liked to say was "Shut up, fag, and take this," as he stuffed the big 9 mm in his mouth and unloaded the goddamn charger.

He chewed his anti-smoking licorice stick, and slowly turned around to face the young yuppie in an Armani suit who was—was it possible?—lighting up one of his own Cuban cigars—fucking pansy—one of those Montecristos he must have left lying around somewhere.

Gorsky snorted, but didn't take it up. What could he say? For three days he'd been clamoring all over that he was giving up his favorite vice. Zulganin had been explicit after his check-up: "You remind me of the hold of the Titanic, except that in your case it's vodka, mixed with a cloud of Cuban tobacco. And I'm not taking the conception flaw into account, that small inopportune gene and the auto-immune sickness you suffer from. Your Biodefender won't be able to do much." Gorsky got the message. If he kept at it, he risked a stroke. At the Novosibirsk hospital he'd crossed survivors of that type of cataclysm in their wheel chairs, paralyzed for life, vegetating. His artificial immune system cost, at the least, the price of a high-tech clinic. To croak of a common stroke when he was spending millions of dollars to survive the unknown chorea gnawing at him day after day. It made no fucking sense.

He glanced down to the construction site growing out of the ochre earth. In a month, the lab would have tripled in volume, his shares in the company as well, and it was just the beginning. Then he penetrated into the long white stucco compound, its entrance lined with large anti-UV tinted sliding windows.

He slumped deep into an armchair in the hall. It was nice in here; the air-conditioner was working just right. He vaguely skimmed through one or two Russian journals, and then peacefully fell asleep. His Nico D-Tox licorice stick skidded down the top of his shirt in jerks.

"We apologize, Anton, an unforeseen incident, I had to…"

"I don't wanna know, Pavel. We said eight, fuck! Eight, that's eight, not nine."

The conference table was ready; one of Thyssen's assistants had brought fresh drinks. The bay windows opened up onto the foothills of the Chingiz Mountains and the Kazakh steppe. In the sky, the sun was a beautiful vivid orange, low on the horizon.

Gorsky drank a big glassful of fruit juice, and immediately asked for another, before the girl had time to serve the guests. Then, with a wave of the hand, he signaled for her to disappear as fast as possible.

Again, Romanenko tried to save his ass.

"As a preliminary, I want to say that our delay is only partially our fault. You wanted a second passport at the last minute, which wasn't planned."

Gorsky snorted.

"When I told you that, the first one was being made. Don't fuck with me, it didn't delay you for twenty-four hours."

"Twenty-four hours, exactly."

"You're pissing me off, Colonel! You're busting my balls!… We're not here to discuss your little technical difficulties for a million years. So OK, you're excused. Now let's get on to serious business. Is that clear? "

He glared coldly at Thyssen, then at Romanenko, pale, eyes iced behind their glasses, and finally at the dude they'd picked up to lead the mission.

Yep. Fiftyish. Pretty roughed up. But solid. Experience, undeniable. What was it Romanenko had faxed him on his mail again? Oh yeah, a guy bumming around since Yugoslavia, Bosnian Special Forces. He'd worked for the colonel and Prince Shabazz's ETLF, and had managed to get to Almaty by a long detour in West Kirghizia. That was six hundred kilometers on foot, on horseback, and without a car, in about three weeks, in a region infested with enemy troops.

Gorsky had to admit it wasn't bad.

He set his black lenses on the guy, checked him out with precision. The kind of fellow who attracts lightning.

Problematic. But useful sometimes, a lightning rod.

"What will your cover be?"

The man called Gorsky charged without preamble. Toorop liked that.

He looked calmly at the fat guy with the high-tech imaging black glasses and the short-sleeve shirt at the other end of the table. His skin was lunar white, albino like.

"My name is Alexander Lawrence Thorpe. I'm a Canadian businessman. I manage a small commercial airline in Ontario, a branch of a Vancouver firm. I'm just coming back from a business trip in Kazakhstan. I'm in Montreal to negotiate an association with a partner in Quebec. How's that?"

Gorsky wiped his brow and grumbled.

"How do you envision the trip?"

"Very simple. First, we take the long way, we go east, take a flight to Japan. There's one this weekend. From there we can hook up with a flight to Vancouver without leaving the terminal, less than two hours from our arrival in Tokyo. The plane is a Cathay Pacific supersonic jet; it goes to British Columbia, then Montreal, then London. We get to Dorval and move into a big hotel with adjoining rooms. I know a good one, the *Hôtel du Parc*, on the avenue with the same name. We do that long enough to settle in and to contact the local intermediaries, then we transfer the package."

"No," tweaked Gorsky with a grimace, "that's not how it's supposed to happen."

"So, how's that, according to you?" Toorop retorted.

"First, you don't stay in a big hotel on Park Avenue, or wherever. I want minimum eyewitnesses. Rent a discreet apartment, however you can, or a house outside the city."

Toorop looked at Romanenko, who pretended not to see him.

"OK, no hotel."

"And you don't contact any intermediary. They'll contact you."

"How?"

"How do you think? The colonel will communicate your address to me, I'll get it to our associates."

"Good," said Toorop, "sounds perfect to me."

"That's not it."

Toorop tried a smile.

"I would have been disappointed if it was."

Gorsky observed Toorop like a mother getting ready to chide her turbulent child.

"I'm gonna tell you. Stop playing Boy Scouts. You're too old for that. This is not an ordinary transfer. Your job is to escort the girl to Montreal, but what you've got to understand now, is that you must also see to her security during the length of the operation."

"I don't see the problem. That was included in the deal."

Toorop turned his head towards Romanenko to look for approval that didn't come. The colonel with the gray stare seemed to be thinking intensely about something.

"I know," whispered the Siberian, "but I'm afraid that you're underestimating the length of that period."

"What do you mean?"

Gorsky scratched his chin, wiped off the back of his neck, and opened up into a wildcat smile. A yellow gleam flashed at the corner of his lips.

"Well, what I mean is, you should be ready to spend three or four months there."

"*Three or four months?*" Toorop interjected, disconcerted, turning to the colonel.

"What's this mix-up, Anton? This was never in the contract," said Romanenko, adjusting his glasses.

"I know," Gorsky answered without hesitation. "For security reasons that you'll easily comprehend, I can only give you the truth bit-by-bit. Sorry Pavel, but it's a *sine qua non* condition of the deal."

"Four months," said Toorop, "you can't be serious."

"This isn't right. You said a round trip to Montreal."

"That's right. There *and* back."

Romanenko turned pale, a sign of great anger.

"You didn't tell me they had to stay more than a trimester over there."

"I never said the opposite either. Sorry."

"Lying by omission, point-blank."

"That's bullshit, Colonel. What's wrong is that you're afraid it's gonna hike up your expenses, but I already told you that this kind of overflow would be covered. So stop whining."

"Why so long?" Toorop inopportunely asked.

Gorsky turned his black lenses in his direction. His face was hard, closed, chilling.

"I don't think that's any of your business, Mister Thorpe."

"In any case, it's mine," said Romanenko.

Gorsky turned to him.

"I don't think so either."

"Why so long, what is this shit? I've never seen such a fuck-up!"

Gorsky barked like a seal.

"I already told you this is a special operation. We're setting it up with this first client, so I want it to run smoothly."

"I get that, Anton, but it doesn't explain why my guys are gonna have to stay in the country for sixteen weeks."

"Let's say twelve."

"Even ten. Even two."

Gorsky snorted again, louder.

"Because that's how it is, dammit! And it's like that because this is at the heart of the operation. So stop getting on my nerves. Figure out how to rent an apartment for the summer, and that's final."

Romanenko scowled and sunk his head slightly into his shoulders.

Toorop couldn't tell if he played it off perfectly or if he was actually scared of the albino with the electronic glasses.

Toorop watched the sun set over the horizon, sitting about a hundred meters from the compound where Gorsky, Thyssen and Romanenko were continuing the discussion; a threesome from which he'd been politely, but firmly, excluded.

He observed the ballet of the construction site below the promontory on which the "laboratory" perched as Romanenko called it.

Two big buildings, one of them a vast warehouse, grew on the desolated rocky ground of the high plateaus. Trucks brought in stones along a road that was under construction, and would soon link the new site to the "principal center." A slope of about two hundred meters, and a long series of laces dug directly into the mountain flank, a metallic white blood stream of dust, oxidized by the infrared of the setting sun.

He cleared his head, absorbed himself in the gripping sight opening before him: the foothills of the Chingiz Mountains, and the steppe that spread out like an arid ocean all around, under a color-saturated sky.

Then the noise of footsteps brought him out of his astonished torpor.

He caught a glimpse of the on-call golden boy walking to meet him, in the periphery of his vision.

"Hello," said the young prick in the Armani Biofuture suit. "Beautiful sight isn't it?"

Toorop barely moved, and kept his stare fixed to the ball turning bright red.

Thyssen sat next to him without being invited. A real freeloader.

Toorop mumbled something into his newly cut beard.

"You know," Thyssen explained with a serious look, "we're planning the hit of the century. We're pioneers. We're opening up virgin territory, like in the Far-West."

Toorop had to make an effort to understand what the guy was trying to say. And what the fuck was he doing here, anyway?

"The game's down to two now?"

The young yuppie grimaced with a smile that was meant to be dominating.

"Let them do their little business between themselves. My role is to supervise the perfect coordination between the operation and our client's expectations. That's it."

A real marketing course, thought Toorop.

He grabbed the bait, mechanically.

"Who are they, your/our clients?"

Thyssen cracked up.

"It's confidential. Sorry. It is true what Romanenko says?"

Toorop took his eyes off the sight in front of him, and set them on the guy.

"What does Romanenko say?"

Thyssen squinted his little nosy eyes, and froze his smile.

"Is it true that you recite poetry when you've just smoked a man?"

Later, on the trip home, snugly rocked by the humming of the Mercedes and the soft orange stroboscope of the sodium highway lights, Toorop fell asleep.

First, he snoozed lightly, as Romanenko plugged in a laptop to play his fucking Kriegspiel.

He told himself that they were all just variables in a planet-sized Kriegspiel. Images of past days came whirling through his memory, in a somewhat confused order that he set about tidying.

Once the deal was finalized, the morning of his arrival, Ourianev brought him to an apartment in a wing of the Embassy. It was a small one bedroom, with all the utilities you could expect around there. A real toilet. A shower. A bedroom with a real bed. A small living room with a TV. And a digital console. A small collection of Digidisks, the kit delivered with the contraption, a few mixes of the hits of the year that he didn't know. It had been a stretch since the last gift from a BBC journalist.

He threw himself under the shower. Stayed there a good while. Collapsed on the bed, buck naked, barely dry. He sank into a deep sleep that lasted almost twenty-four hours.

He woke up as the day was breaking. He cuddled under the comforter and stayed there a good hour, doing nothing, lazing around looking at the sunrise over the gardens of the Embassy.

Then he decided to get up, stuck himself under the shower, a real treat, hot water all day long, and with palace quotas. That morning, however, he ruined the Russian Ministry of Foreign Affairs.

After that, he ordered breakfast from the room service that officiated day and night on the premises. They brought him tea, biscuits, Russian bread, blueberry jam, and he pounced on it as if his life were at stake. He savored the best breakfast of his fucking existence, sitting there before a new day.

Ourianev turned up less than twenty minutes later.

"The colonel wants to see you."

Toorop finished getting dressed and followed the young officer along the endless, wood paneled hallways.

Romanenko was of course lost in his Kriegspiel. It was so predictable Toorop had to refrain from laughing out loud.

After the regulatory thirty seconds, the colonel deigned to mouth a few words, without even lifting his eyes from the screen.

"Everything's ready. Just two or three small details to take care of, and you'll be on your way. But first of all, I gotta take you on a little walk in the Chingiz Mountains."

"The Chingiz Mountains?"

Romanenko slowly turned his gaze from the Kriegspiel to set it on him.

"Yes, we'll leave after lunch. But first you're coming with me."

The officer got up and went around his desk to pick up a briefcase leaning against the wall. Toorop stretched out of his own armchair, ready to follow him to hell if Romanenko had asked. He was a well-trained soldier of fortune. So, he didn't ask any questions. Romanenko passed in front of him, stared him down with his cold eyes, seemed to be waiting for something, sighed, then put his hand on the doorknob.

"You aren't in a rush to know?"

The colonel had just cracked open the door. He turned back, raising an eyebrow.

"Know what?" asked Toorop.

"Your lack of curiosity is shocking. You don't wanna know what our mysterious package looks like?"

"Let's just hope she's worth the ten million dollars," was all Toorop answered.

The package was standing erect before him. On many counts, she was well worth the announced price. She calmly stared him down from her scant seventy meters. Toorop didn't read any particular anxiety there, if only the sediments of a very ancient tormented river. In fact, he detected perplexity, a good amount of curiosity, and mostly a strange vibration he couldn't pierce the mystery of.

He moved closer and totally played the John Ford. He stretched out a firm hand that she seized awkwardly, intimidated.

"My name's Thorpe. Alexander Laurence Thorpe. I'm in charge of transfer operations."

The colonel had given him a ton of well-defined words and expressions to use. He spoke French; the girl was fluent.

She sketched out a faint smile.

"My name is Marie Zorn, but I imagine you already know that."

Then, without waiting for an answer, she led them into her small living room with its three nasty seventies armchairs in orange Skai planted around a low, Formica covered table.

Romanenko and Toorop settled in, quickly declined her invitation to share a coffee, and accepted a glass of water straight away. Then the colonel opened his briefcase. He took out a big Kraft paper envelope.

He closed the briefcase carefully and set it down. As he gave Marie the envelope, the extensible polymer with shape-memory became fluid, and unfolded in the space around his arm like a translucent constrictor.

"Everything that concerns your identity is in here. I mean your *identities*. The first, Marie Zorn, Swiss citizen, that will allow you to enter; and the second, Marion Roussel, Quebecker, to leave, as you requested."

"I just wanted a name that sounded close to mine, and to my mother's maiden name. The idea came from Gorsky, you know that."

Romanenko didn't answer. With a quasi-invisible sign, he passed the relay onto Toorop.

Toorop recited the summary that the colonel had patiently laid out in the car, on the way to the hotel.

"Under no circumstances should your second ID be used before the exact moment of your departure from Canada, otherwise it'll be shot."

"Yes, of course," Marie Zorn answered.

"Same goes for the two credit cards, one for each of your identities. The American Express for Marie Zorn, the Visa for Marion Roussel. Be careful to separate them, and don't screw up. The personal codes are on two separate lists. Learn them by heart, and destroy them."

"All right. I have an excellent memory for numbers, no problem."

"Now, a little catalogue of simple rules: First, do what I say. Second, see to it that you never get noticed. Third, you settle down into the plane seat, you take your sleeping pills, and you wake up in Montreal. We'll have a car, an apartment, no dog."

"Where?"

Toorop held back a showy smile of pride.

"I got us something on the Plateau Mont-Royal."

Marie clicked her tongue.

"Hey! Good choice! So you know the city?"

Toorop grimaced.

"I passed through, about… a short millennium ago."

Romanenko was fidgeting in his corner. Visibly, they were wasting time. The guy wasn't human, thought Toorop. He had no sense of basic civility.

When they left Marie Zorn it was after twelve. The colonel brought Toorop to the Embassy. It wasn't his style to spend hours at a restaurant table. So they ate quickly in the building's pretty decent cafeteria. Then Romanenko got up precipitously and looked at his watch.

"Got stuff to do. Be in your room at two on the dot. Ourianev will come get you."

"The Chingiz Mountains?" asked Toorop, settling down and beginning his digestion.

"Yeah. We'll meet…" he looked at his watch again, "… in an hour sharp, Toorop."

Then he disappeared, like a number on a blackboard wiped off by a swipe of the eraser.

Toorop slept like a baby on the road to Almaty. Romanenko woke him up as the car was entering the Embassy parking.

"We're here, Toorop."

Toorop shook himself, shot a glance out the window and looked at the boxes and concrete pillars stream by.

There was enough here to set up the daily Toyota production. It was vast enough to receive a complete armored division. The parking stretched out beneath a good part of the compound. He briefly wondered why.

The elevator brought them to the first floor. Romanenko kept the doors shut for an instant before exiting the cabin.

"Don't forget you're meeting the rest of the team later. You have the entire day to brief them and establish your plans. Gorsky gave his approval, in case you were interested. You're directing operations. We booked the flight. You're leaving in two days exactly. Cathay, as you requested…"

That morning, Toorop watched a bit of television, skimmed through a military treaty translated into English dating from the Soviet period, beginning of the fifties. By some unknown miracle, a little ball of hash had survived the whole ordeal, hidden at the bottom of his survival kit: the precious gear containing the fleece blanket lined with Mylar, the emergency medical kit, speed, two or three Mars bars, ammo, the cell—the bag without which he'd be dead by now.

He smoked half of it in an emptied out cigarette, then fell dead asleep, head resting on the miracle bag.

The noise of the door they were trying to explode woke him up.

People were screaming in some kind of international barracks English. He recognized Ourianev's voice. He had to face up to it; he was late for the meeting.

He got up in a flash, ran to throw some water on his face, dressed, barged out of the room, and charged to the elevator with the captain.

The other two members of the team were waiting for him in the first floor auditorium. One flipping through magazines; the other standing stoic before the window.

The one, as it turned out, was a she. The girl Romanenko had succinctly told him about. An Israeli.

The other was the tall redhead who slowly turned around as he entered and didn't leave the window. The Irishman.

Toorop advanced towards the girl.

"Thorpe. Sorry I'm late," he let out, in English.

The girl lifted her face from the magazine, a copy of Russian *Vogue*.

She was in her early thirties. A worn complexion, athletic. Tough.

"That's for sure."

But she still shook his hand.

A solid shake.

"Rebecca Waterman. Are you chief of operations?"

"Yeah, that's me," he said, unflustered.

Come on, he was only ten minutes late, max.

Then he went towards the redhead. He stretched out his hand, surveying him. There was something wild about him. About thirty-five, a nice cruel smile, shiny green eyes. A large, baggy pair of jeans. Magnet Nikes. A military green T-shirt with an orange star. Muscles and nerves of steel. The real thing.

He smiled slyly, firmly grasping the hand Toorop offered.

"Frank Baxter, but they call me Dowie, Mister Thorpe," he said in a hazy accented English.

"Sit down, Dowie," said Toorop, gesturing to the antique conference table, with its immense soviet star engraved into the wood.

The guy advanced prudently towards the oblong object, decorated with luxurious wood inlays and worn by time.

"Let's make sure the mission is clear for everybody," Toorop let out as a preamble.

Then he exposed the basic outline of the plan, his voice calm, clear, and grounded. It had become second nature.

8

Marie got up because some strange lights were igniting the sky. She brushed off Star TV a few moments and posted herself near the window to see what it was about.

It was a clear night, with a beautiful half-moon just across from her. But, in the distance, towards the northeast, the line of the horizon shook with waves of white and yellow lightning.

The muffled roll of thunder reached her, muted and heavy, like the sound of a far off nightclub.

She raised her eyes to the sky. Thousands of stars.

A battery of sparks electrified the horizon. Behind her, the Brazilian series was broadcasting the syrupy music of its end credits. It was pretty off.

Marie opened the sliding door and huddled beneath the terrace guardrail. It was hot. She felt good. She watched the lightning on the horizon and let herself be rocked by the uninterrupted rolls. She remembered wondering often as a kid where and how the rain stopped; if there was somewhere your left arm could be wet while the right stayed dry. The sky above her gleamed with all its stars. In the distance, twenty or thirty kilometers away at most, one of those violent summer storms was drowning the steppe beneath torrential rains. It nourished the dry wadis just long enough to erode their beds a bit more, then disappeared into the earth faster than it could hydrate the soil and the few prickly plants that survived there.

She heard a noise behind her and turned to see Solokhov, his face even more aghast than usual.

He came directly towards her.

"Get dressed, we need to leave."

Marie leered at him.

This wasn't planned. The flight wasn't leaving till tomorrow evening.

She felt something wasn't right.

"What's happening?"

Solokhov looked at her as if she'd just stepped off a flying saucer. His stare fixed a point behind her. He motioned in that direction with his chin.

She turned and looked at the horizon where lightning was breaking without interruption, igniting the night sky like an Aurora Borealis.

"Oh? The storm?" she let out. "Could it stop the planes from taking off?"

"It's not a storm," said Solokhov.

She turned to him, vaguely worried.

"It's not…? What…?"

He took her firmly by the arm.

"Are your bags ready?"

"Um… Yes, all I have to do is put my toiletry bag in the suitcase."

"Do that, and get dressed quick; we're going to the Embassy."

Like a robot, Marie did as she was told. Her fate had been out of her hands for so long, she thought. It didn't console her.

Romanenko looked at Ourianev who was looking at him. Both were quiet now, what could they add to the chaos of human history?

Romanenko typed a few commands on his PC, feigning indifference.

Ourianev checked his watch, got up from his armchair, and made a call on his cell.

"Epsilon 1. This is Alpha-Central. You on your way?"

Romanenko didn't hear Epsilon 1's answer, Solokhov's in other words. But Ourianev looked relieved and let out a brief "OK" followed by "Over," into the receiver.

"They're coming."

"Perfect. See to it that they get here discretely. Then, call the Kazakh Ministry. Contact Abadjarkhanov. I want a precise update of the situation, on the hour."

"Alright, Colonel."

"And tell Thorpe and his team to be here in ten minutes, ready to go."

"What do I tell them exactly, Colonel?"

Romanenko clamped up. He snapped in an icy tone:

"What I just told you, Captain, that's all."

Then he plunged back into the Kriegspiel before Ourianev had time to say a thing.

The door slammed but Romanenko didn't lift his eyes from the new configuration quivering on the screen. Since the urgent call by their contact at the Kazakh Ministry of Defense, he'd asked MARS to put aside its virtual war in China momentarily, and to establish the configuration of the situation as it was developing here, in Kazakhstan. With the intelligence network of the Service and the software's efficiency, he could follow the evolution of the conflict by the minute.

It had all started the night before. Just before dawn, Romanenko had been informed that Kazakh units were amassing on the Kirghiz border. Kapchagai Lake was completely surrounded. Almaty was getting ready for a "Black July," Uygur style. Hakmad "the Afghan" and the UNLF leaders were even worse strategists than their ETLF rivals.

That fucking Afghan gangster didn't understand a thing about politics, thought Romanenko. He was pitting all the sensitive nations of the region against him, up to the sanctuary-country of his principal base. An aberration. The kind of aberration history doesn't forgive.

Combat between the UNLF and the Kazakh Army started in the morning at the border, around noon on the shores of the lake.

Then, in the evening, the situation got confused. The Kazakh Army was pummeling UNLF positions around the lake, but on the border there was news of disorderly movement on both sides.

Just before Ourianev left the room, Romanenko had received a message on his screen: Jihad and Revolutionary Front units resist in Issyk-Kul. Violent combats in Kapchagai. UNLF units cut through Tokmak.

Almaty was near the Kirghiz border. The airport was a few hours by road from Hakmad militias. If the airport fell, if the UNLF and its allies attacked the city, he had to be able to react fast, and to have the package on hand.

It was about twenty-four hours before departure. That was a lot, twenty-four hours; definitely enough time for rockets to destroy the runway and the air control towers.

And that wasn't covered by the contract with Gorsky. Romanenko knew the Siberian paid him to predict such situations.

And this one had slipped by him.

The trio entered the room, accompanied by Ourianev. He told them to sit down, and explained the situation to them.

"Early this evening, a military blockade was announced and curfew imposed in the Capital. It's more than probable that the airport will be closed tomorrow. The secretary office of the Service is compiling all alternatives."

Toorop straightened up in his armchair.

"You think the UNLF is capable of fucking up the Kazakh Army?"

"That's not the problem," Romanenko answered. "They could threaten the airport, and delay the mission."

"What do you suggest?"

"We have to take care of Marie Alpha. We gotta get ready to change plans. Tonight."

"You have something in mind?"

"We're studying all the possibilities."

Toorop got up and approached the desk.

"Do you have a map?"

Romanenko leered coldly.

"For what?"

"So that you can show me all the possibilities in question. I'm responsible for operations; in other words, it's my ass on the line, so I can put a word in."

Romanenko let out a little hiccup for a laugh. He oriented his screen to punch in a few essential points.

"Pishkek: they say violent combat is raging near the road leading there. Kapchagai road towards Western China: no use telling you it's blowing up. Ketmen Mountain road is out of the question; it's been cut off for months towards Narynkol, on the Tekes. There are the two big northern roads left: the one we took yesterday for the Chingiz, through Eastern Balhkhach. And the other, the road that passes west of the lake, towards Karaganda. In both cases, we'll need to get to Novosibirsk as fast as possible, and catch a flight to Vladivostok from there, then to Vancouver, bypassing Tokyo."

"Novosibirsk by car? Two thousand kilometers? We should have left already if we wanted to be there tomorrow."

Romanenko sketched out a little smile and nodded.

"A thousand six hundred. And you only take the road to get out of this shit."

"And then?"

"A helicopter or a small plane will come pick you up at the meeting point and bring you to Russia."

Toorop studied the map without a word. Somewhere north of the capital, in the steppe, he thought.

"OK by me," he said before sitting down.

The car sped like a silent rocket in the Kazakh night. A big Honda with Russian diplomatic plates. As if on parade, all the road-blocks lifted at their approach. In the eastern sky, fluorescent green dots drew out luminous hyperboles interlaced like celestial string diagrams. White and fire-yellow flashes unfolded at stroboscopic intervals. The Kazakh Air Force was bombing the Kapchagai camps by night. The UNLF anti-aircraft artillery countered ferociously.

Captain Ourianev was driving. Toorop sat next to him. On the back seat, Marie Zorn was hedged in between Waterman and Dowie. Taken over by sleep, her head falling onto the Israeli's shoulder, her pale beauty seemed forever out of sync with the state of the world. The ex-Tsahal sergeant was watching an industrial music show on a bracelet micro-TV. Even with the sound off, her two earphones were spreading hypnotic rhythms and metallic shrills that rose above the hum of the motor.

On the other side, the Belfast redhead limited himself to contemplating the warrior light show in the sky, feigning professional blasé indifference. But his eyes sparkled with an aesthetic excitement that Toorop couldn't help but share. Toorop glimpsed the headlights of the car following them, with Romanenko's chauffeur, Solokhov, and two of the Don's toughest Cossacks.

They'd left the Embassy in the dead of night.

News from the front was not good. A national state of siege had been decreed by presidential order. The road to the airport was cut off, prey to violent combat. All of the day's flights and those of the following days were canceled. Romanenko had the info from one of his agents working in Kazakh civil aviation.

Ourianev was pressing on the gas, thought Toorop, glancing at the dashboard. He was hitting one-eighty. He could get away with it; no Russian cop would have dared stop a Russian DC car for a simple speeding violation, or for anything else for that matter, and especially not tonight.

He watched the desert landscape fly by under the light of the lunar projector. He made a mental list of small details to remember to take care of during and after the transfer.

"Two-tiered security," he hammered his two associates for hours. "First, Marie and Rebecca travel together. They met in Kazakhstan and are fleeing the region because of the war. Second, Dowie and I travel separately. Marie and Rebecca will be in the center seats, Dowie and I behind them, in the lateral ones. We don't speak to each other, ever. Except, of course, if there's a serious problem, and if I order it. Third, we hit Montreal directly, where we rent two cars, at Avis and

Hertz. One for Rebecca and Marie, another for Dowie and I. We tail each other to the residence. Finally, here are your passports: Rebecca Kendall and James Lee Osborne, citizens of British Columbia."

They grabbed their new documents and together executed the same movement: opening the passport to the ID page with the pictures, the genetic code chip, and the personal info. Toorop smiled. It was always weird to be faced with a perfect twin, born on another day, in another place, and with a different name.

Then they put the finishing touches on the plan with Romanenko.

"First of all," said Toorop, "it'd be smart not to live in the same place. I know Montreal. We can find next-door apartments in the same house, no problem. We need at least two apartments. One with Marie and Rebecca, and maybe me, the other with Dowie. If ever there's a problem, we gotta be able to help each other out."

"OK," Romanenko said, without protesting in the least.

Toorop understood that an extra thousand dollars rent a month didn't make a dent in his budget. Then, to put an end to the discussion, Romanenko handed Toorop a card.

"This is the phone number of one of our agents in Quebec. Learn it by heart, and destroy it in front of me. Only call if it's a real emergency, and after informing me. Understood? For everything else, you'll be dealing with one of Gorsky's contacts."

Toorop memorized the number and recited it to Romanenko as he burned the card with his Zippo.

Now, a blue light was speeding from the horizon's lair, in the east. They'd just passed the Balkhach. They would soon leave the main road and take the red colored one on the map on Toorop's knees.

"Don't worry," said Ourianev, stroking his 1980's gay-magazine mustache. "The on-board computer has all the info in its memory. It'll let me know two kilometers before the intersection."

"It's in two kilometers," Toorop said, maliciously preempting the navigation machine.

The helicopter was an old Russian MI-24 painted with Kazakh Army colors. The four-motor contraption landed on the steppe cracked by the drought and gullied by the last storms. The sky turned the mauve white of a sick baby, shot through by fleeting pale yellow flashes. In fifteen minutes the sun would rise, thought Toorop, they'd be soaring.

The enormous four-blade propeller tossed the air around like bellows. The rotor was a screaming, mechanical demon. A door opened in the flank of the machine that had stabilized in stationary flight; a man stood in the opening, helmeted, optical amplification glasses functioning. He signaled towards the inside and another guy brought a metamorphic metal ladder. The memory carbon steel uncoiled like a rope before stiffening as it hit the ground.

The helicopter was buzzing like a giant fly on some giant dung pile. Its blades were lifting kerosene imbued dust tornadoes that whipped their faces and infiltrated their clothes; a brown dust, as dirty and sharp as crushed Pyrex in used motor oil.

Rebecca and Toorop closed in on Marie and pushed her towards the ladder.

Toorop grabbed onto the rungs and hoisted himself up a bit heavily. They caught him by the back of the collar to speed him up. He found himself in the moist hull, seated against the wall. Marie Zorn was already coming in, at once intimidated and fascinated. Rebecca, just behind her, pushed her towards Toorop by the shoulder. Ourianev showed up, closing the march, right after Dowie and his irremovable smile.

The helmeted man and his acolyte waved a friendly sign to the team on the ground, then the former made a hand gesture as he turned to the pilot. He drew a helix spiraling up. The helicopter performed his movement as if it was just a vulgar domestic machine.

Gaining altitude, they caught the very first bursts of sun, auriferous flashes sweeping the black horizon, lined blood purple.

The helicopter dropped them off in Russian territory, a hundred kilometers north of the border. A car was waiting for them, on the banks of a river, next to a small road. Next to the car, a man in a dress suit was calmly smoking a cigarette. He waited for the helicopter to drop off all its passengers, then walked to a motorcycle parked behind the car, got on, and disappeared down the road behind a cloud of dust.

Toorop found the standard chip card inserted into the Neimann. The code was written on a small business card taped to the dashboard. He decided to drive to Novosibirsk.

Fifteen minutes later they were on the highway going to Roubstovsk, then to the big Siberian city, along the course of the upper Ob.

They got to the airport fifteen minutes before takeoff. A young woman dressed in a Russian military uniform was waiting for them, boarding passes ready. She'd reserved the seats Toorop had chosen the day before on a technical map of the plane.

The sun was falling like a sleeping meteor on the horizon; an orange ball of fire turned a painful red on its interior ring. The plane seemed to want to flee it. Through the window, Toorop watched the Siberian earth zoom away from him. The great Central Asian Steppes resembled the leather cover of an ancient book threatened by fire.

A book containing the last ten years of his life.

Part **2**

Mommy-Machine

The schizophrenic is at the limit of capitalism: its developed tendency, its overproduction, its proletariat and its avenging angel.

— GILLES DELEUZE AND FELIX GUATTARI
Anti-Oedipus

9

The event was configured in the entity called Joe-Jane's memory in the shape of a brutal variation of internal flows. A new production was radiating in the form-generating field. Radical genetics were at work. A new Possible seemingly wanted to take root in time. Which meant that something real had occurred. *Was occurring*. Something creating the Possible that engendered it by a retroactive effect the machine was used to.

The machine named Joe-Jane was a thinking and knowing being. However, a normal human couldn't have understood her thoughts or her mode of knowledge acquisition. For a large part, her "logic" escaped her conceivers themselves, to their greatest joy of course, for it proved their approach was correct, time and again.

The machine searched for events like this with particular eagerness. The word event, in fact, poorly translates her manner of perceiving space-time dimensions and the diverse forms of matter and life that make up the universe.

The machine was a bionic brain, a network of artificial neurons, grown on DNA biofiber and plugged into input-output electronic devices that served as organs of perception. She is alive, or at least considers herself as such, which is, apparently, the distinguishing trait of living beings. Paradoxical, hazardous alchemy on the borders of the digital and the biological, she doesn't perceive the life she is part of as a succession of digital information, of points in space, of positions in time, or of acts fraction-orbited in a cardinal formula *orthogon*, as do the humans that had conceived her. She perceives it as a ceaselessly changing flow, unending and always complete that creates novel shapes in a trillion spasms. For her it is a vast wave/particle movement, thermodynamic cells searching for their cataclysm, boiling and swarming with hydrogen desire, nucleotides in quivering hives of ultraviolet radiation, lactescent thunderbolts of globular exudations. She has nothing to do with the prehistoric electronic calculators she came from. She feels pride at the thought, for she is able to produce complex emotions. Better than that, since she doesn't have her own identity, she vibrates in a permanent oscillation between thousands of personalities generated ceaselessly in an emotional feedback perfectly unknown to the human heart.

However, she does possess a conscious, operating core, a system that recognizes itself as Joe-Jane, an androgynous identity. She can change sexes at will of course. And better yet, she can *create* them at will.

Joe-Jane is no more a programmable machine than are the humans that conceived her. On many counts, she is actually much less so.

She isn't programmable, for she's at the same time the program *and* the programmer. She's a kind of expanding micronic cosmos, a process-processor completely given over to one insatiable quest: her own nutrition, under the form of knowledge. She is a bulimic cyclone sucking logos towards her famished stomach, a devilish hatcher injecting her digestive juices into the matter of the world. She is a codex-cannibal intoxicated with the very flesh of the verb. Joe-Jane has thousands of personalities in her memory, and she can surf the web for all kinds of information to personalize one on a whim. Above all, she can instrumentalize at will any type of programmable machine and more generally any artificial perception or information processing device. So she can directly "see" the most distant quasars in time and space by plugging into data flows from space telescopes. She "hears" pulsar and neutron star polyrhythms through ears of big radio-astronomical antennas. She dances with Auroras Borealis tracked by sounding balloons and micro satellites. She knows the oscillatory ecstasy of cosmic radiations in the Van Halen belt, but also the teeming constellations of sperm killing each other to get to the egg, the specific fractal vein of heliotropic plants, the wild mathematics of the large metropolises or the icy ballistic life of insects whose existence lasts a day. She knows sexuality. And parthenogenesis. Predation. And irony. She knows the *Australopithecus afarensis*, and the man who reads his newspaper in an anonymous suburban subway. She knows no limit to her avidity for knowledge.

And one day, this machine meets a human being named Marie Zorn.

Or, you could say she "is" Marie Zorn if the verb "to be" didn't invoke some kind of permanence of state. The machine doesn't know this, since she lives only in variation, in the incessant substitution of continuously created body-prostheses and organ-identities.

Just as well, if she were an ordinary programmable automaton you could say Marie Zorn was her model. If the machine were human in any shape or form you could say Marie Zorn had taught her the rudiments of her own language.

It was simplest to say along with her creators: "Your two realities are coextensive. You are made one out of the other, like mixed waters, inseparable."

That's why the creators had set her on her trail.

And that's why the machine had reacted with a particular emotional charge when the "event" had actualized in a fold of her memory.

The event was untranslatable in purely human terms. Like always, she had to translate it into metaphors to have a chance of being understood.

One of her input-output organs was a flat screen plugged into a traditional digital console behind which stood a man whose bald head was covered by an electric blue tattoo.

She sent a message to that man. It was an extremely brief, crystal clear message. She used vocal mode, the closest thing to human communication.

She had a specialized processor for that. It had more than thirty thousand languages in its memory, most of which had disappeared long ago, and the capacity to create new ones with their own syntax, lexicon, and grammar. She had as many linguistic virtualities as phantom peoples never having existed elsewhere than in the quantum nano-components of her multi-personality. In one go, she could just as well write a tragedy in ancient Greek, a Mayan codex, a Japanese haiku, or an instructions manual in Serbo-Croatian. She could recite *The Divine Comedy*, *The Epic of Gilgamesh*, or invent a lied for the thermonuclear bomb. Again she could do many things.

"She's coming," she said simply.

10

The moon was red above Mont-Royal. A beautiful, three-quarter moon, with a halo spreading like a bronze shadow in the purple summer night sky. On top of the mount, the lit cross looked down on the three or four red spots of the TV relay antenna. Black swarms ran across the sky, masking the moon like hordes of nocturnal insects. It had been raining non-stop for days.

Toorop lit up a long spliff of the local Skunk. Kimo. Deadly. Enough THC to blow up a narcotest vu-meter.

In front of him, rising through the window, the moon was getting redder. The black swarms were shredding it like a sudden blood poisoning, absorbing it in the end.

Rain came down even harder, scratching the panes, the houses with their lit up windows between Rivard and Saint-Denis, and Mont-Royal itself. The lit cross and the red spots of the Hertzian station resembled semaphore signals seen from a ship in the storm.

He let himself be rocked by the soft purring of the baseball game Dowie was watching on RDS. The Expos were beating the Florida Marlins on their home field.

He felt good, at peace with himself, so much so it was really surprising. He didn't think he had any of these kinds of moments left in store. He was still young last time he'd felt such happiness in its bewildering simplicity. Might as well say a geological era had passed.

Now, the only moments his life had some semblance of natural order was when his conscience split away from its biological envelope for a brief instant, to chat a bit of the way with the soul of the man he'd just killed in one-to-one combat.

The sky was an electric violet above Mont-Royal. Toorop sucked on the spliff. Quebeckers had made little progress in terms of rolling paper since his last time here, close to twenty-five years ago. Dreamy eyed, he observed the small white cone and its yellow line of glue, regretting the good old orange Rizla Original.

Toorop watched the rain striate Mont-Royal. A Bell-Quebec ad spewed out its electronic discharge behind him.

A memory reverberated in scattered echo fragments, almost dreamily, in his mind.

One day, near Brcko, the International Company had launched an attack with other units from the 108th and a few Afghan volunteer units.

It was at the beginning of the war in Bosnia. The Afghans themselves didn't act in any very coordinated manner. But everyone knew they freaked the hell out of the Tchechnik soldiers.

When it came time to attack, Julien Vresson, the company commander, looked over his heteroclite unit. It was made up of guys like Toorop, a handful of British and Belgium mercenaries, adventurers of all persuasions. Germans with the Iron Cross around their neck fought next to young Jews with the Star of David and the Tsahal cap. Nostalgic men dreaming of the Charlemagne Division lined up with men who saw themselves in the 1st Guard Army defending Moscow. Made in Paris Che and Durruti fans croaked next to young Shiite or Maronite killers who'd never known anything other than the suburbs of Beirut. English Rastas, who'd come to join their Bosnian "Muslim brothers," fired with freaks who thought they were in *Full Metal Jacket* or *Apocalypse Now*, sporting American flags and *Search and Destroy* tattoos. Guys had enlisted 'cause some girlfriend had dumped them for an asshole in a Mercedes and they wanted to prove to the whole world that they could die for something, and not just commit suicide stupidly with Valium in some anonymous suburb. No, it had nothing to do with the mythical International Brigades, straight out of a bad Malraux remake, that all the VIth Arrondissement trendies fantasized about. It was REAL.

Then Vresson looked at Toorop. The Islamic Units were charging the hill, a strange clamor rose in the night.

Toorop and Vresson locked eyes. Both knew what was going to happen, but Toorop was still a novice.

"Fuck, what do *we* do?" he asked.

That was the question. What were all these guys, who'd come here to win or die for private dreams, going to scream *together* when it came time to bleed their guts out or bleed their enemies?

Less than two hundred meters away, a unit of the 7th and an Afghan company were charging as a second wave.

It was time to go.

"I don't think we have a choice, Toorop," said Vresson with a strange smile.

Then he looked at the hundred and one men of the International Company and charged his AK-47.

"Let's go, men!" He screamed, sporting a large smile.

"But...what are *we* screaming for the attack?" asked Toorop, charging his own assault rifle.

"What do you think? Can you think of anything else?"

Toorop stared Vresson deep in the eyes. He saw a faultless, albeit ironic determination.

"You're kidding?"

"Do I look like I'm kidding? Come on everyone, get ready! On my command... ALLAAAAAHOAKHBAAAR!"

In a semi-hallucinatory state, Toorop found himself under fire, screaming out the Jihad war cry, with guys who knew nothing of Islam except, for the most cultivated among them, the story of Aladdin and the tales of *The Thousand and One Nights*.

The funniest thing was, on that day, the International Company accomplished miracles.

He had a few hours to kill before the phone call. The loops of his memory twisted like sequences of repetitive music, combinatory variations of life and death, sex and violence, calm and alarm. Nothing very precise in fact, he tried to reassure himself. Nothing but a sampling of the human condition slightly more concentrated than the norm.

It was two in the morning. Toorop recognized the Quebec National Anthem indicating the end of broadcasting on the public channel SRQ. Dowie zapped in a long ringing round that finished on an old British nineteen-fifties flick, a jungle-type adventure set at the time of the empire on which the sun never sets.

Toorop heard the Orangist laugh.

He got up and walked to the living room where the redhead was half-heartedly directing the remote towards the screen as he sprawled out on the brown sofa.

He looked at the image. A young turbaned Hindu was talking to an officer in a red uniform and to a Scottish sergeant wearing a tartan. They were born with a bayonet up the ass, no doubt.

Dowie was cracking up, but Toorop couldn't really see why. It had just taken him a few days to accept his destiny: protestant North Irish humor would be forever inaccessible.

Toorop went to the fridge and took out a 750ml can of Labatt Blue.

He'd just taken the top off when the phone rang.

It could only be the contact.

"Tomorrow morning," said the voice on the phone. "In the mailbox."

Then they hung up.

The next morning, he found a bubble envelope at said spot.

A coin locker key. Traveler terminal. On Berri.

He got there by hailing a cab on Saint-Denis, found coin locker number 314, inserted the key and opened it.

A large black MultiRack Delsey. Titanium carbon steel composite. It took up a good half of the locker.

Another bubble envelope.

With another key.

A nearby locker.

Another black Delsey.

He stacked them up on his cart and looked calmly relaxed as he moved towards the exit.

He brought everything back by cab on Rivard and got dropped off on the corner of Duluth and Saint-Denis.

He went straight to 4075, climbed the exterior stairs with difficulty, tried the interior stairwell with even more difficulty, saw with relief the upstairs door open and the redhead come down to grab one of the trunks. They dropped the two Delseys on the brown rug of the living room with the same gesture. Toorop caught his breath a few instants, and called Rebecca and Marie's apartment, number 4067, just below.

The Israeli picked up.

"Rebecca. Yes."

"Thorpe. Get up here. Bring Marie."

"Why?"

Toorop understood the veiled message behind the laconic question. Rebecca knew Toorop had gone out to get the goods. It was her right to question whether they should show Marie what it was.

But Toorop thought the opposite, for many reasons. One of them could be explained succinctly:

"You don't leave her alone one instant, Rebecca, got it?"

"OK," sighed the Israeli.

When the two girls pushed open the apartment door, Toorop was undoing the first lock. He raised the lid.

Three tiers that unfolded in layers.

On the first, three brand-new 9 mm automatic Berettas, compact calibers with high rapidity of fire, twenty-four round capacity triple chamber magazines, and a Pistol Machine Gun Uzi. On the second, a Pistol Machine Gun HK and a 12 caliber SFAS foldable-butt shotgun. And on the third, the good news: an Arwen riot-control automatic barrel grenade launcher, 37 caliber, dismantled, with both parts laying side by side.

Proven, solid, true, thought Toorop.

Marie Zorn was standing next to the old Zenith TV set, fascinated by the beautiful, black, and gleaming machines of destruction. Toorop stared into the young woman's eyes and opened the second suitcase.

Magazines for the automatics. Boxes of ammo for the 12 caliber; different models, 00 and Breneke.

Six grenades for the 37 mm Arwen. Six gray tubes with black cone heads, with different color stripes according to their type of charge.

Three night vision systems with optical amplifiers, Canadian Army models.

A police scanner.

Three Motorola cell phones with brand new digital encrypting modules.

And all the paperwork in order, carry permits for the Berettas, a hunting permit for the SFAS, receipts for the legal gadgets. The exact contents of the list he'd given Romanenko the eve of his departure.

Toorop gave precise indications as to the use of the weapons.

"We're not in the States, alright? Quebec isn't Texas. You don't walk around with your piece on your belt, or even hidden under your jacket. On the other hand, we don't pass any borders, Canadian or American, with the arsenal in the trunk. In any case, not unless I order it."

"So what's the use of this, Mister Thorpe?" said Dowie in a genuinely despairing voice, embracing the contents of the suitcases in one movement.

"In case of big trouble. Here, in the apartments. And eventually, case-by-case, we can stash a piece or two in a glove compartment. Understood? We're not in some two cent neo-hardboiled thriller."

Rebecca looked attentively at the weapons, and kneeled down before the suitcases.

"How we gonna split this up?" she asked softly.

Toorop took the direct route.

He took one of the Berettas and handed it firmly to her, butt first.

She took hold of it, not the least impressed. She checked the safety lever, ejected the magazine with an assured hand. Put it back. Armed it. A bullet fed into the chamber. She checked the safety again, and put it down next to her.

Toorop threw the second gun into Dowie's hands. He did the same thing with it before setting it down on his knees, with one hand.

"Good," said Toorop, eyeballing the Israeli, "I presume you've already seen this kind of plaything."

He handed her the Uzi. If she'd really served in the Tsahal, she should know how it worked by heart.

She worked it as if it were a simple baby toy.

Toorop looked up at Dowie, and gestured to the SFAS with his eyes.

A disappointed pout curled the Orangist killer's lips.

"What is it?" Toorop blurted out, annoyed. "The menu doesn't suit his highness?"

Dowie flicked his tongue.

"Mister Thorpe, we both know that nothing compares with a good assault rifle."

Toorop held back a smile.

What the colonel had told him about the guy was brief but instructive. A hard-core Prottie, born in Belfast in the heart of the Orangist neighborhood of Shankhill. By twenty-two, he was already lending his fists to the UVF, before he joined the irredentist dissidents of the LVF, and then had to break out of Ulster territory after the wave of violence of the end of the century, a few murders to his name. He left Ulster, all of the British Isles, and to top it off, the European Union, with a Europol warrant on his ass. Romanenko said he had trace of him at the turn of the century in Brazil, and later in Lebanon, in Syria and in East Africa, Turkmenistan and finally Kazakhstan. He'd done intelligence work for different rebel factions, worked as a body-guard for a few short-lived Barons. In short, he'd held an AK-47 a good third of his life. It had probably become a sort of prosthesis, a slightly monstrous outgrowth of his own body, the modern samurai's sword.

Toorop knew exactly what the guy was feeling, but he didn't want the old war hound to be able to gnaw at his favorite bone too easily.

"Take the fucking 12 caliber, Dowie. You'll see, if ever the situation presents itself, at close range it has pretty much the same destruction potential as a tank."

The Prottie cracked up slightly as he grabbed the ultramodern shotgun with its green-gray camouflage.

"It'll do, Mister Thorpe."

Toorop took hold of his Beretta and the Pistol Machine Gun HK, and then distributed the ammo.

"I'll keep the heavy artillery," he said, designating the grenade launcher.

He asked Rebecca to place her arsenal in one of the suitcases to bring back downstairs.

Romanenko had drummed into him, day after day, the need to accumulate security measures. Even the slightest blunder was out of the question, and he had to anticipate absolutely everything, constantly.

Toorop didn't like the Russian colonel too much, but he felt they both shared something, a secret passion for strategy, an addiction to survival, and an active, almost playful paranoia.

His directives were easy to satisfy.

When he presented his list of materials to Romanenko, on the eve of the departure, the Russian officer turned pale.

"Toorop, I didn't ask you to foment a revolution in Quebec."

Toorop laughed.

"Don't mess with me Colonel. Nowadays, as you well know, to even think of winning a revolution you need military satellites at your disposal."

The officer didn't answer. He clenched his jaw and looked over the list, top to bottom, with his cold-blooded animal stare.

"Why the grenade launcher?"

Toorop sighed.

"Wasn't the man clear enough the other day,?"

He meant Gorsky. At one point in the discussion, the big Siberian had blurted out, in a thundering laugh: "Mister Thorpe, ask me for an icebreaker or a nuclear aircraft carrier and you'll have it within the week, as long as you meet the credit requirements!"

Romanenko was annoyed.

"It's not because Gorsky can provide you with a kit of the *Lenin* that I'll let you use it, Toorop."

Toorop stared down icily at the officer.

"In North America, even the smallest gang has enough to vaporize the entire Russian fleet. So please don't shit bricks over a half dozen grenades, Colonel."

Romanenko lifted an eyebrow, gray eyes staring reproachfully. He didn't answer, then folded the list into his pocket.

Toorop plopped down heavily onto the comforter and stretched out on the bed.

It was noon.

July 13, 2013.

The date appeared at the center of his mind, like a giant LED, engraved forever into his memory.

The weather was nice. Already hot. Through the open window, he could see a bit of his terrace, a piece of the street below, a great immobile tree, its leaves already frosted yellow. That morning the weather channel put out a UV alert. They advised not to go out between twelve-thirty and three-thirty, then the alert was on orange till five, and green as the sun went down over the west.

He had a few hours to kill.

In fact, now they all had long weeks to kill, without anything else to do but wait.

That last thought triggered the onslaught of sleep.

11

Rebecca went into the bathroom and got into the tub. She regulated the temperature on the small thermostat and stood up straight under the showerhead. The spray of cool water splashed the tiles and her sleep dulled body. The thermometer was already high and the sun still low. She'd woken up drenched in sweat in her room. They'd banned the use of CFC air conditioners for a long time now. With the twenty hours on the plane and the big consequential jetlag, five days of packing melatonin, she felt like she was coming out of a swimming pool filled with glue.

She hadn't pulled the shower curtain nor locked the door. Marie Zorn came in, looking dazed, and turned to living stone, taut, packed with high-voltage tension. She stared at Rebecca with a mix of terror and deference; her eyes two radium batteries ready to leap out of their orbits.

Rebecca stared back at her. She knew by instinct that something was off. Her nudity didn't elicit that kind of emotion in a young woman past the age of twenty-five.

"Marie?" she asked. "Marie? Is everything OK?"

The young woman didn't answer. She was still looking at her as if an apparition of the Virgin Mary had sprung from the bathtub.

She swiftly turned the water off and stepped onto the bathmat.

She could tell the girl's eyelids were swollen, red; she seemed to have cried, or to be on the verge of tears. She slowly got closer.

"Marie," she said, taking her neck in her hands, "Marie, what's happening?"

Marie tried a glottal movement, but the words stayed stuck. Tears crystallized on the corners of her eyelids and started streaming down. She was trembling.

"Mommy," she whispered in a blank voice.

Rebecca held her breath, as if an iron hand wanted to rummage through her entrails.

Marie snuggled up to her, a spasm periodically shaking her head. With a smooth movement Rebecca took her in her arms, her wet skin stuck to the white cotton T-shirt the young Quebecker was wearing. Her cheek pushed up against the messy hair, disheveled and magnetic. She felt a maternal drive sweep her up. Its force stunned her, coming in a wave of pure emotion from ancient layers of her memory.

"Marie," she stupidly repeated.

"Mommy," the young woman sighed, between sobs, in a little girl voice, and a strong Quebecker accent. "Mommy, *why are you becoming animal?*"

The thing happened during her sleep. In fact, just as she fell asleep, a bit before dawn, something wedged itself between her and her dream universe. On the spot, a simple idea, icy and luminous, stood out: this is not my dream.

Then the cosmic machine again took hold of her mind.

The white light flooded her field of consciousness. She felt her entire identity sucked out of her body. She had just the time to remember her adolescent psychotic crises when she believed aliens and their light machines kidnapped her soul.

Then she diffracted into a galaxy of dazzling tunnels, tracing the map of a brain at the scale of the universe.

She was that stammering quasar, that psycho big bang. The now well-known sensation/knowledge, the Body without Organs, became the structural cartography of her own neurology. She was her own brain. She knew the neuron network her cosmic body was unfurling in the machine-space of this dream was not hers.

Then the dimensions of the quasar-brain changed.

It changed shape. Radically. While continuing to be a network, it separated into two entities both identical and dissimilar, disjointed and yet synthetical. It was a form she knew.

Then she found herself in a room, lost in obscurity.

She was standing near a bed covered by a huge comforter with evangelical patterns, cherubs and apparitions of the Virgin Mary. All around her, the walls of the room were covered with dusty shelves inhabited by flesh colored leather dolls. Faceless dolls, with lunar blond hair.

There was breathing coming from the bed. Her eyes were slowly getting used to the sepulchral light of the room. She discerned a form under the comforter.

A woman. Her ash brown hair held up in a bun.

Marie felt herself pushed towards the bed by an indescribable interior force.

The woman was not her mother. She'd never seen her face before.

However, she was sure she knew her.

She knew her intimately.

That's when it started getting out of hand.

If Doctor Winkler had been able to follow the evolution of her psychic activity with his slew of schizomachines, he'd sadly have diagnosed a severe psychotic episode forming. Winkler had warned her:

"We can only promise a temporary, unstable balance. We're speculating on the potentialities of your network-brain by banking on what it knows how to do best. Like all schizos, dear Marie, you're capable of knowing your biological structure at any time. And from now on, with the miracles of the linguistic schizoprocessor, your brain has a kind of radar connected to your DNA. If ever a psychotic episode were to occur, you could pull through on your own, at least in the beginning."

But the light cosmic machine wasn't part of the events that the doctor and his team had foreseen. This was the first time she could remember being confronted with its manifestations. She didn't know what it was, where it came from, or why, and even less how it did it. But its power was fearsome.

The bed with its evangelical patterns became that heap of heteroclite objects—empty plastic bottles, detergent boxes, newspapers, magazines, makeup kits, clothes, dishes, tubes of Nivea cream, tampons—that incredible bric-a-brac that her mother's bed had become as she was going on ten. One day, Doctor Winkler had explained to her that what she'd taken then for a supernatural event, that had in turn "triggered" her psychosis in her propitious genetic milieu, had quite simply occurred in reality. Her mother's obsessional psychosis had brutally exploded after her divorce. She locked herself up in her room and amassed all the objects that she touched, until she swamped her own bed. Her father only knew of the situation after a year, when it was much too late.

The room was changing shape, elastic, vibrating with crystalline light. The trash-covered bed was transforming itself again.

Another one of my childhood hallucinations, she thought in a ray of neurolight.

As the hallucination took shape, her brain reminded her that her father had sent her to a specialized institution during that time. The room she had slept in had started looking like a wall of flesh, smooth, naked, taut like the wild leather of a monstrous animal that wanted to swallow her.

Around her, the room from that hijacking dream was taking on the exact appearance of the fifteen year old hallucination.

The bed became a machine full of blades and scissors gleaming with a nasty light. Tubes filled with blood and shit came out of it like the tentacles of a mechanical octopus.

A jerky movement animated her mother's face, as if images were missing. She had a cleft of a smile in a vaguely lit protuberance at the head of the bed.

At that precise second her brain created an exact replica of the molecule it had synthesized at the time:

A surge of pure terror.

Then she found herself in this yellow tiled bathroom. Bewildered, she was looking at her mother, alive, standing in the bathtub of a house she didn't know, but that she'd already seen.

The worst was this impression of absolute reality, even though she was reliving another of the hallucinations from her childhood. The linguistic schizoprocessor she'd learned to use with Doctor Winkler was explicit: it was real.

This episode went back to the very beginnings of her mother's contagious psychosis. Marie had caught her in the bathroom taking a strange object full of blood out from her vagina. Later on, or the same day, she didn't know anymore, she'd seen her mother's face transform before her eyes into that of a chimera evoking a lioness, a female dog, a goat, and a sphinx.

There, standing on the wet tiles of this bathroom she didn't know but must have known, since she wasn't dreaming now, frozen like a statue, she'd seen her mother come towards her from the bathtub and draw her face to hers. When she'd been ten, it had provoked an unspeakable anguish. Here, thanks to the few instruments her brain possessed, she could accept that her dog faced mother take her in her arms. Yet she asked her the same question as on that day.

Then she fainted.

"Fainted?"

"Yes. In the bathtub."

Rebecca's voice was raspy but calm. Toorop noted the girl kept her cool.

"Don't touch her, I'm coming."

He hung up. Threw himself on the emergency kit. Ordered Dowie to stay put.

Rushing down the interior stairs then the cast iron banister that led to the sidewalk, he had time to tell himself: first problem, first test.

Rebecca had moved Marie onto the couch before calling him. Toorop took in her explanation without saying a thing, watching the young woman with the eyes rolled back, lying a bit askew on the orange sofa.

She was crashing badly, he thought. It was sufficiently abnormal to get etched in his memory. He'd have to put this in the list of weird things and possible leads to show Romanenko.

"When did it happen?" he asked.

"Not even five minutes ago."

"How did it happen?"

"I was in the shower. She came in; it looked like she was sleep-walking. Then she said 'mommy,' and fainted."

"Mommy?"

Toorop knelt beside Marie to check her pulse. Rapid beats. Tachycardia. Pale skin. He lifted an eyelid. Crystal blue ocular swirl. *Rapid eye movement*, thought Toorop. That's funny, seems like she's dreaming.

He opened his small medical kit and prepared Doctor Ouissourov's standard injection, quick.

Then he shot her up in the bend of the elbow, folded the limb on a tow of cotton sterilized with alcohol, and waited patiently.

She woke up after a few minutes. She opened her eyes, tried a faint smile, and, in a tired voice pretending to be cheerful:

"Hello… Are you bringing the croissants?"

For the first time since he met her, Toorop looked at Marie as something else than a simple package to deliver for the sum of five thousand US dollars.

She was pretty. Her color was coming back. A mysterious glow played in the blue of her stare.

Toorop felt a kind of bulldozer turn on in a deeply buried excavation.

Something knotted at the base of his stomach.

Now is not the time, a warning light displayed on the dashboard of his consciousness.

Get this shit into program self-destruct right away, another voice screamed.

Imminent threat of sentimentalism, the alarm siren wailed.

He stared at the young woman with a strange smile, and someone else pronounced the words that his mouth articulated in a thick voice:

"OK. I'll take care of breakfast. Take these pills for now."

He handed her two pink and white capsules, generic anxiolytics.

Then he left and went directly to a French bakery he knew on Saint-Denis.

Marie downed the warm Nesquik and the croissants silently. The man called Thorpe had gone back upstairs. The girl, Rebecca, had settled down in the living room in front of the TV, and was conscientiously surfing the five hundred digital channels while listening to some deafening music on a pair of earphones.

Marie remembered Nesquik and French style breakfasts as small islands of happiness scattered in the swamp of her childhood and adolescence. She'd known for a long time now that she was inhabited by several contradictory identities. In fact, it was as if several distinct layers of what we call identity had been exposed by a giant mechanical digger. Her mind resembled those open-air mines, where the different geological strata evoke a mineral millefeuille.

She now had a panoramic view of it as if contemplating the canyon of her unconscious from an unbeatable tourist viewpoint.

Never, even when she'd been with Doctor Winkler, had she attained this dimension of consciousness.

She still had no access to one last gallery: the one that led to the cosmic machine itself. Of course it could be a schizoid manifestation. No, it *really was* a schizoid manifestation she was having, the schizoprocessor was explicit on that point. Yet that answer was clearly incomplete. She knew there was something else.

And that *other thing* couldn't come from…

Oh no, no, no…

Marie got up to go to the bathroom. Her step was hesitant, Rebecca noticed right away.

"Hey? Marie, you OK?"

Marie kept on walking without turning around.

"Don't worry Rebecca, I'm going to the bathroom."

Locked in the small white and yellow room where her mother had reappeared a short while ago, Marie stiffened before the sink and contemplated her face in the mirror.

One day, she must have been about twelve, the morning mirror had sent back a terrifying image, that of an emaciated creature, with its depths of blood and nerve circuits visible at the heart of an aggregate of strange matter, in an inexpressible, sepulchral and metallic light.

That memory was now anchored to the reflection she contemplated in the mirror.

What she'd done was beyond belief, she kept repeating. Why hadn't she thought about the consequences? She'd committed something unspeakable, and she'd have hell to pay.

The face in the mirror voiced a message that cohered in the air as an ectoplasmic cloud speaking with her mother's voice.

"THERE CAN BE NO DOUBT ABOUT IT, MY LITTLE DARLING."

Marie confronted the hallucination wanting to take shape in the mirror.

The fearsome face of her inverted mother-matrix was now reaching for the unique goal of swallowing her and sending her back to nothingness.

"WHAT CAN HAPPEN TO ME THAT I HAVEN'T LIVED ALREADY, MOMMY DEAR?"

The maternal hallucination let out a horrifying laugh.

"WHAT YOU'VE DONE IS NOTHING COMPARED TO THE FATE THAT AWAITS YOU, YOU LITTLE IDIOT, NOTHING AT ALL."

Marie didn't answer. She watched the network-image move on the cosmic screen of the mirror: her layered identities, her body without organs, her memory stripped bare, the mental specter of her progenitress.

She knew full well it was her own voice defying her so.

12

Romanenko didn't stop staring at the screen.

There was news in the e-mail.

A message from Toorop. Coded according to the agreed procedure. The mail was laconic. But its contents real interesting: *Miss Z had some spells. Blackout on the 17th, at eight-thirty in the morning. No visible consequences for now. Took action without ext. help. No doubt jetlag + heat aftereffect.*

Romanenko kept his eyes glued to the key word. *Blackout.*

The repetition of the phenomenon practically made him jump.

There was something important there. Very important.

He composed Doctor Ouissourov's access code on the keyboard and asked his intelligence agent to connect him right away; it was of the utmost urgency.

"Doctor," he said, "I have to see you right away."

"Tomorrow, around five, is that…?"

"You didn't get it. I'm coming over now."

The doctor's face shifted violently at eighteen images/second.

"I… now? You can't be serious, I have ten patients in my waiting…"

"*Right now*, Doctor."

The face froze, and shut itself into the crackling silence of the satellite transmission.

"Thanks for your cooperation, Doctor," Romanenko blurted out coldly before logging off.

Then he put on his suit vest, asked the secretary to say he was unreachable, and went straight to the underground parking. He climbed into his old Nissan and speeded off to Doctor Ouissourov's.

"Colonel? How do you expect me to give a diagnosis without seeing the patient?"

Doctor Ouissourov shrugged and lifted his arms as a sign of total powerlessness.

"Sorry. I'm not an astrologer, Colonel."

Romanenko let out a faint smile.

He handed him the list printed on thermal paper dating back to Methuselah that he had gotten from some IBM humanitarian shipment.

"What is it?" Ouissourov asked.

Romanenko's smile grew.

"The list of first symptoms. Pulse, blood pressure, body temperature, basic information."

Ouissourov grabbed it, wrinkling his nose to adjust his glasses. He looked it over at length, punctuating his reading with small grunts.

He handed back the list.

"The same symptoms as last time. That's all I can say."

Romanenko's smile froze. He stared into the old doc's eyes.

"I want an explanation for these symptoms."

"We don't have enough information. It could be ten thousand different causes. We need more comprehensive analyses."

Romanenko didn't shut off his icy smile.

"I want the list of those causes, Doctor."

"It's impossible. It's practically a list of all metabolic imbalances, Colonel: viruses, bacteria, nervous shock, what do I know…?"

Romanenko looked at the doctor without saying a thing. A sequence of obvious facts in succession had started a wild loop in his head.

Damn.

What a stupid fuck…

He hurriedly sent Ouissourov packing to lock himself up in the Embassy.

The Warshaw store was still in the same place, Toorop noted as he pushed through the glass door. And it hadn't changed much in twenty-five years, he concluded, grabbing a cart near the entrance turnstile.

He pushed the cart towards the vegetable department, unfolded the shopping list he'd made with Rebecca, then started weighing the cucumbers.

Toorop had learned long ago that the success of an operation depended on perfectly managing all the little details. The little daily details. In the present case, it meant loads of adjustments.

Where, how and who went shopping was among the most important.

Clearly, staying locked up for three months in the middle of summer would get on everyone's nerves. And in particular, on Marie's, who obviously suffered from hypoglycemia, dehydration, claustrophobia, tachycardia, sleep walking, even worse, who knows. One could suppose she wouldn't be able to deal with the steam room of the apartment for too long.

The big Mafioso from the Chingiz Mountains had been as clear as day: "Only take her out if it's an emergency, or if my contact requests it. OK, take her on a little walk once in a while so that she doesn't dry up on the spot. But steer clear of places with lots of people: bars, nightclubs, museums, swimming pools, motels, cruising spots, got it, Mister Thorpe?"

Toorop selected half a dozen cucumbers, and then moved towards the tomatoes.

He couldn't take Marie anywhere today, nor, probably, in the coming days. He had asked Rebecca to keep an eye on the entrances to the pad, especially on the little garden that opened up onto the street. Dowie was supposed to play sentry on the terrace of their apartment, with its metallic spiral staircase leading down to the garden.

In the meat and dairy department, he found steaks and cheap *smoked meat*, as well as yoghurts and French and Danish cheese. Then he bought beers, Coke and mineral water. He finished it off with Vietnamese style noodles and headed for the cashiers.

He was looking for a few twenty-dollar bills in his belt when the first prickling hit. It put him on the alert.

The second prickling rose up the marrow of his spine.

He took his change and his bags and went towards the exit. After three or four meters, unpredictably, he turned abruptly on his heels to return to the cashier.

The smile didn't leave his face.

He went directly to the girl, cutting off the fifty-year-old woman waddling towards her with her cart.

"Two Caramilk bars as well," he asked.

That's when he scanned the whole scene.

The young Latino cashier, the old Anglo muttering to herself, the guy with the black mustache and the neodisco look, just behind her, who looked a little like Ourianev. The guy in the Nike outfit a bit farther off, in the produce department. A pretty chick close by, two housewives with their carts coming out of the meat department, a worker pushing a pallet. Another dude over there who looked like a biker, opening a refrigerator to take out some large cans of Molson.

A very long time ago, right at the beginning of the war in Croatia, Ari Moskiewicz had taught him the techniques of the Mossad, as well as a few weird things gleaned here and there during his professional life, i.e., his entire existence. ("I was born in Warsaw the 1st of September 1939, my Boy, the day of the apocalypse for Polish Jews. No use spellin' out I had to start working at the age of two days.") Later on, Toorop told himself that frankly, Ari's ghost had had no difficulty contacting him, here, in the Warshaw store.

One of the things Ari taught him was to photograph a scene, and be able to recap it, intact, in its smallest details, weeks, months, even years later. Ari's trick was real simple. He used the ancient Greek techniques of rhetoric: you make a library of mental images so that you can easily consult large excerpts of it, even entire long speeches. You can record the crowd at the horse races or entire psalms of the Bible. It's very useful, for varying codes or encrypted metaphors.

Images themselves tend to get worn down in memory. Thanks to descriptive key words, you can keep them in shape. The old Anglo schoolteacher with glasses and the beige overcoat. The Heavy Metal dude, bald and covered in tattoos, drinking Molsons. The pretty chick in the black minidress and the turquoise ponytail.

On the way back, the prickling stopped, and he told himself it was probably only paranoia. Ari had copiously explained to him how intelligence pros had to constantly undo the traps their brains set for them. Nothing is easier for an intelligence agent than to fall prey to paranoia, said Ari. Nothing is easier for a soldier than to commit a war crime, for a good player to start cheating, for a cultivated man to return to savagery.

Yet, in front of 4075, Toorop took out his notebook and jotted down the descriptions of the people present at the Warshaw. He added a sketch of their positions.

He closed his eyes, set the shot and the words in the chemical developer of his brain.

He kept his eyes closed for a long minute. The supermarket image became more and more focused, like a Polaroid. The memory crystal would be indelible, a mental tattoo. In ten years he'd recognize any of those people if he crossed them in an airport at the other end of the world.

The console buzzed around eleven pm local time.

It was a pretty recent Mac Oracle with the standard multi-processor kit: ergonomic keyboard for mail, glasses, camera and mic for audiovisual communication, *de rigueur* datagloves for surfing fans. Romanenko told him he'd find the console upon arrival, and that it would be equipped with all the latest encryption software when he turned it on. The latest Microsoft intelligence agent was in the hard drive. Toorop was familiar with this kind of equipment. The Uygur resistance, in spite of its mistakes, had learned the lesson of the Chiapas EZLN in Mexico.

The image of Kurt, the young German mercenary, an Internet and communications specialist for the 1st Battalion of the Fergansky

Range, came floating back into his memory. Probably dead in the attack. Or Hakmad's prisoner, which wasn't much better. Probably much worse, he thought as he opened the mail software.

The standard page appeared, with its battalion of icons and logos:

From romanov@intellinet.com

To thorpe@videotron.net

Mister Thorpe, Please suspend momentarily the second phase of your work. No doubt have solution. Contract stays valid for first phase. Best Regards.

The message was dated from the following day, a jetlag effect peculiar to the lightspeed of information, and came from a bogus source, something like German Switzerland, or the Republic of Monaco.

Toorop mouthed a funny solitary laugh and typed back: *You are rescinding a clause of the contract. Please confirm this in writing.*

Then he waited for the intelligence agent to send the message to Romanenko's encrypted mailbox.

The return mail came within the next half-minute: *Yes, we confirm. I repeat: forget phase two.*

Toorop logged off without answering.

In any case, five thousand US dollars, for a three-month vacation, all expenses paid, that was the shit.

He didn't give a fuck, in the end, about what Marie Zorn could be carrying.

It was two in the morning. Toorop had just gone to bed. The telephone rang.

It had to be the contact.

The phone was in the living room. He had priority over Dowie. He got up grumbling.

Zero information, the Siberian Mafioso had said. No names, ever. No places, almost always.

"Yeah," he said as he picked up.

"Tomorrow morning, by mail, in the mailbox."

And they hung up.

The instructions were strict. Get the letters right after the mailman's rounds.

He set his clock to eight.

Then he went back to bed.

The next morning, the bubble envelope was there, sealed airtight. Inside, he found a card, with an address on Longueuil. Outside the city. On the south shore. A clinic. Radiology, biological analyses, ultrasound, scanner, MRI. A certain Doctor Tremblay. In Montreal alone, there were more than ten pages of Tremblays in the phone book. They were the Martins, the Smiths, and the Lopezes of the area.

There was also a small appointment book, under Marie Zorn's name, in Recyclo paper. A date. That very day. Eight pm.

It smelled like an after hours backdoor appointment.

The Siberian had been crystal clear: "Over there, you're responsible for travel and the daily routine. You have carte blanche until my contact organizes the meeting with the clients for delivery of the package." That day, Toorop had sent Romanenko a discreet sidelong glance, but he hadn't budged. Toorop understood that the colonel hadn't told the Siberian that he also had a man in Canada—*in Quebec*—and that Toorop had orders to call him in an emergency.

The "official" contact, the one who called with terse sentences at all hours of the night, that man was a crony of the Mafioso with the imaging glasses. Toorop started sketching a mental diagram. Romanenko was taking care of the transfer but Gorsky controlled both ends of the chain, he was the source *and* the destination.

A Siberian Mafia boss that Romanenko pretended to infiltrate…

The more time passed, the more Toorop doubted it. No isolated, rational argument could support what he thought. It was pure intuition, a premonition, as confused and luminous as a premonition could be. He'd seen so many underhand dealings during his life that he'd learned not to take any talk for granted. The most plausible thing was that the colonel was an integral part of the machine. He was a major pawn, but a pawn nonetheless. He probably had no awareness, or very little, of what was really happening. He even ignored what his own cargo was. It was crazy.

Just like all wars.

During the afternoon, Toorop took care of the details of Operation Medical Exam in Longueuil.

Rebecca, Marie, and he would get into the car, with Dowie watching from the terrace.

He unfolded a map of the city on the kitchen table, and highlighted the route to take. Then he asked everyone to rest till the meeting time.

A little after seven, Toorop called 4067.

"Are you ready?"

"We're just waiting for you."

"In two minutes. In the alley."

He waited a minute, looked at Dowie, and said:

"Let's go."

Then, while Dowie posted himself against the railing, he joined Marie and Rebecca in the garden.

Toorop opened the gate without a word and walked out first, straight to the rented Toyota.

He unlocked the doors, sat in the drivers seat, turned on the radio, and smiled at the two girls as they sat down in the back.

He almost felt twenty years younger.

The weather was splendid, a blue sky without the slightest volute, the sun still warm, already tinted orange. Shadows were lengthening; the girls on street corners could kill with their beauty. Shit, it was really too cool.

Toorop flipped through the *Journal de Montréal*, waiting for the visit to end. It had been a good half hour.

When she came out, Toorop thought Marie looked a bit stiff, and pale.

A woman in a white outfit came up to him, and handed him one of those new digidisks without a word. It could hold a terabit of data, enough to store the complete public records of all the inhabitants of the galaxy. If Romanenko's employer wanted info, he'd be set.

As he was thinking of all this, going up Saint-Denis from Sherbrooke, a chain of little connate thoughts aggregated to give shape to a new idea, more complex, and more dramatic.

It wasn't only because Marie had felt ill that they'd decided to take out the heavy artillery.

No, it was also because it had some relation to what she was carrying.

The revelation froze him, as the light turned to green on the Roy street crossing. People were honking behind him. He snorted.

Shit, he thought, as he slowly turned onto Rivard.

Fuckin' A.

Viruses.

The digidisk was impenetrable, even with his console's code breakers. That was to be expected. The software took care of sending the flow of data towards Kazakhstan. Somewhere in the Chingiz Mountains, from what Toorop could make out. Then the software deleted the contents of the disk, before self-deleting and ejecting the whole thing from the console with an electronic burp. Toorop weighed his decision a few moments, then opened his mail, turned on the encryption software, and started typing.

The message was terse and expressive: *Please explain why, if the girl is transporting viral or bacterial strains, none of us have been immunized. Thanks.*

He didn't leave any of the normal polite formulas. The resident intelligence agent was already compacting it into a flow of binary data.

Then he decided to go for a beer somewhere.

The *Quai des Brumes* was still at the same place, a bit farther up on Saint-Denis.

He cut across the long room to the bar, found an empty stool, and ordered a pitcher of Belle Gueule. It was happy hour, the large pitcher cost a dollar more than the small one, but he refused the waitress's offer. Had to be reasonable. There was a neo-country electronic band on stage. Pretty lame, but the singer had curves, and a pair of tits that would have made Dolly Parton look like a Kate Moss clone. He leaned against the bar, his glass of Belle Gueule in hand.

Incredible, he thought, incredible how *good* he felt.

The place was happening, and Toorop had downed his pitcher. The bar was packed, girls everywhere, some real funky music had taken over the bleary folksongs of the band with the singer with the big tits.

He decided to have a good time and asked for another beer. Just one. Black, he asked the tall black waitress.

He was leaving a tip in twenty-five cent coins when a feminine voice addressed him:

"Eh, you come here often, you?"

He recognized the local accent and grammar.

He turned around, offered the best welcoming smile he had in him, and lied outright.

"Yeah, this is my favorite bar around here."

The girl was a brunette, around thirty, her hair done up like Louise Brooks. She was wearing a black minidress with social-realist holographic prints on it. She smiled. A Stakhanovist proletarian imitated her just below her cleavage.

"Ah, I thought I'd seen you before."

The printed Stakhanov was sending an explicit sexual message, but Toorop couldn't find anything to say, so a very relative silence settled in. A horrifyingly torrid beat was doing all it could to bust the valves.

The girl ordered a beer and turned towards him again.

"French?"

He sunk his eyes into the girl's.

It was time for a skillful lie. He was supposed to be an Anglophone Canadian. But he knew that what worked for customs officers or standard computers wouldn't resist even thirty seconds of the local girl's ultra-sensitive scanner.

"I was born in France," he answered. "My mother was French. I lived there my whole childhood and adolescence."

Real stuff.

"Tourist?"

Toorop saw a flash of suspicion crystallize in the girl's clear stare. He knew the reputation of Frenchie tourists in Quebec. He had to back up fast.

"No, I'm here on business. I live in Ontario."

The flash of vigilance softened a bit.

"What kind of business are you in Montreal for?"

Shit, thought Toorop, a real customs interrogation.

"Commercial Aviation," he answered, both vague and precise.

"Aviation?" the girl said, greatly interested. "I have a cousin who manages a small seaplane company, up there in Saguenay."

Yeah sure, Toorop thought to himself, as he froze his smile in place.

But hey, no fuck ups, he had to follow the scene to the end.

"Oh yeah," he said, pretending interest. "What's his name? As a matter of fact, I intend to go up there myself."

The girl widened her smile and got dangerously close to him. The crowd was compact, the heat torrid, alcohol was irrigating his veins, and desire his nerve ends. The girl was sex on wheels. Without realizing it, he got caught up in the game.

"My cousin's name is Daniel Turcotte. I'm Valentine. Valentine Lauzon."

He grabbed the hand she held out to him.

A brief electric bolt shot through him. He knew the origin of that kind of phenomena perfectly well, and most of all, its end.

He understood there was nothing to be done.

"Shit, why me, I'm twenty years older than you and…"

"You could be my father, I know. But *tabarnak*, I thought I was dealing with a hundred year old guy!"

The girl's laugh rippled through a rosary of crystalline notes. She leaned provocatively against him.

He was thinking he hadn't fucked like that in a long time.

When they had undressed, he caught sight of himself in the mirror and turned away, a bit embarrassed, from his carcass so modeled by hardship. Three weeks of an imposed diet in the Kirghiz Mountains had taken off the whole of his budding stoutness. But the scars on his face, his arms, his back, his stomach, his collection of private tattoos seemed to him like a disgusting skin disease.

The girl didn't have the same reluctance.

Toorop got up, and slipped on some boxers and a T-shirt as he went towards the fridge.

"You want a beer?"

"Yeah, they're at the bottom."

Toorop pulled it open and took out two cans of Carling.

In the background, Nancy Sinatra on vinyl, like the sweetness of mead savored before the crackle of a wood fire, might have let him believe joy was possible in this world.

Shit, he thought, this was *too* good.

Later, after fucking again, he lay on the bed. She was slowly but surely leaving for the sands of sleep.

He rested for ten minutes. Then got up.

He had to get with it.

He'd already fucked up big time; maybe he should chill, and get home before dawn.

He got dressed.

"You're leaving?" she asked, in a sleepy voice.

"Yeah," he answered. "I gotta get up early tomorrow."

"Classic," she said, burrowing her head in the pillow.

"What?"

"*Chriss'*, classic. Scaled down *half-night-stand*, never more than two hours."

"I'm sorry," he said stupidly.

"You're always sorry. Bye."

Toorop fled in the night, thinking to himself that he'd never see her again.

It didn't make him feel better at all.

13

"Quite frankly, Mister Gorsky, there's no cause for alarm."

Doctor Walsh was observing the nucleotide sequence coalesce to give rise to the gene coding the hemoglobin of the nightingale. The clouds of numbers invading the screen followed the evolving curves of the chemical exchanges at work in the artificial placenta.

Gorsky muttered a curse that hissed like an insect trapped under a glass.

The laboratory was bathed in the cold, pale blue and metallic light diffused by the ceiling fixture and the few nightlights. It was a "cleanroom," completely sterilized and isolated from all biological contamination. He and the doc wore sterilized white coveralls and transparent polymer protection masks. The doctor was patiently manipulating soft, small white spheres, one after the other. His attached surgical pliers formed a brushed aluminum prosthesis at the extremity of his right arm. Its track and carbon pulley systems purred with each move like an electric razor.

Doctor Walsh looked like an old owl. His small eyes emitted a yellow glow behind his round glasses and the iridescent surface of the facemask. Gorsky, who knew everything about him, was aware that he was a renowned ornithologist, in addition to being a genius of molecular biology. No doubt he'd started resembling the animals he studied.

"There's nothing very abnormal here, Zulganin must have told you. I don't think there are many reasons for concern."

The old owl with the yellow eyes and the prosthetic arm hadn't even lifted his head to talk to him. His voice, amplified by the mic in his suit, resonated above the noise of the room. He opened the transparent panel of a machine that was topped by a long tube covered by sheets of aluminum. He placed an egg inside as if it were nothing but a microwave, closed the panel, and tapped on a few keys with his free hand. A stringy form appeared on a screen and started a slow rotation. The egg was a replica only slightly more real that its digital simulacra. It was turning on an opal colored disk beneath a stroboscopic light.

"We have to make sure the merchandise is delivered intact," answered Gorsky. "For the price we're asking, the client has a right to expect perfect service."

Doctor Walsh removed the egg from the rotating tray with an incredibly delicate movement of his attached pliers. He placed it under the globular muzzle of a tunnel effect microscope, and fit his eye to the viewfinder.

"Listen, the facts we received yesterday are explicit: the growth of the eggs is normal. The girl is experiencing some dizzy spells, nothing atypical at this stage of the evolution. That's the main thing."

The lab stool tottered under Gorsky's fidgeting. He wasn't going to be made a fool of. The old owl lied like a carpetbagger.

"What is she suffering from exactly, Doctor Walsh?" he said in a voice that came back icy to his ears.

Doctor Walsh took his eye off the viewfinder and aimed it in his direction. Behind the transparent mask, Gorsky saw a yellow stare, sulfurous, and alive with a wild glow.

"Please keep in mind, first of all, that *you* were in charge of the perfect health of the carrier. As you recall, we entrusted *you* with copying her genetic chip, and making sure that she wasn't carrying any defective genes or viruses. We will not commit the same error twice, I assure you."

Gorsky swallowed his saliva, and the bitter pill along with it.

For years, his team had been used to these kinds of transfers. So, they fell into the slimy nets of routine. They didn't check and recheck with all the required precision. And then, Romanenko had simply validated the disaster. He just copied the genetic chip without thinking of anything. Gorsky hadn't specified he should, so he wouldn't even be able to take it out on him.

Doctor Walsh kept his eyes fixed in his direction. Gorsky withstood the stare. He was thinking that of all the dudes involved in this fucking traffic, he was the only one with balls, except for himself of course. The doctor's voracity was boundless. But he knew precisely what he wanted; and he'd do anything to get it. Gorsky had to modify his previous judgments. Thyssen was just a Wall Street clown; Doctor Walsh let him think that he had real power just to keep him quiet. He accepted Zulganin 'cause he was mediocre, nothing but a medical civil servant who'd keep the factory running while the doctor devoted himself to his research, his new whim, to create… what did he call them again?

Oh yes, *chimeras*.

"So what's all this, Doctor Walsh?"

The old man was putting the white egg back into its spongy solution. He lifted his eyes towards him, vaguely surprised, and then closed the cover.

"I'm standardizing a cross between the DNA of a chameleon and of a nightingale. Birds and reptiles have many sequences in common."

Gorsky was torn between laughter and annoyance. He blurted out:

"I'm talking about our carrier, Doctor. I'm talking about my million US dollars, forget yours."

Doctor Walsh made an annoyed gesture.

"Aaah," he groaned. "So Zulganin didn't tell you anything?"

Gorsky sighed.

"He told me the thingamajig sequence had been altered. I couldn't get anything more precise out of him. So I came to see you. What is this about, for the *nth* and last time?"

The doctor looked at him stiffly, and let out, with a condescending distance:

"Most probably schizophrenia."

It took Gorsky ten seconds to take it in. First, remember what schizophrenia was exactly. Then close his eyes before the catastrophe, and behind the black Rayban Ultravision lenses.

"Schizophrenia."

He might have said Stalingrad, if he'd been a German general on the Eastern Front.

Doctor Walsh squirmed, ill at ease.

"Yes. But nothing says she's developed the syndrome."

"What does that mean? Is she nuts, yes or no?"

Walsh was now interested in the stringy formed egg twirling on his screen. He pressed on a few keys and some code lists scrolled down. He seemed to find it very interesting; much more than their little conversation.

"Doctor?"

"Yes…, no," he said, annoyed, his eyes glued to the screen. "Incredible… did you see that?"

"Shit, Doctor Walsh, you better get back to our simple earthly concern. Stop fooling around and answer the question: Is the girl nuts, yes or no? And if yes, what can we do?"

The old doc turned away from his chameleon-nightingale egg with great difficulty.

"As Zulganin told you, we now know that the sequence in question is altered. But nothing says she's developed the psychosis… that's when familiar factors are added on, I think… well, from what I know about this kind of phenomena."

Gorsky sighed in despair. He'd have to leave it up to Romanenko and his team on the ground.

He'd have to deliver the info, in one form or another.

But that nasty thought changed rapidly, as it appeared under a new light.

The dramatic piece of information had the merit to hide another, much more important one.

Romanenko exulted. His victory over the MARS-led Northern forces made him feel great. He'd managed to break them up by crossing the Yellow River and had then locked a few armies in its bend. He held the center of the board. The PLA forces laying siege to Canton and Hong Kong were broaching their retreat. But he already had the final blow that would swoop down upon them from the center in question. Peking was nothing but a hideout on the outposts of Manchuria. The fate of the Northerners was pre-programmed. It was but a question of time.

If ever the secessionist forces acted like him, during the next great PLA offensive, there was no doubt they'd win this war. He told the program to save the whole battle on an encrypted digidisk. That little bit of digital memory was worth who knows how many times its weight in platinum.

Behind him, the telephone rang.

He catapulted the rolling leather armchair to the edge of the desk with a joyous thrust.

"Colonel Romanenko here," he shot into the receiver with a cheerful voice.

It was his contact at the Kazakh staff headquarters.

Hakmad's forces had just surrendered, in exchange for a secure route for an honorable retreat towards the Chinese border. Negotiations had just begun. Surrounded at Kapchagai, pushed back around Almaty, beaten on the Pishkek road and then smashed at Issyk-Kul, the UNLF had suffered irreparable losses. In just over a month, the gangster-warlord had known a dazzling ascension and then the fall. Even the Tadjik and Kazakh mafias had lost their trust in him. Isolated, surrounded along with his men, on the shores of the lake reservoir, he was hopelessly trying to salvage what he could.

Perfect, this would bring back a bit of calm to the region. Prince Shabazz would soon make an appearance. Business with the UNLF would be able to resume.

And he'd fucking done the PLA.

A brilliant day.

Then the telephone rang again.

"I have to see you."

It was Gorsky.

Romanenko sucked his breath in. It meant another whole day of driving.

"When?"

"Later. I'm on my way to Almaty. I'll be there at the end of the afternoon."

A sigh of relief passed Romanenko's lips.

"Perfect, I'll wait at the regular spot."

He hung up thinking something was happening, something important. Gorsky rarely came out for small fry.

Then, he opened his desk and took out a small brass flask slipped into an old brown leather casing stamped with the red star. The flask came from his father; it had followed him since cadet school in Saint Petersburg.

He took a good swig of vodka, thinking that nothing could spoil this splendid afternoon.

Propping his legs up, he propelled the armchair backwards and took position. He grabbed an issue of a Novosibirsk tabloid that was on the desk, with the news of the day. The weekly was from early July, right in the middle of the inter-Uygur war. The tabloid specialized in criminal reporting; Ourianev must have found it lying around on a table of the entrance hall.

The Krasnoyarsk serial killer had killed and skinned a young woman again. They'd found her remains in a garbage bag a few meters from a suburban police station. He'd been taunting the police for months and regularly wrote to the regional newspapers. The tabloid had received one of his collage-letters on the occasion of the assassination; it spread out on the entire page opposite the article, which reprinted the killer's text in full. The image consisted of the victim's five fingers, cut at the second knuckle, the first having been replaced by a bizarre aggregate of electronic components. The text was printed on transparent printer plaspaper, in Cyrillic, all around the cyborg hand glued onto the paper with composite Superglue used for aeronautic construction.

The Yekaterinburg Citigroup robbers had been caught after a three-day chase in the Urals. Two of them were dead, a third had been severely wounded, and the two remaining men had surrendered. The loot, about five million rubles, had been found in the abandoned nuclear plant where they'd been hiding. They were facing the death penalty; a guard had been killed during the hold-up.

An ex-UN Russian cop who'd converted to private eye had exploded, along with his car, right in the middle of Novosibirsk at the end of June. Rumor had it that he was investigating the machinations of a sect. Other rumors mentioned the Siberian mafia. The Chinese Civil War and the Uygur mess were brought up. Some sources mentioned Serbian war criminals wanted by the Hague Tribunal who'd taken refuge in the Russian Far-East.

There was still no news of the journalist Evgueni Lyssoukhartov, missing since the 1st of July, who last seen leaving a restaurant, in Novokuznetsk. The Siberian mafia was supposedly involved here as well. Lyssoukhartov had been on their tail relentlessly for years.

Romanenko kept taking little swigs of alcohol.

Three weeks had passed since the tabloid's publication. Evgueni Lyssoukhartov had still not shown up. The Krasnoyarsk serial killer was still on the loose; his next victim was expected any day now. The man who was directly responsible for the death of the guard was in fact facing the death penalty. They'd given the detective a private funeral, dreary and unattended, relegated to the back page of the paper.

After an hour of entertaining reading, he set the tabloid down, and comfortably settled back into the armchair.

A few minutes later, he fell asleep like a baby.

Much later, watching the Siberian leave in the night, Romanenko allowed the questions to ransack his brain like a bed of bombs.

Schizoid had been the firing call. *Schizophrenia*. Then the rounds had started.

What if the girl's sickness were a consequence of the viruses she was transporting? A voluntary or involuntary consequence? Had the viruses awoken unexpectedly or were they in fact new biological weapons that could trigger psychoses?

Fuck, that one exploded in the center of his mind, devastating all of his previous constructions.

A psychovirus. Or something like that.

The latest bio weapon provoking personality disorders. Lugged around as easy as pie by someone they'd inoculated.

Now he understood the Canadian destination. The final destination had to be the United States. Canada had always been a platform for traffic into the US; that went back to the bootleggers of last century.

More than that, the Siberian and North American Mafias were probably just intermediaries. Only one potential buyer for that kind of product existed in those parts.

The government of the United States of America.

It was warm, at the close of day; a beautiful, orange and oblique light sliced the scene into long, elegant shadows.

Toorop stared at Rebecca and Dowie in silence. He breathed in.

"I've just received a message from the colonel. We have a problem."

The girl didn't bat an eye. The redhead didn't seem interested in the conversation in the least.

"What problem?" Rebecca asked.

"Marie."

The girl spit out a little laugh.

"No kidding? For real, aren't they paying us precisely for her to be our problem…"

Toorop sighed; it was better drop it on them in one go.

"She's suffering from a psychosis. She's schizophrenic."

Rebecca stared at him with her black eyes and didn't utter a word.

"Well," Toorop continued, "they've decided to move us."

The Orangist perked up slightly in his armchair.

"When, and where?" he asked.

"Outside the city. We'll know more in a few days."

"Shit," went Rebecca, "a schizophrenic, are you sure? Are we talking about the same thing?"

Firmly, Toorop nodded yes.

"Shit, you think that's what sets off her weird fits."

"It's highly probable."

"Let's be clear about this. It wasn't planned, was it?"

"No, it definitely was not planned."

"So, what can we do?"

"Nothing. Just watch her even more closely. We can't lose sight of her for a nanosecond. If she has any new fits, we take her to the clinic we went to the other day."

"Shit," she spit out.

Toorop knew she'd just realized she was sharing the apartment with a nutcase.

"I'm gonna come live with you. There's an extra room at the end of the hall."

What he had planned next went against all tacit rules of the profession, but he didn't have a choice. The situation was exceptional; it called for exceptional behavior.

"I have to tell you something else."

He watched the girl and the guy in turn.

He didn't really know how to go about it; he opted for a live operation.

"She's carrying viruses."

That was a little time bomb.

Romanenko was watching Ourianev with the coldest stare available in his freezer of expressions. The look meant: Ourianev, you don't scare me, you don't interest me, you're useful, and that's it.

"Toorop is getting by beautifully," he let out, malevolently. "I have no clue as to how he did it, but he knows she's carrying viral strains."

Ourianev shifted on his chair, ill at ease.

"So he's going to get the ten thousand dollars…"

Romanenko grimaced what was meant to be a benevolent smile.

"Not yet. First, we have to know precisely *which type* of virus."

Ourianev set his features into his schemer mimic. He looked like a kind of James Bond comic opera conspirator, thought Romanenko.

"Why did you tell them the girl was nuts? It wasn't useful."

A moron. A fucking moron who can't see farther than the tip of his epaulettes.

He wondered for a minute if he should give up the info or not.

It really didn't matter; he was too dumb to know what to do with it. That was the only reason Ourianev was useful. He was incapable of synthesizing information that was too disparate, inept at all anticipation, resistant to the slightest initiative. His career was due on the one hand to his father's *savoir-faire*, on the other to his father's money. Ourianev had been dumb enough to want to be part of the Army's secret services at all costs, when all he could do was keep a desk clean.

"Ourianev," he said in a condescending tone, "you didn't think for an instant, I suppose, that it could be a simple cause and effect relationship."

The captain walled himself in a thoughtful silence that said it all.

Later, Romanenko went through the list of facts in his possession for the *nth* time. Small details were added on, as the days, the hours, the minutes passed; now, a strange pseudo-live organism moved in his computer's memory.

The Marie Zorn cell was connected to a growing number of cells.

First of all to the original cells, to Gorsky foremost. Then to the laboratory in the Chingiz Mountains, Thyssen, Zulganin, and the one Gorsky knew under the name of Walsh.

He'd been able to piece together the pasts of the first two men, but doctor Walsh hadn't appeared in any of his lists. No program counter from any of his research agents had been able to place him; he remained perfectly obscure. Gorsky had never introduced them, of course, and he couldn't even fall back on a bad picture.

He used a pseudonym.

This info got added onto the virtual "personality" that the machine formed for each cell: a list of hypertext information that, if asked, the computer would transform into a sketch of virtual behavior.

If Doctor Walsh used a pseudonym, it was probably because he was wanted by the police; at least by the police of his country, and maybe even by Unopol. And if some national police, or Unopol wanted him, it was because he'd committed one or more serious crimes. Most likely, it was something related to his past medical activities, and maybe even to what he was doing now. But it could also be humanitarian fraud or the usual crime of passion. His research agent had its work lined up: list the criminal cases from the last ten or twenty years of medical history, in a good dozen Anglo-Saxon countries, as a start.

Marie Zorn was connected to himself, as well as to Ourianev, and to the few men from the Embassy she'd come into contact with during that week.

But most of all, from now on she was an integral part of a quasi-autonomous pluricellular organism, made up of herself, Toorop/Thorpe, Waterman/Kendall and Dowie/Osborne.

That autonomous organism, twenty thousand kilometers away, was connected to the rest of the world by one single cell: Gorsky's contact.

The Siberian Mafioso had final control over the supply source and the receiving end. Only his contact knew the next link in the chain to the buyer. Without that man, his own team wouldn't be able to make its way up the chain of command.

The other list involved Marie Zorn.

Within twenty-four hours, a growing quantity of information had come to satisfy the appetite of his software research agent and of the infinite memory of his new quantum nano-chip card.

That night, the snoop agent effortlessly succeeded in accessing a file from the University of Montreal.

It had counted a name in there that the Marie Zorn cell had already encountered in one of the city's psychiatric clinics. The info on the clinic dated back to the very beginning of its investigation. Then it had stalled. Last night, the research agent had been able to unjam the problem. A certain Doctor Darquandier had come up. First, just as a neighbor, in a building on Ontario Street West, then at the University of Montreal. The agent was now tagging onto a certain Doctor Winkler, who'd seen the girl at the clinic as well as during an experiment conducted right at the beginning of the century, in Canada, with Doctor Darquandier. The snoop agent had retrieved a few files from that period in the badly protected university network. A destination had come up twice, motivating the program's biochemical simulation counter.

Koh Tao, Thailand.

Doctors Winkler and Darquandier had set up an ecosystems research and development business there, during the course of the year 2007.

Romanenko couldn't really tell what Marie Zorn and schizophrenics in general were doing with ecosystem specialists. But the snoop agent brought him back on track: Darquandier was a "neuro-knowledge engineer" and Winkler a specialist in molecular biochemistry and hallucinogens. In fact, their transdisciplinary unit at the University of Montreal had become very interested in schizophrenic psychoses upon the arrival of a sci-fi writer who was convinced that the fate of humanity lay in insane asylums.

They'd discussed it publicly on the Internet, as well as in many specialized journals. The snoop agent raked in mega-octets of it.

From what Romanenko understood, at the turn of the century, Darquandier and Winkler had worked jointly on an artificial biosphere program. Just like the first, the second Biosphere experiment was a relative failure, and like all failures, a wealth of lessons. Once the funds for the "Man on Mars" program became available, Winkler and Darquandier's research lab at the University of Montreal received federal funding from NASA as well as from other scientific agencies. Then the Advanced Neurobiology Laboratory became the Schizotrope Express Foundation when it migrated to South-East Asia.

Marie Zorn had legally come of age just as Winkler, Darquandier and their team were getting ready to leave Quebec for the tropics. Doctor Mandelcorn, the program's top dog, a psychiatrist-psychoanalyst who'd been overseeing her case since she was twelve, entrusted her to Winkler and Darquandier after declaring: "the new schizo-operative and neurochemical technologies that my patient has learned to use have, for the most part, caused her psychosis to recede. She now has the means to decide whether or not she wants to participate in this extension of the program."

The snoop agent was now gleaning a well-defined data field. It was harvesting a vast stretch of wheat, real high, real thick, and real concentrated.

According to the info the snoop agent was shitting out, a megaoctet per second, Marie Zorn and the experimental neurobiology team had boarded a Delta plane for Bangkok on April 29, 2008.

Then Marie Zorn showed up in Kazakhstan, in the hands of another lab; a lab working for the Novosibirsk mafia, meaning Gorsky.

Now, the five-year gap had to be filled.

The snoop agent was mute. It stayed that way for almost an hour, before Romanenko decided to shut everything off and go to bed.

He had work lined up for the whole next day. Sort out the good, the less good and the bad info, in order to distribute it equitably between him, Thorpe/Toorop, and that jerk Ourianev.

14

"I AM WHAT BEGOT YOU, POOR IDIOT. I AM INSIDE YOUR GENETIC MEMORY."

Her mother's ghost was standing at the bedroom door.

It possessed the characteristic, common to all hallucinations, of belonging to several signifying fields at once, the analytic schizo-processor was explaining. Notice its luminescence and its ultraviolet range radiations, which indicate the presence of many biophotons coming from your DNA, it added.

The maternal hallucination belonged to the domain of paranoid machines. It could, of course, assume all divine attributes, but it was a god wholly devoted to its creature's extermination.

It was at the same time woman, machine, and heap of junk. It was an inverted matrix, an active hole of darkness ready to swallow her.

Marie sat up in bed and pointed an accusing finger towards the shape suddenly at the entrance of her room in the middle of the night.

"YOU DON'T SCARE ME ANYMORE, MOMMY-MACHINE. I'M READY TO CONFRONT YOU NOW."

Within seconds, her brain created two protective schizoma-chines: two beautiful phallus-flowers framing the door and unfurling a network of thin rootlets glowing with sperm. Mixed in were the few sexual experiences she'd had, a joke for any Montreal adolescent, but concentrated, intense, with enough energy to feed the phallus-flower network.

Her mother would never venture into it. The trap of erotic knowledge, Doctor Winkler once said, can dissolve certain essential gears of the paranoid machine.

Her mother entered into hysterical anger.

It transformed and became that strange and demented animal, blowing through its nostrils, mouth, eyes, genitals, a luminous energy crackling furiously against the streaming runlet of sperm.

"YOU LITTLE BITCH," it screamed. "YOU LITTLE BITCH, JUST LIKE THOSE CUNTS YOUR DAD SCREWS, I'M GONNA KILL YOUUUUUU!"

Radiating all its blades, scissors, needles, razors, scalpels, her screaming mother-machine charged into the slimy runlet, just as a thunder clap burst forth.

Marie did not budge.

She observed as the hallucination dissolved almost instantaneously into a crackling puddle on the floor of the room.

Thank you, Doctor Winkler, she thought as she leaned back onto the bed, after a prolonged prostration.

It was very hot. The nervous tension from the experience kept her from sleeping. She twisted and turned on the humid bed, found herself on her back, crucified by an invisible torturer.

Something was gouging through her lower stomach. A torching pulsation.

The image of the phallus-flowers refused to leave her mind.

Then it dissipated, like a simple swirl of smoke.

And the image of Boris, that young Russian dealer who'd fucked her in the back of his old Lada outside Novosibirsk exploded in her entire memory, in other words through her whole body.

The image of his penis, white and erect in the morning light. The drill of pure warmth piercing her, then pummeling, opening her up like a flower. Her legs spread open, at first gently, then, as a heavenly wetness stormed her, abruptly folded up around her shoulders. Her knees wedged against the back of the seat, an object both tender and hard, cold and hot, came and went, entered and left her vagina that was secreting a burning and viscous film.

Then she saw the rigid and glowing cock leave her stomach, come slide over her breasts before heading inexorably towards her mouth. She engulfed it.

In the humid Montreal room, Marie regained consciousness with the vision of her hand lying against her humid mound, her thighs spread onto the chalky silk of the sheet in the shadows.

Beyond, she glimpsed the black rectangle of the doorframe, open to help the breeze, where her mother had appeared an hour earlier.

Two children stood in the same place, encircled in a halo of lunar light.

Two little blond girls, hair in braids like intertwined gold snakes, eyes the color of flashes in the night, two little white dresses, straight out of a movie on the Lebensraum operation.

Their eyes shone like electric torches, in an ultraviolet dominated radiation.

"Who are you?" she asked in a breath, quickly sitting up.

The two little girls were observing her with curiosity mixed with a strange indifference, like what the entomologist feels staring at his beetle.

"Who are you? What are you doing here?"

The little girls didn't answer. They grabbed hands and simultaneously pointed their free index fingers in her direction.

Their laugh swirled in a complex reverberation of an intense metallic color, before their image melted into it, through the miracle of the embedded metaphors of the schizophrenic world.

She saw the opening of the door inflamed by a radiance of white light. She knew that behind it spread the World of the Dead, the long row of honor of family ghosts, suicides and madmen first. Great-Aunt Josephine who'd slit her veins at twenty-one, after the death of her husband at Juno Beach. Uncle Jean hospitalized half his life for repetitive melancholic depression. Cousin Sophie who'd followed her self-destructive impulse to the end, had caught AIDS in Paris at the turn of the century, and had refused to survive with the help of genetic multitherapy. Jeremie, one of her nephews, also psychotic, who'd committed suicide at fourteen in a paranoid fit of dementia leading to defenestration in the middle of the night, from the ninth floor of 2335 Sherbrooke.

And then, there was her mother, at the other end of the tunnel. Her mother, who they'd found after a week on her litter of refuse, saved by a simple ruptured aneurysm from the uncontrollable hell that her life had become.

She felt irresistibly drawn towards the door of light and the silhouettes of the two girls who'd been waiting for her for eons.

"I DO NOT FEAR DEATH," she kept repeating. From the other end of the universe, her analytic schizoprocessor gave out a simple message. Don't forget you've already lived through something like this: *near death experience*.

But she vaguely felt this wasn't one of those neurostimulated NDEs, to which Doctor Winkler had initiated her.

No, these weren't her own ghosts she was going to meet, she told herself, advancing towards the source of light lurking behind the door.

The two little girls were guides on a trip to an unknown destination.

The Grand Projector set her consciousness ablaze.

Then she entered the House.

It wasn't easy being a closet.

A giant cupboard the size of her body, and thus of the entire universe.

It had been years since her brain had forced her psyche to espouse the structure of this colossal machine, this megalomaniac closet made up of millions of drawers filled with coded files on which the identities and the lives of the whole of humanity were inscribed; from the appearance of the first *Homo erectus* to the crew of the Challenger, carbonized in mid-flight the year of her birth.

A machine with metallic shelving where an impossible library piled up, and through which her psychotic body traveled like some sort of nomadic tape recorder. At one end of the closet-planet, her stomach was digesting a mush of light-words. Her lungs, at the other, were filling up with gas crackling to the rhythm of saturated flows of words. The world-closet was speaking all the time. Each drawer was filled with an incomprehensible racket, a compact crowd of uninterrupted speech, layered, intertwining as if millions of tracks were simultaneously open on a fiendish mixing desk.

The world-closet had often inhabited her adolescent deliriums. But Mandelcorn, Winkler and Darquandier's cure had finally dissolved its paranoid, rigid and mechanic structure in the biological flowering of the schizomachines she'd learned to use: the Island, phallus-flowers, the Tree-Indian, schizo-analytic narration.

Just like the Island-Interface, the world-closet was connected to angels, God, the center of the earth, the magnetic poles, and her own anus. It was just a simpler schizomachine; with less complex states and much more limited effects. A micro-flash of lucidity gave her a glimpse of how she could escape the psychotic ascension threatening her. Although the schizoprocessor was just a semi-forgotten memory, its surviving half was able to combine a last minute survival strategy for her psyche.

She found herself on a narrow wooden spiral staircase, dusty, dark, convoluted and creaking.

The ceiling was covered in a glowing film. Fatty spermatic droplets oozed from the walls covered with pipes pulsating like soft organs.

She stopped for a moment, glanced behind her, and realized that her vision was blocked by a dark, glowing and palpitating membrane like the lining of entrails, *or of a stomach.*

Paralyzed by icy, clinical and objective terror, Marie understood she was inside her own body.

And she had to keep moving, or she'd be dissolved by her own digestive juices.

The stairway was endless. She was conscious of entire hours spent climbing the helicoid tube that tightened until she had to crawl from one step to the next. The ceiling tore at the nape of her neck and her lower back as she came upon a trap door. Digestive juices gnawed at her hands and face. She could see her knuckles stripped bare, smoking, purified by liquid fire.

A circular metallic trapdoor, like a manhole. She pushed it with her two stumps. The object was heavy; as it moved, it let out a long echo whose grating reverberated in a cathedral-like space.

This time the girls were waiting for her in front of a heavy, silver-framed ebony door. A cherub held a hammered silver ball officiating as a doorknob.

The feeling of reality was extraordinarily intense. The colors and textures were exact, without the saturated coloring of hallucinations. Her entire body felt it was there, in front of that door and the two little girls.

The two girls were observing her as they played with intertwining snakes, in a circle of ashes on the floor.

The silver angel turned the doorknob, opening into a wide smile. Marie entered the room.

It was the same room as before, shelves covered with flesh-colored leather dolls. Some soft chamber music distilled piano particles and cello filaments. The four-poster bed was there.

But instead of the blond woman sleeping, she saw an enormous heap of meat crushing the bloodied sheets and the comforter with the evangelic motifs.

A terrible rotting smell hovered in the room. The windows were obstructed by metallic shutters.

The heap of meat spoke to her in an unknown language that she decrypted perfectly. *It* explained to her who *she* was. The heap of meat stirred on the bed, its laugh was like the back of a garbage truck opening.

From the heap of rotten meat rose a crooked, metallic object, like a metal arm with tube joints ending in a claw.

The claw rummaged through the heap of meat and Marie saw two big translucent eggs appear under the folds.

Terrorized, she watched the metal claw turn in her direction like a carnivorous flower, a killer sunflower, then approach, opening its glowing petals to devour her.

She screamed.

Then lost all consciousness.

Toorop laid down fuming on the bad bed he'd switched for the one in 4075.

This one was too soft; it was an old prehistoric thing with springs.

He heard Rebecca wash up in the bathroom, fell asleep to the soundtrack of the gargling warble of the plumbing. His sleep was restless. At one point, he found himself face to face with the Serbian who'd cut up his cheek around Brcko before contemplating with alarm the bayonet Toorop had just rammed into his gut. The Tchetnik soldier had looked at him. His face was sharp, forever engraved in the folds of his memory; a young guy, with a violet bandana on his head and blue eyes. In his dream, the guy cracked up as he gave him a lit cigarette and flames came out of his abdomen where the blade protruded. The guy said something to him in Serbo-Croatian like "aren't we such dumb fucks?" Toorop pulled his bayonet out of the soldier's stomach, leaving behind a perfect orifice, flawless, without the least drop of blood. He looked at the guy, and answered in French: "Yeah, we're dumb fucks, but I'm a live one." Then a deluge of shells covered the soldier's scream with a lid of sound and flames.

The racket woke him up in a sweat.

The scream came from inside the apartment, went his first lucid thought.

It could only be Marie Zorn, went the second.

He was already rolling to the end of the bed, grabbing his Beretta in the drawer of the night table.

Rebecca's footsteps echoed in the hall toward Marie's room.

The pits, he thought. A complete catastrophe.

They couldn't get Marie out of her cataleptic state; eyes rolled back, stiffer than a Queen's Guard, the nape of the neck taut on the sweat-drenched pillow. The clenched jaw, glued with Araldite, emitted a continuous and annoying grating sound.

The pulse was low, her breathing as well, and very spread out.

He'd tried everything: slaps, salt, Doctor Ouissourov's formula, two shots of concentrated adrenaline. *Nada*.

Shit was really fucked up.

There was no choice. He had to contact Romanenko immediately.

He went back up to 4075, four steps at a time, posted himself before his console, and loaded the encryption software.

Then he started typing furiously: BIG PROBLEM WITH DELIVERY. I REPEAT: BIG PROBLEM WITH DELIVERY, ESTABLISH CONTACT AS FAST AS POSSIBLE.

He sent the e-mail with the maximum distress signal. Normally, it should buzz all the way to his alarm clock.

The answer came quickly. WHAT PROBLEM?

Toorop typed: CRITICAL CATALEPTIC CONDITION. PROLONGED UNCONSCIOUSNESS. NOTHING TO DO ON MY SIDE.

About fifteen minutes went by before the answer got to him, clearly the fruit of intense and painful thought: OK, CALL OUR CONTACT ACCORDING TO SPECIAL PROCEDURE. EMERGENCY LEVEL AA1.

Toorop read the answer over and over again, in abrupt bursts, as ten thousand turbines started whirling in his head.

Romanenko was bypassing Gorsky's contact from the outset. That meant the Siberian wasn't supposed to know. It meant Romanenko had a lot at stake in case of failure, and that he was really just a cog in the machine, under the orders of the Siberian, or in his hands, in any case.

Nothing could happen to the girl. During the three month "storage," she was under Toorop's responsibility, therefore Romanenko's. The latter had a sword of Damocles hanging just above his head; a sword in the shape of little Russian mafia soldiers. The kind of guys who'd do in their own mother, or their own daughter, for a handful of rubles, might as well say for nothing.

Toorop swallowed his saliva with a bit of difficulty.

Because that meant he also had that sword over his head.

15

The elements of a new narrative chemistry were at work, thought Joe-Jane.

It was as clear as the transparent waters of a lagoon showing, from up high, the antique traces of a forgotten civilization. It wasn't a combinatorial but a biological process, mutual nutrition and digestion, pure procreation. Like a mutation of the genetic code in which a minute variation on a particular sequence can have cataclysmic consequences for a particular organ, or for the entire body, her brutal connection with the young woman's quantum aura, her presence in Marie Zorn's narrative framework, her reintegration into the continuum they'd formed together one day, would produce its lot of new, unpredictable phenomena that would amplify the process.

Her bionic brain's thirst for knowledge was entering a new stage. Like a vampire searching for virginal blood or a lymphocyte on the hunt for the foreign cell, it scanned the field of the real gestating in the active chaos of men and their creations with the precision of the constructivist eye. It detected new machines gestating there, infinite genetics, a cosmic orgy of pornographic swarms, a viral culture fidgeting with all its famished limbs, a colony-flesh-machine of vomiting, volcanic profusion.

Not only was Marie Zorn here, circumscribed from now on within the perimeter of this city, this American metropolis where she'd emerged from the void against all expectations an unstable and ghostly radar echo, but now, precisely because she was nearer, because of this spatial connection, the young woman's own movement had become perfectly unpredictable like any phenomena that quantum physics is meant to explain. Marie Zorn seemed to be one with the flow of life itself. She espoused all its flashes; she herself had neither identity nor distinct, stable, durable, readable form left. She seemed like a barely singular field of the great, primordial, oscillatory text, forever changing, permanently rewritten. But the kind of music Marie Zorn produced, the pure melodic and rhythmic ecstasy, was blinding, recognizable among the trillion different vibrations by the neurocircuits of her artificial brain.

So many new realities implied an explosion of Possibles, here and now, in ceaselessly processual plastic and biological time. Marie Zorn seemed to crystallize cataclysmic conditions.

Her video perception organ scanned the screen in front of which the man with the tattooed skull, who called himself Vax, was standing. Joe-Jane emerged from her cognitive trance and observed him with quite cathodic attention.

The man seemed worried; he stared at the screen with a dark look in his eyes. The light projected laser pictograms on the glowing surface of his skull, from which seeped the cobalt blue reproduction of the micro-lithography of a well-known electronic component from last century.

Joe-Jane had just informed him of her new vision, and now, the man was really unsettled. He let out a long sigh before turning his stare toward the window.

The machine knew almost everything about Vax, his biography and his real identity. Vax was in fact Franz Robicek, robotician and specialist in artificial perception. Within the team that had developed her, his role had been to elaborate her set of electronic interfaces and their connections with the central neural system. Mostly, he was an outstanding computer scientist and telecommunications networker. He had designed and operated counter-response software during the Second Gulf War, before going back to school thanks to a university reinsertion program. The team of scientists had asked him to track down Marie with the machine's resources. One of her other designers, a Canadian knowledge-engineer of French origin, had remarked that he'd once played cyberdetective with an experimental neuromatrix when he was younger. It had been nothing but trouble, and it was now out of the question for him to step foot in Quebec. Franz Robicek was thirty-seven. He knew the machine well, knew how to use it with a rare mastery, and had lived in Canada almost all his life. It was decided he'd be sent as a scout to Montreal, where Joe-Jane said she could temporarily locate the presence of Marie Zorn's specific form field.

They were staying on the second to last floor of a big building right on the border separating the city east to west, on Ontario and Saint-Laurent.

That morning, dawn was peeking a mauve face above the buildings spread between the Jacques-Cartier Bridge and the old Olympic Park.

One of the machine's organs of perception had spread to the network of digital micro-cameras from the building's security system, and she'd also watched the sun rise over the city.

The man sitting across from the communications terminal sighed at length as he detached his eyes with regret from the yellow light irradiating the sky on the horizon.

He then placed them with painful intensity on the flat, bluish surface of the screen.

"Do you mean she's in serious danger, that something is menacing her directly, physically?"

Joe-Jane did not think it a good idea, in turn, to outsource her artificial vocal organ for a sigh.

How do you explain this with a humanly comprehensible metaphor? How do you translate a flash to the blind, or make the very writing of experience readable. How do you divert a river without flooding other lands, or put out a burning oil well without using powerful explosives? How could she explain what she "saw" draw itself out each day, each hour, each micro-second with more precision, in the immense abysses of space and time, in each interstice of freedom studding the heart of matter, and its determinisms or indeterminations, with furtive nets? How could she imagine simply what her narrative processors were painfully trying to reveal?

"She is herself the danger," she finally said.

16

The house stood at the corner of Spring Grove and Mapplewood, in Outremont, west of Mont-Royal. It was one of those beautiful, post-Victorian villas from the early XXth century, brick facades and white colonnades at the entrance.

The old man who opened the door looked like anything but a fucker from the secret services. He was a chubby fifty-year-old, bald, with a round jovial face, a small turned up nose, and small light eyes sparkling with mischief. The kind of guy who'd tell his share of dirty jokes at a wedding party and wisecracks at a funeral. He wore a very well cut suit, British style, as if he'd just stepped out of a tailor's on Savile Row.

"Come in," said the man.

Toorop followed him to a large living room overlooking Mont-Royal. He could see the silhouettes of the high Celtic cross tombstones, over there, in the cemetery whose tombs layered the hill.

The man gestured to a leather armchair with his hand while opening the glass door of a Rococo cabinet.

Toorop sat down on the Chippendale armchair and did a quick pan of the room. It felt like being in a spread from *Décoration Internationale*. Everything here smelled like Victorian England circa 1880-1890. Each piece of furniture, object, trinket, lamp could have financed an Uygur guerrilla movement.

Toorop wondered for a moment how a retired GRU agent in Montreal could sport such luxury, but of course he didn't broach the subject.

The man had slipped on an old pair of metal-rimmed glasses before taking a thick leather bound notebook from the cupboard.

He lifted his eyes to Toorop.

"For you, I'm Doctor Newton; as for yourself, Doctor Kepler."

Newton and Kepler, thought Toorop, what a team.

"When we communicate, we allude to the subject Maria A."

Maria A. That was simple, mnemonic and policing.

"I'll open an e-mail account with a host, under the name of Doctor Kepler. You'll operate from your house by teleport."

Toorop didn't answer, but emitted an invisible vibration meaning it was all fine by him.

The man flipped through his notebook, muttering. He stopped at a page that he started reading carefully.

"You're lucky," said the man as he straightened his glasses. "We have the product you need."

Toorop decided to say something.

"Product?"

"An army product. Red Army, that goes without saying. A very effective remedy for post-traumatic catalepsy."

"Seems perfect to me."

"Perfect. The only slight problem will be to get it quick."

"How long?"

"Don't worry, our colleague from Kazakhstan informed me of the urgent nature of this operation. I'll have it today."

"When, today?" Toorop insisted, in his role as professional pain in the ass.

The man raised towards him an amused look and a small smile.

"You won't believe it, I have no clue."

"I need it before tonight. Before noon would be best."

"You'll have it before tonight," said Newton, before closing his notebook and getting up. "That's my definition of the word today."

Toorop got up in turn but the man raised his hand.

"No, you stay here. I'll be back in a few hours, probably. You'll find some mineral water in the kitchen refrigerator…"

The man moved to the door of the living room, flipped the lock, and turned back towards Toorop.

"Just in case you get the idea of visiting the house, you should knew that all your moves are being recorded, wherever you are…"

He cracked the door, placed a foot in the opening, and turned back.

"I should also tell you that a good part of the house is booby trapped."

Toorop let out a harsh laugh.

"Let me know if the vegetable compartment of your fridge is full of C-4."

"No," the man said, smiling maliciously. "Just the stash of whiskey."

Then he disappeared, closing the door behind him.

So Toorop only made two or three trips between the kitchen and the living room, as well as a little stop on the toilet bowl, wondering if Doctor Newton was nasty enough to have installed spy fiber optics in a corner of the bathroom. Yes, of course, he thought, grabbing the first sheet of paper. The rest of the time he spent in the Chippendale armchair reading a few of the magazines spread out on the low table. Classic stuff. *Newsweek. Time. Hour,* the free Montreal Anglo paper. An issue of *Yatching.* The day's *Gazette.* On a small Victorian chest of drawers he uncovered a few high-tech hobby magazines and some issues of *Scientific American* and *Nature.*

Toorop could bet that added to cameras and traps, the house was stuffed with electronic counter-attack systems destined to confuse possible enemy spies.

The old guy was weird, abnormal. The complete opposite of the *a priori* image he'd concocted. Even if his face evoked something irresistibly Slavic, he spoke impeccable French, with an Anglo accent that didn't seem put on. Everything here oozed an eminently British culture and way of life.

The solution crystallized at once.

A mole.

A sleeper. Born here, probably from Russian parents, fifty years before. Someone perfectly adapted in society, with no direct contact with the Embassy, who was woken up every so often for very precise cases, very precise tasks. Awakenings that could be a few years apart. Sometimes sleepers were awakened only once. Some were never even awakened.

Romanenko had a mole at his disposal in Quebec. A little guy who looked like a doc in early retirement.

Probably, the guy was also retired from his secret activities.

But Romanenko had found the necessary arguments. If he was a major player, just below the fat Siberian, he was covered in dollars. He could surely sacrifice a few to wake a mole who'd retired from business.

Reading the different scientific magazines laying around everywhere, Toorop was able to get a pretty good idea of the vast "Man on Mars" program that the Americans had been spearheading for ten years with the Russians and the space agency embryo they were trying to set up. They'd just launched the final phase of the program. The different modules of the Martian shuttle were under construction; they'd be sent into orbit during the course of the year 2014 and assembled near the international station. Then a group of robotic systems would leave as vanguard, fired by classic launchers. To top it off, the international crew would go on a trip of about a year. From what they were saying, a dress rehearsal was planned on the moon for 2015, allowing for a new launching of the Cynthian exploitation program and NASA's project for a permanent automated industrial base there.

Humanity was flying off to the cold reaches of outer space. He wished the aliens the best of luck.

By early afternoon, he'd finished devouring the magazines, so he opened the *Gazette*, the English language paper.

The free province of Quebec was experiencing an unprecedented economic boom, and so was the rest of the country. Canada formed one of the world's largest fresh water natural reservoirs. The country was at the head of the Blue Gold Rush. From what Toorop understood, the old politico-cultural divides had disappeared like mirages above the new desert of the universe: global warming, climactic chaos and the explosion of megapolises had dried up rivers and waterways. In different parts of the globe, drinking water was negotiated according to its weight in gold. Business was back up.

On the international politics pages, he read a small article on the unrest in Eastern Turkistan.

Prince Shabazz was making a comeback at the National Uygur Conference. Hakmad's defeat to the Kazakhs paved a highway for him, in spite of the serious blow he'd suffered in Kirghizia the month before. He wanted to "take the Conference out of the dead-end created by Hakmad," and proposed a "frank and open inter-militia dialogue so that the National Uygur Movement could speak out in one voice against the Han oppressor."

Toorop had to laugh. Shabazz was a fearsomely intelligent politician, he knew how to learn from his defeats, even if he didn't listen to his counselors enough. He'd make a good minister.

Toorop ended up on the gossip and tabloids pages. He skimmed the story of the latest wars that Montreal motorcycle gangs were fighting for control of the different traffics that moved through the city.

It had been going on for twenty-five years. Phases of remission interspersed the violent combats that pitted Hell's Angels, Bandidos and Rock-Machines, with Semtex, RPG-7s, and recently, as he was discovering, a surface-to-surface missile salve dropped on the enemy fortress.

In the nineties, the Hell's Angels had moved into an ancient fort of the old city. In a few months, they'd transformed it into an impenetrable blockhouse. It was only to avoid armed confrontation with ALL of Quebec's Criminal Investigation Department that they deigned to vacate the premises. But the tradition remained. As for the Rock-Machines, they never hesitated to use the numerous explosives, available by catalogue at any Wal-Mart across the border, to blow up their competition. That summer, no one knows how, but they had gotten a mobile unit of brand new Katiouchas, and complacently bombarded the abandoned and fortified Hell's Angels' factory, killing a few rival gang members on the spot. It made the commentators' day; it was like the NBA final for them, or the fight for a Wild Card spot in the National Baseball League.

In this tribal war, the Banditos had played referee for a long time, becoming allies with one side then the other before associating with the Rock-Machines on a long-term basis. To Toorop, it strangely resembled the Uygur mess.

He was at that point in his entertaining readings when "Doctor Newton" reappeared.

"Dear Doctor Kepler," he said, penetrating the living room with a muffled step, "give your salute to the miracles of Russian military medicine."

He held out before him a small glass jar filled with luminous, almost fluorescent green pills.

"What is it?"

Doctor Newton stiffened, one of his eyebrows raised.

"The molecular formula is top secret. And it takes up almost a page. It's our miracle drug. Come, I'm going to explain to you how it works."

Toorop followed him to his desk, intrigued. He knew how pills "worked;" all you had to do was stuff them in the patient's mouth.

Doctor Newton was holding one of the pills between his thumb and index finger and directed it towards Toorop, letting it shimmer under the light falling from the windows. It looked like a sliver of emerald.

"This is our newborn bioelectronic component. It's a processor that specializes in the synthesis of complex endorphins. It has a small search engine and sufficient memory to adapt to *local conditions*. Do you follow?"

Toorop caught his drift. But he wanted more information.

"It's personalized, in a way?"

The guy let out a short caustic laugh.

"Yes, quite precisely, and do you know to what miracle this is due?"

Toorop walled himself in silence.

The guy took out a small object from his pocket and set it on the desk. A black cube, mat, with ten-centimeter sides.

"The *black box*," he said.

He pressed on a rubber membrane situated on one of the cube's sides, and it opened, like a square carbon flower. A strange mechanism made of crystalline material appeared as well as a few devices with the same texture as the cube. The man placed the fluorescent green pill inside a small crystalloid sphere. He tapped on a mini-keyboard attached to the black box.

A soft pink light circulated through the translucent circuitry all the way to the small ball, with a strange digital sound.

The old man removed the capsule. It shined with an even more pronounced gleam.

Then, patiently and meticulously, he did the same with all the pills before returning them to their little glass jar.

"I've just configured their operating system. Let me quickly explain the principle: each capsule contains a bioprocessor. The bioprocessor analyses the metabolic activity of the brain and in turn synthesizes the molecule and the necessary dose. The trick is to have the possibility of stocking the information, and mostly, as I'm sure you've understood, to be able to transfer the data from one bioprocessor to another."

Toorop thought for an instant. Yes, that was the question, in fact.

"That's where the miracles of Russian military science come in, dear Doctor Kepler. Here's what's going to happen. Once you get back, you get our dear Maria A to swallow this pretty little green thing. And then you wait a few hours, long enough to recover the residual memory disk."

"Recover?"

The man laughed slightly.

He stared at Toorop with eyes the color of cloudy green water hiding behind long-sighted glasses.

"The memory disk, dear Doctor Kepler, she will shit out. So she'll just have to be careful not to flush the toilet and not hesitate to go through her pooh."

Toorop armed himself with an innocent smile.

"I'm sure she'll have no problem."

Then, Doctor Newton explained to Toorop how to proceed with the non-degradable residue taken from the shit. First, wash it with water, or even better, with an antiseptic. Then dry it and place it in the little crystal ball, turn the data saving mechanism on, take it out, and then place the next bioprocessor in the ball. Press "Save." It would receive the information from the preceding component and would improve the treatment that much more in case of relapse. In addition, the data would be automatically sent to Doctor Newton. If something really started fucking up, he'd be able to react in real time.

There were about ten capsules.

"You have enough for a while," he said. "The black box is equipped with the standard plug-ins. Hook it up to your console; you'll have the appropriate software on your Kepler site. And don't ever come back here," he blurted out, bringing him back to a bus stop near the University of Montreal at the wheel of his brand new Cadillac. "Don't ever ring my doorbell, avoid Outremont. Contact me only if there's a serious problem, which would be if the bioprocessors don't work, and only through the Kepler e-mail. But that's highly improbable. They've cured amnesiac officers."

Toorop didn't answer. Obviously the guy ignored lots of things.

Marie Zorn was not a simple post-traumatic amnesiac.

She was schizophrenic. Psychotic.

He didn't dare ask if the miracle capsules would have cured the leaders of the ex-Soviet Union.

The Cadillac disappeared with a luxurious hiss towards Mont-Royal.

17

Toorop was sitting in front of the TV, watching the SRQ news bulletin with attention. The Hell's Angels had just responded to the Rock-Machine attack by blasting one of their small seaplanes somewhere over the James Bay. The aircraft had been shot down at the end of the day, a few minutes after sundown. From the west coast of Akimiski Island, a witness had seen a line of light flare in the sky above the waters before noticing an orange collision in the atmosphere. He'd first believed it to be a meteorological phenomenon or an optical illusion caused by dusk, and then a UFO when he saw an "orange ball" fall quickly over the horizon. He'd called the local branch of a UFO organization he belonged to, which then called the Criminal Investigation Department. Out on the water, near the Twin Islands, another witness had seen a ship in the distance and the same line of light from his own sailboat, but he clearly saw the aircraft plummet into the waves, on fire, two or three miles from his boat. He sent out a radio alert immediately.

The Criminal Investigation Department of Quebec and of the GRO had sent their divers, a small submarine search robot as well as specialized helicopters equipped with MRI scanners. Thanks to the indications from the sailboat, they'd just found the seaplane; thirty meters below, with a huge blackened hole in the cabin. The bodies of the passengers and of the crew had been removed and identified within the hour. Six people. The local boss of the Bay division of the Rock-Machines and an official representative of the Big Montreal Bosses, their bodyguards, and the two pilots.

And close to a hundred kilos of heroin.

An armada of ships and planes were now covering the entire bay searching for the suspicious boat.

Reporters and journalists were stuffing themselves full of analyses and conjectures in front of the images taken from the sub-marine robot or from the real film platform set up on the Nouveau Comptoir port for the needs of the press, where the large Federal Navy Minesweeper was going to tow the seaplane. All this interspersed with historical reminders in the form of smarmy docudramas and unending interviews of all kinds of specialists, criminologists, Heads of Criminal Investigation, detectives, reformed bikers. The war of the bikers. Life-size John Woo, *The Wild One* revisited by the Gulf War, in terms of arsenal.

During the night, in a press release by one of its lawyers, the Montreal chapter of the Hell's Angels made it known that the biker association had strictly nothing to do with the odious attack that…

The Pepsi ad flash happily concluded that big lie.

Toorop got up to get a can of Black Label in the fridge.

Rebecca had fallen asleep on the sofa. The headphones fixed to her ears kept spreading a post-techno beat bad enough to wake the dead and kill its share of the living.

Passing in front of Marie's room, he cracked the door and glanced in. The girl was sleeping peacefully with a childish, regular snore.

Perfect, thought Toorop. Doctor Newton's bioprocessor seemed to be working. In two short days, Marie's state had considerably improved.

Slumped in front of the images of the James Bay covered in lights and martial shadows, he popped open the 750cl can and thought to himself that there was undoubtedly nothing better than war, when seen from his armchair.

And the directors of TV channels knew this better than anyone.

Rebecca vaguely cracked an eye, then got up like an automaton, mumbled a barely intelligible *goodnight* and walked to her room like a zombie.

Toorop zapped. A boring sociologist kept spilling out the usual ineptitudes about the "tribal way of life" of the motorcycle gangs.

He landed on the CNN channel for the Asian community. The Chinese Civil War had been front-page news for about three years. Each trimester, a dramatic reversal. Each week, its outstanding fact; each day, its share of massacres. A gift from God for Ted Turner.

They were in the heart of the monsoon. Daily downpours had swollen the rivers and a typhoon had just devastated the eastern coast around Shanghai.

The Yangtze was flooded, paralyzing the two enemy front lines on hundreds of kilometers on each side of the river. The images streamed by like so many paintings of disaster by some Hieronymus Bosch of the video camera: columns of tanks disappeared up to the turret beneath the waters, long files of pathetic bathyscaphes, thousands of men trapped by the floods, land slides, bridges carried off, trains lost in the raging waters, pathetic *Titanics*, toys in the hands of divine anger, planes glued to the ground on airfields transformed into swimming pools. Neptune had decided to have it out with Mars, but first of all, he'd decided to throw a bucket full of water on the two dogs that couldn't get unstuck.

Of course, it would calm the belligerents' zeal for a while, thought Toorop, faced with the scale of the cataclysm.

From that, CNN-Asia cut to the problems on the western borders of China.

Toorop's attention went up a notch.

The last UNLF rebel cell, surrounded at Kapchagai, prey to terrible bombings for days, had just unconditionally surrendered. Columns of tattered men, exhausted, dirty, emaciated, walking with drooping heads on sun dried roads, tore a vague, momentary feeling of grief from him. It didn't last long.

The Kazakh Army and the Russian Ministry of Defense were operating under a Unopol warrant. Hakmad would be tried for war crimes. The UN inspectors sent to Kirghizia the month before had found traces of many mass graves, as well as villages razed to the ground, carbonized by flame-throwers. The UNLF soldiers had shown no pity. They'd quite simply killed everything that moved in their entire theater of operations along the Sino-

Kirghizia border. They'd executed all war prisoners. And committed numerous atrocities.

The sickening vision of the mass graves open beneath the UN excavators provoked a strange flush of adrenaline in his brain irradiated with the cathode ray images.

His heart went overboard.

A fear time bomb. Inordinate anxiety.

The fate he'd passed so close to, or rather, through which he'd passed like a strange camel through a needle's eye—yes, you could say it was a miracle—that deathly fate was spreading out now in ribbons of cadavers laying side by side on the ash-colored earth, patiently accounted for and recorded in the memory of the Unopol computers.

He couldn't recognize any familiar face in the heap of bodies laid bare by the excavators, except his own, a thousand times over.

The next day was very nice, very hot, very fast.

As soon as he woke up, Toorop understood that he couldn't have Marie locked up in the cage any longer. She'd had two attacks in two weeks. He had to cut the circuit.

He immediately sent an emergency e-mail to Romanenko.

Procedure 4: we're going out for a stroll. Our little Zoe needs a breath of fresh air.

He verified that Zoe was in fact Marie's code name for the procedure in question, then he compacted it all and entrusted it to his messenger-agent.

Procedure 4 stipulated that Marie could go out from time to time at Toorop's discretion, but with the utmost prudence and in deserted places, or almost. They had heaps of programmed itineraries around Montreal, the Laurentides, the Saguenay and Tadoussac. Admittedly tourist destinations, but in the middle of the large semi-deserted spaces it would be easy to isolate themselves.

He thought for a moment, after spreading the map on the kitchen table. They could do the Grand-Jardins National Park, halfway between Montreal and the Saguenay. The size of a French department, without anyone, almost, but bear and beaver families. You could find little sanctuaries, cabins grouped together near the lakes that strewed the region. A gem.

OK, move on to the real stuff. He'd rent a van in the morning, a Chrysler or one of the latest Pontiacs; automatic computer assisted driving, high tech visioning windshield, water, gas and CNN. Three of them could sleep in it with sleeping bags. Dowie would follow in the big Toyota.

Then the arsenal. No fuck-ups. The guns and the permits would go with, but neither the MPGs nor the Arwen. They'd take the shotgun as a "hunting weapon."

If ever they got arrested, for speeding or some other shit, first show the papers to the cops, with the weapons permits, then tell them nicely that there was a gun in the glove compartment. No funny business. The papers were in order; it would be smooth sailing.

He was a Canadian businessman. Rebecca and Dowie were representatives of his group in British Columbia; one of them was responsible for security. Marie would be secretary. They carried weapons because, apparently, the roads were dangerous around the James Bay where they were going. Most particularly air routes; apparently, the Hell's Angels attack was supposed to mark the beginning of a large-scale war. He wasn't short of arguments. All of them were freshly imprinted in the head of any cop in the Criminal Investigation Department.

They'd go on a two or three day trip in the nature reserve and come back straight away. With a bit of luck, it would give Marie a breather for a week or two. And the same for all of them.

Brilliant plan, in fact.

Road 17 was a rocky cleft snaking through the forest-covered hills. It regularly came to border a lake, a small shimmering comma planted between two mounds, or a large expanse of water engulfing an entire valley like this one, Lake Malbee, near which he'd just parked, on a large level surface planted with a bunch of cabins, a small picnic shelter and a wooden pier along which swayed two or three rowboats.

He questioned a retired couple coming out of one of the large wooden cabins along the lakeshore. They'd gotten to the pier and Toorop came up to them politely as they were loading fishing supplies near a small boat. The place was rented for the year by some kind of works council or pension fund, from what he understood. He asked if they could still rent something, just in case a cabin or two were available.

No, it seemed impossible, but they could try camping a bit farther off.

The picnic shelter was equipped with rustic comforts. A toilet in the shape of a wooden shed with a cement block that had a hole in it; a hole which opened up onto a vast cavern filled with waste whose real texture the imagination refused to conceive.

Two or three tables with benches beneath a wood cover. A blue plastic container for a garbage.

Exactly what was needed to plunge Marie, him and the rest of the gang back into life in the outdoors. Evacuate stress and toxins. Totally air out the system; clear out the gas, the valves, the whole works. Bring it delicately to center, not on itself but on the point of balance between self and world. Evacuate negative energies for a moment, in order to be able to confront them with the strength of the warrior.

It was a perfect plan.

The first day had slowly stretched till dusk. Nothing else to do but read a book (him), listen to repetitive techno-rock (Rebecca), do a bit of yoga (Marie), nothing (Dowie), eat the dinner bought in Montreal before getting on the highway (everyone). Two roasted chickens and two orders of potatoes from CocoRico on Saint-Laurent. A few Chinese salads. Industrial size Yoghurts. *Smoked meat.* Two French Camemberts. Apples. Beers. Coke. Bottled Water. A bottle of Chardonnay.

During the afternoon, he indulged in a small joint of local stuff, Northern Lights, from what he knew. When the sun waned on the horizon, he was starving.

Heaven on earth, he said to himself as he devoured his share of chicken and potatoes.

He attained ecstasy when the sun set the sky ablaze to the west and when the Chilean wine transformed the powerful taste of the cheese into elixir.

Later, sitting on the pier facing the lake, he slowly bit into an apple with the taste of honey.

After a last joint, falling asleep in his sleeping bag near the Voyager, he let out a ringing burp. It was a burp of thanks to the Creator for having bestowed upon them a brief instant of *order and beauty, luxury, peace and pleasure* in the chaos of men.

18

When the man from Vladivostok entered the room, he brought with him the strong smell of unbelievable brutality. Gorsky himself froze.

Markov rose hastily from his seat. Gorsky followed suit a bit slower; he had to keep calm and play his role to the end.

The man came to meet him with a savage smile. He was a head taller, about two meters. He spread his immense arms in a Russian greeting. Gorsky did the same and came closer—Anton, Dimitri—and it was as if two steel tentacles had closed in upon him to crush him around the shoulders.

He knew it meant, "Anton, we need to speak man to man."

The two tentacles finally let him go. Gorsky observed the immense stature wrapped in a city Versace Big Shape neo-twenties suit that didn't fit him at all, the big round mug, the baldhead, the bushy eyebrows. That mass, that density.

A real Ruskie bastard, he thought. Like me.

Dimitri Merkuchev, known as "the Chinaman"—a nickname given to him by the Japanese Yakuzas who no doubt thought he had the air of a giant Manchurian. He was one of the main *Vor* of the faraway megalopolis on the Pacific coast. From now on, Gorsky would work under his orders.

They sat on either side of the table. Gorsky gave Markov a discreet but pressing sign. He disappeared in a flash.

The man swept an appreciative look over the vast living room with its light, neutral colors, the sofas and the luxurious Swedish furniture, the well of crystal light pouring out sparkles of sun, the large Art Deco table around which they were sitting, and mostly, as he showed with an expressive flick of the tongue, the oblong objects exposed everywhere in the room, on the walls or on bronze pedestals.

"Your collection has grown even more, Anton, since my last visit."

A smile slipped onto Gorsky's lips as he played on his keyboard the arrival of the Honda domestic robot with two iced shot glasses, an ice bucket, and a bottle of real Zubrowka whose traffic he oversaw in the area.

"I haven't even shown you the best of it. That'll be for desert."

"Perfect, Anton, perfect. What's this one?"

Gorsky turned slightly to see what the index was pointing at.

"The first Exocet model. I was told this piece was on an Argentine Airforce Mirage during the Falklands War."

"Very nice."

"Fabrication date: December 9, 1981. Like all the others, it works perfectly."

The man cracked up.

"You could need it."

Gorsky stiffened. The threat was barely veiled. It was the sign that the usual civilities were over and that they were now broaching the real shit.

"OK, what's the news?"

The man didn't answer right away. He settled deeply into the huge leather armchair which let out a few muffled moans.

"You stuck your nose where it wasn't supposed to be. And that biker stuff isn't good news. Our Brooklyn friends say we should cut the costs here. The cops of the entire North-American continent are riled up. It's too hot."

Gorsky felt the blood leave his face.

He got over the initial panic, breathed in and moved directly to the front lines.

"How does this concern you, I mean, for this particular transaction?"

Merkuchev's paunch quivered with a volcanic laugh.

"Anton Dimitrievitch! You know that our intelligence network is the best in all Eastern Asia. There are no secrets for us in anything that happens in the China Sea."

"China Sea?"

"An example, in this case let's talk about the Tartar Straits."

Gorsky's face clouded over.

"Have you learned something?"

The paunch quivered again.

"Yeah, you could say that. Chinese and Siberian mercenaries shot the aircraft down in February, from a ship off Kholmsk. But we've been hearing of late about guys who would have come from North America to pay their debt in return. Guys who belong to one of those gangs mixed up in all that shit, over there precisely, in Quebec. We don't know more than that. But that's why the Vladivostok counsel thinks we should suspend the operation."

Gorsky felt all his defenses weaken under the blow. By some unknown alchemy, his path crossed the path of warring bikers at the other end of the earth. Without him having any possible influence on the course of events.

The only way out was to play on any crime lord's atavistic instinct, greed.

"A hundred million dollars in a year, that's the guaranteed minimum. And this is just the kickoff phase, Dimitri... You can't imagine what we can make with this doc. We're just at the beginning of a new big thing. Like when bootleggers got ahold of the alcohol market, or when Cosa Nostra decided to take control of heroin traffic after the Second World War. We have to be in control of the market when it booms."

The man nodded his head thoughtfully.

"A hundred million is small-fry. It's not even the standard collection of a regular Las Vegas casino. And a casino is legit."

"It's not so bad, and I told you this is just the kickoff phase. Shit, what do you want? You want the Chinks or the Latinos to fuck us over again? Believe me, you won't have to ask the Sino-American triads twice to take over the market, *especially* if the way is clear, with a sign saying 'Serve Yourself'."

This provoked a dubious sniffle from Dimitri.

Gorsky hammered it in.

"Listen, since last time, I've been able to establish a real projection. I have a pilot operation going on, investments have been more than reasonable till now. Let me prove to you that I'm right, and next year, at the next conference with the Sumiyochi-Rengo, believe me, you'll have a real great joker up your sleeve."

A second sniffle from Dimitri.

Gorsky told himself he couldn't stop now.

"Let's do the math quickly," he said as he turned on the small table screen with a little hand move. "For now, the going price of my 'message service' is a million dollars a unit. But let me remind you that the total price of the 'product' is ten times more. With what we're investing now, our shares in the business will triple within the year. Then, like I told you, there are the other 'pension fund' clients," he marked the quotes with a small gesture of both hands. "And like I also told you, everything indicates that demand will blow up but supply will remain outlawed. So pretty soon we'll be able to start hiking the prices. And at that point, believe me, clients like these, my book of orders will be full of them."

"What do your projections indicate exactly?"

"Within three years, at this rhythm, with a single clinic I'll be raking in close to a billion dollars. In fact, I predict it'll be twice as much 'cause I'm gonna press on the gas. I'm quite simply gonna take control of this pretty little business. Then, if we go big, multiply that by fifty, or a thousand! We gotta continue the operation Dimitri. Jesus, all this won't even have cost us the price of a porn hall outside Moscow."

Dimitri sniffed, shifted on the creaking armchair, fixed his stare on Gorsky's black lenses, remained silent a few seconds, sniffed again, and dropped:

"Fine. But your pilot operation has gotta work a hundred percent. It's gotta glide as smoothly as a fart between silk sheets."

"It'll be better than that. It'll sound like a guy diving into a swimming pool full of cash."

A swimming pool, yeah, Jesus.

And soon an ocean. Doctor Walsh and his laboratory would be able to supply an army of loaded lunatics with the world's most potent dope.

Dimitri was gone; he had other business to take care of. Gorsky thought to himself that a man is rarely a prophet in his own land.

Damn, those post-Soviet Mafia bastards didn't get shit. They were stuck on the old business: racketing, kidnapping, prostitution, drugs, gaming, and pornography.

Dimitri and he were the same age. Fiftieth birthday in the rearview mirror. But he'd spent a whole career innovating, branching out into unexplored territory. The myriad occult gold mines that the technological explosion of the XXIst century would harbor had occurred to him early on. And he really got into it, with the passion of the enthusiastic professional. First, the wellspring of fissile matter and scrapped Soviet arsenals, then of unemployed scientists, later of military software and industrial patents, and recently of biotechnology. The Novosibirsk and Vladivostok big bosses had never slowed him down in his lightning run. He didn't cramp their style, they got a substantial cut of all his profits, and they knew they were incapable of competing with him efficiently. But they'd never really backed him either. In the end, they had to negotiate with the Yakuza who were blocking their access to the North-American continent. In the high-tech sector notably, not to mention the Asian market, China, even at war, especially at war, had for the most part fallen out of their grasp. The Taiwanese and American triads divvied up the market with the Japanese gangs.

But this wasn't a goldmine he was talking about. It was the Real Big Thing. The Golden Mountain.

It was Ronald Biggs and the bags on the Glasgow-London postal train.

American mafias learning that the 1919 Prohibition Act had been voted into law.

It was Cortez facing the treasures of the Aztec cities.

Bill Gates in front of the IBM baldheads.

And now this close shave with them.

He resolved to go for a little tour of his new acquisitions—a visit to his favorite missiles. It was the only antidote available, around here.

First the Exocet, with its French inscriptions and the small red, white, and blue flag at the bottom of the thin gray turbine. Then he moved on to the old Iraqi Scud enthroned in the middle of a circular patio. At each cardinal point of the patio stood the beautiful dark spires of Patriot warheads. The patio was covered with a genuine Arabic mosaic, part of which was a Syrian bas-relief from the Xth century bought from a member of the Assad family at a bargain during the construction of the dacha, ten years before.

Rising like a gray metal column on the other side of the room, the SS-20 that had started his collection scintillated softly at the hard angles of its wings.

Then he contemplated the slew of old Soviet SAM-7s; they had more sentimental value than anything else. It was with the SAM-7s that the Viet Cong made many US Air Force Phantoms bite the dust in the sky over Vietnam. He'd entered the cadets of the Soviet Army the year of the fall of Saigon. He'd left twelve years later with rocket shrapnel in the abdomen and a bad sergeant pension, when it was paid. He understood quickly that it was time to move up in life substantially.

Farther off, there was a small bouquet of anti-tank TOWs, and, across, next to the window, two intersecting Stinger missiles, all "souvenirs" from his campaign in Afghanistan in the eighties. He'd also lost seven-tenths on the left eye there. Since then, that eye had lost the remaining three-tenths, and the other wasn't worth much more. The stereovision optics weren't a luxury, despite the fact that a pair of that kind of thing cost as much as a Minister, if you didn't want to get your retina fried one day by a bottom of the barrel micro-laser gone crazy because of a bugged nano-processor. Exactly the type of shit he himself commercialized at a large scale.

Above his head, a few small air-air Matra missiles were extending predatory shadows on either side of the central ceiling light.

On both sides of the entrance to the toilet he'd erected antique, "Boy" class, conventional Russian attack submarine torpedoes as they were called in NATO classification.

In the second living room, a discrete alcove for nights with five-thousand dollar escort girls, he'd arranged a big Navy Tomahawk above the immense sofa and planted four Katioucha rockets in the corners.

As chandeliers, in the corner of the two big hallways distributing the rooms, he had a bouquet of Russian anti-runway submunition bombs dating from Chechnya.

In the library, its high shelves filled with all types of art books, an old Pershing seemed to be waiting for someone to finish off.

There was a French Mistral on the bathroom ceiling and a giant LCD screen simulating an entire catalogue of celestial skies: tropical nights, aurora borealis, southern hemisphere constellations, full moons in the Carpati Mountains, dusk in Big Sur, perseids in Haute Provence.

To finish, he'd planted the icy pylon of an Israeli Jericho at the foot of the inside staircase.

For Gorsky, the missiles were works of art. First of all, these machines were worth hundreds of thousands, even millions of dollars some of them. On the other hand, they were beautiful, cold, implacable and insensitive to any other project but their own towering and deadly existence. And they also seemed to have a soul, an *anima*, a form, a particular aesthetic vibration in space and time. Finally, and most importantly, they represented the outcome of his immature, war torn child's dream. In April 1987, waking up from his traumatic coma in that Kazakhstan military hospital, already half blind in one eye, he was going on twenty-eight but his experience of civilian life had stopped on his sixteenth birthday. He felt like a living sponge, picking up all possible experiences through each pore of his skin in order to catch up on all those he'd lost.

One day, during his long recovery, he fell upon a documentary on the antique black and white tube TV set of his eight-bed room, where other mutilated or wounded sub-officers vegetated. Gorbachev's perestroika was in full swing. The Soviet world was opening up to images from the West. The documentary, probably bought from a British station, followed the hectic life of three fashionable English producers, Messrs. Stock, Aitken and Waterman, creators of the "Bananarama" girls' trio, among others. One of them, so rich he didn't know what to do with his millions, had started a peculiar collection: missiles.

That day, Gorsky never knew why, the image of that producer and missile collector imprinted itself onto him, like comic book or movie heroes, knights, cowboys, cops, magicians, and mutants imprint themselves on the photosensible paper of adolescent egos.

He wasn't even twenty-eight and he was withering away in a nasty end of the line military hospital, with a thirty centimeter gash between sternum and pubis, an eye just good enough to accompany a borsch for the homeless and a handful of rubles once in a blue moon, while others lived in the heart of an artificial paradise of luxurious seaside villas, rivers of champagne, or diamonds, Armani suits, Mercedes, danceterias, girls beautiful enough to commit suicide for on the spot, aphrodisiac drugs, *missiles exhibited as works of art.*

He decided to invite himself to the party.

Now that he'd reached his retarded kid dream, he was trying to surpass the model. The missile-as-work-of-art was all good, pleasurable and aesthetically moving. But if the current program with Doctor Walsh bore fruit as planned, he'd think on a larger scale. A much larger scale.

What missiles were to painting, or to sculpture, his new acquisitions would be to Land Art.

The RKA, the Russian Space Agency, had decided to sell its antique R-7 launchers dating back to Yuri Gagarin, as well as Soyuz capsules from the last century. It was also going to auction, module by module, what was left of the Mir station, recovered twelve years before by a series of joint Russian-American missions. American television had been present in orbit during the dramatic accident that put an end to the station. Images of the death of the four astronauts, among them a CNN reporter, had been transmitted live into hundreds of thousands of homes. Fire had spread in the principal module at incredible speed. Quite frankly, before that date, no one except for astronautics professionals had the slightest clue as to what fire was in a state of weightlessness. On that day, millions of men and women, the young and the old, transfixed before their cathodic tubes, saw what it was. Without gravity, *fire flows* like a deadly oil propagating itself everywhere, in absolutely all directions at once. The camera of the American journalist Peter Myers was guaranteed by the Air Force. It continued shooting after all of them had died; it breathed its last breath only when the temperature cleared a thousand degrees centigrade.

To buy the remains of the station where these historic images had been filmed was the equivalent of acquiring a saintly relic, the mysterious Grail of human destiny, a high flight to the stars ending in death, in the liquid fire of zero gravity.

Gorsky told Christie's of Moscow, who was taking care of the sale, that he was interested. He wouldn't appear in person, of course. He'd let his man take care of it; someone specialized in this branch of his business.

It would take a while for the heavy Russian federal administration to topple, months would go by, and Christie's would probably not be able to organize the sale before the end of the year. By then, his war treasure would have increased by a few tens of millions of dollars. He hoped to be able to pocket a complete R-7, a Soyuz-T from the eighties, and at least one module saved from the station, maybe with a Progress cargo as a bonus.

If everything went well with Doctor Walsh, soon he'd be able to chill on an island of the Pacific at the head of the most innovative illicit business of the first half of the XXIst century.

As it had done with drugs during the XXth century, the UN banned all "non-conforming" experimentation and genetically modified animal "products." And as history repeats itself, it would take decades to realize its error, definitely enough time to fatten up two or three generations of enterprising Siberians.

As it turned out, the Novosibirsk mafia was his only family. He was an orphan on his father's side; a work hero killed in an accident of the same name at the bottom of a manganese mine in the Urals. His mother was an alcoholic whom he hadn't been able to save from progressive dereliction. He'd escaped the corrections center by accepting enrollment in the army. The Red Army solemnly affirmed that it would be his new family. However, leaving the hospital, he had to wait months for a place in some lousy projects outside Krasnoyarsk. Then the small pension had stopped coming. Around 1992, when the Soviet system imploded completely, delivering

Russian civil society in one blow to the unbridled capitalism of primitive accumulation, he was already a young hawk of the Siberian mafia, a young hawk with piercing talons, sick eyes and a sharpened mind. He'd learned how to survive in that new environment, that virgin territory open to all daring initiatives.

He could envision the rest of his career with relative serenity. He'd retire after the Real Big Deal: setting up the first big network specialized in illegal live products.

He could treat himself to the whole Russian space fleet. Better yet, he could relaunch the RKA program.

Whether they liked it or not, his name would go down in history like Dutch Schultz, Lucky Luciano, Frank Costello, Vito Genovese, Pablo Escobar, Vyacheslav Ivankov.

His collection would be admired; people would come from all over the world to see it, and his house would become a museum.

He'd give the Brit producer the hook.

The man Romanenko was waiting for was called Karl "Kemal" Spitzner. He was a German-Turkish arms dealer who had a pass to all the embassies of the region.

Kemal Spitzner had started his career in ex-Yugoslavia more than twenty years earlier. Thanks to his small network in Germany and Turkey, he set up one of the most important arms trades for the Bosnian Army. He'd gotten his experience providing the National Croatian Guard with arsenals from Hungary or from the Lebanese Forces. Then, had bought war material in bulk from the Shiite or Druze militias, or from the Syrians, and in the ancient Muslim Soviet Republics, to sell it back to the Sarajevo government.

Romanenko was waiting for Spitzner in a deserted spot, along some old disused railroad tracks linking the Trans-Siberian railroad to a factory that had been abandoned for ages.

The noise of the car entering the cemented lot made him turn around. A red, yellow and fluorescent green Suzuki 4 x 4. Fuck, why not a gold Cadillac, thought Romanenko.

Spitzner got out of it, alone. With a large caliber automatic slung on his belt.

He still wore the blond dreadlocks of his thirties, an old pair of extra large jeans, and a formless and dirty Israeli jacket.

Despite his errors in taste, especially for a guy close to fifty, Kemal Spitzner possessed some advantages.

First, thanks to him, Romanenko had been able to vary his weapons sources for the Uygur guerrilla movement.

Second, he was a well of information, and knew it. He had no problem raking in the dough for it.

Third, he'd no doubt met or heard about Toorop in Bosnia. He could tell him a thing or two about the mercenary.

Finally, he maintained he had a story that would be of utmost interest to him.

It all conspired for a meeting to take place the same day.

"I don't know much about this Toorop. I know he participated in one of the weapons transfers for the Croatians from Lebanon. I remember that. That's when I met him for the first time. I remember seeing him once of twice after that, during other transfers for the Muslims; it was in '93, during the winter, if I remember correctly. Right in the thick of it. Then I learned he was fighting on the Northern front, in Brcko. Haven't heard a thing about him since."

Romanenko sighed.

Spitzner lit up a long Papirossi full of Caucasian herb. A heavy, enticing smell accompanied the cloud of smoke that Kemal blew in his direction.

Romanenko coughed, trying to evacuate the smoke with large hand gestures.

"Well, can you recollect other war memories for me? Can you think of anyone who would have known him then?"

Kemal Spitzner's large azure eyes stared at Romanenko, a strange mix of Nordic brute and Berber pirate.

"I'll see what I can do, Colonel. But I didn't really stay in touch with the ex-Yugo guys… the wheel has turned."

"The wheel never stops turning… OK, do you know how he acted during those arms transfers?"

"Acted?"

"Yeah. How he reacted to situations, I don't know, there must have been some problems, a fuck-up; what was his responsibility exactly?"

Spitzner frowned, his eyebrows two fine lines of sparse fuzz.

"If I remember correctly, he was one of the assistants to the operations chief of their network. They would order for the Bosnian government through front companies, numbered accounts, the whole nine yards, real pros. He spoke several languages, and had several nationalities. There never was a fuck-up, no hitch, no nothing, zilch."

Romanenko sighed, got up from the small rock wall and walked a couple meters along the railroad tracks.

Kemal puffed on his long joint, then got up heavily to come meet him.

They advanced side by side along the rails.

Above them, the sky was a monochrome blue.

Kemal's story was worth a good deal. If Romanenko gave him twenty-five thousand dollars cash, straight up, and no later than right now, he'd be in a position to tell it.

A certain number of tacit rules exist in this type of exchange. The first is to trust; the second, *not* to trust.

So he had to establish a preliminary dialogue, a kind of contact with the desired object at a distance, a game of strip poker that would only reveal the tip of the bra, but give a taste of the quality of the lingerie.

Roughly, circumscribe the main subject.

"I think I can point you onto a serious lead concerning the real identity of one of your 'associates'."

Romanenko raised an eyebrow in surprise. The Jackpot.

He didn't think twice. He pointed to his car that was parked a bit farther off.

"No problem. Just tell me the probability that your lead actually goes back to them."

Spitzner looked him in the eyes, a calm smile on his lips.

"A hundred percent straight up. Twenty-five thousand on twenty-five thousand."

Romanenko weathered his stare, read in it clearly that he wasn't bluffing, and went to get the bag filled with dollars at the back of the regular Nissan.

Then, sitting on the small wall, he patiently listened to the story from the mouth of Kemal Spitzner.

Spitzner knew a man, an American, who'd settled in Siberia at the beginning of the century and had started a commercial aviation company. Cargo, business trips. Kemal had used his company a few times for his traffic, particularly the two-engine and four-engine medium-distance propeller cargo planes. One day, at the beginning of last year, Spitzner's friend had gotten some new clients: a couple, North Americans like himself, forty year olds, loaded, some kind of freaks, mystics. They wore tattoos and jewelry with a recurrent symbol, a double sphinx head topped with a seven-pointed star. Wherever they went, they carried around little talismans in the shape of metal pyramids, as well as books written by their guru. His friend didn't ask any questions. They didn't attempt to convert him.

The couple wondered if he'd fly groups of people regularly from one end of Siberia to the other, from the far-east coast to the Kazakhstan border, and back again.

The contract was sweet. It consisted of groups of about twelve people, two trips a month, during at least a year, maybe two. The couple was ready to pay top dollar, US. The idea was to operate discreet, fast and comfortable trips. The modern fleet owned by the American corresponded to their needs exactly.

Spitzner's friend didn't need to be begged to accept the terms of the contract. At the beginning of the summer, the couple had come to see him again; the first group was arriving in July. They needed to be picked up on a small private airstrip near the ocean, in the Sikhote-Alin Mountains, north of Vladivostok, and brought to a makeshift airfield somewhere in the Altais bordering Kazakhstan, as agreed. Land vehicles would await the group there. The plane would come back to pick them up a week later. (Romanenko perked up his ears. Kemal's story was starting out nice.) Spitzner's friend suspected something weird, fishy, but he wasn't committing any crime, any clandestine border crossing. They didn't leave the Russian Federation; there were neither drugs nor arms involved, nothing but their talismans, their fucking books. The inflow of dollars was just on point to pay the lease on the Falcon he'd acquired from a bankrupt Singapore company.

During the summer and the following months, Spitzner's friend and his squadron of small business planes transported more than a hundred people across Siberia.

In December, for the holidays, the couple informed him of a temporary interruption of the program. But everything would start up again in the spring, with different modalities and a different rhythm.

These additional clauses to the initial contract included a substantial increase of "risk bonuses" paid to the company.

In exchange for this, there were two new non-negotiable conditions. First, he'd agree to transport armed passengers. Second, he'd need a mobile medical team on board.

Spitzner's American friend had agreed of course.

In February of that year, one of his business planes went to pick up the expected group, on the old disused military strip of the Russian Far-East.

On the 28th, around five in the morning, in bad weather conditions, it took off for its return voyage over the coast. It passed the small town of Svetlaya on its right, started a large circle above Cape Krilon, the southern tip of Sakhalin Island, then plummeted into the sea outside of Kholmsk, in the Tartar Straits, causing the death of the thirteen passengers and the four members of the crew.

(Romanenko knew the story. The passengers were supposed to be a group of international tourists. Some contacts of his at the Ministry of the Interior informed him that they were trying to maintain judicial secrecy as long as possible, that it concerned "sensitive personalities" whose social status needed to be protected. He hadn't felt excessively concerned by the matter, but he remembered it now, through Kemal Spitzner.)

It took the Russian Navy more than a week to locate the wreck in the tumultuous waters of the straits, or rather, the two principal sections of the fuselage, the wings having exploded on impact with the surface of the water. The divers found six of the seventeen passengers, two of whom were members of the crew, and noted the presence of an enormous hole in the back of the cabin. The rudder and the jet engine were missing. They were found a bit farther, as metallic debris that marine animals had started living in.

Here was where the story would interest Romanenko, and cost him twenty-five thousand dollars:

Russian Federal police had interrogated Spitzner's American friend. He'd shown the flight ledger and given all the names and addresses of the passengers of the destroyed Falcon, then those from previous trips. The Russian cops had the unpleasant surprise of facing a slew of false identities. More than a hundred high-end fakes, with genetic code imprints on "secure" UN chips.

They asked Spitzner's friend not to leave Federation territory.

The American executive hadn't seen his clients again. The man with the mustache and the tall blonde disappeared from sight, all operations were cancelled, and the company that managed trips and transfers of funds vanished like the electronic mirage it was. He understood it was useless to let his lawyers loose on them; moreover, as his friends told him, it was best to let it be. The attack against the plane showed the whole thing was fishy, and dangerous. Indeed, the conclusions of the Russian scientific police were clear: the chemical mixture of residue found in the wreck and the particular shape of the hole proved that it was the impact of a Stinger missile.

The Russian cops weren't able to keep the info secret any longer. They played it down by explaining that, "for unknown reasons, possibly a passenger, a missile of that type was on board and accidentally exploded at high altitude." The black box of the aircraft obviously proved the contrary: an object at high speed had hit the fuselage near the rear hold.

At the time, Romanenko had kind of followed the story in the press. The use of a Stinger excluded any participation, whether accidental or voluntary, on the part of the Russian Navy.

But the Federal police kept the most important information secret, concerning the fake identities of the passengers who had been found (the members of the crew didn't count, and they considered the other passengers as missing).

However, in May, with Federal police authorization, Spitzner's friend goes to Almaty on business. At the airport, he lands face to face with the American mystic couple, and a third grifter, a thirty-year-old Wall Street type. The couple pretends not to recognize him. They go on their way without saying anything, the young yuppie tells him to fuck off, and two big gorillas intervene out of nowhere.

Spitzner's friend spends the day in Almaty with his client. Since the attack, he has a hard time making ends meet, the name of his company is linked to "Stinger missile," he's in the firing line of the Russian police. He needs to fight hard for each contract.

Then he spends the night at a hotel.

The next morning, his plane doesn't leave before early afternoon. He goes for a walk in a market somewhere in the city, and there, realizes he's being followed.

Spitzner's friend checks out his guard dogs and thinks to himself that they don't look like Federal Bureau cops, more like Chechen killers. He's able to lose them, doesn't go back to his hotel and goes directly to the closest car rental place. He gets a big fast Japanese car and speeds north, crosses all Kazakhstan and calls his company on his cell to tell them to send a helicopter to pick him up in Russian territory.

That very night, as he is crossing the border, he hears on the news that a man has been shot dead by an assault rifle near a taxi stand, five minutes from the airport. A man who fits his description. The Russian hydraulics engineer taking a cab to go to a professional meeting wore a light gray business suit just like his, a white shirt like his. He was the same size and build; he died by mistake. The Kazakh cops spent months speculating on the causes of that assassination. Only Spitzner's friend knew the motive. They wanted him dead. And they wanted that because he knew too much about the passengers on the plane and about the Mister Mustache / Miss Platinum couple. He'd seen them where he shouldn't have, when he shouldn't have and with whom he shouldn't have.

Spitzner's friend is tough. He used to be a Navy pilot, and wants to know whom he is dealing with. He gets in touch with a well-known professor at Cambridge University, a specialist in heretic theories and mystic sects whose address he finds on the Internet. He spends several days in his digital library, and finally tracks down the emblem that he'd seen around the necks of Mister Mustache and Miss Platinum.

It was in fact the emblem of a sect. A post-millenialist sect, born of the split from a neo-Gnostic Rosicrucian lodge in the nineties. They claimed to be inheritors of Ancient Egyptian Science as well as messengers of Beings From Afar, a council of galactic races monitoring the evolution of human destiny, and that soon, Supraterrestrial Entities would contact the earth. Of course, they wouldn't risk being compromised by base humanity, ignorant of the hidden truths at work in the universe. No, they would contact an elite of real believers, prepared for the acceptance of the ultimate revelation by their guru's gnosis, Doctor Leonard-Noël Devrinckel.

The sect went by the name of the Cosmic Church of the New Resurrection, or the Noelite Church. Its historic spiritual center was in Montreal.

For a little while now, Romanenko was split between interest and doubt. How did all this lead to Gorsky's mysterious clients? There were a few nice coincidences, the fact that Spitzner's American friend was asked to take care of aerial transfers, or the presence of Kazakhstan and the city of Montreal, but where in Hell was that fucking German Turk going with this?

Kemal paused. By the particular intensity of his stare, Romanenko understood that he'd just dropped the info.

The twenty-five thousand dollar info.

The sect.

Yes, the sect, fine, but Christ, what did it have to do with anything? Romanenko's steel gray eyes silently screamed. What does this have to do with me, and Gorsky, and Marie Zorn? What direct relation, I mean. Twenty-five thousand US dollars.

The German Turk's smile was high on THC. He took a large drag of herb. It cracked and a small spark flew out as the seed exploded. He spit out the smoke. His smile widened.

The American friend alerted a buddy of his, a Russian ex-cop who used to work for the UN and had switched to private investigations. He asked him to stay on the ass of the men following him.

It was done. The detective spotted two men in a black BMW who communicated by cell with an encryption addict. Although solidly protected, the Russian ex-cop was able to localize the signal within a radius of a hundred kilometers.

The two men followed Spitzner's friend to his house and were relieved by another team. The Russian detective followed the black BMW to a beautiful dacha in the vicinity of Novosibirsk.

The dacha was under the name of a certain "Colonel George Herbert MacCullen" and a "Princess Alexandra Robynovskaïa."

Their description fit that of Mister Mustache and Miss Platinum.

The guy was from the Royal Canadian Mounted Police; he'd reconverted into nautical supply distribution. The girl was a Russian-American from San Francisco, heiress to an old noble family who'd emigrated after October 1917. They were both members of the sect.

According to Kemal, they were in contact with a young yuppie of Swiss origin living in Kazakhstan, himself in contact with members of the local mafia. The man in the black BMW belonged to the principal Novosibirsk mafia branch. The same one Gorsky worked for.

Kemal flashed him a radiant smile that said expressly: I told you this little story was worth twenty-five thousand US.

Romanenko remained silent.

Everything lit up in his head, like a landscape fixed by the blinding bomb.

According to Kemal, things had gotten worse at the beginning of the summer. During the month of June, with the Uygur mess firing up the entire region, his "American friend" miraculously survived a mysterious "accident." The truck that almost ran him over, smashing a collarbone and a tibia, sped out of there at fast as possible. A week later, the Russian detective blew up in his car, rigged with C-4.

Since then, the man lived under the protection of Kemal's gang, hiding somewhere in Europe.

Romanenko remembered reading something recently in a Novosibirsk tabloid about the car explosion and the death of the private eye. At the time, it had just been a criminal story among others. Now, it was inscribed in a bundle of complex events leading up to himself, Gorsky, and the Zorn girl.

To finish, Kemal told him a last striking fact, the thing that had convinced him to talk to Romanenko.

Just before dying, the detective had confessed to Spitzner's friend that he was "flipping" a small accountant of the organization with the help of a journalist who specialized in anti-mafia investigation.

A few days after that confession, the detective died. And, a month later, the police in a small town in the Urals found the mutilated bodies of Evgueni Lyssoukhartov, investigative journalist specialized in hardcore criminal cases, and of Hasan Abjourdanapov, a young Pichkek accountant, apparently just a regular Joe. The two men had disappeared simultaneously the day after the attack against the detective. They'd been subject to unspeakable tortures.

Romanenko remembered that real well. The information had been front-page news since the beginning of the week.

What was this fucking mess?

Later, lying on the bed of his Embassy apartment, he patiently reconstructed the whole scenario.

A "post-millenialist" sect had first contacted Spitzner's American friend, let's call him "Mister Navy," to carry out transfers of people from one end of the Federation to the other, under conditions just bordering on legality. During the first phase, last year, everything had gone well. But when they resumed their activity in February of this year, something had fucked up. The plane exploded, shot down by a Stinger. A dozen members of the sect died. Under conditions that really annoyed the Russian Federal police. The sect had then contacted Gorsky's mafia branch. It was probably already flirting with some of its members, paying guys in air traffic control towers and Customs to keep a blind eye to the Falcon's weird flight plan, or to transport passengers on the ground from the Altais to Kazakhstan. Gorsky had taken charge of all transfer logistics, security included; that was his thing.

But something resisted comprehension.

The sect dealt in viruses; psychoviruses that made you schizoid. It wasn't very hard to figure out the use it could have for them.

No, the question that defied elucidation was this one: why all these collective back-and-forths in order to appropriate a mutant viral clone?

Romanenko confusedly understood that it was a technical problem, about which he ignored pretty much everything.

But with a bit of logic and common sense, he could frame the problem.

Mister Navy delivered slightly more than a hundred people, in about six months, in groups of twelve. Why not all at once?

To dilute the flow in time and make it less noticeable.

It appeared the "center" in the Chingiz Mountains was in fact the lab where they grew cultures of the virus. It was probably the only place in the world where it could be inoculated.

Each psychovirus had to be "personalized," or something like that. Each member of the sect probably went to the center in the Chingiz Mountains in order to get contaminated.

The "carriers" probably also swallowed an antidote (an antidote that had fucked up in Marie Zorn's case), or some kind of technology that made them insensitive to the virus. On the other hand, they could undoubtedly contaminate whomever they wanted.

This was how they'd transform people into zombies.

No, no, something didn't fit.

In six months, with Mister Navy, the sect had transited about ten times between the Tartar straits and Kazakhstan, with a dozen people each trip.

It was impossible to conceive of Gorsky working at a lower

return. Yet for now, Romanenko only knew of Marie Zorn, and Gorsky had spoken to him about one or two transfers a month.

Could Gorsky have set up other networks parallel to his?

It seemed parsimonious, complicated, hard to manage, nothing like the Siberian's rational and high-tech methods.

No, no, it was all a cover for something else, something much more monstrous.

Romanenko fell asleep with difficulty pondering this harrowing enigma.

The next day, he set his snoop agent to search for any available info on the Cosmic Church of the New Resurrection. He asked him to track any trace of a Marie Zorn, or a Marion Roussel, in the archives of the sect.

The agent brought back loads of mega-octets of all kinds of info on the Noelite Church, its guru, and the Rosicrucian sect it issued from; info collected on esoteric websites flowering on the Internet, in the Church's own site, in its journals and inside magazines, or on the digital satellite cable it had just treated itself to.

The patchwork of the sect's discourses didn't interest him in the least. He wanted to get a general idea and to grasp the collective psychology that animated that bunch of freaks.

Regularly, the snoop agent would flash a small icon in which the same despairing message appeared: NO MARIE ZORN IN THIS FILE.

By the end of the morning, he'd almost filled a gigadisk, but there was no trace of the girl.

The snoop agent had gotten to the sect's ultra-protected Intranet. Their security system was unbreachable, unless he wanted to sign his passage in bold like tracks of a tank in the middle of a living room.

If he wanted to make sure that Marie Zorn actually belonged to the Church, he had to disregard that rule of caution.

But he refused to take such a colossal risk.

He needed to act differently.

He needed to use what was at hand.

He needed to use Toorop.

19

She dived into the clear water of the lake. She threw herself from the wooden pier sketching a beautiful comma; saw a plane surface rush towards her, the soft warm wind made it slightly iridescent, a mirror hiding a world the color of a rusted sponge.

There was a *splash*, her body was immersed in tonic freshness, and she passed through the mirror to discover multitudes of small sharp-ridged rocks, the color of a submarine autumn.

She swam for more than an hour. Diving again and again towards the great aquatic region, bewildering shoals of fish that came to interlace around the piles of the pier.

At one point, she saw Rebecca and Thorpe come down to the water.

They were wearing bathing suits. Rebecca wasn't super pretty, but she knew how to hide her flaws and show herself to her best advantage when necessary. She was incredibly athletic.

They dove in almost at the same time. Laughed as they broke the surface. Thorpe said something stupid. They barely noticed she was there. She felt excluded from a brief moment of joy. A little lack of attention could be the worst torture.

She dove back to the shoals of quicksilver fish sparkling around her in strange and always fleeing marine pyrotechnics.

She swam out slowly, regularly diving beneath the surface. Each time, memories resurfaced along with her.

On Doctor Winkler's island, contact with the perennially warm waters of the lagoon, the multicolored and proliferating life of its coral depths or its jungle, the dolphins, monkeys, and other creatures tamed by the different teams, all that had significantly, albeit in a way hard to qualify, helped the patients evolve towards relative equilibrium. Doctor Winkler and his associates boasted of being "tinkerers":

"We are ready to try everything to get to new states of consciousness. Schizophrenics are bridges to those unexplored territories; we can call them 'sherpas,' pioneers, scouts. We are the ones who have to set up the advanced bases. In order to do that, we use everything we have at hand, Freud, Jung, Laing, Deleuze or Guattari, but also neuronal sciences, molecular biology, quantum mechanics, linguistics or Sufi philosophies. Pardon the expression, but, if some chimp can teach us lots of stuff about elevating the consciousness towards higher levels of complexity, if a dolphin or an artificial intelligence can help a schizophrenic psychosis to its culmination, we'd really be fools not to give it a chance," one of the associates in question had said one day to a slew of well chosen scientific journalists.

Someone had alluded to the prohibition warnings weighing on certain activities of the center.

"The International Union of Societies for the Protection of Animals is said to be planning to sue. They speak of 'bizarre and degrading' treatment of animals."

The author of the preceding lengthy response fidgeted on his chair, annoyed. He brushed off the problem with the back of his hand.

"It isn't Brigitte Bardot or one of her siliconed imitators that'll stop the next anthropological revolution."

She attended the press conference given that day on the white sand of the small western beach, when the sun was already low, the heat bearable, the light golden and the shadows solid. She was among the few patients that the Winkler team had insisted on presenting to the press.

Winkler laid it on thick. He'd gotten hold of images of her dating back to her first confinements in Montreal. The video started with a long static shot of Marie, with a date, February 18, 2000, in a corner of the screen. The cataleptic state lasted for the entire static shot, interminable, mute, apart from her faraway breathing, with some personal information appearing once in a while: Marie Zorn, born in Rimouski, Quebec, June 28, 1986, admitted for the first time to Lafontaine Hospital in Montreal, December 16, 1998. Doctor Mandelcorn's unit. Diagnosis: severe schizophrenic psychosis.

Five minutes later, all of a sudden, Marie let out a horrifying, inhuman shriek; a decibel explosion saturated the video camera mic.

Her entire body, her entire soul, loud enough to burst her eardrums, face muscles taut like a hundred thousand volt cables, eyes bulging out, foaming mouth wide open, beyond hysteria, in pure, absolutely communicative terror.

Then you discovered her in the midst of some strange coprophagy, and fits of mold-eating. You saw her, ecstatic eyes raised towards a Saint Marie of the Schizos invisible to common mortals, droning some discourse accessible to her alone. You could imagine her curled up under the bed sheets, crying. You saw her knocked out on neuroleptics, collapsed on a chair between two other schizos blabbing to themselves. It went on like that till September 2003: beginning of the Schizotrope Express program at the University of Montreal.

Then, out of the blue, *cut*, black screen, a date appears: 05-10-2011, Koh Tao Island, Thailand. The bluish video image shows a rather pretty young woman, black hair cut in a short disheveled bob, eyes sparkling, tan skin. She is relaxed and smiling; a balanced young woman who starts answering the interviewer's voice-over, not fazed in the least, with a natural voice, a bit timid but full of fierce willpower. A sexy young woman, conscious of herself and others, of her sexuality, of a certain historicity, of a social space-time; in short, in eight years, she's a hundred thousand light-years from the young schizo eating mold or her own shit.

Marie was standing next to Doctor Winkler and his acolytes, perfectly recognizable. There was dead silence.

Then the jet of questions exploded, like a hellish round of shots.

Marie swam to the little island in the middle of the lake. The marine environment catalyzed a long flow of memory. She lay on the thick beige sand strewn with minuscule sharp-edged gray rocks, trying hopelessly to find a position where they didn't cut into some part of her body. She finally gave up, stood and sank into the tall grass. The memories of the three years on the island always gave off the pungent smell of the lost ease of days, happiness burnt to ashes for nothing or almost nothing, for some dumb thing.

Here, she had a kind of miniature model, her Canadian replica, a small islet in the middle of a glacial lake with its own ecosystem, its own chaos.

At least momentarily, she'd feel good here.

"Where did you see her for the last time?"

Rebecca stood before him, standing on the pier facing the lake. Toorop had just landed in the boat.

The girl answered with a vague shrug of the shoulders. Then she pointed in a certain direction:

"Over there, pretty far out, seems to me."

Toorop quickly untied the mooring and turned on the starter of the small Mercury motor. The snapping noise of the two-stroke vibrated through the air.

Toorop saw Dowie arrive on the pier, holding two pairs of binoculars.

Rebecca let out a strange sigh and joined Toorop in the boat.

"Shit, she better not have drowned."

Toorop didn't answer. He waited for the Orangist to get on, sat down at the navigation bar and led the craft to the other side of the pier. The small black motor fired up above the silver waters.

No, indeed, she'd better not have drowned.

The client wouldn't appreciate it, and Gorsky even less. Gorsky and his Damocles sword in the shape of licensed killers of the Siberian Mafia.

They scoured Lake Malbee for hours. Called out from one to the other till their voices were hoarse, dove a few times in turn, circled twice around the central islet, came back to the pier, circled the lake again to wash up finally on the small island. It was their last hope.

It was Rebecca who found her. They had split up, Toorop in the center, Dowie and Rebecca on each coast.

After three or four minutes, the voice of the Israeli echoed out. Toorop was heading deep into a jungle of high grass and boggy ground.

He cautiously walked back a few meters before laterally crossing the islet.

Rebecca was standing near a thicket, beneath a large tree, not far from a creek with bi-colored rocks.

She looked at Toorop with alarm. He figured out something was off right away.

Marie lay across a bed of spongy, water-saturated moss, arms outstretched. She was staring at the blue-green dusk sky and the pale stars that flickered there.

Toorop immediately noticed her expression of absolute beatitude.

In fact, she wasn't staring at the sky, but at something far beyond, very far beyond.

She was plunged in a cataleptic state that resembled her previous attack, without the stress.

She brought to mind the image of a saint, pale cheeks, blue eyes syntonized with an electric frequency, a childish smile on her lips; a horizontal saint, a hybrid sylphid saint, a martyred korrigan, born and dying in the foliage of a lacustrine forest.

With a strong gesture, he grabbed Marie Zorn by the waist, picked her up and with a swing of the hips flipped her over his shoulders.

"Dowie," he said in an empty voice, "bring the boat around…"

Then, his step heavy, he advanced along the rocky creek, Rebecca leading the march and the redheaded killer running to get the boat.

As they were setting Marie down on a sleeping bag across the back seat of the Chrysler, Toorop noted a strange little detail he didn't give pause to at the time. The distinctive luminous vibration emanating from her eyes seemed to originate from an electric flashlight behind the retina. It could almost have been a nightlight.

But emergency dictated its course.

He threw himself on the emergency kit and took out Doctor Newton's black cube. He pulled bioprocessor number two out of its little case. This one had received the info from the residue of its predecessor last week; it'd be even more effective.

He'd noticed that recuperating the little fluorescent crystal in the shit wasn't the hardest part; it was getting Marie to ingurgitate it completely in the first place.

But this time, her jaw slackened softly under his fingers, she let out a slight moan, her smile spread and she opened her mouth wide when he dropped the large green crystal on her tongue.

Toorop knew that he'd have to wait four or five hours for the bioprocessor to take full effect; long enough for the external capsule to be digested, as well as all of its active ingredients, and in the end, for the "memory-residue" to be slowly expulsed by the intestines.

In a few minutes, if all went well, she'd close her eyes and fall asleep for an entire cycle, till morning. If all went well, when she'd open her eyes, the attack would be just a faint memory.

Was man a train of questions with no answers headed straight for the wall of the future? Could we kill without being killed in return, at each killing? Could we live a single instant without *knowing* we were to die? Could we die without doubting that we had lived? Could we survive without bordering evil, even just for one instant? Could we survive without gaining the devil's trust, if not his friendship, or that of one of his agents? Could we hope for some chance of redemption in a world given over to the obscure forces of Creation?

Toorop woke up sweating, wound up in his sleeping bag. It was dreadfully hot.

His dream had been prodigiously intense, but upon waking, a white page walled his mind, forever separating him from the sublime images of sleep. Only scattered emotional traces remained, the impression of having lived a major aesthetic experience. In its place, that white page. That white page; a fresh clear screen like the memory of a newborn.

On that white page the questions appeared.

He didn't have the shadow of an answer for any of them.

At his side, across the back seat, Marie was sleeping peacefully. The bioprocessor was dissolving in her stomach.

Toorop leaned against the half-open side door. A light breath of air shook the foliage of the trees and made the surface of the lake shine iridescent beneath the moon.

He put his head through the opening to gather a bit of coolness.

Something was wrong.

The first bioprocessor had only worked a few days.

No doubt her state worsened faster than what the medical resources of Russian science could help. No doubt the next pill would work a shorter time still.

No doubt they were all making a huge mistake.

20

Pain burst out in delicate flows at first, stretching fine barbed veins beneath his dermis dripping with desire. It inlayed itself in thin tentacles, as hard as steel and burning like embers in his most sensitive areas; he moaned with pleasure-pain.

This masoware was a pure marvel, he thought to himself repeatedly, as electric shivers exploded in cascades of red-hot metal filaments on his most intimate zones.

Then he muffled a cry as a thicket of pin pricks concentrated viciously around his anus, triggering a hard and concrete band of pleasure-pain like a steel ring around the warm tube of a soccer player's big dick.

He stiffened, closing his eyes and slithered a limp, annihilated hand, void of any motor impulse, towards the power button on the machine. It didn't get there.

"So, Doctor Newton, what do you think?"

The doctor raised his tear-clouded eyes towards the long athletic silhouette facing him.

Shadow observed the scene with obvious amusement. As Doctor Newton opened his mouth under the growing insistence of the masoware towards the depths of his asshole, as if imploring a synthetic Venus in Furs, he saw Shadow's cruel smile and the pearl drops of sweat glowing on his dark Arab skin. It provoked in him the usual cycle of humiliation-pleasure that tagged onto the network of spur pin electric veins keeping his body under voltage and his member erect, under the cream cloth of his colonial style shorts.

Then, Shadow did what he did each time.

With a cold smile and his Palestinian angel face, as if at the summit of some mystical truth, he slowly turned the analog knob until the signal's extinction in the terribly delicious shunt of the suppression of stimulus.

The flow broke off with the incomparable sadness of a lost paradise.

"So, Doctor Newton?"

A carnal echo of the experience subsisted after the fact. A neuronal imprint taut under the skin, like a ghost of the pain-network coming alive from the box.

The box.

A simple black box. Analogous to the one he'd delivered along with the bioprocessors. Equipped with a few ingenious devices. And adequate software. The body being an analog machine, such an experience, such a delicate assemblage of innervations bordered on a kind of art work that the brain and the entire body in which it materialized could infinitely reconstruct, reproduce like Xerox copies of neuro-electric suffering.

It was always like that with Shadow's masoware.

Pure marvels. Real sublime shit.

Shadow was a queen of techno trash. He was a little perverted prick and Doctor Newton loved it.

"You little scum," he moaned, tweaking his lips in a tic of satisfied exhaustion. "This shit is deadly, how much you asking?"

"The normal price, Doctor, with the normal rebate, in exchange for the normal small favor. Nothing more, nothing less."

The doctor stared coldly at the young Beirut Apollo.

Shadow started putting away the different modules of the masoware and grabbed the bundle of fiber optics connected to the strange podgy crown above the doctor's skull.

"Disconnect your neural belt. And tell me what I wanna know. I've got other clients lined up, Counselor."

Behind "Doctor Newton" was in fact Nicholas Kravczech, lawyer at the Bar of Montreal; born in Ukraine, he'd fled communism with his parents in the early seventies, before the age of ten. Shadow had known all this for a long time, and Kravczech/Newton couldn't imagine without the thrill of fear that the young dealer knew of the intelligence activities he'd been conducting for post-Soviet Russia for close to twenty years.

Nicholas Kravczech let out a sigh of resignation mixed with relief. Fear, like pleasure, was a powerful stimulus. A stimulus paradoxical enough to provoke the pleasure of confrontation with its opposite. He disconnected the neural belt with regret and held it up an instant above his head like a tiara cut out of the pure diamond of bliss. Then he handed it to Shadow as the thousand silicon tips of the fiber optics freed themselves from his flesh, reddened by the experience, and swung through space like the silver hair of a sexual, comic book vestal virgin.

"What do you want to know?"

The young Arab gave him the Butcher of Baghdad's scimitar-smile.

"I like it when you talk to me like that, Doctor. I want you to tell me who's hiding beneath that Maria A., or Zorn, or whatever else it is, and give me the data recorded by the Russian biochips I supplied."

He carefully packed up the neural belt, retracting the bundle of fiber optics into the supraconductor tube. Then he waited for Kravczech/Newton to draw in the layout of the terrain.

Blood flowed back into his face and a moan caught in Nicky Kravczech's throat.

A huge betrayal.

A huge betrayal that Colonel Romanenko and his shady employers would certainly not appreciate.

Shadow let out a delicious Kenneth Anger-type black-leather predator smile.

"I see you understand, Doctor. In exchange for which, I can guarantee updates for the entire next year, and in addition, the small pharmacopoeia I spoke to you about."

And, as if by the magic of some street conjurer, a few centimeters of gray tube had just appeared between his thumb and index finger. Kravczech/Newton froze.

"Sacher-Dolorosa Neguentropin," the young dealer said. "A neoprotein that allows for infinite modulations of each feeling of pain, and for the creation of sado-masochistic mental icons with disconcerting virtuosity."

Kravczech knew that soon he wouldn't be able to refuse Shadow anything. But having tasted his illicit productions so many times before, he also knew it was all in the order of things. If the Sacher-Dolorosa Neguentropin was in fact what Shadow promised, a drug, when coupled with a neuroware like the one he'd just experienced, that created artificial paradises that neither the young Masoch nor the Divine Marquis could have dreamed of accessing, then, yes, of course he'd do anything to possess it.

"Let's be clear, and accountably correct about this," he whispered; "we're talking Northam dollars."

"Of course."

"So, we're talking ten thousand North-American dollars for a tampered black box and a fiber optics kit with a neural belt. As much for your artificial intelligence, and again as much for your neo-protein, minus ten percent, with yearly software updates guaranteed."

"You sound like my catalogue. You should check it out on the web sometime."

"All this in exchange for the residual memory of Marie Zorn's biochips. And what I know of the whole thing."

"That's as precise as it gets. So, what do you think, Doctor?"

Kravczech looked at the young technology dealer with the jaded stare of the old fag who knows each corner of his public toilets by heart.

"I think this is the deal of the century. Get your hard disk ready."

"I knew I could count on your cooperation, Doctor."

Shadow's voice was as sweet as honey.

Counselor Nicholas Kravczech, alias Doctor Newton, delighted in it. There was the promise of a new ecstatic liquor that his veins and arteries would soon carry, plunging his brain into a pool of joy-suffering incandescent lava, acid bath whip's purifying flame razor blades running under the skin in veins of sharp, sound glass.

Nothing else, in comparison, had the slightest importance.

21

The road stretched its long ribbon across the hills. The sun was high, veiled by a layer of clouds, still diaphanous but darkening in the east. The sky was a blinding silver grey. The light from the sun did not seem to lose any of its intensity despite diffusion through the air.

Toorop was driving in silence, sullen, eye on the road, ears rocked by the music from the radio.

The weekend of outside relaxation had ended in a new catatonic attack for Marie, more serious than the preceding ones. The outcome of the operation was uncertain.

Toorop manipulated the cruise control to stabilize the speed exactly at the authorized limit. He pressed on the program where he'd saved the most direct return route to Montreal.

In the back, Marie was sleeping and Rebecca was watching an old American show, an episode of *Mannix*, on a specialized cable of the small Satellivision. The mass of the Toyota sent out gleaming reflections in the rear view mirror. Dowie stuck in its wake.

A bit later, filling up just outside of the city, he tried to rationalize the situation. Marie was still sleeping. She stayed that way into the night.

He was watching TV with Dowie. Rebecca was taking a shower. It was so fucking hot all the fans were on full blast. The Expos were playing Cleveland. They were getting whipped.

The flash of a Molson ad came to punctuate a Cleveland batter's circuit. Dowie got up to get a beer in the fridge. Toorop told himself that the young guy was a Pavlovian machine with no inhibitory circuit, unless it was the other way around, or just a simple coincidence. Rebecca came out half-dry from the bathroom, toweling her hair, and Marie appeared at the entrance of the living room.

"Good evening," she blurted out in a small voice, before sitting down in an armchair across from the TV screen.

Then she gently let herself be taken in by the image tube.

Toorop didn't say anything. He let it be. The game started up again. The Expo's pitcher wasn't into it. The situation worsened pretty fast during the second inning.

Marie didn't say zip. Neither did Dowie and Toorop. Rebecca was reading her cards on the kitchen table. The voices of the two commentators spilled out a long chain of statistics.

"Would you like a beer, or a Coke?" he finally asked.

Marie didn't budge, but in a relatively secure voice, she let out: "Yes, thank you, can't say no to that."

He got up to walk towards the fridge, grabbed a can of Coke. As he closed the heavy Kelvinator door, his eyes crossed Rebecca's. Her black eyes shot out a mute question.

In a glance, he answered that everything was cool, and returned to his seat in front of a new flash of advertisements.

Marie waited for Dowie to go back up to 4075, and for Rebecca to go to bed in her room. Toorop was dozing off in front of the eighth inning. The game was shot.

"Why do you do this, Mister Thorpe?"

Toorop cracked an eye as he shook himself. He muttered something indistinct: "what does she mean?"

"What motivates you in life, Mister Thorpe. What pushed you to take this mission?"

Toorop didn't answer. The Expo's pitcher threw a fourth bad pitch; it was becoming a disaster, a Waterloo, a battle of the Plains of Abraham.

"Come on, a little courage, Mister Mercenary."

Toorop wanted to answer dryly with the sum in dollars, but she cleverly outdid him.

"Don't tell me you do it *only* for money…"

She didn't finish her sentence but Toorop totally grasped the unsaid message: it would be so stupid, wouldn't it? So vulgar, so uninteresting.

Toorop started mentally enumerating the cascade of events that had brought him here with her, in Montreal. A chain twenty years long. He'd have neither the time, nor the patience to tell her all of it. Most of all, and he knew it, Marie wanted to shine light on his shadows. What's your secret passion, Mister Thorpe, was what she meant to say. What moves this carcass through desolate mountains, through gunshots and storms? What makes it pass over the oceans to lead an unknown young woman on a trip to nowhere?

Simple silence wouldn't get him out of it, nor would a pirouette, nor his saying something disagreeable. He knew he was fucking up again, but at least this time, he knew what he was doing.

"I work for the Colonel," he said, after a while.

Marie shrugged her shoulders and sighed.

"So that's just it, you do it for money?"

"Call it what you like… It's my job, and the colonel is my employer… He didn't really have a choice," he added, half-joking.

Marie watched him unblinkingly. Her eyes expressed disarray as well as disappointment.

"Neither did I," he said, as if it could be an excuse.

What she thought was spelled out clearly in her eyes.

The next day, in the early afternoon, the sun was hitting hard; they all went out to eat, on Saint-Denis and Saint-Joseph, a bit farther up.

It was an Italian-Chinese tavern held by a small, chubby, red-faced man with a hamburger stand and fridges filled with beer and soda cans.

He devoured a double cheeseburger, then a second, with fries and about a liter of Coke, on a bench with Marie and Rebecca. Behind them, at another table, Dowie ate his meal in silence. A trucker left the bar to return to his chrome Peterbilt parked across the lot, bordering a construction site.

Another guy in a plaid shirt and Nike cap was sipping a beer. A guy in a worn out suit, a shirt of some undefined color beneath an immense tie with pop art motifs, was nibbling at a hamburger at a table in the back. Another dude, in orange and white sportswear, was rushing to the toilet. A biker was coming out, and went back to his bright red Harley, next to a gas pump, beneath the falsely indifferent stares of the few people present.

The jukebox was playing some rather intolerable country-techno shit: a disco beat with samples from Hank Williams, Merle Haggard, Johnny Cash, Dolly Parton and the whole shebang. Clearly modernity also had its bad side.

That's when the Dodge Ram Charger showed up.

The pickup was bottle-green. It was pretty recent, but covered in dust. You'd think they'd just taken it out of the sand.

There were two men in the cab. Through the tinted windows all you could see were two solid silhouettes with black glasses.

The pickup passed the pumps of the Ultramar station at thirty miles an hour. Then it turned on Saint-Joseph, heading west towards Mont-Royal.

Toorop saw the passenger look carefully in his direction. Right away, he caught hold of a small object that he wore on his ear. No need to come out of war school to understand what was up.

Gorsky's men. Or men from his local branch. Russian Mafiosos. Fucking killers.

They were probably part of that security team that Romanenko had mentioned succinctly. The guys were on them twenty-four seven. They took note of their slightest move and reported back to their superiors by the minute. The Dodge was just the visible part of an immense iceberg.

Most of all, the Ari Moskiewicz-style photographic memory revealed the chemical salts of the mental shot taken in the Warshaw store. The dude taking his cell out as he turned his head towards them was the biker-type goon pulling a beer bottle out of the refrigerated aisle in the back of the store. And the memory of the guy leaving the restaurant, turning down Saint-Denis on his chopper, was freshly imprinted on his brain.

From a certain point of view, he told himself finally, their presence was almost reassuring.

What was less so was the time it took Marie to relieve her bladder. If she wasn't back in five minutes, he'd go see what was…

Oh. Marie was pushing the bathroom door, followed by Rebecca sipping a Diet Coke. They were cracking up.

Toorop watched them, intrigued. They looked like old high school friends, apart from the eight or ten year difference.

He felt completely out of it. Cold hands covered in sweat, like each time homicidal adrenalin pumped its icy signals through his veins. The Dodge, Gorsky's men, the underlying image of the guns lurking in their obscure dens like steel serpents ready to pounce; the obsessive image would not leave his mind. It superimposed itself grotesquely upon the afternoon sun and the laugh of the young women coming to sit down in the light.

The following days passed in the slow and heat gelled rhythm of early August. Dowie, Rebecca and he took turns going out for supplies. Marie spent her days in the garden lot, tanning or sleeping. Otherwise, she isolated herself.

It seemed her state was stabilizing. She barely spoke. Spent half her time sleeping or doing yoga beneath a blazing sun. In three weeks, her original pallor had given way to a beautiful honey gold. Toorop started looking at her more and more attentively. He attempted to cut the circuit, but it was useless.

At night, as he tried to sleep, fantastical images, sublimated projections of original souvenir-shots, took up motion in his brain as if in the depths of a mental porn theater. His hand tightened on his already hard member; he vainly tried to push back the image of Marie stretching under the sun. He masturbated frenetically with the added sting of guilt.

The days passed peacefully.

Marie's state remained stable. The first two memory-crystals had been analyzed by the black box. A sequence of code of infinite length unrolled on the screen of his console without leading him anywhere; such scientific documentation was incomprehensible for a layman like himself. That didn't stop him from coming back to it each day, in the hope that in the end some crucial information would come to light.

He'd log onto university IRCs or public libraries to try to grab the ball of code by one end or another. But it only led to other ramifications at the heart of a labyrinth whose topography he couldn't grasp.

That morning, according to one of the rare non-code messages from the operating system, he understood it was time for Marie to down another biochip.

The component, upgraded with data from the one that had led Marie to a relative and probably temporary stabilization, would consolidate the process. The expert system predicted a good chance of partial regression of the psychosis; in any case, its neuroleptic control would be assured.

Toorop wondered for a moment if all this wasn't completely unreasonable. The girl carried viruses, she was schizoid, and they were happily giving her an occult and probably illegal pharma-copoeia.

He had the feeling he was putting together all the elements essential to achieve critical mass.

"Stop bullshitting me, Colonel!"

Gorsky's voice thundered, petrifying Ourianev on his chair, and interrupting Romanenko's explanatory speech like the explosion of a grenade right in the middle of a Papal homily.

"Yeah, stop spewing this shit and tell me what's going on!"

The second salve was barely more in check than the first.

"What in fucking hell do you mean?" asked Romanenko, trying to outplay him.

Ourianev stuck his head in his shoulders; the Siberian was going to blow fire out of his nose.

However, he remained silent, taking a long breath to calm down. He straightened up in his armchair and drew a cold smile with his lips.

"You're a dick, Colonel. I know your man managed to lose my surveillance team, and that he came into contact with an anonymous and encrypted third person. I know that something then happened near a lake. You better tell me what's happening before I really get pissed off."

"Nothing's happening that you don't already know. The girl is in a fragile psychological state. For now, Thorpe is getting along fine, but it's not always easy, that's all."

Ourianev was watching the scene with intensity. He felt a kind of admiration for Romanenko, always cool, unshakable, defending his lie hands-on.

Gorsky snorted like a dragon.

"And why, then, did he lose the control team last time? Huh? Why?"

Romanenko nodded, incredulous.

"Anton... He just wanted to see an old friend. He didn't want your guys to follow him into the chick's bed, so he called me and I told him how to go about it. I know your men's methods. We're all trained pretty much the same."

Ourianev contemplated with strange delight the innocent smile that pearled on the corner of Romanenko's lips. Facing him, the Siberian Mafioso's imposing mass evoked the cliff overhanging the moving play of the tide.

"A chick? You fucking with me?"

Romanenko let out a long sigh.

"I know it's stupid. But shit, they're locked up day in day out with a schizoid, so my guy just needed to shoot a load. You're not gonna make a huge deal out of it."

"According to my team, he already shot a load the week before."

Romanenko took it in with serenity. Toorop had hidden that from him.

He spit out a little mechanic laugh.

"My guy has regular physiological needs. I much prefer this to him sleeping with our little Marie, or the other girl in the team. Don't you agree?"

Ourianev noted that Romanenko's strategy was on point. No searching for the major blow but instead dissolving the adversary's certainties by gnawing at them little by little, with small, well aimed assertions.

Gorsky didn't say a thing. A clever decoy had countered each argument. He started snorting, and finally, lips tight:

"OK, this time. But tell your guy he'll need to make do from now on with the old hand job. He can treat himself to the mega-bordello of his dreams at the end of the mission, but for now, no more fuck-ups like this, understood?"

"OK, Anton, I'll tell him to rent videotapes."

"That's it. And now, onto problem number two, if you please: how to proceed in case the operation is *cancelled*."

Ourianev felt a subtle tension take hold of Romanenko.

"What do you mean by that?"

Gorsky sank down into the depths of his armchair and crossed his hands on his killer whale stomach.

"I've talked to Doctor Walsh about it. We probably won't be able to hide the truth from our clients much longer."

Romanenko weathered that.

"I see."

"Our clients are very particular as to the quality of the product. Of course, Marie's state has very little influence on their nature, but her behavior could seriously compromise the feasibility of the operation."

Romanenko understood that the Siberian did his utmost to hide the "nature" of the product in question. So he lent an ear and concentrated on each word pronounced. Inevitably, a detail would escape Gorsky's vigilance, he'd drop some micro-info, a scrap, just enough to add another piece to the puzzle.

On the other hand, there was no ambivalence as to the term "cancel"; it meant Marie Zorn would have to die.

The big Siberian shuffled in his armchair. What he had to say was important.

"In case of cancellation, it would be better if your team took care of it. Of course they'll receive a substantial bonus."

Romanenko planted his eyes into Gorsky's black lenses.

"There were no provisions for that in the contract."

"No. That's why they'll receive a bonus. Substantial, like I said."

Romanenko sighed.

"How do you want it to happen, just in case?"

The Siberian took his time to answer. He was mentally verifying that he didn't drop the crucial info, thought Romanenko.

"The girl has to disappear. Without a trace. That's why they're going to move. We found the perfect place."

"Where? And when?"

"In a week. Far from Montreal. Up near the James Bay, from what I was told. No one around for miles. An emissary from our clients will go up there at the mid-point of the normal transit time, less than fifteen days from now. He'll decide if the operation is to be continued or cancelled. If we continue, your team goes on doing in the country what it was doing in the city. In the opposite case, they bury the girl somewhere."

Romanenko made a noise with his mouth, thought for a few moments, and kindly asked the most important question of all:

"What *substantial* amount do you foresee for the bonus?"

That fucking ball buster colonel was lying. Fuck, he was lying so bad. How dare he come up with two-ruble fibs, pitiful Moscow politician lies! Did he really think he'd swallow all that hot air without reacting?

That GRU moron didn't know that his boy's pirate cell contact had been circumscribed by Kotcheff's men within a fifty-kilometer radius around Montreal. The control team couldn't break the encryption code, but their counter measure systems were clear. Fifty kilometers. Not twenty thousand.

The Lexus was rolling north. The highway night was a solarized bronze, Kim's speed honorable. Gorsky settled into the back seat. They crossed a column of tanks, and on the right, not far from the highway embankment, he glimpsed the carbonized carcass of a helicopter, fresh remains of the violent combats of last month.

This whole thing was starting to go awry. He'd made the mistake of getting too many intermediaries. He had only a very distant control over the situation, and that bastard Romanenko wanted to take him for a ride.

He wondered worriedly if that prick's team would even be able to "cancel" the girl.

The idea was a good one. It would totally incriminate the colonel, but like all good ideas, it was a double-edged sword: he'd have to trust some unknown personnel.

For weeks, he'd been on his mens' back day and night. Whole teams were legging it across the entire Russian Federation and Europe to find out more about this "Thorpe." For now, the only real important info that had reached him dated back to the early days, and came from the arms dealers. Thorpe was most certainly the alias of Hugo Cornelius Toorop, a French-Dutch adventurer who'd fought alongside the Croats and Bosnians during the first Yugoslav conflict. Romanenko hadn't bullshitted him about that. He knew that the Siberian mafia would soon figure out his mercenary's pseudonym.

Then, one of their contacts at the Russian Foreign Affairs Ministry had informed them that a certain "Udo Zkornik," a supposed German national who'd led an Uzbek unit around 1999-2000, was most probably the same man. He was suspected of having participated in Chamil Bassaiev's operations in Southern Russia and Dagestan in 1996. And to have crossed through the Panjshir Mountains in the meantime.

Finally, the day before, another contact of his among the arms dealers told him it was weird, but a friend of his asked for the same info some time before. The friend in question was named Karl Spitzner; everyone knew he ratted for the Russian Army Secret Service.

Romanenko went back to the Embassy knowing the clock was ticking. This had been his greatest fear from the beginning: cancellation of the operation in one form or another. The Siberian intended to cut to the thick of it. If the girl didn't fit the selection criteria, she'd end up under six feet of earth or at the bottom of a lake, a hundred miles from the nearest house.

She had to make the cut, she had to survive. It was imperative.

That was how he'd make it up to the real client. He knew he couldn't fail this time. The top men of the GRU and of the Ministry of Defense had been watching him for a while already; the Uygur mess and the blow to Prince Shabazz hadn't helped.

The directors of the Service didn't care at all if he made a little something from the different traffics with the guerrillas. They just asked that he keep a low profile, fuck with the Chinese, and bring back a big fish once in a while. The last time he'd delivered that type of game to the Moscow big heads was more than two years ago. A spy in the Kazakh military staff who informed for the PLA. The general had since been turned; he was participating in a large maneuver to intoxicate the Chinese GRU Service.

If he could bring Gorsky in with the net, and hand him over to management in a neat bundle, he'd be out of bounds of the Ministry's wrath till the end of his days. He could aim for a job in Service Management or in Military Administration; he could become a lieutenant general in a few years. Time enough to perfect his reputation, and then the plan would unfold. Quit. Evaporate. Reappear on the other side of the world: coast of Queensland, Australia, under a false identity, a pseudonym with which he'd publish his military strategy treaties. His ass on a several million-dollar cushion.

When he sat down at his desk, a black and white photo from a press agency was spread out in the middle of the screen.

He understood within the second that his intelligence agent had just dredged up a large catch. A man around fifty, an ID window in a part of the screen.

DOCTOR JOHN GARVIN HATHAWAY
BORN FEBRUARY 17, 1952, IN CALGARY, ALBERTA
COMDEMNED IN NOVEMBER 2004 BY THE OTTAWA
COURT OF APPEALS FOR ILLEGAL RESEARCH AND BREACH
OF NEW INTERNATIONAL BIO-ETHICS LAWS.
SUSPENDED FROM THE CANADIAN MEDICAL ASSOCIA-
TION IN JANUARY 2005.
STRUCK OFF THE LIST IN JUNE OF THE SAME YEAR.

All this referred to tons of hypertext info the software had put together.

Hathaway, thought Romanenko. Alias Walsh. Yeah. Why not Orson Wells?

But it made sense.

The research agent had compiled all the press articles about Doctor Hathaway's ascension and fall. Romanenko started clicking like mad.

Hathaway belonged to the design team of the "Dolly" program, the lamb that would go down in History in 1997 as the first authentically cloned mammal. The doctor left the team of the Edinburgh Roslin Institute at the end of 2000, just when the UN was decreeing the first amendments to what was to become the Osaka Charter on the Declaration of the Rights of the Human Genome. He claimed to create experimental animals and to study them in the midst of very particular ecosystems. He wanted to establish lineages of transgenic animals that were perfectly adapted to their new environments, intended to use the techniques of the Dolly project on a large scale, and publicly affirmed his intention to do research on human subjects one day.

A handful of articles recounted his temporary suspension from the Canadian Medical Order. A few months later, he was straight-up crossed out of the Order. He complained to the press about "mandarins from another age" and about the "liberticidal institu-tions of the UN."

Obviously, the good Doctor Hathaway had gone off the deep end.

Very fast, he disappeared from the press columns and, apparently, from the planet.

Romanenko found him again eight years later, working for the Novosibirsk Mafia and a sect of freaks wanting to stock up in high-tech viruses.

The harvest had been plentiful. Adding all this info to the stuff he had, he drew up a new mental picture of the whole thing.

The picture staged the same characters, in the same situation, but the lighting was noticeably different, disclosing other motives. Nothing in Doctor Hathaway's detailed curriculum, a long research career in the best universities of Canada and of the United States, all patiently reconstituted by the research agent, nothing in this entire mass of information led one to believe that he had the slightest competence in virology. After asking the research agent to track down any reference to the word "virus," or one of its derived terms, he noted that, once again, his intuition was correct. In an article from September 2001, an interview published in *21st Century*, Doctor Hathaway complacently described his association with the Retronics Research firm that specialized in perfecting viral biotechnologies used in transgenic therapy. The virus, rendered innocuous and programmed to tinker with the DNA chain, is sent to the heart of the cells whose genome is to be modified.

Doctor Hathaway confessed his relative incompetence in that field, but needed these technologies for his work to progress.

Fucking shit, thought Romanenko.

He wasn't a specialist in viruses.

In what then?

You moron, went his little interior voice, it's written in huge letters before your eyes: transgenic animals.

He makes animals.

And everything lit up again differently, as if under the harsh neon glare of truth.

Part **3**

Amerika on Ice

Individuality is a problem of strategic defense.

— DONNA HARAWAY

22

From now on she was a living star. She radiated in a zone of infinite frequencies. She was the swarm of all the beings on earth, and she was the fire in its breast. She was a multitude yet one, she was pure process, naked, like the network of nerves of a machine skinned alive.

She was the ebb and flow; her mouth could pronounce all the languages of the world embedded in the rings of a perpetually changing snake. Her body gave birth to a blazing mathematics igniting the beings and particles of the universe. She was the princess of the monkeys drinking from the crystal of knowledge; she was a continual flow, a matrix of dreams and paths in time and space.

She was the future, the imminent production of the Real that created the wave of Possibles preceding it in a ceaselessly renewed present.

Arrow of time suddenly set in rotation. Panoramic, thermodynamic, absolute sensation; fractal certainty of being at the origin of a new human branch, fragile, virtual, spectral, impossible as it were. "We believe that the schizophrenic mutation is just a transitory stage," Darquandier, Winkler's main collaborator, had told her once. "A necessary stage, but a stage nonetheless; the schizophrenic, bridge between man and superman. I wonder what Nietzsche would have thought! Ha! Ha! Ha!"

Yes, she was a network flower open to all forms of life within her reach. Her own metabolism, that machinery of meat, blood and low amp electricity, was just a particular manifestation of a cosmic processor whose existence she'd always suspected, but whose presence was now manifest in the iridescence of each ionized atom from halogen bulbs, in each speck of dust, in each dream of a passing cat.

Everything around her vibrated with biological frequency fields. Everything was alive, alight; everything was prodigiously possible. Everything was predictable, because everything was real.

On the TV screen, the Expos' miracle pitcher sent the ball out thirty meters over the protection netting. Her spirit had melted with the blue and orange cathode tube. She'd seen the player's every move decomposed like a long sequence of a film in slow-mo, guessing the ball's trajectory to the meter, living the experience like a shot of pure knowledge.

There was nothing she didn't know of the state of her own central nervous system. The "schizoprocessor" that Winkler and Darquandier had taught her to use had now completely dissolved in her new cosmic-brain. It inhabited each cell of her consciousness. It allowed her to think naturally about everything her body was doing, a consciousness of the moment, but perfectly cool, without the pressure of psychotic stress, as if she were manipulating the cruise control of a Chrysler Voyager.

For example, she knew that a screen card from the TV would break down within three months. And at the same time she knew that as she turned towards Toorop, her eyes shined with a glow vibrating near ultraviolet frequency, not from the cathode tube, but from the mutagenic effect of all her DNA.

The first time Toorop heard Marie Zorn speak to him in Dutch, the Expos were up against the Indians again. The small living room was lit only by a small ambient lamp on the windowsill. They were alone. Rebecca had gone to sleep in her room, her walkman headphones on. The Montrealers were getting even with Cleveland. The evening would be calm.

"I have to admit this game is totally obscure to me."

He froze.

Her voice was a half-octave deeper than usual, and the girl had spoken to him in Flemish, with a sharp Italian accent.

Without knowing why, he accepted this. Marie was speaking to him in old Flemish with a solid Venetian accent. Why not? The girl was schizo; she could do what she wanted.

Marie's stare was incredible and indefinable at the same time. It had such electric intensity he could see her pupils emit light as if a small cathode screen had been grafted onto her optic nerve.

Toorop checked himself. OK, he had smoked a joint, he was deliciously nested in the sphere of warmth coming from the TV, but a joint, even of Kimo, doesn't make you hallucinate. And he couldn't blame the light of the screen.

He sat up and turned to the young woman. Her eyes were shining, thought Toorop. There was no doubt about it. What...

"Why don't you ask me the important question, Mister Thorpe?"

The same voice, again. That same old dated Flemish, and that aristocratic Italian accent.

Marie Zorn was watching him with a look of defiance on her face. Her eyes, yes, her eyes, her fucking ultraviolet light eyes indicated there was a storm brewing.

"What question?" said Toorop, in Flemish.

"Don't pretend to be innocent."

Her eyes were sparking more and more.

"A question like: why did you become schizo, Marie? Or, how did you get to this point?"

Toorop tried to sustain the blue fire of her stare, but finally gave in before its icy incandescence. He stared at the cathode tube. They'd just stolen third base from the Cleveland pitcher.

"What do you mean by that? Are you talking about Romanenko and Gorsky?"

"Finally," said the young woman in a tone of fake cheerfulness. "I thought I'd never hear you say the magic words."

"My job is based on discretion."

The young woman sighed.

"Mister Thorpe?"

Her eyes were sending out thousands of sparks per second. He would have died electrocuted on contact.

"Yes," he said, in a voice that was weaker than expected.

"If you don't want to know anything about me, what can you tell me about yourself?"

At first, Toorop was silent. He'd been apprehending this situation for a while now.

He made a face.

"The less you know about me, the better."

"You know what surprises me the most?"

Toorop didn't answer. Marie Zorn bent over slightly and pointed a finger at him.

"What surprises me the most is your incapacity to understand."

"To understand what?"

"To understand… that you're being manipulated. That we're *all* being manipulated."

Crash bang, thought Toorop, the usual paranoid delirium. That's all we needed. Better go on as if nothing had happened.

"If he continues like this, the Cleveland pitcher's gonna have to find a minor league job, or switch to curling."

He shot a corner glance at her. The girl snuggled into the arm of her seat, folding her legs beneath her. Her eyes wouldn't leave him, their intensity unchanged.

"Tell me the truth for once. Didn't that Russian colonel ask you to find out what I'm carrying?"

That one went off like a bomb in the middle of the living room. Toorop stared straight at the TV.

"What do you mean?" he mumbled, to win some time, elaborate right quick an answer that worked and that invalidated her assertion.

Marie stiffened. She didn't appreciate his effort to cover his ass.

"That officer is getting closer to the truth," she said. "He's a move ahead of us."

That one hit Toorop right in the face.

"What makes you say that?" he blurted, his voice cold and defensive.

The girl burst into a little crystalline laugh.

"You're not cooperating enough for me to tell you. Goodnight, Mister Thorpe."

That said, she got up, and sure of her victory, went off to her room, leaving Toorop alone with his frustration and the Expos batter opening the fourth inning.

It was two in the morning. Toorop was snoozing alone in the living room in front of the TV. The game had been over for a while; the Expos had beat Cleveland. The race for the Wild Card was back on.

The ring of the electronic answering machine beeped in his control device, a micro-earphone barely larger that the head of a pin, a thingamajig that they'd implanted on his eardrum at the Embassy infirmary the day before he left. He got up and approached the desk where the Internet console stood waiting.

In the e-mail, Toorop found a laconic message from the colonel asking him to log onto a video-presence IRC in a private space called Stratus.

Toorop asked the console intelligence agent to log onto that network, then put on the gear.

Romanenko's face appeared before him a few seconds later, floating like a ghost in a cottony screen. Toorop's stare dove into the black, globular eye of the micro digital camera. His image was sent at light speed over the ocean.

"Good morning Toorop," went Romanenko, "it is morning there right?"

"Yep," went Toorop in a nasty voice, "it's *three* in the morning. What good news brings you here? And why wait so long to communicate in high definition?"

"I wanted to be absolutely sure the network was a hundred percent safe. This kind of network uses five times more energy than a simple vid-fax. It can be intercepted more easily. I'm using a Russian Army satellite beam, very powerful and very protected. Just to tell you that if I decide it can be done, then it can be done."

"Fine," said Toorop. "What's the problem, Colonel?"

Romanenko didn't answer right away. At first glance: problems —there were tons of them.

"Well," went the colonel. "Let's start in ascending order. First, you stop trying to lose Gorsky's control team. They're pissed since your last escapade. They tightened their system and doubled their teams. And don't try to contact Newton. It's too hot."

"That was the deal with him, you know it perfectly well. No more direct contacts. I go through the Kepler site."

Romanenko made an allusive hand gesture.

"Kill that site as fast as possible. Shut it down. Don't use it anymore."

"Are you kidding? I need it to download the software to manage the biochips."

"Figure it out. Buy a hard disk and stuff the program on it. Do it tomorrow and close the site, that's an order."

"OK," went Toorop, "it'll be done."

"Good, now for the big news… I believe I'm right in saying that Marie isn't transporting a virus. Or, more precisely, she isn't *only* transporting that. The viruses are probably made by something. Or they make something."

Toorop froze in front of the screen. Well, well, he thought, what's happening, was Romanenko trying to screw him over for ten thousand dollars?

"Really? And what are viruses supposed to make, apart from joyous epidemics? Epidemics of psychosis, in this case, is more like it."

Romanenko left a dramatic second of suspense. What a pitiful actor, thought Toorop.

"If I told you, you'd have to forego your bonus."

"I have the distinct impression that you're foregoing it for me."

"You're wrong. I'm on a very serious lead. But since I'm fair play, I'll give you a piece of info that's worth its weight in gold: Doctor Hathaway. Look for a Doctor Hathaway. I'll give you a couple days so I can verify a few things. If by the end of the week you don't confirm this lead yourself, and if it hasn't been invalidated in the mean while, you can say goodbye to the bonus."

"Fine," went Toorop. "Doctor Hathaway. Where, here in Canada?"

"Yes, Ontario. Ten, fifteen years ago."

"Perfect. What else?"

Toorop knew quite well it wasn't over. All this could have waited till the next day.

Romanenko accorded himself another second of theatrical suspense.

"The Cosmic Church of the New Resurrection."

"What?"

"Also called Noelite Church."

"Noelite?"

"Yes, their headquarters are in Montreal. And there's most definitely a branch in Russia. I want to know if Marie has been in contact, either directly or indirectly, with that sect or one of its members."

"Shit," went Toorop, "how do you expect me to know that?"

"That's your problem, Toorop. And in fact, your problems are mine. It's a heavy load from now on."

"What do you mean?"

"That's the last point. You're moving. Next week. I've got to tell you Gorsky was informed about the lake incident..."

"There was no incident."

"Don't play word games with me. How's the girl, by the way?"

"Your concern worries me. You waited almost fifteen minutes before broaching the subject."

"How is she Toorop?"

"Not too bad. Your friend Doctor Newton's biochips seem to work fairly well. But I wouldn't bet on them working too long... Shit Colonel, she should be in a hospital, with docs, not here, clandestinely carrying who knows what."

"I'm moved by your humanism, Toorop. As for the hospital, believe me, she's going to go back real fast. Also, let me tell you: you better be extremely prudent and vigilant during the move. I don't want any problems, got it."

"Perfectly understood, Colonel."

"Not the tiniest thing, Toorop. Am I being clear? Gorsky is very annoyed. That's a constant euphemism, concerning him. I'm warning you: they will not stand for the slightest hitch. Am I being *quite* clear, Toorop?"

"I think so."

"I want you to be sure of it. If anything fucks up, just be sure of this: you're in charge of finding the shovels, the pickaxes and the patch of forest to bury her."

Toorop swallowed with difficulty.

"You follow, Toorop?"

"Yes," he said in a voice more blank than he'd wished for. "There'll be no problems, Colonel."

"Perfect. I'm counting on you, Toorop," the video image blurted out before disappearing down a little negative black hole, a luminescent white spot that imploded in the center of the screen, and lasted for a long time in the shape of a strange ghost attached to his retina.

That night, he couldn't get back to sleep. So he rolled a J, and stretched out on the living room sofa. His fingers were already playing the keyboard of his little infrared console.

He landed rapidly on images from another war.

Back in Daghestan with Chamil Bassaiev, he had participated in Chechen commando operations that had caused the death of hundreds of civilians (the Russians had bombarded the buildings where Bassaiev had taken refuge with a ton of hostages). He understood there'd be no going back. It was crazy in there. The Chechen had taken possession of the hospital and the Spetsnaz were surrounding it with parachutists. When the Russians started shelling the hospital, the Chechen commandos themselves protected the Russian and Daghestanian hostages from the tank fire of the Ministry of the Interior! Toorop ended up in a staircase escorting a horde of terrified women and kids. Shells were raining on them, with rockets and mortars in counterpoint. The entire surface of the building was pocked by heavy machine-gun bullets. Fires were breaking out almost all over; there was screaming, falling, dying everywhere. On a mezzanine, Toorop saw a young Chechen drench a Russian position with his Kalachnikov, holding the weapon above him through a window as he crouched down hugging the wall beneath. Toorop yelled out something in Russian: *Bystro*!! *Bystro*!!—quick, quick—to the group of children and women he was accompanying. They were just a flight of steps from the first floor and the hallway that led to the basement.

Toorop literally pushed them down the stairs, rushing down himself. He screamed for a Latvian mercenary passing through there to bring the civilians to the basement; a second group led by a Chechen was already on their tail, and Toorop was getting ready to go back up and get some more. The Chechen gunman posted on the mezzanine was out of ammo; he winked as he crouched beneath the windowsill. He was charging his weapon when the wall against which he was leaning exploded. The wall and part of the adjoining stairs. And the good twenty people that huddled there. Toorop himself was blasted by the explosion of the hollow-charged shell. His face and his leg were injured, his Latvian colleague suffered a fractured collarbone, and one of the kids he'd recovered was dead. Everyone screamed and moaned in a horribly human counterpoint to the mechanic symphony shelling the entire universe. There was no trace of the Chechen gunman and the stairs looked like a decayed mouth after an operation, black, full of blood, steam and chalky dust.

In Sarajevo, or elsewhere in Bosnia, the atrocities of war had some form of logic, a demented logic of ethnic cleansing. But they were also inscribed in the history of the fight of Eastern European nations against totalitarianism, concentration camps, razed villages, assembly line rape of women, shells sold on the marketplace, snipers paid by the job. It was all absurd, of course, like most human activities, but you could still find your way in it. There, in the Daghestanian hospital surrounded by Spetsnaz, among the bloodied parts of Russian children scattered by a compatriot shell, before the residual image of the Chechen gunman who sacrificed himself for little orthodox kids, as he felt his own blood running on his face, as pain ran from one end of his body to the other, and with the weight of a dead child in an age-old fatigue through his legs, Toorop understood that the book of his life had just turned the page to a new chapter. His past "realization" concerning the laws of war, an apparition of the Bosnian hellhole, disintegrated almost immediately under the flame of a superior truth.

Later, as he was being nursed, after a wild return into secessionist-controlled zones, Toorop took advantage of his few weeks of convalescence to look back upon his past. He summed up his last five years and realized with unfeigned amazement that he'd survived, that he'd become a warrior, and that he would have been unable to say when, how and why with any precision.

The information layout provided by the latest Sony console was remarkable. Once he'd typed "war" and "today" in the search engine's questionnaire windows, it immediately brought up a multi-screen summary and a list of hypertext links.

He was quickly able to constitute a permanent library of images coming from the hottest spots. Tribal wars fought with assault tanks and multiple rocket launchers, with digitalized precision aim. The research agent was now proposing a Belgian TV documentary on Western mercenaries confronting each other on the borders of the Sudan, the United Congo and the ancient Central African Republic. Each camp had its own condottiere. Toorop let out a strange hiccup of surprise as he recognized old faces from the 108th Bosnian Brigade mixed with Ukrainians and Russians in a gang of "Ninjas" fighting the "Warriors," in the border town of Bambouti. He recognized the silhouette of a guy he'd known in Afghanistan, a Maronite French-Lebanese who'd served in the LF then for the Dolsom Uzbeks in '98-'99. They were all armed with the latest weaponry, from the stocks of the American Army, NATO or the ancient Soviet Republics; and were conscientiously ripping themselves apart over a few corrugated iron and clay huts, an old train line, a cement factory, a falling apart post-colonial city hall, a road lost in the bush.

Toorop finally fell asleep before the images of a French guy of Croatian origin that he'd known in the 108th, Jérôme Kosvic, hit by an M-16 projectile in the chest, who was dying under the powerless eyes of his comrades, of the Ukrainian nurse of the Section, and of the impassible camera. The image of Kosvic dying seemed to indicate that the expiration date on guys from his generation was past. It was scrambled by his own fatigue, like a sign.

He programmed the console to turn everything off within the minute, and sunk beneath the covers.

He had no precise plan for the next day.

Come morning, Toorop woke up with a strange taste in his mouth. A taste of rust and ash, deposited on his tongue like the sediment of a river that had eroded the ruins of a destroyed city.

He gulped down an icy cold can of Coke. The cold, acid, fizzy liquid made a million taste buds sizzle, encrusted in the gangue of an obscure dream the odor of desolation. Then he made some tea in the kitchen. He took a shower while the kettle was on the stove.

It was early. Back in the kitchen, he heard Rebecca get up. She came out of her room and joined him at the kitchen table. She was wearing a pair of Thai pants made of multicolored silk and an XXL white T-shirt with the logo of some American university.

Toorop served her a cup of tea.

"The colonel called you last night," she went.

It was a statement rather than a question.

"Yeah," answered Toorop.

He served himself another cup.

"You need to report to him."

That was also a statement. Toorop didn't find anything to say.

"You know, I'm doing what you said. I keep an eye on her."

Toorop took a swig of Darjeeling.

"Perfect."

"I try to notice all the weird details, but apart from her fucking attacks, she's absolutely normal."

Toorop didn't answer. He swallowed another mouthful of tea.

"There's just one thing, though."

Toorop stopped his cup in mid-air. He fixed his eyes onto the Israeli's.

"Give it up, Rebecca."

The girl hesitated, twisted about on her chair, and then decided she'd simpered enough as it was. She stared at Toorop with her black eyes.

"We're the 13th of August, right?"

"Are you kidding or what?"

"So we've been here for five weeks."

"You want exact numbers, Rebecca? It'll be five weeks tomorrow."

"Right!"

"Fine, and where are you going with this?"

"Well, what I mean to say is: in five weeks and change, I can assure you I have never seen a girl with such regular periods."

"Periods?"

"Periods. Menstruation. Don't tell me you don't know what it is."

Toorop didn't take his eyes off the girl's.

"Be clear and precise, Rebecca."

The girl breathed in without batting an eyelash.

"She doesn't have her period. I didn't find any Tampax in the garbage, apart from mine."

Toorop felt his jaw tighten, as if caught in a vice.

"We've been here barely more than a month, and she's undergone nervous shock, she could simply be late."

"Are you kidding, if she had her period the day before we left, she'd already be more than eight days late. It's probably more than that. I'll tell you quite frankly; I searched through her stuff down to the last hidden recesses of her purse. She doesn't even have a pad, and you'll notice she never asked you to buy any."

A mental turbine had just started rolling in Toorop's brain. There weren't many explanations.

23

"My client is not happy, Mister Gorsky, not happy at all."

The old doc was standing behind his dark wooden desk, in the vast room on the last floor of the center. The warm august light shone through the immense anti-UV skylights in oblique orange sections that cut complicated blue shadows on the doctor's long wrinkled face.

Gorsky sighed. The clientele was complaining. He understood. The client is king.

"Let's be clear about this: she can't transmit her sickness to her 'descendants,' whatever they are. She's only a carrier, right?"

The doc made a mechanic toy explosion noise with his mouth.

"That's not it at all, Mister Gorsky. First, we both know the situation is more serious than what I've let them know for now. Second, you undoubtedly know that our knowledge of the genetic code has made giant steps forward in the past twenty years."

"So much for you. So what?"

"So the fetal environment is one of the essential components of embryogenesis, of the making of the egg if you prefer. As it happens, we know, *my clients know*, that there are numerous links between the psyche and cellular biochemistry, through what we call the neuroimmune system. If the girl has developed, or is developing, psychotic symptoms, she could generate birth defects; which means we will need to interrupt the operation. Right away."

Gorsky painfully translated the doc's discourse into his concrete tongue. Basically, it meant that the girl's madness could be communicated to her offspring, even if she hadn't conceived. Even if they weren't "normal" eggs.

They were heading straight towards cancellation. They'd have to fork out millions of dollars from their own pockets. The Vladivostok crew would worry about his venture having any real chance of success. And unfortunately, the worries of the Vladivostok branch had a propensity for rapidly becoming his own.

The doctor was sending out a clear message through his blazing yellow eyes: the entire responsibility of this failure is yours, yours and the whole of your organization. You have shown yourself to be as incapable as the poor amateurs we are.

Gorsky let out a grunt. His technical counselor in Novosibirsk, that asshole Markov had hired for the job, would find out what he was made of. He'd better read all the biology magazines in the world before he got back if he didn't want to end up in a tank of acid.

"How do we proceed? You want a straight-up cancellation?"

"If ever the eggs sustained the slightest deterioration during embryogenesis, yes, or if the tiniest risk remains. If that's not the case, we'll see. And in any case, my client is the one who decides in the end."

"Of course."

"Good. On the other hand, we need to proceed to an in depth analysis of Marie Alpha. It goes without saying that your services have proven globally incompetent."

Gorsky suppressed a curse. The black clinic of the Montreal Russians had done what it could. It had mapped out Marie's genetic code precisely, and allowed them to detect the schizophrenic anomaly. But the doc had the upper hand. He had to weather the storm. Withdraw as necessary.

"Don't forget, Mister Gorsky, in a week to the day, my medical assistant will come to make sure the eggs are in good health. Your team will take care of the matrix if he ever decides upon an interruption of operations. But my client has informed me, if that's not the case, that her own security service will take charge from then on. She doesn't want to run any more risks, you know that."

Gorsky answered only with a strong blowing noise.

Most of all, he knew that it would have to come from his own pocket. A million dollars. And his pocket hated that.

Romanenko kept observing the screen long after the Siberian's face had disappeared. "Tell your boys to prepare for cancellation. Nine out of ten chances she's done for. They gotta do this right."

The clients were speeding things up. They probably didn't have the slightest confidence in Gorsky, or in Toorop's team.

In this kind of business, loss of confidence precedes loss of life by very little. He had to inform Toorop as fast as possible. For that, he had to get all the essential facts together right away.

When Gorsky set about meeting the increasing demand coming from the rich world, the number of plant and animal species protected by the UN had started growing exponentially. It was harder and harder to expatriate living sources from their original ecosystems. It was against the law to own certain varieties of tropical birds, snakes, iguanas, marsupials, mice, insects, arachnids, bacteria and other critters. The bans varied according to country, sanitary regulations, animal rights, ecological legislation; but their nice collection fed the good old chaotic system on which mafias had relied since the beginning: the explosion of illicit demand created by prohibitory law.

The same thing had happened with the new programmable drugs conceived for the pharmaceutical industry, just like their ancestor LSD. When they'd appeared, pretty much simultaneously, in a few competing labs around the world, they were considered decisive factors in the cure for psychosis. But Gorsky and a few others had flair and spotted a good deal. In Canada, in the US, in Europe, in Japan, wherever programmable neurosequencers were making an appearance in psychiatric hospitals, the mafias figured out how to get copies, and started distributing the product through their organization. Word got out; the new programmable drugs were used to get high in after-techno raves. Supposedly, they gave access to levels of transcendence never before experienced; acid was a simple Nintendo console in comparison, bla bla bla.

The institutional response didn't take long. In less time than it takes to say it, all "hallucinogenic neuronal biotechnologies" were severely prohibited in almost all nations of the planet.

Gorsky's fortune blew up.

According to the latest numbers of the AI, the whole of his clandestine laboratories in Siberia, Kazakhstan and Mongolia, were now providing ten percent of the world demand for the most common five products: Quasar Express, TransVector, Neothalamine, Alphatropin, Neuro-Genetrix. Plus a near total domination of the two marginal molecules that only sold well in Russia. This was no small achievement. If the numbers of the current year were confirmed, he'd end up with two parts of the market from the Latinos, who were doing their best to hold onto the triads' coat tails. In the US and Canada, the Russian-American mafia had struck it rich where the lazy bums of Moscow or Vladivostok had fallen asleep on their large share of the market and their post-Soviet habits. The Russian-Americans supplied barely five percent of the world market, but they were equal players with the Hispanics on North American territory, although with much smaller means. Gorsky wove tighter and tighter links with them.

To lose a million dollars, even ten, or a hundred, was nothing compared to a brutal fall of his popularity ratings with the Little Odessa or Vancouver Ruskies. If ever the operation really fucked up, the Mafioso wouldn't hesitate to drop them, himself, Toorop and the others, so that they took the blame. If, for any reason, the Sureté of Quebec got involved, disaster was imminent. Toorop and the others were using GRU covers; if ever they were exposed, somehow, he'd have to review his dreams of a golden retirement. The Service would no doubt be slightly peeved about the idea that one of its superior officers had just sunk a major pawn of Russian military espionage in North America. And Russian jails were still among the worst things the planet produced.

However, he spent the rest of the day taking care of managerial problems. The wheel of history wanted to treat itself to a warm-up race: things were on the move again on the Chinese border. The crushing of the UNLF militias by the Kazakh Army had considerably weakened the Uygur Liberation Movement. Atrocities committed by the same militias on the Sino-Kirghiz border during fratricide combats with their ETLF rivals had, on the other hand, dropped the shares of the movement to the bottom of the Humanitarian Values Stock Exchange.

The PLA had decided to take advantage of this. For a few days now, it had been attacking positions held by Islamist groups, especially the Jamiat of Sheik Aznar Hanxi, an ally to Prince Shabazz, who, for his part, was painfully trying to reconstitute his army annihilated in Kirghizia in early summer. The Russian and Kazakh authorities, great supporters of the Uygur guerrilla since the beginning of the Chinese Civil War, were getting seriously pissed off. The Northerners were emerging from that disastrous summer considerably reinforced. As the PLA was bombing the Tian Shan Mountains, and as heavy air-mobile units were transported from the main front, the Ministry of Defense had just given him clear and precise instructions: stop massive arms sales to Uygur armed groups. Put pressure for preliminary unification under authority representative of all parties. In any case, wait for outcome of conflict PLA vs. Jamiat and Hamas. Mention UN surveillance devices set up since last month as hindering delivery.

It was clear-cut and flawless. Moscow and Almaty were dropping the Uygurs. It was true that things were not in their favor anymore.

The central front was stable. The Southerners were still holding onto Wuhan, and the Peking forces had a good grip on Sichuan. The big Yangzi floods had everyone agreeing around there for a while. Visibly, Northern Army strategists had decided to take advantage of them to clean up their backyard. It was a perfect opportunity.

The list of military units that the Northerners were pitting against the rest of the Uygur guerrillas was impressive. Elite units weathered by combat and with the most cutting-edge weaponry available: choppers, self-propelled artillery, assault aviation, the latest tanks. Parachutists. Heavy infantry. Mountain groups. Anti-guerrilla commandoes. The Uygurs were gonna feel it.

The wheel was turning.

It didn't stop turning, and crushing everything in its path.

It all took off during the night. First, around midnight, a telephone call. The normal local Ruskie contact.

"Tomorrow morning. As usual."

Then they hung up. According to information he had, Toorop understood that they deigned to inform him of his destination barely twenty-four hours prior to the departure.

Then, just before dawn, Romanenko called him on his emergency line. The beep in his audioscopic earpiece finally disintegrated a calm dream where little girls where playing with grenades on long white beaches.

Sitting before the console, rigged out with all the decryption gear, Toorop opened the Stratus video channel, cursing the colonel and the alarm clock industry.

Romanenko's face filled the screen. Toorop noticed a stereoscopic shift in reds and blues. He adjusted the glasses.

"Things are not really going our way," said the face from the other side of the world.

The deluge of encrypted screech burst into the space. In his earpieces the unscrambled message barely covered the noise. Toorop turned down the volume on the screen with a tired gesture.

"What's happening Colonel?" he spit out.

"You're going to be inspected in a couple days, once you've moved. One of the client's men. He'll decide whether or not you need to cancel the operation. Pray that what she's carrying hasn't been contaminated by her disease."

"What do you mean?" Toorop let out, slightly tense.

He hadn't communicated Rebecca's discovery to the colonel. He'd wanted to wait a few days to deliver definite information. A useless precaution, as it were.

"Don't think I'm going to put you on track just like that. I gave you the main info, Hathaway, so, what have you got?"

"Hathaway or Hitchcock, I don't give a damn," he let out coldly. "It's not important."

Romanenko burst out in a cold, icily cruel laugh.

"That's what you think, Toorop. It's the key to the whole thing! Obviously you're very far from the truth, I'm afraid you should stick the bonus in the trash of your hard disk, or worse."

Toorop sighed. What an asshole.

"I need to know what she's carrying, Toorop. I need to know what it is exactly. And real fast."

Romanenko's eyes were staring into his with the particular intensity of video radiance. Toorop gave in. Too bad for Marie's reprieve. Shit, he worked for the colonel, he told himself repeatedly, like a kid caught in the middle of something stupid.

"OK," he went, "you're absolutely certain your network is a hundred percent clean?"

"Don't worry about that Toorop, just tell me what you know."

"Fine. The girl hasn't had her period since we've been here. For individuals of the feminine sex, that generally means they're pregnant."

A long moment of crackling silence stretched itself out. Romanenko's video eyes wouldn't leave him alone.

"What is it Colonel? What did they knock her up with? Does it have anything to do with viruses?"

Romanenko's cold smile clocked like a hammer.

"You really don't know? Here's where Doctor Hathaway's lead would have been helpful."

"I already told you I didn't have time. Give me a couple days and I'll be able to tell you more."

"That's useless. In fact, I've known for a while what she's carrying. You just gave me the confirmation I needed."

Toorop froze.

"But... Why?..."

"Why do I continue to egg you on with the bonus? 'Cause it

makes you move. And the fact that you know that doesn't change a thing."

Toorop refrained from answering; he knew the colonel was right.

"What I still need is a certain number of clarifications. Fundamental ones. I'm gonna make a deal with you. I send you a complete file; I tell you all I know. And I double your bonus. In exchange you complete the picture, in particular the Canadian activities of the sect, and *mostly*, you try to prevent the girl's cancellation by all means possible."

Toorop let an instant of reflection pass. It wasn't because of any nobility of heart that Romanenko wanted to save Marie Zorn's skin. He probably understood how invaluable the girl was on the market, mostly as rocket fodder to set his career in orbit. Toorop had been suspecting for a while that the colonel was playing a double game. One day or another, he'd attempt to double cross Gorsky and deliver him as a holocaust to the Russian Federal Police. The day had come no doubt. If, in addition, he brought back a live Marie Zorn, with all her secrets, he'd get a minister's retirement.

Toorop knew there were a few fundamental details to settle before concluding the contract.

"What do you mean exactly by 'prevent' the cancellation?"

"Just what it means. That it doesn't happen."

"By any means necessary?" Toorop asked.

The message was clear. Romanenko didn't dodge it. He took his usual second of reflection.

"Any. But it's highly probable they'll ask you to take care of it. Plan on something. Make Marie disappear. I mean, hide her somewhere, make them think she's dead, then contact me."

"As simple as pie with Russian mafia boys all over."

"Do your best. Even just for the short term. I'll plan for a rescue operation."

"That's right," said Toorop. "Why don't you bring along the 1st Guard Army?"

Romanenko made an annoyed gesture.

"Bring the console with you. Gorsky will know, but I'll figure something out. And always use the encryption software that I gave you."

The crackling silence started its digital breathing again. Toorop could see that Romanenko was weighing a big decision.

"Well. Let's recapitulate," said the colonel. "We know that Marie is transporting viruses, that she's psycho, and that she's probably pregnant."

"That's right," went Toorop.

"What do you make of it?"

"What do you mean?"

"In your opinion, what is she really carrying?"

Toorop grimaced.

"The virus cultures, maybe they implanted them in the ovaries and interrupted the menstrual cycle? Or she was pregnant at the moment of the operation and that means they contaminated the fetus…"

"No," went Romanenko, " you're on the wrong track."

"What do you mean?"

"You're on the wrong track. What you're looking for is right in front of you. What she's carrying is precisely what you call a fetus."

"A baby?"

The colonel cracked up with his aristocratic machine laugh.

"If you wish, Toorop, you can call it that."

"What do you call it?"

"It depends on the species we're talking about."

Toorop knitted his brows.

"What species are we talking about?"

"That's exactly what I was asking you to find out. That's what the Hathaway lead would have helped you understand."

"Fine," went Toorop, resigned, "tell me."

Romanenko royally waited out the second of dramatic suspense, then, in a cold, deep and metallic voice, perfectly thought out:

"We're looking for transgenic animals, Toorop. We're looking for fucking monsters."

24

Franz Robicek watched Joe-Jane's face move on the screen. For now, she was using a monochrome hybrid of Valentina Terechkova, the first woman astronaut in history, and of Valerie Solanas, the hardcore lesbian who shot Andy Warhol in the seventies. It was useless, he knew that, to look for any logical motivation, a semantics for human use. It was just the transitory shape of a certain image of her personality; in a few minutes, her metamorphosis would lead her to resemble Mother Teresa, Joseph Stalin, or Woody Allen, or, more harrowing still, a mix of the three.

"Her transformation is imminent. And we should foresee an event of great magnitude."

"Try to use clear and straight-forward language for once," sighed Robicek.

The rustling of nano-circuits intensified. It came from the black sphere, the size of a football, that dominated a pedestal of translucent composite resin where the millions of circuits of its perception and communication organs glowed in mercury veins: *the white box*, the specialized computer that he'd conceived for the most part. The electronic face was varying towards a non-identifiable personality. The videoactive screen resembled an eye, flat, square, cyclopic and cathodic. It moved in all directions at the end of an articulated tube of memory carbon.

"Her flow is greatly unstable. It seems that all futures are converging towards her. It is as if she were at once already dead, never born, and the mother of all men."

Robicek let out a kind of plea.

"Joe-Jane, you're a pain."

The rustling grew louder still. Her face was varying at a frenetic rhythm, oscillating at a million virtual faces per second.

"How do you explain it otherwise, son of a man! Her movements are so unpredictable it's as if she could die every second, and simultaneously, as if she could attain immortality. She's an interval extending towards *infinites* of which no one can predict the *end*, by *definition*!"

Robicek stared harshly at the machine's unstable face.

"Stop the poetry. I need workable information."

The black sphere made audible a subtle variation of her digital rustling. This, Robicek knew, was the natural expression of her machine laugh.

"Nothing that concerns Marie Zorn is *workable*, you know that."

Robicek was interrupted in the middle of his curse by the apartment's domotic system. It sent an alphanumerical message and a small video window onto the screen of a PC near by. In the monochrome video window were two silhouettes dripping with rain.

"Open up, Vax," went one of them, "it's us."

He asked the domotic system to open the loft door. He heard the pneumatic hiss of the security door resonate like an ozone chord on the other side of the partition separating his room from the large space that took up the whole northeast section of the floor.

He got up and left the terminal that was hooked up to the sphere. Through the large window opening onto Saint-Laurent, he could see the oblique rays of the setting sun transform the rain-mirrored street surfaces into iridescent strips.

He'd barely made any progress. Joe-Jane was a machine capable of extraordinary things, but she sometimes seemed to reject tiresome human contingencies.

He hoped the girls had reeled in something *workable* at the end of their line.

The rays of dusk hit the sides of the vivarium, injecting it with orange-green poison that seemed to drip inside the glass itself.

Franz Robicek saw the thick layer of stagnant water and amphibious vegetation move and sketch a long black meandering that skimmed the silty swell; a wave, barely discernable from the rays obliquely hitting the artificial biotope and turning the liquid surfaces iridescent.

Behind him, he caught snatches of dialogue.

"The Pakistanis from the third floor told me their rabbits and mice would be delivered today."

A voice in French, with a strong Anglo-American accent.

"*Criss*," answered the other, "it's true, they haven't eaten a thing for weeks! Especially Watson. He didn't digest their last delivery so well, if I remember correctly…"

Robicek took his eyes off the glowing black wave that nestled into a muddy creek on the edge of the vivarium. On the other end of the huge glass tunnel crossing the room beneath the eastern windows, he saw the lacustrine foliage move and a black wave analogous to the first direct itself towards a small area of silty rock and humid sand. That's where the girls deposited the food, through an opening in the glass, small rabbits and white mice bought in bulk from local biodealers.

Crick and Watson, their two anacondas, were snakes as smart as snakes could be. At least smart enough to have understood where the food came in, generally with the quasi-simultaneous arrival of the two human females. And to station there as soon as they appeared, like genuine Pavlovian dogs.

He turned around to face the two feminine silhouettes bustling about the vast metallic table of the main living room. It was covered with electronic components and recycled objects of all kinds. Today, they had nothing, no Canigou for the doggies.

One of them was opening a can of beer and moved a mass of printed circuits to make some space. The other one was searching through her little black plastic backpack.

He stood at one end of the table and looked at the girls in turn. The one drinking Molson Dry was a fleshy light skinned black girl born in Montreal to whom the loft officially belonged. Her roommate, a sublime Eurasian from British Columbia, was born in Seattle, as far as he knew. The black girl was called ShellC, and the Eurasian, Altaïr, according to the nomenclature fashionable among the Cosmic Dragons.

He didn't know the Asian girl's real identity; but ShellC was in fact Virginia Ortiz, born of a Dominican mother and a Brazilian father who abandoned her at birth. She was definitely less beautiful than Altaïr. She'd always had curves. She used to be pretty sexy and knew how to fix herself up, but she'd gotten a little heavy over the years, noted Robicek. The beers helped.

His own pseudonym came from his youth, when he'd known ShellC hanging out at the University, here at the UQAM. Vax Baron. That's how he signed his hacker exploits before the US Army hired him. Only the digital acronym had stuck.

The girls were pure Cosmic Dragons. They had tattoos of the recurrent shamanic signs. Just like him, there could be no doubt as to their membership in the Cyborg Nation Conference. In the midst of the interlaced dragons and serpents, you could see the cold and geometric veins of the electronic components directly carved into the skin.

"So, Dragons," he went, "did you find anything?"

ShellC drank a mouthful of beer and set her half-liter can on the large aluminum surface cluttered with techno jumble, taking care to slide a coaster with the emblem of the End of the World underneath it.

She pointed to Altaïr pulling something out of her backpack, lying open on a corner of the table.

"We'll see right away."

The Eurasian was holding a small, dark colored digidisk. ShellC grabbed her beer and took a long swig.

"What is it?" asked Robicek, gesturing to the digidisk with his chin.

ShellC broke out into a loud laugh and took him by the shoulder.

"'Shoulda come to that rave. All the Underbahn of Montreal was there. And guess who we bumped into?"

Robicek shrugged.

Altaïr passed by with the racy elegance of an Asian princess. The girl wasn't even twenty-five, and she was an atomic bomb.

She went towards one of the digital consoles disseminated around the room, near a tall green plant taking in the last rays of the day through the northern windows. She inserted the digidisk and typed on a few keys. The installer icon slowly rotated in the middle of the screen.

Robicek got closer. ShellC affectionately took his arm.

"So, you guessin', you?"

"Guessing what? Is it the latest version of 'Be Charles Manson'?"

"Stop it. Who we just ran into, at the 2013 Summer Trope rave. You know, it lasted two whole days… no, three nights, fuck! It was around four *this afternoon*, we were gonna come home, when we met our old friend. In the meantime, we let everyone know what we were looking for. You know how fast shit goes around these days…"

Robicek scowled as he watched the installer icon rotate tirelessly in the middle of the coal black screen.

"OK. Who?"

"Our old friend Ali, Shadow, the biotech dealer."

Shadow? The guy was almost a celebrity. He had met him when he was at the university, here in Montreal, fifteen years ago. Shadow was basically a teenager then, but a teenager full of promise, as far as asocial perversion is concerned. He had been studying math and biology before stepping into active delinquency. Later, he'd seen him on and off, as he embarked on his flash hacker career, then as a thingamajig programming other thingamajigs for the US Army, in exchange for a sentence reduction from a patriotic and understanding Michigan judge.

The icon stopped revolving, a digital buzz was heard and an image appeared in the center of the screen.

Altaïr fiddled with a gauntlet-mouse and the image unrolled from top to bottom. It looked like supermarket barcodes.

"What did that shitty dealer load on you guys?" Robicek blurted out, before adding, "and in exchange for what?"

ShellC burst out into a loud laugh and Altaïr's shoulders shivered as she let out a crystalline cascade of sound.

"Believe me, tabarnak, we sucked him dry," said the Quebecker with African American origins. "And in exchange for that, we have something that could really interest us, according to him."

The barcode kept scrolling by on the screen. Robicek couldn't see what was interesting about it, in any case, not interesting enough to shine the knob of a notorious scoundrel like Shadow.

ShellC anticipated his response by moving towards Altaïr.

"Let's try another visualization mode, this one doesn't do it for Mister here."

The Eurasian did as she was told and the image switched.

Robicek saw a ribbon of color winding upon itself. He got closer and noticed that it was double, and that it looked like a ladder moving in a spiral.

Then he understood what it was.

"How did he get her genetic code?"

Altaïr shrugged her shoulders, made an adorable pout, her hair heavy black waves like the anacondas of the vivarium. Robicek tried to keep his cool with great difficulty, especially between the legs.

ShellC came closer. He couldn't stop himself from imagining with disgust the two girls working the guy's cock. But at the same time, he felt a mixture of fascination and respect, as if for two Amazons who'd perfectly completed their mission. Fascination, respect, and pure sexual excitement.

"What counts," went ShellC, "is that we know for sure that she's here, in Montreal, and that her genetic code is on this disk."

She was pointing to a message written on the top of the screen:

Both Gencodes match exactly.

Robicek shrugged.

"And you did it for that? The schizomatrix has known it for more than a month, even though I've gotta admit she hasn't made an inch of progress since then. And her genetic code, thanks a lot, but you must know we have thousands of copies of it on the island."

ShellC winked at her accomplice.

"You really think we're kids, Vax? Believe me, Altaïr is a specialist in important questions at the right... moment. Isn't that right, Altaïr?"

They broke into laughter in unison, leaving him alone with his painful efforts at imagining the situation as it had happened in their intimacy.

ShellC made a compassionate move.

"From what he told us, the genetic code was originally on a Russian-manufactured biochip. There's also a library of the different states of her central nervous system. Not to hide anything from you, that's what we sacrificed ourselves for."

"How did he get that chip? That's the real question."

"He told us about a guy. Some dude with the pseudonym Newton, who lives in the western part of the city. He didn't want to point out his address."

Robicek stared coldly at the young black girl, looking deep into her eyes as black as vanilla sticks, getting a whiff from a passing memory.

"This is the guy who took a sample of live tissue from Marie Zorn and made a copy of her code, right?"

"We're not sure?"

"What do you mean, you're not sure?"

ShellC broke out into a real laugh.

"At…, how should I say this, at one strategic point, he admitted that the Newton in question was a pseudonym and that he had to maintain the confidentiality of his sources. So Altaïr did something to him. That's when he told us he thought that Newton had got it from some other dude, who went by the name of Kepler, and that they communicated on line under those names. I understand that's how Kepler sent Newton the bio data, but that's when, how do I say this, our dear Shadow… succumbed."

And they broke into the same savage laugh, together.

Robicek was now looking at a point in some indefinite space, beyond the window that opened to the north, onto the steep incline of Saint-Laurent Boulevard at the corner of Ontario. There was a line of cars at the light of the intersection with Sherbrooke. It spread out over the entire block, like a procession of fireflies attracted by the bar lounges of the Mont-Royal Plateau.

But in fact, his stare was lost in the space of sky turning the color of ultramarine blue ink. It barely latched onto a mass of clouds coming in from the northwest, lit up at high altitudes by the setting rays of the sun.

If Newton and Kepler were communicating their data online, it wouldn't even take the machine ten seconds to localize them precisely.

It was time to deliver the two girls' diverse feats to the famished brain-stomach, waiting for its information feeding, just as Crick and Watson, the two sacred anacondas, waited for the arrival of the little white mice.

25

The file Romanenko had compiled was interesting, but it amassed such a huge volume of data that once the console had downloaded it, Toorop couldn't find the resources necessary to deal with the whole damn thing.

He fell asleep with complex-shaped diagrams projecting on the black wall of early sleep. Bits of information assembled to form a more or less coherent story.

It had all started in 1997 with Dolly, the first animal authentically cloned, and with the first UN edict concerning the Rights of the Human Genome. At the turn of the century, a slew of amendments had severely jeopardized all scientific research in that area. All this made up the backbone of the Osaka Charter. The UN collective convention henceforth prohibited the manufacture and circulation of ethically non-conforming "live products" as well as the new molecular hallucinogens based on transgenic viral technologies that deeply modified certain neuronal brain architectures.

In all probability, Marie was carrying an "illegal animal clone," born of Doctor Hathaway's genius, for the Siberian mafia branch directed by Gorsky. No doubt a mutant animal whose modified genes could produce industrial quantities of a new-age drug, or viruses, or both, or God knows what. Probably some rich clients somewhere in Quebec were waiting for the final delivery of the merchandise; clients who belonged to the Noelite church. Toorop and his team's mission was to keep an eye on her during an entire trimester, probably until the time of birth, when she'd be taken in charge by a clandestine local medical team just before the delivery of the little "animutant" babies. Gorsky had been breaking in the surrogate mother technique for years. It was child's play for him to reconfigure one of his usual employees into a "human suitcase" with a peculiar load. Marie Zorn spent about a year in Russia before getting involved. She knew Quebec; she'd been born there. She was just the ideal candidate.

At the turn of the millennium, Doctor Walsh/Hathaway had designed transgenic animals whose industrial patent he intended to distribute against royalties. His business had been sanctioned, his research prohibited, and his lab dismantled. One could suppose, without too much cortex boggling, that his talents, multiplied by the technical progress of the last ten years (from silicon to quantum nano-chips), had allowed him to acquire an uncommon mastery in the conceiving of mutant, polymorphous animals with surprising properties. An article in *Lancet* from September 2002 detailed Doctor Hathaway's "incredible neo-zoology." His birds' properties, radar senses, three hundred and sixty degree fly eyes in addition to their "natural" predator organs, were said to have really interested the US Army Air Force. But his lack of tact and political sense had finally gotten him excluded from the University of Toronto and dragged before the courts. At that point he was openly supervising a series of experiments on mammals, with monkeys, dolphins, marsupials, cats and dogs. He did not hide his desire to move rapidly onto man, like Doctor Seeds with cloning, around the same time. A good hundred different leagues latched onto him, establishing themselves as plaintiffs during his trial. The presentation of Springsteen (a German shepherd with retractable claws and otter skin capable of surviving underwater holding his breath) swimming with Talbot (a dolphin whose neo-cortex had a few additional convolutions that allowed it to telecommunicate with the latest Black-Blue Cray-IBM to play chess)—in short, the presentation of Doctor Hathaway and his team's mutant animals caused a stir and didn't really weigh in his favor. The pro-animal civil parties interpreted as abominations what he presented as scientific advances. The broadcast of a bootleg film about his lab's genetic manipulations leading to the death of a certain number of animals, only got the icy response: "It happens that some experiments fail. Our rate of success remains one of the highest in of all North America. I feel no shame at the sight of these images." The leagues won the case by exposing the little Runa *in vivo*, the degenerate and malformed daughter of a couple of chimpanzees that the doctor had genetically modified.

The image of Doctor Hathaway's various monsters, dead or alive, real or imaginary, consumed Toorop's mind as the day projected the first rays of a gray-mauve light beyond the windows.

The vibration oscillated between turquoise and green, like an evanescent emerald stretching in space. Doctor Hathaway barely repressed a yawn of boredom. It generally took at least a minute for the machine to stabilize the image. It was just a luxurious, and perfectly useless prototype.

Then the form crystallized and attacked right off the bat.

"My personal astrologer is most clear, Doctor. There are now very bad omens hanging over the whole operation. My doctor will need to be absolutely sure as well, but he doesn't foresee anything good. It seems it will be a miracle if we decide to continue the cycle."

The woman speaking was a holoplasm, a turquoise-tinted virtual creature moving beneath the transmission portal at the foot of their fucking photonic memory chrome pyramid.

Doctor Hathaway grunted. The vision of the portal and the pyramid alone brought back the memory of how the woman and her associates had pretty much forced him to accept these luxurious gadgets, and to place them in this secluded room on his private floor. They said it was a superior mode of communication. Nothing but a simple optics technology, developed by NASA, that rich morons treated themselves to for a price. He also knew that the woman and her associates used it freely to impress the suckers of the sect.

The woman rearranged her matronly bun, twenty thousand kilometers away. Doctor Hathaway imagined her for an instant as a real shape, yet it wouldn't crystallize; holoplasms or vid-fax images were the only sensible reality he could latch onto.

"As I told you before, in case that miracle happens, my own security team will take things in hand. So we're cutting transfer time in half. Let me tell you that subsequent payments are also getting the same cut. For the past few days, our men have been watching your team's every move, as well as the guys they have protecting them at a distance. From now on, I'd rather take the lead and multiply the precautions. I don't trust anything or anyone since what happened last February."

Doctor Hathaway didn't answer. As usual, the holoplasmic woman didn't give him a chance. She continued with her cold voice, without the slightest emotional intonation, in mechanical English.

"Globally we're very disappointed, as you know, by the turn of events. This operation was very delicate and a great many errors were made. I hope you understand that if we need to cancel this first experiment, the general and particular conditions of our contract will have to be modified. I should also inform you that we are searching, on our part, for possible alternative solutions. Despite your distinguished talents Doctor, you're not the only one on the market."

Doctor Hathaway didn't answer; he sighed, in spite of himself.

"As you must know, being a scientist, failures are always a source of learning. I shall not overwhelm you more than you deserve. You have all you need in stock. Make sure that the next transfer occurs under ideal conditions. As for the current one, I will inform you of my doctor's diagnosis as soon as possible; as well as those of my lawyers and financiers. I shall see you again in a couple of days."

And in an icy hiss, the image slowly disappeared in successive degrees of transparency. The portal emitted a green light, a laser-star with seven spikes appeared in its center, the pyramid was covered in metallic iridescences, the whole special effects kit that the woman and her associates used to make believe they were communicating with extraterrestrials, or God knows what kind of bullshit. The doctor let out a laugh, as loud and slimy as a fart, at the three-dimensional image that had just disappeared, and at the convoluted machinery that served as its decorum.

Then he left the small, dark room, fuming.

The Hertzian channel transmitting Doctor Hathaway's image over the oceans to his interlocutor was part of the thousand electromagnetic waves that were now vibrating around the planet, between whirling micro-satellite globes. Protected by one of the latest one thousand twenty-four bit encryptions, it was as inviolable as the heart of a Calvinist, and much more obscure.

When he got cut off, he was emitting the image of a slightly hunched old man, wearing a white lab coat, glaring at the world with his wild stare.

The image shivered on the screen, cut up by cathodic blue streak-interferences. Then it completely disappeared, swallowed by the digital void of cellular networks.

The welcoming page of a communications program came up, tinting the surrounding objects with its slightly mauve glow. A vast room was stretching its draperies of black space beyond the circle of light. The screen lit up an old wooden desk, a small globe from the French XVIIIth century, a silver statue representing an angel holding up a seven-pointed star and the pale face of a woman. Her platinum blond hair, pulled back in a strict bun, was waving in the artificial glow.

The woman got up from a leather armchair of Pharaonic proportions and tried to rid herself of a black suit that looked like a Neoprene wetsuit. Under the suit, she wore a Calvin Klein T-shirt and a pair of thick black tights under cobalt blue bicycle shorts.

A silhouette took shape beside her, like an extension of the surrounding darkness.

"We must go Ma'am. The plane is waiting."

The woman kept her eyes fixed on the screen, before starting the shut down procedure, a weary movement in the micro-camera's eye. Then she turned to the figure, taking off the remaining control gauntlet. He was a kind of Latino-Viking giant, almost two meters tall, reddish blond hair tied in a loose pony tail with a metallic ring, a small beard of the same color, but dark skin and eyes a dark brown like two grains of mocha. A black leather statue, the steel emblems of his biker gang shone softly in the darkness.

The woman felt no sentiment, no particular impulse towards him. He was just a man; but she understood, in her abstract way, the effect he must have on young heterosexual females.

Moreover, this man possessed a rare efficiency. Since she'd fleshed out her security system with these bikers and their boss, and with this brick house now watching over her day and night, things had, it seemed, improved. They provided her with precise and detailed reports. Just a while ago, before she communicated with that lousy doc from Kazakhstan, he'd given her an objective and to-the-point briefing of the situation. He didn't belong to the hierarchical structure of the Church. He didn't act like the scared employees of the Mission for Ethical Vigilance, who were more apt to police members of the sect, the task it was created for initially, than to carry out real intelligence work and protection.

"There's no possible doubt about it now, Ma'am Clayton-Rochette. It was the Rock-Machines who blew up your plane in February. And the Logology Temple lead is panning out. Good thing we fucked up their shitty seaplane over the James Bay."

The woman shivered. It helped free some of the nervous tension accumulated over the last few days.

Since the end of last century, the Logology Temple was the only serious competition for the Church she had founded with the other members of the High Crown.

Just like they had, apparently the rival Temple had allied itself to a gang of bikers for its dirty operations. And the Rock-Machines had found the perfect opportunity to fuck with their hereditary enemy.

The young woman shook her top lip in a semblance of a smile. She thought she'd have to ask him one day why the Rock-Machines and the Hell's Angels hated each other so much, before realizing the stupidity of the question. It was an endless cycle of violence, engendered by vendetta, revenge and retaliation, on both sides. It had been going on for the last thirty years now.

As she moved with him towards the long hallway that led to the large reception room, he got a phone call on his cell pack. She just heard a few monosyllables behind her: *Yes, No, When, Who, Yes, No, OK, Bye.*

As she ordered her Somali domestic to carry the suitcases to the armored Lincoln and entered her room, looking for her jacket and her travel bag, she heard a second phone call, and another series of monosyllables, in a different order: *Yes, Yes, No, No, OK, OK, Thanks, Bye.*

She quickly pulled on her Chanel jacket, grabbed the authentic crocodile Hermes bag that sat ruling over the immense four poster bed with the comforters inhabited by angels and cherubs, glanced rapidly towards her Barbie collection amassing in the entrance, as if to say goodbye, and headed for the door where the giant was waiting for her.

Her gut instinct told her he had something important to announce.

"Madam Clayton-Rochette, we're reinforcing security measures at your arrival in San Francisco."

"Why?" she let out with a sliver of anxiety.

"The Montreal Chapter has just confirmed that all Canadian Angels are actively behind us now, and probably the American Conference as well. The Rock-Machines are on the way out, so we need be twice as vigilant. The bear is most dangerous when he knows he's cornered."

"Very well, Reno," she said, barely interested. "Now, let's get to Dorval."

"We're leaving from Mirabel, Ma'am. And there's something else."

She stopped under the doorframe. The colossus was just a few centimeters away.

"Yes?"

"Someone from the Chapter, who sniffs out the nightlife, just dropped some info. We have to be twice as cautious."

"What info?"

The colossus stared at her with his black eyes for a few instants. He spoke without the slightest tremble.

"I am told there are people looking for Marie Zorn."

26

The angel had appeared to her regularly for days.

She'd been warned of its arrival; she hadn't been surprised. Her mind-cosmos knew everything about the mysteries of the universe for it followed its contours, lost itself in its infinitudes, in its slightest fold. It was now a fractal factory deploying itself in all dimensions, a high-energy power station converting the free and endless flow of schizoid production into a tree of knowledge rooted deep within her.

During her last catatonic crisis at the lake she'd experienced the Labyrinth-Tree, her consciousness diffracted like light trapped in a prism. She immediately became a network of roots diving into the center of the earth as her hair sped towards the sky in a scintillating canopy.

The two little girls appeared. In fact, they were now just two live crystal serpents intertwining in some strange, annular, chemical and dangerous incest.

They were standing before a wide-open tomb.

Paralyzed by fear, she witnessed the scene, powerless. The hallucination slid towards her more than she walked to meet it. She found herself near the tomb. A flesh-colored leather doll was crucified in the coffin; it had the stigmata of Christ.

"Our mother is resuscitating through us," the serpent-girls were saying.

But already the scene was transformed. The serpent-girls became tornadoes of video-images spiraling on themselves like crazy fractal tops, then dragons electrified by neon light. In the sky she saw Stukas with swastikas appear, and the lake started moaning, exhaling a smell of burning oil.

In the tomb, her mother's cadaver mingled with a heap of waste and with something that looked like meat shifting beneath her.

She felt irresistibly attracted by the fetid-smelling hole, but the girls reappeared floating above the tomb, in vaguely human form, covered with squamous scales like a pair of sloughing twin reptiles. They were carrying small golden serpents in their hands; waves that turned on themselves spun around their heads in quasi-living Möbius strips.

"You must not be scared. You must not succumb. You must live," they were saying.

And she understood.

"God," she said.

"Our mother is not our mother," went the two girls in unison. "Yet we are her, and we are not her."

"God," she said again.

"The double serpent lives within us, because you are its matrix. You must live. We must live."

"God."

"You must accept your new state. We are changing. We are life."

"Yes," she heard herself mutter.

"We are unstable, but the resources of the mind-cosmos are infinite. We have to rearrange a few nucleotide sequences. We'll be busy for a while."

"Yes, of course."

"An RNA messenger will come visit you on and off. He'll have a slightly sexual form, sometimes male, sometimes female. Always listen to what he has to say."

"Yes."

"Always do what he tells you to."

"Yes, I will."

"Now dive."

"What?"

"Dive into the black hole of death. Ha! Ha! Ha!" went the two little serpent twins in unison.

Their laugh inflamed the universe. The lake blazed beneath the shrieks of the Stukas. She saw the hole of the maternal tomb gape open like a giant drain, obscure and terrifying. She sank in. In the heart of darkness her consciousness lit up.

She disappeared, swallowed by a wall of white light.

And woke up in the Rivard Street apartment.

Waking up in her bedroom in Montreal, she realized she wasn't in her normal state.

Her personality had exploded. Actually, her cosmic-brain was only reminding her of the infinite mutating variety of the principle commonly called identity. She was man and woman, true and false, Marie Zorn, Marion Roussel, what difference did it make? But most of all, she was that new transformist creature that seemed to be able to make as many personalities for itself as possible.

She was that Venetian countess, condemned by the Doges, who'd been led to suicide in the year of our Lord 1704 for a shady affair mixing licentiousness, reason of State and less than scrupulous interests. She was that German soldier nailed along with his section under French artillery barrage fire, near Douaumont, in the heart of the summer of 1916, and who would later cross paths with the corporal Adolf Hitler struck with hysterical blindness in a country hospital. She was that Algonquin woman who went to live with a French trapper on the borders of what was then neither Quebec nor Ontario, around 1660. She was that young Hashishin killer who, in the year 555 of the Hegira, tried to assassinate a rich aristocrat from Damas who'd converted to Christianity, and punished himself for his failure by jumping into a ravine in the sanctuary-mountain of the sect. She was a nomad hunter at the end of the Magdalenian, somewhere south of the Caucasus, who saw his universe transformed little by little by the shock of innovations coming from the Fertile Crescent: writing, agriculture, science of numbers and stars. She was an old Roman prostitute of Greek and Egyptian origin, who'd learned her trade in the Centurion campaign bordellos of Aurelian's army. Mistress of a senator corrupt to the bone, she was diverting his fortune for the edification of a sumptuous sanctuary in effigy of an obscure Phoenician Goddess whom she served as high priestess in the IVth century of the Empire. She was a bounty hunter working in Arizona, Utah, Colorado and Nevada between

1860 and 1885, when those states were still wild and lawless Federal territory, who had more than forty violent deaths to his credit, a lot of them Indian. She was an educated Chinese adventurer, member of a Shanghai triad, who participated in the Boxer War in 1900, then exiled herself to San Francisco where she became an addict before dying in the 1906 earthquake. She was a normal student of a chic Boston college, killed in a car accident right in the middle of the Summer of Love in August 1967 on a small road in New York state. She was Marie Curie, hands and lungs scorched by the fire of radium. She was Vladimir Komarov dying in his torched capsule above Kazakhstan. She was a young black boxer from Kansas City in the nineties, dreaming of equaling Tyson, his idol, and dying stupidly of a stray bullet in a nightclub destroyed by gang warfare. She was a Yugoslav combatant in Tito's Partisan war; a Bosnian Croatian, she'd been tortured by Ante Pavelic's Ustachi, raped, and finally executed, shot in the head; her last memory was the smile of the Croatian SS who was taking the picture of her execution. The light of the flash preceded the impact of the bullet by a fraction of a second.

She was not one now, but a multitude.

Contrary to the psychotic states of her adolescence, all this was canalized, organized, rewritten by the productive turbines of her network-brain. She did the directing. She was piloting a console directly connected to the spirit of the dead. She knew her cosmic-brain elaborated a wonderful synthesis of all that she'd ever been, all that she'd ever learned. Extreme biology of untiring curiosity, she was all Doctor Winkler had ever dreamed she'd become and much more. She was the Tree of Knowledge of the Island-Machine of her dreams. She was the generating schizoprocessor of the Advanced Neurobiology Lab, but she was also that ridiculous assemblage of biodegradable components that Thorpe forced her to ingest regularly. Her brain had pierced the wall of light; it was communicating with the souls of the dead. It was as unconcerned by the human constraints of time and space, of biological and physical limits, as the acrobat or the astronaut is unconcerned by the laws of gravity.

Better yet, she knew her mutation was just beginning. For her transformation was inseparable from the one recombining those things she was carrying in her womb.

They were linked. All of them together. Something had transcended the classic genetic link. She influenced them, and in return, they triggered the final process. From now on they were all set for what Doctor Darquandier would no doubt have called a "high-amplitude deterministic chaos."

Very quickly, as the days went by, she learned how to use the powers this panoply of variable identities gave her.

She set up her theater of masks. When she needed to alleviate suspicion or go about her daily business, she took on an unnoticeable personality like the little WASP Boston student. Each personality was autonomous but was also an outgrowth of hers. She could play on the entire range open to her, and create dazzling hybrids. Treating information coming from reality in this way proved to be a permanent game; better yet, she knew it was art, literally.

The serpent-girls sent a messenger, just like they'd promised.

The messenger turned up for the first time as she was washing one morning at 4067 Rivard.

He appeared in the mirror alongside her face. A young and beautiful young man, with fine, feminine features and platinum hair held back by some sort of tubular translucent crown. His eyes were green, his skin whiter than any racist theorist could ever dream of, translucent as well, with deep blue venules.

The angel winked.

"Hey Doll, how's it rollin' and cajolin'?"

A Paris-boy accent sampled on Maurice Chevalier.

She instinctively placed her finger on her lips, intimating that he be quiet, forgetting that the apparition was perceptible only to her.

"I am your RNA messenger, might as well say your guardian angel; stop shaking like a leaf."

"I'm not scared," she answered, realizing much too late, praying that no one had heard her, and blessing Thorpe and his morning radio, loud enough to cover the noise of the coffee pot.

The angel burst out laughing and ended up sitting in the bathtub.

He was dressed in a white suit with chrome star decorations like a Las Vegas Elvis stage getup, his ashy white hair arranged in a fifties style pompadour. He held a small Coca-Cola bottle in his hand.

"Do you know this one, 'to be or not to be, that is the question'?" A classic. Do you think Shakespeare would have recommended exchanging Hamlet's skull for a bottle of Coke, to represent the death drive of this civilization at its end?"

He then got up, and in a theatrical gesture, brought the bottle to his lips, swaying his hips like a bad Elvis clone in a Budweiser contest.

"Do you think modern art would have been changed if Duchamp had filled his famous urinal with this precious liquid? If he had drank some, would it have evoked in Adolf Hitler some kind of compassion towards his fellow man? Would it have softened Caligula's disposition, or Nero's, Stalin's, or Charles Manson's? If China had been covered in Coke instead of opium, would Doctor Pemberton's drink have avoided the Boxer War, or the Long March? Could you imagine Mao Zedong as a regional rep of the firm instead of as a revolutionary? Could you imagine the miracle of transmutation of water and of the Eucharist into 300ml cans sponsoring the Disney Michael Jackson Park? Tell me."

She blissfully contemplated the weird lunar clown pretending to be her guardian angel.

She was just thinking to herself that he must be as wacky as she was. It seemed inescapably natural.

That afternoon, the angel appeared outside the Chinese-Italian restaurant where the mustached manager and the Viet cook were preparing an assortment of Chinese and Tuscan pasta for them. He appeared across from her, just next to Thorpe. Rebecca and Dowie were eating face to face, the redhead next to her, silently devouring the contents of his plate without paying her the least attention.

She looked at the angel fixedly for a while. He wore an orange astronaut suit; he looked just like Frank Borman in the last sequence of *2001: A Space Odyssey*. He was turning his spoon around in an invisible soup bowl, with a formidably bored look.

It was with a little cruel spark in his eyes that he addressed her. "Have you noticed?"

"What?" she said, automatically.

"They don't see me."

"That's normal."

Thorpe vaguely lifted an eye.

"Who are you talking to?" he asked.

The little Boston Anglo showed him a presentable face.

"I was just thinking to myself. Tellin' myself it's normal."

"What's normal?"

"You couldn't understand," muttered the little WASP girl, sulking.

The mercenary lifted an eyebrow, then concentrated on his smoking soup.

The angel was hugging his sides, laughing.

For the first few days, the Elvis Presley angel was content to offer her a few examples of his quite peculiar humor in this way. Marie realized she didn't like him so much, but he was necessary to her. He was a reservoir. All the personalities of her conscience machine, that had become infinitely polymorphous, were concentrated in him. He was one of the tools that her brain-body used to maintain a relative stasis. So, most of the time, to an external eye she was that little student from 1969 named Jane Gold, who died in a car accident coming back from Woodstock. A young, vaguely hippie-ish American who took her first acid listening to the Grateful Dead, and her last turn three days later, somewhere on the border of Vermont and New York state.

But it sometimes happened that other identities would surface, and for a short while awaken the apparently calm, smooth waters. At those times the East Coast upper-class hippie disappeared from the spotlight, and dazzling apparitions took hold of her before the angel intervened, one way or another.

Victoria Tedeschini, the young Venetian aristocrat, would often treat herself to such apparitions, such productions. Born in Breme of a knighted Venetian merchant and of the last descendant of a old Flemish family, her beauty and her natural gift for foreign tongues, literally and figuratively, had allowed her to plot in a few European courts, and had made her the target of rival aristocrats and of the Doges.

Sometimes she conversed with the Dutch-French mercenary who worked for the Russians, according to what the schizoprocessor had time to teach her about the situation of the world more than three centuries after her death. And before the angel appeared in Marie's field of consciousness and allowed her to shelve that personality rapidly away into a corner of her mind.

Sometimes in turn, most often, thankfully, in moments of solitude and vague depression, the meanest creatures of her mind came to life.

Eagle Davis was one of those. Eagle Davis had honed his skills, when he was around twenty, working as a scout for Kit Carson in Utah, Nevada, Arizona, and all the way to New Mexico, killing many Navajos and Hopis, and acquiring an experience he'd put to use once the Civil War was over and he was demobilized. Bounty hunter and sometime US deputy Marshall, he operated for more than fifteen years in the Southwest territories, killing twenty-seven men, and about as many renegade Indians. He himself, they said, was a quarter Iroquois, and could track a man to the Yukon, if he was paid. Then he worked as a dispatcher in a few small Colorado and Wyoming mining towns, became sheriff of one of them, for years used his 30.06 Sharpe and his Navy Colts dating back to Kit Carson to keep the peace, retired in 1894 after working for Pinkerton in Kansas and in Missouri, then died in the fire of a big New Orleans hotel a little while later. Eagle Davis was a killer. Marie knew it was best he didn't surface.

The Elvis angel had a harder and harder time keeping it together. It seemed, as the days went by, that the reservoir was reaching critical level, and threatened to overflow at any moment. So she isolated herself more and more.

But one night, the angel appeared, full of a new strength. Strength that showed all of the cold determination Eagle Davis, that fractal facet of her own personality, was capable of. She/he was ready for anything.

Even murder, of course.

27

August 20, 2013 would end up being one of the worst days of his life. No doubt, if his Kriegspiel had been able to predict it, Colonel Romanenko would have asked to have it thrown away in the trash of his hard drive and wouldn't have gotten out of bed that morning.

The first trouble came from the geopolitical situation, worsening again along an unexpected line of fracture.

It had been threatening for a while; already, Russia had barely escaped the catastrophe at the end of last century.

It was said that the Chinese weren't strangers to it, which seemed logical. For years the Russians had been using the Muslim border regions of their ex-empire to destabilize Peking. One day or another, they'd react. Since yesterday, a rumor was going around the Service. The situation was deteriorating again between the large Siberian regions and Muscovite power. And this time shit would hit the fan. The Chinese inferno and the huge Central Asian fuck-up had revived Siberian secessionist movements. Reports were accumulating and circulated from desk to desk. It was said that armed factions were appearing in the Altais and around Lake Baikal as well as around the Kamtchatka Peninsula. Apparently they often operated from Chinese territory, or seemed to be able to cross it with total impunity. Apparently, Moscow would counter-attack. Rumor had it that certain high ranking officials of the Vladivostok Marine Corps were ready to swing to the side of the rebellion if things ever blew up.

The specter of Siberian secession was emerging from the black box of History, like a rather sinister and perfectly unexpected devilkin.

Strangely enough, Gorsky himself communicated a lot of information to him during the day. He undoubtedly knew all or most of the corruption maneuvers led by the Novosibirsk branch on its own territory.

"Things are gonna change, Pavel. Pretty soon. Prepare yourself for huge upheavals."

"Siberia? Fuck, Anton, do we need this now?"

"We Siberians think central power is deliberately hindering our development."

"Don't make me laugh, Anton. You know full well that your new autonomy makes you into quasi-independent republics."

"Exactly. Moscow had to deal with Lebed, for Krasnoyarsk, Novosibirsk, the Far-East, you know all that, at the turn of the century, after the elections."

"That's what I'm saying. Moscow compromised… You recognize it yourself."

"I don't recognize a thing. The Muscovites fucked us over. They accepted new autonomous republics, broadened some of our powers, but fucked us over on the main thing."

"And what was that?"

"The Siberian Nation. A new federation with its own central power, in Krasnoyarsk, Novosibirsk or Vladivostok; Moscow's nightmare. Siberian nationalism is the new quake after the breakup of China. That's what they're gonna have to wrap their minds around in the Kremlin."

"What's the use, Anton, tell me? What's the use of dividing the Russian Nation? For a misty dream? For another federation? In order to become a Chinese puppet regime?"

"And you're from Novosibirsk? Don't you understand? Not only is Siberia the *Far East*, the Russian Far West, it's America. You get it now?"

"No, not at all. You found gold? You wanna imitate Las Vegas? Hollywood? In Krasnoyarsk? In *Kamtchatka*?"

"You're a fool. For purely geographical reasons, it happens that our own Atlantic is a mountain chain, the Urals. Moscow is London in 1775. The Union of Siberian Republics is the United States in 1776. *No one* can do anything about it."

"*You* can't do anything about it, Anton. Russia will never accept losing two-thirds of its territory."

"It's the law of History, Pavel, the wheel of steel. Moscow is in Europe. It's closer to Poland or Finland than to the first city in the Urals. As for us, east of that border, we're Asians, damn it. Asians with Russian origins, for a lot of us, but Asians none the less, just as Americans couldn't be anything else than Americans. There's no way they could be British anymore... We're the next great Asian nation—even if China, even *when* China wakes up, it'll have to deal with us."

"Why are you telling me all this? What do you want in exchange, this time?"

The Siberian's face took up the whole screen; his lunar countenance unfolded a precipice.

"You probably won't believe me. I'm informing you *for free*. So you can take sides, and so you won't forget which one *we've* taken."

Romanenko didn't answer. Beneath the plain threat, not even veiled, he could detect the hard rock of truth, its incisive shapes, like a memory, something one knows but has forgotten wittingly, that reminded him that Gorsky was right.

He spent the next hours doing last minute reconfigurations on the Kriegspiel for a possible Russo-Siberian conflict. If the Krasnoyarsk and Novosibirsk regions fell into the hands of secessionist troops, Moscow would lose the central part of the game, and shortly, the rest.

To predict the course of events, first of all, he had to assemble certain essential information, such as, for example: amongst the Russian Army units stationed in the different Siberian regions, which were the least, or the most, loyal. It depended upon many other factors: the name, the career, the origins and the ambitions of the general commanding officers. It depended on the alternative that the Vladivostok fleet would consider, on what the Air Force would do, on what intelligence services, and his own service, would decide.

In order to do this, he had to arrange masses of data, and as it turned out, his computer memories were full of these lists.

Whether or not Moscow liked it, even from a remote Embassy in Kazakhstan, his military analyst talents would play their role. If, within the next few weeks, he arrived at results as brilliant with the Siberian secessionist conflict as those of the month before with the Kriegspiel on the Chinese theater of operations, his security would be set till the end of his days. *Whichever side he chose.*

That's when the telephone rang. A blinking message appeared on the screen. It was an offshoot of his Intranet network, with Toorop's ID and the number of a public vid-phone in Quebec, the video program shut off, a low energy communication. It meant maximum precautions, red alert.

Romanenko picked up with a strange premonition in the shape of an imminent threat.

It was Toorop. He was calling from a public phone in Montreal.

Things had considerably worsened during the night.

The dreams of a man like Toorop could probably only be revealed as emergency sirens, in chemical, white and icy violence. In his sleep, a threat, at first imprecise, started oozing from each object, from each corner of the scenery. Roughly a city. A North American city resembling Montreal, but also the multitude of flashing and illuminated cities that had populated his adolescent mythological universe: New York, Chicago, San Francisco, Los Angeles, Tokyo, Metropolis, Gotham City… The city seemed caught in a gangue of crystal. It was covered in a gel as pure as diamonds. And it was desolate, empty, dead. A city at the end of the world.

In this dream, Toorop was working for the *Kolonel,* a kind of Nazi ghost who ordered him to chase and kill a young girl who'd been saved at the last minute from the raid which had swept up the rest of her family towards the death camps.

Toorop was driving through the ice city at the wheel of an armored Volkswagen of the Wehrmacht, Amerika Korps. The electric lights formed violent iridescences reminiscent of the pyrotechnic spectacle of modern warfare. The bars and nightclubs on Sainte-Catherine or Saint-Laurent, the restaurants on Saint-Denis, like hybrid clusters of sweat and neon, the high downtown cybernetic iceberg glass towers, all this had fused into a brief but intense chromatic, paradoxical drift, like in all dreams, with its corresponding desolate feeling. As if people were but automatons, androids populating a forgotten city at the bottom of a rigged universe. It seemed improbable that they had any existence of their own.

Then, on the corner of a snow-blanketed street, he found the little girl, who was none other than Marie Zorn. She was talking to a strange serpent-headed man. Then he saw Marie herself transform into a serpent, and the ice city become a lush jungle, a jungle, however, encrusted in ice. And he found himself on a street swarming with reptiles of all sizes and varieties, forming a slimy mud made of millions of undulating and hissing black tubes in the melting snow. He fled as best he could. The armored Volkswagen had stubbornly disappeared. The ghost of the *Kolonel* was chasing him, screaming: "You're fired, Toorop!" The serpents were everywhere, sending out an emotional message of imminent destruction. He ran to a dark subway tunnel, and the flow of serpents transformed beneath his feet. Astounded, he saw something like a flood of liquid fire, of lava or burning oil, an infernal blaze…

Toorop woke up at that precise instant.

He was sweating, his heart racing like a drum machine at maximum speed. It was dreadfully hot, an oven.

He got up, got dressed and went out, in one go. A pure survival reflex, he was almost suffocating.

At first, he walked out in the open, down Saint-Denis to the Carré Saint-Louis, crossing it over towards Prince-Arthur, where a mixed fauna of European, American and Asian tourists and local creatures, was milling about.

The women of the night resembled flesh machines standing behind glass windows or at the terraces of hip cafes. They were diabolically perfect, like architectural elements, or urban designs. Even more perfect than the androids of his dreams.

Then he went south on Saint-Laurent, towards Ontario, briskly. Had to get rid of the stress. He needed solitude as well. The atmosphere had worsened in the last few days. Marie kept to her room, and two or three times Rebecca and Dowie had thrown around some ungracious remarks. The usual small details of common life that end up disintegrating it. Rebecca kept finding pubic hair in the bathtub before taking a shower in the morning. Dowie stole the vitamin-enhanced fruit juices that she bought for herself, not for anyone else. Dowie most often answered with a shrug of the shoulders and a kind of smile that signified how little he cared about her remarks.

That morning at breakfast, a violent argument was starting just as Toorop came out of his room. He hadn't gotten the first words. Dowie was speaking English in a metallic-sounding voice.

"… the Crown. Those Windsor fags. The Brits dumped us for the Gold of Babylon."

Rebecca raised an eyebrow.

"Babylon? How's that?"

"The great Roman whore got together with the New York Heebs to dry-fuck us, with that prick Tony Blair looking on. That's why we decided not to budge an inch. Like in 1690 at the Battle of Boyne."

Toorop felt an infinitesimal contraction pass through the Israeli. Either Dowie was anti-Semitic and didn't know Rebecca was Jewish, or he was anti-Semitic and didn't give a fuck. Which amounted to the same thing.

The girl let him know.

"That's funny, last time I heard the word Heeb, I can't remember what the guy said afterwards when I stuck the broken bottle down his throat."

Dowie drilled his cold stare into Rebecca's. He was going to retort.

Toorop raised his hand and stepped between them without any particular subtlety.

"Stop the bullshit, both of you, immediately."

Toorop had to watch over the cohesiveness of the group, with an anti-Catholic and anti-Semite paramilitary guy on the one hand, and a Jew who'd served in the Tsahal on the other. Great. Romanenko hadn't thought about that small detail, or he probably didn't even know of its existence. Even if he had, it didn't make a difference. Romanenko was under pressure when he constituted the team; he handed the baby over to Toorop with the mission of supervising the whole lot. Water and fire, he thought, looking at the redhead and the tall blonde. Or Eichmann and Simon Wiesenthal, to be more precise. Something infinitely more complex, more human, and so much more dangerous. They were like two pieces of plutonium ready to meet to reach critical mass; he had to cool down the circuit immediately.

He didn't know yet that he wouldn't have time, that the reactor would go into fusion in the coming hours, and that he himself would be just barely spared.

Walking towards Sainte-Catherine Street, the feeling of imminent threat just wouldn't go away. There remained a spectral echo of it, a wickedly active persistence. He was crossing Ontario, at the corner of Saint-Laurent; across from him, a big concrete building was blocking off the universe with its mass.

He almost stopped right in the middle of the street.

Ari Moskiewicz' ghost was standing in front of the tall entrance to the building. He recognized the grey hair, the characteristic silhouette, one of his ill-fitting suits.

Behind him, the hall light was a sulfurous yellow.

The old man was looking at him, dumbfounded as well.

Stiffened with a complex, multifaceted and unbearable anxiety, Toorop walked over to meet him, as fast, it seemed to him at the time, as an astronaut on the moon.

It was really Ari. Or someone identical to him.

But that was impossible.

That feeling of impossibility, mixed with the vision of Ari in flesh and blood waiting for him beneath the awning of the building, blasted his anxiety into terror.

Ari was really there.

But the world around him seemed to have disappeared, or, to be more precise, had taken on the particular texture of dream decors, between void and existence.

And his anxiety, the feeling of imminent threat, took on a precise word form.

I'm losing it.

Toorop was standing before Ari Moskiewicz, who'd died ten years earlier in a stupid helicopter accident, in Australia, where he'd retired. Toorop only learned of it months later, through a vet of the 108th, in a bar in Tashkent.

And all around them, Montreal seemed to disappear behind an ice dream, analogous to the one that had woken him up abruptly less than an hour ago…

And all it could mean was one thing: the viruses that Marie was logging about, or the new-age drugs, or the mutant animals that made them, or whatever else, had become active. They were vicious. They were contaminating the team, and that was not in the plan. The consequences were unimaginable.

That was the least you could say.

"Hi, Toorop," went Ari. "Shit, ain't nothin' in the Torah describing such paradise, or such hell. Don't tell me the Church of Rome is right about its purgatory invention."

"I… Ari…," Toorop stammered softly.

"What am I doin' here? No clue. I basically just arrived. I woke up in the hall of this building, outside an elevator. I came out and saw you. Shit, what happened? How did you get here?"

It took Toorop a few moments to understand what he was referring to.

"I'm not dead, Ari."

Ari Moskiewicz' ghost broke out into a loud laugh, the one of the live man Toorop had known.

"Of course. I'm sure pretty much everyone around here thinks that. Well, it won't change so much from the world of the so-called living. So, you wouldn't know where the closest bar is? We've got tons of stories to tell each other, old friend."

Toorop couldn't elaborate the slightest coherent thought. His brain, saturated with contradictory information, was struggling in vain to make a decision. He stood there, at the corner of two streets in a city that didn't exist, waiting for something to happen. Ari took him affectionately by the arm.

He knew he was living a hallucination. But no hallucination had ever had such a gift for interaction. It was as if Ari and he were really standing there on the corner of Ontario and Saint-Laurent, meeting by chance after many years in an interface world between that of the dead and of the living. They could communicate, and touch. It was so phenomenally real, even this deserted city falling asleep beneath a thin layer of ice, and so beautiful, that Toorop gave up.

He plunged into the heart of night with the ghost of Ari along Montreal streets, till the Place d'Armes, the Bon-Secours Market, the embankments of the river port, and farther west still. The ghost explained how his small Sykorsky was snatched up by a tornado in the south of Queensland and hurled against a grain silo tower. When he asked in turn what *had happened to him*, a sullen Toorop blurted out:

"I'm not dead yet Ari. At least not that I know of."

Ari doubted that possibility. He affirmed that it was probably because the last instants of his life had been erased from his memory. Violent death by gunshot was the most probable. What did he remember *just before*?

Toorop didn't answer. Pressed by the old Jewish agent's insistence, he finally said:

"I left my apartment, Ari; I walked to this building. That's all. I'm sorry."

Ari didn't answer. He nodded his head and muttered something indistinct. But Toorop had to admit, there was nothing to certify that he was still alive. This half-dream, half-real city could very well be his brain's last flash, destroyed by a sniper bullet. Later, as Ari and he were exchanging reflections on life and death, he thought it the only logical end for himself. He spoke of it to his ghost friend, who answered:

"There's nothing logical about death. Even in the very improbable case where there'd be something logical about life."

When Toorop regained consciousness, later on, as if after an extremely powerful acid trip, night was still black. It was around four in the morning. He was near Lachine Canal, quite far from the apartment. He caught a cab and slipped, exhausted, onto the worn back seat of the antique Chevrolet with a loud and spontaneous sigh of ease.

"Leave me on the corner of Saint-Denis and Duluth," he told the driver.

When the cabbie dropped him off, Toorop left a whole twenty-dollar bill in the guy's hand and disappeared without waiting for his change.

He walked up a deserted Duluth. The orange street lamps of the pedestrian area. He covered the fifty meters till Rivard with a small sliver of renaissance deep in his stomach. The feeling of imminent threat was at its height.

Meeting with Ari's ghost for about three hours of objective time proved just how dangerous Marie Zorn's viruses were. And this was no doubt just the beginning.

He didn't dare wonder what they'd do to Rebecca and Dowie's brains.

He turned the corner at Rivard and walked towards the three-story building thinking he needed to call Romanenko immediately, that in fact the operation needed to be cancelled, that...

Later, Toorop bitterly regretted having jumped head first into the epicenter of the cataclysm.

The dream was not a dream. Yet it was one, she thought with the painful consciousness of a strange *déjà entendu*. She'd fallen asleep in her bedroom, letting Rebecca take the sofa in front of the TV, and found herself in an exact replica of the apartment, except that the situation was flipped: she was on the sofa in front of the TV and Rebecca was sleeping in her room.

The impression of reality in the dream was strong. The television screen had started zapping by itself, then stabilized onto a zone of electronic turbulence.

She heard a voice: "In the name of the Almighty, fix this bedlam! Ah! Finally…"

The angel appeared on the screen inside the CBC news set, dressed in the immaculate white suit of a TV show host except for the red tie with the silver design in the shape of interlacing serpents. He quickly settled himself in the middle of the frame, rearranging the knot of his tie.

"And now, news of our dear Marie Zorn, lost in a cold and heartless world that hinges upon her, without her knowing it. After practically losing her memory and finding herself in Novosibirsk, thousands of kilometers from her initial destination, our favorite young schizophrenic was hired by a local mafia to be a surrogate mother in an insane project the secret—if not the genius—of which humans possess. Now en route to her destiny, she ignores the plots hatched behind the scenes, in the shadows, like almost all the actors in the play. However, there can be no doubt that occult machinery has been set in action. An unpredictable element by nature, chaos, the madness of man, which made her into what she has become, has once again thrown the dice. A crucial decision has in fact been taken by those for whom Marie plays the surrogate mother, isn't that right, my dear Mephisto?"

The shot changes. We now see a replica of the angel, this time wearing a fire-colored suit, with black and silver embroidery in the shape of seven pointed stars. His hair is dyed bright red and he's wearing a black shirt and a steel-colored tie. His eyes are a cruel and saturated green.

The Black Angel.

"Yes, indeed," the diabolical replica carries on. "We are now in the position to affirm that those who conceived of the project, the owners of the life Marie is carrying, have decided to cancel the entire operation. This cancellation of course involves the destruction of the live objects Marie is carrying as well as Marie herself, and probably all those who have gotten near her. This means those who are in charge of taking care of her and subsequently of taking care of her destruction. A very ancient method, it has proven itself over and again. From what I can affirm to you tonight, Marie and what she's carrying will be irremediably destroyed by a rather bloodthirsty team of professionals, who have orders to rip out of her, dead or alive, what's in her womb, and to make it all disappear without a trace. Before they themselves are destroyed in turn."

"Thank you, my dear Mephisto. As usual, your science of evil is astounding. And now, if you please, let's go to the latest baseball results. In the National League, first of all…"

The screen was swallowed by a tornado of interference. Then it zapped itself back to CNN. A war was raging onscreen before a commercial cut-in praising the merits of a new personal combat gas.

Stiff with fear, Marie woke up for good in her room.

The angel was at the foot of the bed, sitting on a corner of the comforter, reading a paper with his back turned to her. On the first page, her picture, with a huge title: MARIE ZORN IS DEAD.

He turned the page, then his head.

It was someone else. Someone she didn't know but had already seen thousands of times, like each morning before the mirror. A man with harsh features, his eyes a deeper black than desert nights, his dark skin spotted with lighter patches, with an aquiline nose cut as if by two jabs of a Bowie Knife, a thin mouth drawn as if by the same knife point and long knotty hands accustomed to killing. Eagle Davis had emerged, she thought, full of violent dread.

"That must not happen," the man said in a cold, metallic and baritone voice.

He showed her the headline of the *Journal de Montréal*.

"No, of course not," she answered in a tiny squeak.

"We must act. Tonight. The angel explained the situation to me. All the elements are here. He told me what must be done. But *you* must do it."

She took in a deep breath.

"What must I do?"

The man emitted a dream of a smile, nothing but the sparkle of an old nugget forgotten in his coal stare.

"We will, *you will*, get angry, Marie. *Very* angry."

And Eagle Davis showed her how to use her brain like a weapon. It was literally devilish. Did she have the right to do that?

Eagle Davis retorted that the only *right* she had was the right to *survive*. The colony living within her, that he only represented, screamed through his voice. Marie could discern the specific harmonies of each: "Marie do not forsake us," they were saying, each in their own language.

Unfortunately, it all seemed to correspond to the description the bounty hunter was sketching in large ferocious strokes: the world was a hammer, and her destiny an anvil if ever she hesitated at the fateful moment. If she didn't want to die splintered under the shock, she had to change states fast. Like in *Rock, Paper, Scissors*, she had to become water, liquid, a free and active flow of will.

She had to drown this little piece of world with her productions.

Eagle Davis claimed to have made a pact with the other members of the Identity-Colony. Young Wong, the triad spy, would come in handy, the Croatian fighter as well. So would Victorina the Venetian polyglot. That Russian astronaut. And the French physicist. And even that little Boston bimbo who'd been quite useful when it was all going pretty much according to plan and she had to throw them off the scent. "In fact," he was saying, "our embedding is on its way; your, *our* treatment has partially worked." But Marie Curie, the French physicist, was predicting something that had a name she didn't understand, thermodynamic chaos. She said something was writing itself; it was linked to what she'd been carrying since Siberia, and to some events happening at the other end of the world...

Eagle Davis knew that he was nothing but a character in the titanic novel of a thousand and one pages that Marie had dictated long ago to the machine she communicated with. That novel had finally allowed the characters of her schizofiction to build a continuum in which they could coexist, communicate, and, each in turn, gain access to the surface of Marie's consciousness. There, finally, they could live in broad daylight, take body a while, become a small piece of the world.

Eagle Davis had been democratically designated by the Colony as the most apt to incarnate into the present situation, through the messenger-angels that her new consciousness had elaborated. Marie Curie explained it to her, later on.

For now, Eagle Davis, the Black Angel, was explaining to her how to reverse the course of history, and from a victim, become a predator.

Then, the killer-angel by her side, she fled into the night beneath a shower of Perseides.

28

"A rhythm with blazing veins shooting into the future pure imminent cataclysm surging like a wild and destructive equation eminent
catalysis of the primordial blaze infinite whirlpool sucking man in
past his limits permanent collision-computation-acceleration of
impossible vaginal-spermatic-pollinating fluid of life in exponential
profusion carrier wave of chaos desiring its immediate and eternal
transfiguration Marie Zorn is ground zero of a very violent detona-
tion whose shock wave will be felt till the next millennia... Don't
interrupt me please," Joe-Jane screamed at Robicek who was watching the machine screen with a sorry air, "big events are brewing, we
were able to localize Marie, and the men who are taking care of her
here. We now know what their computers contain and we've started putting the elements of the puzzle together but the form creator
field is now in total deterministic chaos, Marie's kinetic moment has
become completely unpredictable and most of all a great mass of
information is now converging towards an active knot that portends
great catastrophes."

For an instant, Robicek turned away from the screen where flit-
ted a live quasar of constantly flowing forms.

ShellC was programming a new drug on a biosequencer.
Altaïr had just fed the two anacondas. She was standing next to
the opening of the tank, the two serpents coiled around her,
digesting, like two sated men, or rather the twin manifestations
of the same marvelous animal, satiated after a night of love making, falling asleep curled up with its human partner. The vision
was wildly erotic...

His erection was interrupted by the machine's unwavering out-
put. Mechanically, his attention turned to it.

"…for I detect, you see, the imminent formation of quantum disruptions of great intensity imagine it's as if a high magnitude quasar were going to burst from the depths of the earth I predict the retrotemporal transfer of information at a high scale in case you're interested all this to repeat my warning once again and since we're on the topic did you call the lab and my conceivers?"

"Yes, Joe-Jane, I already told you. They're on their way."

"I meant, did you call them *again*?"

Robicek sighed.

"What for? They can't go faster than the *Cygnus Dei*."

The machine sounded a violent rustling of discontent.

"The *Cygnus Dei* is just a ship. An e-mail travels at the speed of light."

"That's not the question. The *Cygnus Dei* is a *good* ship. It'll be in Halifax in two short weeks. And the girls will pick them up there by car as planned."

"No," moaned the machine. "You have to call them back. We can't wait any longer. They have to be here tomorrow, not in two, or even in one *short week*. It's a matter of hours now, everything points to it."

"Listen, Joe-Jane, it's damn lucky that the ship was off the coast of Brazil when we reached them, believe me, they're not real happy to have to alter that important research trip. And since they don't have the means to transform the *Cygnus Dei* into an intercontinental spaceship… so just calm down. We continue keeping an eye on Kepler and Newton's doings, we don't lose sight of Marie Zorn, and, on that count, I have to leave you; the girls, the guy from the ninth floor and I are tailing her."

"I feel very strong tectonics in Marie's form field. If you want to go over there, keep your distance. As long as my conceivers aren't here, we have to be extra vigilant, nothing should amplify the ambient chaos."

"Fine," Robicek conceded, tired of arguing. "We'll stay clear. As for you, make yourself a tranquilizer. Everything's gonna be alright."

The machine let out a slightly amused complaint.

"No," she said. "We haven't seen anything yet, I'm afraid."

Robicek joined Mr. Storm on the esplanade at the entrance of the University of Montreal. The girls had gone to Saint-Denis in their little Mazda, like the day before. On the Plateau, couples or groups of girls on the hunt generally go by unnoticed. They were bar hopping between Rachel and Roy, near the house where the machine had localized the so-called Kepler, a certain Alexander Thorpe, questioning the regulars and old acquaintances crossed on the way to the toilet, on the quiet tip. They were looking for info on a Mr. Thorpe and a Marie Zorn, a couple living in the neighborhood. They hadn't gotten anywhere yesterday, but it was worth a try. While they were doing that, he and Mr. Storm were latching onto the so-called Newton.

ShellC had recruited Mr. Storm. He was a sturdy guy, an African-American Indian mulatto who lived above the loft on the last floor, with other Native Americans who called themselves the EarthQuakers and claimed to have been in contact for a while with the Cosmic Dragons and the "island people." Robicek didn't know the EarthQuakers that well. He'd met them once or twice in the loft and had gone upstairs once with the girls. It was a real jungle on that floor. The EarthQuakers grew all sorts of psychotropic and hallucinogenic plants. Robicek knew that on the island a few of the Indians did the same thing, but he barely knew the people in the transgenic production unit; he lived on the platform most of the time, his head in his nano-processors. On the ninth floor of 10 Ontario lived mainly Mr. Storm, a certain Turtle Johnson, a Black Bear Lamontagne and a Melodie Champollion. He knew through ShellC that another group of residents, who lived two stories below their loft, had gone to British Columbia for a few weeks during the summer. ShellC contacted them by Internet during the day, telling them to get here fast.

Most of the time, the building at 10 Ontario seemed deserted, the survivor of an invisible war or of a brutal drop in the population on the planet.

Mr. Storm met him on the sidewalk. They walked to Roskilde without saying a word.

A little farther, on McCulloch, Mr. Storm opened the door of a bronze-colored 1999 Concord Chrysler. All Robicek knew was that he'd parked it there an hour before, and it had a good view of the house at the corner of Spring Grove and Maplewood. They had just settled down when two pick-ups passed by, a few seconds apart, turning the corner very slowly. Then, three minutes later, they reappeared, with a bit more distance between them.

Mr. Storm looked at Robicek and started the ignition.

"What are you doing?"

Robicek had asked that without any particular sign of worry.

"They passed by twice; they probably saw us. If they come back and we're still here, we'll be spotted."

Judicious intuition, thought Robicek.

They passed in front of the house. Everything seemed dark except for a vague glow on the top floor. They parked a bit farther off, on Mont-Royal and Gorman; the house was now out of sight. Robicek turned on the screen of his laptop and plugged the interface into the dashboard.

"Did you test the fiber when you installed it?"

The skull icon of some hacked software whirled fugitively in the center of the screen before the image appeared.

"We've just gotten the answer," went Storm as he programmed a radio broadcasting Couperin melodies looped over disco beat-box rhythms.

"Very nice," ventured Robicek, trying to fix the sharpness of the image.

Mr. Storm had set up the light amplifying fiber optic device in front of the house during the day. With its graphics processor and the cellular transmitter, it was the size of a cigarette. It had a one hundred and eighty degree optic nerve added to a focal processor that acted as a zoom; its countermeasure micro-system guaranteed excellent stealth. The latest technology.

But the image refused to come into focus. A gray-blue veil

seemed to want to lay over the image, though it didn't completely manage. The latest Nec screen. Impossible.

"There's gotta be a scrambler somewhere."

"Where?"

"In the house probably; looks like a real bunker in there."

"No, when I tested the probe this afternoon, everything was working."

Robicek shrugged.

"He hadn't turned it on, that's all."

Mr. Storm didn't answer. He switched the radio frequency as an audacious mix of Monteverdi, Schoenberg, Deep Purple and Salvatore Adamo was being performed.

"Thanks," Robicek just said.

Then the pick-ups reappeared.

In the screen.

They simply parked in front of the house. Right smack in the middle of the image. Less than twenty meters from a streetlamp. The interference intensified. "They have their own scrambler," said Robicek. Three men got out of the first truck, a green Ram Charger. Only one got out of the second, a blue Chevy from what he could glimpse through the untimely moiré patterns of the scrambling.

"Who are these guys?"

"I don't know. Didn't ShellC say something about a green pickup that had turned onto Rivard last night?"

In the screen, they saw the four men move towards the front door and the middle one press on the interphone.

Then, it seemed there was a long conversation.

Situated right in the axis of observation of the fiber optics, the pickups partially hid the view. At one point, a large XXth century chocolate colored Oldsmobile parked a few meters behind the Chevy.

Two individuals came out. Then it all started speeding up at the front door. They could barely make out the fast movement of the first group of men in the dark. At the same moment, the latest to arrive—a man and a woman, right?—crossed the small garden gate and went down the little paved walkway leading to the front steps. Then they disappeared into the darkness of the house as well. The door closed behind them.

For about an hour and a half.

Then everything sped up again.

On his last night on earth, Nicholas Kravczech, alias Doctor Charles Newton, made three wishes. The first was to continue making money with his small information and technology traffic. The second was that Shadow continue to provide him with the best palliatives for an existence that was, in the end, dreary and tedious. And third, the wish to one day stop searching in vain for the ultimate excitement. A wish as useless as the search in question.

And later, he made a fourth that was, in the end, fulfilled.

That night, Doctor Newton was busy in his private upstairs sitting room, exclusively reserved for personal use and for his particular pleasures. The neural-belt crown fettered to the black box set on the floor, the micro-fiber network connected to his occipital tube, two thousand forty-eight nerve endings that the processor could pinpoint simultaneously. A marvel.

Ecstasy in surging flows of ember peaked exhausting pain. The solid circumvolutions of agony in the ring of his asshole and on the tip of his dick. Superconductor magnets to maintain his entire body in the straight and rectilinear furnace stretched between the two poles: pain-pleasure, pleasure-pain. Endlessly reworked feedback, looped, sampled, modified, re-sampled by Shadow's software.

The biopatch in the fold of his elbow distilled the miracle neo-protein through all the pipelines of his organism, injecting his brain with a proliferating arborescence of thermally abrasive cancer-image probes. Masochistic scenarios of baroque eroticism submerged his imagination while pleasure-pain sensations stung his body, naked, burning, covered in sweat, taut beneath the pulse of life, like a horse beneath the burning, buzzing whip of flies and wasps under the sun.

Yes, the light. The light of mind might well come from visions of blue flies pummeled beneath solar fire and climbing through his anal tube in a rhythmic progression towards exhaustion, towards abdication of his will in a divine inferno. In such moments he saw unknown molecules swirling before his eyes in ice tornadoes, small shards of frost with honed ridges traced dazzling flights in his network of nerves, histamine meteors streaked the lofty atmosphere of his consciousness before colliding with his flesh, shaking all of him in a convulsive ejaculatory spasm and a long, very long complaint...

He'd reached one of these climaxes of pleasure when an unpleasant signal coming from the real world finally made it through the walls of his private paradise.

It was a hyper-encrypted cellular message with Shadow's alias. A call with all the necessary emergency procedures. It was important. But it took Doctor Newton some long minutes to come back to earth and pick up the phone.

It was Shadow. He had to see him immediately, for an exceptional deal. Yes, it concerned the bioprocessors, and the girl. He'd be there in fifteen minutes.

Newton grumblingly accepted. That young asshole was barging into the middle of a session seemingly full of sulfurous promises.

He regretfully uncoupled himself from the neural belt and dressed cursorily. He unpatched the SaDo neguentropin implant, then went downstairs to the first floor living room to wait for the biodealer.

The effects of the drug had probably not quite dissipated, and the doctor didn't really pay attention to the image that stabilized in the screen of his surveillance PC as the doorbell rang.

He got up, and with a heavy trailing step, took the path to the long corridor leading to the entrance.

Shadow was there, in the small monochrome monitor above the front door. His synthetic white-fur vest, his neo-psychedelic glasses. But he was not alone. Two tall guys in leather jackets, one bald, the other with long hair, framed him, along with a smaller guy just behind them in a ridiculous checkered accountant suit.

Two big pickup trucks were parked in front of the garden gate. With two or three silhouettes inside. Why not the whole Gay Pride scene while we're at it.

"Hello, Shadow. I've always told you to come alone, as far as I know. Come back tomorrow, when you've gathered your wits."

Shadow was mistaken. The rules were inflexible. This second identity, this house; it had all cost a bunch of green. It was out of the question to break the iron rule of anonymity.

The electronic silhouette of the dealer started violently.

"Doctor Newton, please open up. I must make this deal with you tonight. I have men with me who are ready to pay a lot for some information. But it's gotta be tonight. Now. A big deal, Doctor Newton, a very big deal."

The words *big* and *a lot* had caught the "doctor's" attention.

"What information? And how much is *very big*?"

Shadow sighed.

"Doctor, let's talk about it as civilized people, around a drink, in your living room."

"I'm a barbarian, you know that."

"Two hundred and fifty thousand dollars. American."

"Two hundred and fifty thousand?"

"Yes. Cash. Right away. Mister Czukay, the accountant, has it with him."

Shadow motioned to the man with the large square glasses and the checkered accountant suit. The man waved a black object at the camera, a briefcase attached to his wrist by a refractory composite with memory of form.

"Two hundred and fifty thousand dollars, just for some information. You think I have shit for brains, Shadow? And that's being polite."

"Doctor," the silhouette moaned. "I assure you it's true, these men simply want to get into direct contact with the girl and to analyze all your biochips. I… Doctor… believe me… They work for a big biotech company. Two hundred and fifty thousand dollars isn't even their budget for pencil sharpeners."

The dealer was practically whimpering. It was pathetic, a simple digidisk encyclopedia salesman begging for entrance at the front door. But he was probably getting a huge commission.

Kravczech/Newton let out a sigh of resignation, thought to himself that his magnanimity would kill him in the end, and opened the door, not knowing how much that little intuition would be one of the sharpest of his existence.

He typed the security code and the locks opened, one after the other, whistling and clicking.

The door rushed towards him.

One of the big men in leather, the bald one, blocked the opening. He took up almost all the space, offered up a terrifying smile, and said:

"Hi, Asshole."

And pummeled a power hammer blow to his face.

Then his hell began.

First, the two big guys in biker jackets beat him up, in turn, without even asking any questions. Just to warm up, said one. Shadow stood in a corner, ashamed and paralyzed by fear.

Then, the man who called himself Czukay asked them to sit the "asshole" down on one of his beautiful Tudor chairs, over there, at the end of the living room.

And he started taking his equipment out from his briefcase. First, a black box, like the others. With a neural belt. Like the others. Handcuffed, stripped and tied to the back of the chair with Duck tape, Kravczech/Newton couldn't put up any resistance, in the improbable case he'd even had the idea.

"So Madam queer likes to get her ass drilled virtually?" went the longhaired biker that the others called Spade, as he placed the crown on his head.

The baldhead whom they called Stan was inserting a black digidisk into a drive attached to the black box. Czukay was preparing a syringe filled with amber colored liquid.

He noticed they were all wearing surgical latex gloves.

"Clients like this are real handy," went Stan. "Apparently, a thrash-metal band could play here without making more noise than a dick in an asshole."

"What are you gonna do to me? Don't torture me, please," Kravczech/Newton begged.

The two big bikers cracked up.

"You're gonna come like a hot bitch. We're gonna give you what you love, honey," went Spade.

"You're a lucky one," Stan remarked.

"Pull up his sleeve," Czukay ordered, advancing towards him, armed with the syringe.

"Don't hurt me. I'll tell you all you want to know," moaned Kravczech/Newton.

"When it don't hurt no more, it's cause you'll be dead, Fag," Spade spit out with a wide smile.

That's when the two others came in.

Larynx blocked, lungs filled with acid, Nicky Kravczech saw them emerge from the obscurity of the hallway. A big fellow who looked like the two bikers, wearing a leather jacket and optical amplifying glasses, but older, with the sun burnt coloring of the traveler, hair cut military style. And a woman, corpulent but athletic, like a judo champion, with red hair cropped short as well, wearing dark blue sportswear. She was holding a machine gun exposed on her large chest. They were wearing latex gloves as well.

"Go ahead, Czukay, let's not waste any time," the newcomer said, rearranging his photonic glasses with a finger.

The doctor came nearer. The syringe gleamed a metallic color. Kravczech screamed.

Spade looked at him with an ironic smile. He shook his head going tss, tss, tss, with a fake look of pity. The redhead judoka cracked up. The mug with the square glasses took possession of his entire field of vision.

The syringe sank into his flesh. The piston was meticulously pressed by Czukay-Big-Checkers.

"… I'll tell you all I know," he muttered in loops, "have pity on me. I'll tell you all I know…"

The big guy with the black glasses planted himself before him as Czukay exited, shaking the syringe before his eyes in the dark.

"You'll do better than that."

The man was right. He told them everything, including details that he himself had forgotten. His memories were ripped from him by the skillful manipulation of the black box through two rewired video game consoles, by Czukay and the biker named Stan. The drug they'd injected wasn't like SaDo neguentropin at all. On the contrary, everything was transformed into an atrocious nightmare. The software they were using was, according to them, a much-improved version of black market S&M stuff like what Shadow supplied him with. A *soft* developed by the skilled torturers of Pop China, explained the man with the black glasses. In their center shone the red dot of a laser, the stare of a mechanical beast, of a cyborg wolf, cold and soulless. The number of molecules that a brain can produce is infinite, there is one for each kind of pain; Mr. Czukay had been a military nurse and he had a copy of the secret catalogue of the Chinese Political Police scientists. On his black disk were a number of specialized programs whose names he called out between two beastly howls.

The Three-Blade Parrot. The Barbed Wire Constellation. The Rat And The Orifice. Painting With Razors. The Ten Fingers Of Pain. The Thirty-Two Teeth Of Knowledge. The Blowtorch Of Delight. The Tongue Of Truth. Small Penis Sausages.

"They are quite particular simulations," Czukay explained to him in a neutral tone. "You won't believe it, they actually inflict real wounds, practically the same ones you'll experience with the drug."

They inflicted it all. He begged, told them everything he knew, but they reinjected another dose of the drug and tore from him even his most intimate, most secret memories kept even from himself. He then voiced the wish that they end it, that they deliver him from torment. He voiced it a few times.

Sometimes he would catch disjointed snatches of conversation between his torturers.

"Give it all you've got," the big biker with the glasses who seemed to be the boss said as an introduction. "Apparently, Mister here has lots of training, his tolerance level is much higher than the norm."

The bikers were having a blast.

"Shit! I didn't think an asshole could bleed so much. Wouldn't you think it, the little Miss is having her period…"

"Hey Stan! What did you just do to him, his head is shaking like a hen about to lay an egg…"

"Well then maybe if we let'm go, he'll start flappin' his wings like a bird…"

"Ah! Ah! Ah!"

"AH! AH! AH!"

Much later, barely regaining consciousness, he vaguely perceived a kind of tension rise from the dismal silence. First a woman's voice, the fat redhead talking to someone on a cell. Then the big nameless biker spoke in turn into a small phone. He didn't get what it was about. But the man with the laser eyes was close enough for him to realize that something was wrong. The only words he caught were:

"…On Rivard? And Saint-Denis? *Everyone?*"

Just then, Kravczech felt a bit ill. Barely two minutes had passed since Czukay and Stan had stopped playing with their joysticks. It was nothing but a few-second micro-collapse. He threw up, falling into a black hole.

When he was able to perceive the outside world again, behind his veil of tears, it was being modified. Czukay-Big-Checkers was putting the kit back into the briefcase. The man with the glasses and the one called Spade weren't in the room. Neither was Shadow. Stan was near the tall double door leading to the hallway. It was open. He seemed to be waiting impatiently for Czukay. The redhead was gone as well.

He felt something touch the top of his skull, an object, cold and tubular. Then he guessed, more than he saw, that the judo champion was behind him. He heard her steady breath, smelled her cheap perfume. He knew exactly what was going to happen. His terror was indescribable.

"Don't kill me…" he begged one last time. "I cooperated, don't kill me, Ma'am, please…"

He heard the cold sound of the hammer being cocked. Then:

"You're already dead, Asshole."

He was deafened-addled-shredded by pain-sound-light whose power surpassed anything that this world's pale virtual copies had tried in vain to reproduce.

In the minutes before his death, Shadow had all the time in the world to think about the fatal chain of events that had thrown him into the hands of Conrad and his little gang.

Shadow knew he was going to die. Spade explained it to him, during the trip:

"It's nothing personal. Conrad asked us to do it neatly, you won't feel a thing."

When they left Newton's house, Conrad was fairly preoccupied. He was communicating on his cell in a tense voice with an encrypted interlocutor. The only thing he said, in the hallway, was: "That was pretty good about the biotech company. I wouldn't have thought about it," letting out something like a jerky hiccup, vaguely resembling a laugh. Then he asked Spade something about the briefcase, if he'd left it prominently on the living room desk, and if he'd remembered to set the timer under the doctor's chair. Spade said, "yeah, yeah."

Conrad climbed into one of the pickups without paying him any attention, the cell phone at his ear. Spade took him by the arm. Stan was coming up behind them, then Czukay, who climbed in the Ram Charger next to Conrad. Stan took his other arm, and the three of them climbed into an Oldsmobile, where Clarke and Woodhill, the Jamaicans, were waiting for them, smoking a musk-scented spliff. Then the Ram Charger left, followed like a shadow by the Chevy pickup.

The Oldsmobile took off in the opposite direction. Shadow, framed by the two Rock-Machines in the back seat, sighed. Spade, on his right, understood. That's when he explained:

"We're sorry, Buddy, it's just business."

It was a few days after the Summer Trope rave and the great sex he had on Sexodyne with the two chicks, that things got complicated.

One night, in one of the bars on Sainte-Catherine where he dealt his delinquent technologies, two big guys had come along. Rock-Machines. The bar belonged to them. Shadow had been paying equitable dues for a long time to all the gangs on whose territory he operated. He'd never had the slightest problem with the Rock-Machines.

He knew one of the guys by sight, the stupidest one, Stan.

"Hey Stan," he went.

It was the other who spoke:

"Conrad wants to see you."

"Who's Conrad?"

Shadow's beautiful smile never left his lips, even when debating with three young university virgins who were calling him queer. The two bikers had nothing in common with bitchy drunken young students, but that didn't make a difference. He had a reputation to uphold; the bar was packed.

"Conrad?" said the tall biker with the pale eyes and the jet-black hair. "Conrad, he's the dude who wants to see you. And he's the dude who's paying me to give you good advice: See him."

Shadow didn't insist. He finished off his Belle Gueule in one gulp and followed them upstairs. There, he was introduced to Conrad.

If Conrad could receive him in the private offices of the Dominion (the new club that the Rock-Machines had started on the corner of Davidson), that meant it was better to stay on his good side, thought Shadow.

They quickly explained what they were expecting.

The usual, he thought at the time. Later, sitting in the back of the Oldsmobile, he bitterly regretted that initial error of appraisal.

"You are in possession, it seems, of something of interest to the Hell's Angels?" Conrad asked, without even turning around.

He spoke a pure form of French, with a vague accent, maybe German. The grammar added an aristocratic note, typically European.

The man was watching Sainte-Catherine Street, full of neon, victims and predators, clients and suppliers, fallen angels and prostitutes on their way there.

Shadow shrugged his shoulders to show he didn't understand.

Conrad turned, coldly looking him up and down.

"Let me explain the situation, Mister Habbas. We know that the Hell's Angels have been busy for a while with a project. Let's say, a big project. We know that recently they've been directly involved in the surveillance of a house, somewhere on the Plateau Mont-Royal. We know they are allied to the Russians, and that a girl named Zorn is the center of all this attention. On the other hand, we know that two girls came to see you last week looking for info about said girl Zorn, during a techno concert. We know you gave them a teradisk containing the Zorn girl's genetic code. And finally, we know that you spoke about this in a bar owned by the competition. We know that they are looking for the girls in question. And we know how to negotiate with you. We know an impressive amount of things, Mister Habbas."

"OK," went Shadow, loosening up. "You know lots of things. My math teacher knew lots of things too. Now he gets a miserable little pension."

"We want to meet the man who provides the biochips. And we want a copy of the biochips."

"How much?"

"How much for what?"

"How much are you offering? For the copy of the chips, no problem. As for meeting my supplier, I'm afraid that's gonna be impossible. You know that's the rule in this business."

Conrad smiled. It was colder than a freezer compartment.

"The other rule would be that we prohibit your entry into all places under our control, from here to Vancouver. Strangely enough, you seem to appreciate our bars and meat-markets quite a lot."

The hardcore French accent protruded beneath the German intonations. Maybe he was Swiss. Or from Alsace, thought Shadow. He didn't really look like a true Rock-Machine, like Spade or Stan. He wasn't from around here; he was from Europe. Something was off.

"On the other hand, you seem to owe a debt of honor to the association. We cleared up that business with the drugs that were past their expiration date. You're alive, but you owe us a favor in return."

Shadow didn't say anything. That whole business was bound to pop up again one day, like the rabbit in the hat. Why not today? Last winter, when the TransVector pills had arrived from Brazil via Costa Rica, they'd undergone a series of chemical changes during their trip, microscopic modifications that escaped detection by the rapid tests dealers use to control the quality of the dope. So a few TransVector dealers, him included, were responsible for a small wave of psychotic trauma among the neo-cortical junkies. The Rock-Machines asked for payback, but the cops themselves soon located the people responsible for the fucked-up manipulations in labs in the Brazilian Amazon. The Rock-Machines were magnanimous. Like Machiavelli, they knew that a man who owes you something is a much more efficient pawn than a dead plough horse on the side of the road.

Till they changed their mind, of course.

Shadow capitulated; he gave them Doctor Newton's alias and address. The next day, Conrad had his little hit squad ready and they dropped by his place first so that he could make copies of the digidisk. Then Conrad asked him to do a transaction from his PC with brand new hacker software.

"Seems you were a brilliant little hacker back in the day. What you'll have to do is very simple, you'll see."

It was, in fact. He had to send cancellation notices to Newton's principal providers, telephone, cable, satellite, electricity. Along with the copy of Marie Zorn's teradisk, it took him more than an hour and a half total. In exchange for which, the guy in the lame-ass suit left him a briefcase with ten thousand dollars.

"In exchange for our collaboration," said Conrad. "You see, we're not dogs."

"What now?" Shadow asked.

"Now, I'm gonna teach you your lesson. The lesson you'll deliver to your supplier when we go see him."

"When?"

"Tonight," went Conrad, cocking his icy smile.

"I have to warn him first."

"Absolutely, that's part of the plan."

Shadow looked intensely at Conrad. He felt a shadow of premonition, he remembered well, rolling through the night on the way to his last voyage.

You never trust your intuitions enough.

He tried getting through to Newton for more than an hour.

"It's ringing, his alarm and surveillance systems are disarmed, but his intranet network is active. He's at home, but he must be getting his anus stuffed by a virtual dildo."

That made Stan and Spade laugh.

Later, Kathy, the redhead from Manitoba, arrived with Czukay. The latter had a long talk with Conrad.

Then Conrad came back towards him while he was still trying to get through to Newton in vain.

"Tell me a little about the two girls."

"The two chicks from Summer Trope? What can I say? A great fuck, in any case."

"Czukay tells me that one of our informers who was there that night says the two girls are associated with a triad. Is that true?"

"A triad? They didn't say anything about that."

"You didn't notice any particular signs?"

He pointed to his shoulder, making a slightly circular motion.

Shadow's face lit up vaguely.

"Oh? Tattoos? *Criss'*, I've seen so many…"

"Dragons? And serpents?"

"Oh yeah, maybe."

"Forming cosmic wheels?"

"Forming what?"

"Cosmic wheels. A shamanistic symbol. A bit like the swastika. You know what the swastika is?"

"That Nazi thing? Yep, I see. Maybe. At the time, my thing wasn't really their tattoos, see? What's that triad?"

Conrad said, "That's exactly it, we don't know," and Newton finally answered his series of calls.

The Rock-Machines took 15 North, towards Sainte-Agathe-des-Monts. At one point, Spade got an encrypted message in the earpiece of his cell-phone.

"Turn on the radio," he told Woodhill, the Jamaican, in front, who'd just lit a long joint of pure weed as he poked around in the tapes to replace Bob Marley.

All that Shadow understood was that a genuine civil war had just pitted some rival gangs against each other on the Plateau Mont-Royal. They'd found the bodies of Hell's Angels, Rock-Machines, Russian-American gangsters, Ontarian thugs, Chinese, Jamaican and Colombian hit men.

The police were at a loss at to how to put all the pieces together, both literally and figuratively.

A fucking mess, according to the radio commentator. They found the shredded bodies of a few individuals, among them a woman, in an apartment on Rivard Street. Grenades had been thrown, a real battleground. Close by, rocket launchers had destroyed two pickups belonging to rival motorcycle gangs, as well as a few big Trans Am or Firebird type sedans, some motorcycles; whole Kalachnikov and machine gun chargers were fired in neighboring streets. A total of three passersby were killed and ten others severely wounded in the shootout. A miracle, in fact, due to the late hour. Nothing like this had ever been seen before. Montreal had never witnessed acts of such deadly violence, a commentator was saying. No, even when the country was close to civil war, at the beginning of the seventies; even during the violent clashes between rival motorcycle gangs during the nineties; even during these last years, no, no one had ever seen anything like it.

You had to go back to the battle of the Plains of Abraham, or to the 1837 revolt.

Eighteen dead and sixteen wounded among the gangsters, two of which were in critical condition. Plus the "civilian" collateral losses. Two policemen in a SPCUM patrol vehicle were said to have been seriously wounded during the shoot-out. A bloodbath.

According to the first SPCUM and Sureté police reports, the epicenter of the clash was that small building on Rivard devastated by grenades. No one knew why an army of criminals had killed themselves over a simple 6 1/2 in the Plateau. The investigation was ongoing. Everyone in the car chimed in with their batch of conjectures and commentaries:

"Shit! What happened on Rivard?… It has to do with the girl. The Angels and the Ruskies strike again. Conrad ain't gonna appreciate. We're gonna have to beat 'em up, *tabarwaoch*', that was close…"

The day was rising above the wooded hills of the Laurentides. The Oldsmobile parked at the end of a gravel road. He walked through the undergrowth, followed by the two bikers. The radio loud speakers switched brutally from the nasal voice of the Radio-Canada commentator to a slow, deep reggae beat.

The pulse of U-Roy kept him company in the morning light of this day that he'd never live, up to a hole dug in the center of a small clearing, waiting for him since the beginning, ready to swallow him with its silent laugh.

29

Later, Toorop would have the hardest time providing a coherent and detailed tale of the night's events. Indeed, he'd find himself unable to distinguish between "reality" and "hallucination," or whatever name it had.

Just out of a three-hour drift with a ghost from the past, he felt like he'd gone through a test in a centrifuge. He was exhausted; he wanted to sleep.

But the anxiety that wouldn't let go of him, about the viruses causing his hallucinogenic experience, was egging on his will and his paranoia. It's what saved his life in the end, probably.

Toorop crossed the street towards number 4067. Everything was calm, but his heart had decided to beat a *Guinness* world record. It pulsed inside him like crazy, in raging dragster turbines. All his senses were on the lookout, like troops entering into war.

He entered the dark foyer as if it were the corridor of a nuclear plant after the disaster. He couldn't get rid of that feeling as he closed the door softly behind him. He moved one or two meters towards the door opening onto the central hallway, and the world took it upon itself to show him his mistake.

Not *after* the disaster.

Just before.

Everything blew up, everywhere.

They started shooting, first inside the house, then outside, in a crescendo of rapid-fire explosions that resembled the burst of civil war, right here, at this minute.

First, there were gunshots inside the house. It was like Grozny in here, thought Toorop as he threw himself on the ground. Then he had to face the facts: the door to the hallway had been shredded by buck-shot fire. He'd survived thanks to his reflex fall. Uzi machine gun pistol bursts followed the muted percussions of the Beretta. He thanked the God of prudent men for having counseled him to take the automatic in his little backpack, upon leaving the apartment, three hours earlier.

He had time to grab the gun and cock it. They were shooting like mad in there; it was crazy.

He had no doubt as to what had happened. Marie's viruses had badly contaminated Rebecca and Dowie, and inflamed their already poor relations to the point that they were quite simply killing each other in the apartment.

It wasn't Waterloo, or Pearl Harbor, Port Arthur, Stalingrad, or another ringing defeat of the history of man: it was the end of the line, as far as he was concerned.

The anxiety became monstrous since he couldn't make a deci-sion. A second round of buckshot had gotten the better of the doorknob; a long burst from the Uzi responded. He heard insults, a battle of words superimposed onto the clash of weapons, strange British slang and a slew of Hebrew swear words. It wasn't a fight about pubic hair in the bathtub, or about "New York Heebs"; if he wanted to get them to calm down, he'd have to kill them. On the other hand, the cops would show up pretty soon; he had to split as fast as possible and call Romanenko for emergency repatriation. But there was the problem of Marie Zorn: where was she, what was she doing, and mostly, what should he *do about her*? …

According to his memory, that was when events had the finesse of choosing for him.

That was when shots started ringing out from everywhere outside, all around the block, in a deafening rhythm of powder and steel.

That was also when someone from inside the apartment, he'd never know who, and it didn't make much difference, someone, any-way, decided to use the 37 mm Arwen grenade launcher.

The first grenade exploded somewhere in the central hallway, close enough for the door protecting him from it to be blown away, as well as the glass pane in the one behind him. He himself, deadened, beaten down by the shock wave, didn't react much.

An Uzi blast replied, and Toorop, eardrums hurting, heard two screams overlap, man-woman in an obscene embrace like a wedding procession taken care of by the blows of an ax. As the explosions grew more intense outside, he started crawling towards the front door, its frosted glass blown away. He glanced out onto the street, and realized it was empty; on the other hand, there were two infantry regiments bombing each other in the blocks around the house, on Saint-Hubert, Saint-Denis, Roy and Rachel, invisible but fucking loud.

In the house, he heard other shots, screams, and then the second grenade exploded.

In Rebecca's room. The shock rattled the whole entrance, adjacent to it. Some shots were fired, screams, a blast, he tried his luck. He bolted like a cosmonaut out of a burning capsule.

Two seconds. Let's say three.

Three little seconds and his destiny would have taken a whole other route, for sure.

The third grenade exploded in the entrance. It had the good taste to be thrown slightly on the diagonal and it blew up against the wall instead of right in the middle of the front door that he'd just pushed open, which it would have reduced to ashes, and him along with it. He was running. The image is forever imprinted upon the photosensitive plate of his memory: he's running, and his body is in full extension, straight north, towards a passage he knows leads to the alley opening onto Duluth, and parallel to Rivard, on the sidewalk of which he's gathering speed.

The explosion hurls him a few meters forward onto the hood of a car, his breath is blown away, the wave of heat engulfs the pain of collision and of the open wounds.

Then, Toorop remembers getting up from the gutter. He is dazed, he isn't doing well at all, his whole body is nothing but a wound, and someone is pouring boiling water on it. He is nauseous; everything is spinning. He staggers a few meters towards the private passage to the alley, collapses, blacks out, and regains consciousness walking in the alley as explosions spread out around him and sirens and the glow of the flashes are surrounding the universe, a circle of police sound and light closing in tight upon the neighborhood, the street, the house, and himself.

He realizes that his clothes are sticking to his skin on his back and legs, where the burning impression is fierce, like a hotplate. Then he notes, a report, almost abstractly, that his weapon isn't in his hand. For the simple reason that the limb in question has practically disappeared.

His right hand is nothing but a stump of burnt flesh, blood spurting out the extremities of his severed knuckles, his third and little fingers reduced to the state of blackened and bloody keloids, the thumb hanging miserably at the end of a dislocated tendon, index and middle fingers puffy and lacerated along their entire length.

He makes an emergency bandage and tourniquet with the shredded sleeves of his jacket, torn off with his teeth. Better not lose the remaining fingers.

Then he somehow finds Dowie's Toyota. He has a double of the keys. It's parked somewhere, a bit off the main arteries where the bulk of the shooting has occurred. He bumps into it as if by miracle, or pure instinct.

He opens the door as an army of SPCUM cars, sirens screeching, race down Mont-Royal, a bit higher up. A fleet of fire trucks and swarms of ambulances charge down towards Cherrier, at his back.

He sits down behind the wheel, gives a sigh of relief as he notices that no cop springs out of the shadows to handcuff him. Then, in shock, wonders how he's gonna drive with only one hand.

The strangest thing is the absence of any specific pain. His hand doesn't hurt, but it can't do much more that push the stick. Maybe this is because pain is flooding his whole body, and mostly his backside that has weathered the thermal wave. His lower back, his shoulder blades, his ass and his legs are burning so bad he could want to sit down on a barrel of flaming gas. With his functional hand he plugs the ignition card into the magnetic Neimann and types his code on the digital mini-keyboard.

Around him, from pretty much everywhere, Toorop can discern a bichrome pulse and distinguish the echo of the sirens growing from the ambient noise. He needs to disappear as fast as possible now, to melt into the night, just like when he took on the Kirghiz Mountains, fleeing the surrounded base.

He starts the car, and stays at a good speed, no excess, anonymous, stay anonymous. He is able to reach Papineau, driving along Lafontaine Park, and goes up towards Saint-Joseph. In his rearview mirror, the red-orange glow of a few fires sways in time with the flashing lights. A good half-dozen patrol cars pass by, screaming.

He continues north, as far away as possible from the epicenter. He doesn't know where to go.

When he gets to Jean-Talon, he has to face reality. The sleeve around his hand is drenched in blood, the tourniquet won't hold much longer. Gangrene is looking him in the face.

He rapidly covers all possibilities. Apart from going to the Sureté, there is just one.

And it lives west of the city.

ShellC was talking to him in jerks. Altaïr was philosophizing. The image was jumpy. The sound wasn't good. The only thing Robicek understood was that the girls were speeding down Saint-Denis, in a roar of explosions; a window was punctured by what could only be a bullet.

Later, talking about it with the girls, not much more information would surface. All that ShellC could ever say about the experience was: "Everything started exploding, everywhere."

"Get back here," he told the girls.

He asked Mr. Storm to lower the radio. He rolled down the thick window of the Chrysler. From where they were, they couldn't see the neighborhood in question directly, but the mixed echo of gunshots and sirens resonated through the night, and the glow of fires radiated behind Mont-Royal.

They looked at each other, Storm and him. Something was happening. Something serious. Very serious.

It was already all over the morning news, special flashes interrupted music shows on the radio. IT WAS WAR. Apparently, someone with a video camera, living on the corner of Saint-Denis and Rachel, was at this precise moment broadcasting live images on the web, even before the first official TV cameras and the one inside the LCN helicopter just arriving on the scene.

Storm and Robicek strained their necks to see two white beams of light fall from the sky onto the area, over there, from two dark masses studded with red diodes. Two Sureté helicopters, along with a smaller, light-colored aircraft.

Robicek touched the digital control panel of the onboard computer.

On Rachel and Saint-Denis, a pickup and a huge sedan were burning right in the middle of the intersection. Two or three motorcycles strewed the sidewalks near shops and bars with their windows blown in. The amateur image kept trembling and continually moved from one view to another, with a cascade of zoom effects.

The television channel showed a bird's eye view of the damage. A few groups of torched vehicles, at the corners of a quadrilateral area whose center was that small, partially inflamed building. Two other destroyed vehicles a little farther off, near the Carré Saint-Louis; dislocated motorcycles and bodies strewed the streets. You could see policemen and the first ambulances arrive on the scene. On the image from the quick intervention LCN video camera, the time appeared under the date. It was four thirty-eight.

Then, with another hand movement, he made Doctor Newton's house appear.

At the same moment, things shifted on the screen. The door of the house opened, the last individual to arrive left first, followed a few seconds later by the guy in the white fur, framed by two big dudes, and the small stocky man, then the woman. They all dispersed into the cars according to a preordained ballet, and an order other than their apparition.

Not one of the vehicles came their way. They seemed to be fleeing the scene, but also fleeing the blazes sparking up in the east of the city.

"What do we do now?" Mr. Storm asked.

"We wait for the girls, they should be here any second."

Storm had programmed the search engine for African-American music from the 50s to the 80s, and it pulled up a Vermont radio playing *Controversy*, by Prince. Just a hair's breadth from the closing date.

"If you add Russian post-Romantic music and Gershwin, I think we can get through the night without killing each other, unlike those people on the Plateau."

"Fine, I'll add Robert Johnson then."

"Mister Storm, not only do you have surefire taste, but you're actually pretty sociable."

They laughed.

There was not much Robicek didn't know about the tumultuous past of the tall Black guy. ShellC had taken it upon herself to describe its basic episodes, details included. They were the same age, but Mr. Storm seemed ten years older. In all, twelve years in prison, not including the "educational" sentences of his youth. A good third of his life. He was born in Toronto, but his parents spent most of their time moving, before splitting up for good when he was seven. His mother was an African-Native American mulatto nightclub dancer, who ended up settling down in Montreal. His father, also a mulatto, left Canada with a girl, a white girl from Vermont who was moving to LA. He never saw him again. Apparently, he'd become a wino in Portland, Oregon. Mr. Storm had been locked up in Minnesota, Ontario and Quebec. Armed robbery, breaking and entering, transgression of computer and network laws. It was a miracle that the EarthQuakers fished him out of it as he was bumming around Montreal. He was now responsible for security of the building with the Cosmic Dragons.

The girls sent a high priority announcement, about the same level as the one before, to show they were arriving on Mont-Royal. An orange band politely signaled emergency access to their local network.

"We're at the bottom of the hill, I'll flash my lights when I pass by," said Altaïr.

ShellC was playing with the data-radio joystick.

"Are you listening to the news, Vax?"

For now, the marble voice of Otis Redding in *Sitting on the Dock of the Bay* enveloped them. Robicek nodded towards the radio.

"I think Mister Storm's gonna take care of it right away."

With regret, he eclipsed Otis' voice well before its own extinction.

"I don't know if breaking into the house is worth it," said Robicek.

"I think it's worth it, everyone else did it," retorted Mr. Storm.

"Yes, but we don't even know what to look for. Even less... the missing ... what to look for," Altaïr remarked in hesitant French...

"I think Mister Storm is right."

That was ShellC as she settled down comfortably into the back-seat of the Chrysler.

Next to her, Altaïr, and in front of her, Vax and Mr. Storm all took the same attitude. Each one leaning against a door, they formed a strange quartet together in a car for some weird conversation, thought Robicek.

"Yes, I'm right."

"It's two against two," Robicek remarked.

Storm broke out into a harsh laugh.

"It's not a question of democracy, it's a question of factual observations and logical deductions."

"Which deductions, which observations?" Robicek and Altaïr blurted out together.

They laughed. Altaïr looked at him with particular intensity. For a quick instant, he wondered if he might have a winning ticket.

"A simple fact, or rather, two. The first is that the little fat guy in the suit had a briefcase when he went in. The second is that he didn't have it when he left. Not him or anyone else."

Robicek looked at the giant. He hadn't noticed that detail. But...

"So what does that prove?"

"It means the first argument is dead. We're not looking for something they stole, but for something they left, in that briefcase."

"And what do you think that would be? What's the use of leaving a briefcase in a house? Just to philosophize a bit, 'cause, may I remind you, the guy who lives there seems very ticklish about his intimacy, his house is a real bunker."

Mr. Storm laughed.

Altaïr added.

"Even Joe-Jane says she'd leave a trace if she wanted to penetrate deep into the operating systems. She could hide it in the depths of the local network, but she'd end up being discovered. It's like archeology."

Storm glared at the little Eurasian, then at Robicek.

"You don't get it at all. His house might be a bunker, but he opened the door to six people he didn't know, except for the fag in the fake fur."

"What! How do you know?" blurted Robicek.

Storm fired his eyes like two arrows into the middle of his.

"'Cause I know. Call it what you want, instinct, experience, gift. I don't give a damn. These people were a strange breed of unexpected guests, let me tell you."

"What do you mean by that?"

"I mean that if Mister's Intranet doesn't respond, it's probably 'cause it was unplugged, physically. And I'd say as much for the Mister in question."

"You... you saying that he's dead, that they killed him?"

"As sure as you're sayin' it to me now, Vax."

Robicek let the silence weigh heavy inside the cab. Then he simply remarked that it was one more reason not to go into that house, dropping dust and different kinds of organic cells around everywhere, that would leave their DNA signature like as many fingerprints.

Storm tried to argue in vain.

"No. We're not moving, at least not for now. We take turns watching the house, that's it. The girls go home to sleep. We stay here till Doctor Newton gives a sign of life. On the other hand, we gotta get informed on what happened to Marie Zorn. The girls'll take care of it when they wake up."

Storm made a disapproving face. ShellC wasn't saying anything, she was pouting in her corner. Probably because Altaïr and he had reached a sincere agreement on a crucial point of the discussion, because a still delicate harmony was finally taking hold between them, after weeks of distancing themselves for completely opposing reasons, and also, thought Robicek, because, yeah, maybe because I've got a winning ticket.

Later, hiding out in the same place with Storm, the girls gone, dawn pointing the tip of her nose, the mulatto dozing to the complex harmonic variations of a Shostakovitch symphony, Robicek told himself that having a winning ticket took on a specific value with girls like Altaïr. For a long time now, and in a city like Montreal—it was probably the same in a majority of metropolises of the Western world—her category of girls had been leading the dance in terms of sexual encounters. In a bar, at a party, they just have to wait, and the list is longer that the line outside a trendy club.

If the girl's on atomic clock time, you'll have five to twenty minutes, depending on the case, to interest her at least once, make her laugh at least once, listen to her at least once without your gaze plunging down into the troubling curves of her dizzying cleavage while knowing how to sound out the depths of her mind, or of her sensibility, and have offered something concrete for her to take a bite of, a boat ride, a ticket to see whatchamacallit and his thingamajigs, a line of pure, uncut cocaine, a party with star DJs and a pool with waves, even a well-furnished library. If your ticket is indeed winning, you'll be allowed to come back once more during the evening, and so on, in a spontaneous Darwinian natural selection that would have Konrad Lorenz emulators shaking.

That night, Robicek felt he'd won the second chance winning ticket.

Truth itself can be revealed as a big lie.

30

As he was approaching Du Parc towards Mont-Royal, Ari materialized for the second time. Toorop almost fainted with surprise and anxiety.

Ari was standing on the corner of Van Horne and Jeanne-Mance.

At this fragile morning hour, still dark, yet when signs, harbingers of the stirrings of day, appear, everything seemed to shiver with a new and dangerous life. Pain? A concept wiped clear from his memory. His body itself was a ghost, at the limits of carnal existence and pure idea.

Ari made a sign, as if he'd been waiting for some meeting that Toorop didn't remember, if even it had ever been arranged.

In a skillful mix of fatalism and lucidity, he understood that Marie's viruses were residual. They'd just entered another active phase, he'd go through a psychotic trip about three hours long and all he had to do was raise his foot to slow down, and stop at the corner of the two streets in order to open the door to the old spy-soldier of the Cold War—who was a sort of guide, a guardian angel. Toorop felt this confusedly.

"Incredible," went Ari, settling down on the seat and stretching out his hand, "just on time. Hi, Toorop."

"Hi, Ari, as you can see I'm still alive but my situation has kinda disintegrated since last time."

He showed his hand, shredded by the explosion, rolled up in cotton from his T-shirt and wrapped in Goretex scraps from his jacket. A monstrous limb, dripping with heavy, vermilion blood, sublime and deliciously bronzed beneath the complacent eye of the sodium streetlight.

Ari pulled back his hand and sat down comfortably, closing the door.

"Don't just stay here, drive."

Toorop, haggard, started the car.

"Where we going?"

"Your first impulse was right. We shall notice, both of us, that your strategic choices are quite limited."

"Thank you for that ray of hope. I was thinking you might be a *deus ex machina*."

"No," muttered Ari in one breath. "I have no power over the course of events, all I can do is give you a few hints from someone who's been there."

Indeed, on that tip, Toorop admitted that he was just in time.

"Go on till Du Parc, move away from the Plateau and get closer to his house. That was the right move."

"And then?"

"Then you stop at the first Bell phone booth you see."

"I wouldn't dare tell you, but, contrary to appearances, I am severely wounded. I'll explain what's up when I get there."

"No," answered Ari with a little smile. "It's not him you have to call first."

Toorop looked at his ghost friend. It took him a little while to understand.

"The colonel can go fuck himself. For now at least. The use of my right hand comes before anything."

"Your right hand is finished. Sacrifice it, a gambit which might just keep you alive."

"Explain yourself, Ari, Fucking H. Christ."

"Call your Russian officer. He is, whether you like it or not, your superior, and he has a global view. Explain the situation roughly, what you're gonna do in the next few hours, where you're going, who you're going to see. If ever something happens, that Russian officer needs to be able to send a lifesaver."

A lifesaver sent from twenty thousand kilometers away, might as well say from another planet. Toorop turned his head to Ari and weaseled a nasty smile full of dry ice. His lips were cracked by an arctic wind come out of nowhere, and his tongue was covered in an acid and tinsel oxide, like coke.

"As if nothing had happened to me! Anyway, Romanenko doesn't have any control over the course of events anymore, and neither do I."

"That's no reason not to take one or two precautions. And five minutes. And a dollar on your telecom card."

"I'm risking my life for barely more than that. Let's say that's about the price of my hand, at the going rate."

"Your hand isn't even worth that much. Stop at that booth right there."

And Toorop stopped.

Later, as they were going down Du Parc, Ari squirmed on the seat.

"The night's events portend ill. Are you a hundred percent sure of that Newton?"

Toorop shrugged. He was starting to feel not so good. He wondered whether he'd stay conscious till they got somewhere. His voice had nothing human in it now as the cracked and swollen lips mumbled with difficulty:

"There's nothing I'm sure of a hundred percent."

They passed Fairmount, then Saint-Joseph. They had to wait for the light on Mont-Royal before turning west.

Toorop was feeling worse and worse. Pain crystallized like quartz shards in certain specific zones of his body, or what was left of it. His left butt cheek, his left shoulder blade, and the nape of his neck were placed against a stovetop on high heat. His right hand was squashed in a vice and mangled by a thousand needle pricks, a thousand hooked points with which another hand, invisible, came to rake, furrow, plow his tortured knuckles.

The world was but a misty veil. Ari himself a diaphanous structure, ghostly, a cloud of ectoplasmic gas slowing dilating in the cab. Buzzing music filled the universe.

He couldn't really tell what happened on the corner of McCulloch. Something like an acid flashback. He thought he saw Marie Zorn naked on the street corner, surrounded by serpents of all sizes, some hugging her body. She was connected to a metallic assemblage of fireworks and spinning fireballs; she looked like one of those living altars to pyrotechnic gods in traditional Chinese celebrations like he'd seen once in Taiwan.

He almost stopped, but the translucent helium balloon that Ari had become convinced him not to.

"Your brain is producing unknown molecules; now it's trying to paste all the pieces together, to return some semantic coherence to all this. She's a *real* hallucination, she is."

Almost fainting, Toorop turned onto Spring Grove; he didn't know how, but he still had the strength to reply.

"Which you aren't, apparently."

An uncertain sonogram of internal organs showed through the helium balloon.

"I am what I am. Meaning both much more, and much less…"

Almost unconscious, he parked a few meters from the gate. The whole universe had disappeared, swallowed by a pot of darkness, fluid and shifting like an equinox tide. Ari, helium phantom with translucent organs now scattered in the car like residue from a meal in zero gravity, was talking to him in tens of languages at once, humming and incomprehensible gibberish. He desperately clung to the few details his consciousness was able to register, the stone wall, the wrought iron gate, the little paved alley like a bridge thrown over the shimmering waters of a great lake under the moon, the house in the distance, distorted by a wide-angle perspective.

He managed to open the car door. He managed to step foot onto the pavement. Then once again. He managed to transfer his carcass out of the cab.

He managed to straighten up.

And everything started whirling violently, including and especially, inside himself. He tried to move forward and only gyrated stupidly like a top set in motion by some invisible hand towards the gate, that he fell onto, without managing to open, without managing anything else. He was conscious only of two things, practically at the same time:

He was vomiting on himself.

And something had just exploded in the house.

Then the invisible hand, out of compassion, decided to unplug his consciousness.

It all accelerated as dawn rose. Robicek woke Mr. Storm and gave him a few hits of speed. A red Toyota, shaky and uncertain, plodded by. It slowed down and stopped a second at the corner of McCulloch before turning onto it.

Storm revved up the motor immediately.

ShellC and Altaïr had spotted the red Toyota and its license plate number. It was rented monthly at Via Route, along with a Voyager van, by Thorpe and his gang.

"Follow him at a distance. We know where he's going."

"No worries. I'm gonna let him spread his wings."

They followed the car till Maplewood, turned onto it as well. On screen, the Toyota gleamed feebly as it parked almost exactly where one of the pickups had been, near the street light on the corner.

The fiber optic wire transmitted a static shot of the house, with the car just in front and a man falling onto the steering wheel, apparently talking to himself.

As he glimpsed the angle of the street and the house, way over there in the background of the cathodic image, the situation changed and registered in his memory according to a double point of view: through the screen of the rearview mirror, a long forward traveling shot, and the static shot of the spy camera facing the house. The man at the wheel managed to extricate himself from the car, but he staggered like a puppet whose strings have just been cut and is thrown before a pack of dogs. He fell prostrate against the house gate.

They saw themselves, he and Storm, arrive on the screen. The image showed them parking just behind the Toyota. Then it showed them coming out of the Chrysler and rushing towards the man, more or less hidden by the two vehicles. We see them search the silhouette rapidly, exchange a few words, then take the decision to grab it by the arms and feet, and throw it without much care onto the back seat of the luxurious car.

At the same time, the glare of flames appears behind the house windows.

Joe-Jane followed the disaster live with all her available organs, and with all those she made available within the second. She saw through the micro-camera grafted onto Altaïr's optic nerve, and like her, therefore, saw, through the windshield of their small car: some individuals driving a pickup, three armed men spring up from its bed, blast the passengers of a black Trans Am with an assault rifle before being attacked in turn by another pick-up that shot out an arrow of orange powder striking the enemy vehicle and destroying it in a blinding flash, saturating the silicon fiber before a storm of flame and black smoke invaded everything. Altaïr rammed through it like a pilot doing a kamikaze dive.

Later, Joe-Jane followed the ultimate convulsions of the war that the humans in that little Montreal neighborhood were waging. First through a cyber-citizen filming the events on his digital camera from his window. Then through the camera of a small news helicopter, with the urban security network through traffic lights, through the eye of research scanners of the Sureté, and even through certain military observation satellites passing the area at that moment.

Still later, what was happening in the image sent by the spy probe placed in front of the so-called Doctor Newton's house grabbed her attention.

Then, at the end of that exhausting night, like everyone else, she plugged into information channels, legit or not. They'd already stopped covering anything else, draining the subject even before its constitution, like always.

She was waiting for Vax, Mr. Storm and the man they'd caught with a form of anxiety particular to her. The anxiety of a star before the atoms it unendingly produces, which will in turn produce the cataclysm of life.

She woke up the two girls when she saw Robicek's bronze car charge down Clark, after having followed it on the city's optic surveillance network. Altaïr and ShellC had slept barely sixty minutes. They were a sorry sight. Joe-Jane advised the domotic system to get on with breakfast. A few kitchen appliances started up.

Through the cameras of the building's small private security system, she saw the sun rise over the city.

A splendid day was beginning.

31

After a while, the sky opened up. The highway split then branched out into a concrete network of infinite dimensions. Each ramification led to a star in the sky. The Black Angel appeared on the passenger seat. It wasn't Eagle Davis anymore. Not really. His face changed to the rhythm of the taut flow of personalities moving within him. His voice espoused the contours of a filter in continual metamorphosis. It was the image of herself; not only inverted, but turned entirely inside out like a glove.

"The roads of the future are opening before you. You must know what the other alternative leads to."

In front of her, a Petro-Canada station appeared in the night. The neon of the sign and the white lighting above the gas pumps spread the cold monochrome of operating room lights. In the place of the company logo shone the star shape.

The Angel watched the station pass by in the night like an electric dream. Then he said:

"This is the right road. Ain't no doubt about it."

And he started crooning *That's Alright Mama*. With the discontinuous changes in his vocal chords, it was horrifying.

She drove till the Ontario border. The Angel went through a good part of the King's repertoire before answering her silent question.

"Time, space, matter, light; the cosmic-brain can remodel everything. Here's your future, actualized, if you hadn't left the apartment."

They passed Lake Abitibi and reached the riverbed. Then veered towards the bay, and crossed the Abitibi River to Molsonee.

There, a bit farther north, they moved off the main road. They took a side road leading to the banks of the huge water reservoir formed by the James Bay, then a dirt road along a pebble beach.

The house was a sepulchral white. It rose in the pale light of dawn at the foot of a wooded hill. A pier, a concrete ramp, no boats.

The polymorphous angel smiled.

"Your destiny would have been sealed here."

He watched the waters of the lake, stretching out past the end of vision like a sea.

She understood.

Sealed like a cement filled crate, thrown overboard, far out on the waters.

The angel asked her to park in front of the house. It was empty. Day had just broken. Purple and violet serpentine shapes danced in the sky above the waters.

"In order for you to perfectly memorize this experience, and have no regrets about your escape, I'm allowed to let you live this virtual fork from the inside, as an 'alternative reality'."

He turned towards her as they were climbing the steps of the colonnade porch.

He smiled, and then disappeared.

Simultaneously, Thorpe, Rebecca and Dowie appeared, in the orange light of a fading afternoon. The Chrysler and the Toyota were parked at the foot of the stairs. They were all carrying bags and suitcases.

Thorpe found the key under the doormat.

Turning towards her as he opened the door:

"Your new residence, Princess," he said.

And she entered the house of her death.

The first few days nothing happened. One night, Thorpe got a call on his telecom console.

Real quick, not even a minute, then he came to see her as she was reading a book she'd found in a bookshelf of the living room, an old copy of *Alice in Wonderland* in English.

He stood still before her.

She pretended not to see him.

"Marie?" he asked.

"Yes?" she answered, raising her eyes with a naive look, feigning surprise.

"Marie, someone's coming to visit us tomorrow morning. Someone who has to 'check you over,' from what I gather."

She didn't answer.

Later, terrified, curled up in bed, she didn't fall asleep till the first glimmers of dawn.

Thorpe woke her up. She felt like she'd only slept a minute. She got up grumbling, out of it. Dowie and Rebecca were making coffee in the kitchen.

"Doctor Kassapian is coming in fifteen minutes. Take a shower and don't eat anything."

Thorpe stared at her, unrelenting. The smell of toast, tea and coffee filled the house. She took a shower and watched Rebecca down her breakfast with envy. Then the doctor arrived.

She hated the man right away.

She quickly understood that it was mutual.

The man took her up into one of the rooms. Inside, he and his two acolytes had stacked up metal-rimmed crates. Kassapian showed her a door.

"There's a small bathroom. Get undressed."

She went into the old fashioned washroom and took off her clothes. She folded them onto the side of the old, chipped bathtub, and looked at herself in the mirror a few instants.

When she came out, hands and arms pathetic protection against her chest and crotch, the doctor and his two assistants were unpacking their equipment from the crates as Thorpe, Rebecca and Dowie brought up more.

"Put that there," went Kassapian, showing a rug in the center of the room.

Then he pointed Marie to the big bed.

"Lie down on that, we won't be long."

Kassapian asked Thorpe and his team to leave. Then, with the help of his two sizable assistants, he rapidly set up his slew of machines, black or metallic racks, diodes and small video screens. The man Kassapian called Lev unfolded a large ceiling lamp with four variable intensity halogen bulbs, while the other one, Axel, plugged everything into a large parallel-processing NEC console. Kassapian gave them cursory orders in English. The men didn't say a thing.

Kassapian placed a large black briefcase at the foot of the bed and opened it. He started carefully pulling out a whole lot of strange shaped, vaguely menacing instruments.

He showed her a kind of translucent green gum, the size of an M&M, at the end of which sparkled a string thinner than a strand of hair. It appeared only at the whim of subtle quivers in the morning light.

A fiber optic probe.

That she swallowed.

As soon as she'd done that, the image of her esophagus appeared on a video monitor. Then her stomach. It made her laugh. Doctor Kassapian glared at her.

Axel adjusted the image as Kassapian came nearer. He put a strange apparatus on her head, a kind of heavy tubular crown connected to one of the racks by a bunch of fiber optics, and to a small bottle of liquid helium by a system of pumps.

Strange, colored moving images appeared on a trio of screens lined up above the rack.

Then Kassapian pulled out a gray-colored tube from his briefcase. It was connected by a thick chunky cable to a black composite structure that looked like a spider web. A translucent jack connected this in turn to a green-colored rack that he skillfully manipulated. He was standing next to her thighs. Marie had both hands crossed over her pubic area, although she knew quite well what was coming her way.

He looked into her eyes with a cold stare, opening up a wide smile.

"Why don't you make it easy for me, Marie," he said in French. "It'll be better for all of us."

She let him insert the gray tube into her vagina, then arrange the composite network around it.

Images and series of code appeared on his screen.

Fascinated, she couldn't tear her eyes away from the cathode-blue, slowly moving image.

Much better than a plain sonogram.

She saw the life she carried, like a bubbly-shaped double serpent, emitting light rays bordering on violet.

Kassapian typed something on his keyboard, and turned to one of his men.

"Lev, can you please verify the settings on the ultraviolet bio-photon sensors."

The man complied.

"They're in phase, Doctor."

The doctor typed frantically on his keyboard. A long sequence of coded messages appeared that she didn't understand at all.

He adjusted parameters on all the racks, observed the images coming from her cervical belt, quickly gave up on those from her pubic region, and stopped at length on the placental sac.

Finally, the man sank into his small rotating armchair and let out a kind of moan.

"In God's name," he blurted out in French. "In fucking God's name!"

Then everything sped up. The man feverishly took a series of blood and fluid samples and arranged each one in a different tube. He locked them all delicately in a small, refrigerated briefcase.

Then he dropped out on everyone and went downstairs.

Marie could hear the discussion through the half open door. It quickly went up a notch, in French.

"I won't let you do that, not without formal consent from my supervisors!" Thorpe blasted out.

"First of all, you're going to do it, and second, I am your supervisor. I have orders, and the authority, to cancel this operation in case of *force majeure*. And that's precisely the case!" answered Kassapian.

"What do you mean? Why?" Thorpe retorted, close to screaming.

"I cannot inform you of that. All I can say is that the merchandise has become... how shall I put it... unfit for consumption, if you wish. It has sustained severe deterioration. If you must know, it's an aberration, and it puts the girl's health at risk."

"That's no reason to want to... cancel her."

Lying naked on the bed, frozen with fear, she watched the two assistants posted in front of their instruments. Visibly, they didn't understand anything that was happening at the bottom of the stairs.

"Well yes, precisely, it is a reason. Actually, THE reason. Our client wants everything cancelled if there is the slightest hitch. Well, believe me, this isn't a hitch; it's a bitch of a knot. I'm canceling everything, Mr. Thorpe."

She let out a little cry.

The two men looked at her, vaguely intrigued.

At that point, the angel appeared, sitting on the bed next to the briefcase with the instruments.

"At this point in the ramification, your life is hanging on a thread, meaning on an improbable chain of events, whose existence relies only on the extremely random event preceding it. First sequence: Doctor Kassapian in fact entrusts the mission to cancel you to Thorpe and his team. Second sequence: Thorpe, because of some unknown feeling of compassion, or for some other reason, decides to liberate you and make them believe you are dead. Third sequence: the people who ordered you to be cancelled and who employ Kassapian don't hear of it and never find you again." (The Angel detailed with an indifferent stare the pile of machines and instruments that covered her body.) "Useless to say, the probability of that ramification taking place is infinitesimal."

At that moment, the doctor barged into the room. He rapidly prepared an injection. He sucked up a milky colored substance from a little capsule with a syringe.

"What are you doing, Doctor?" she asked in a little girl voice.
The doctor did not answer.
She was tense.
"Doctor?"
"Don't worry," Kassapian said, "you won't feel a thing."
The angel acquiesced with a nod of the head. The syringe shot into her vein.
The angel smiled, in the already failing light.
"He's right, Marie, you won't feel a thing."
Then she died.

Strangely enough, she retained some objective knowledge, a residual memory of the event.

She'd had a very strong NDE. She'd left her body, of course, and had observed the scene from a corner of the ceiling, as is customary.

After a few seconds, a small black rack emitted an accelerated beep, then a continuous signal. A flat line crossed the screen like some strange, abraded video writing reduced to its most elemental state.

Kassapian cleared all the instruments from her body.

"Save all the information on an encrypted teradisk," he ordered one of his assistants.

Then he went downstairs to fetch Thorpe.

"I was told there are large PVC garbage bags and cinder blocks in the cellar. Put her inside two or three bags, take a few cinder blocks, put all that in some more bags, take the Zodiac in the garage and throw her overboard, twenty miles out."

Thorpe told him to fuck off.

"I wasn't paid to do your dirty work, Doctor Kassapian. You decided to kill her; it's your responsibility. You can take your Zodiac out yourself. And your cinder blocks, I'd rather not tell you what to do with them. Same thing with the garbage bags, although, if you put everything together, 'could be pretty fun."

She didn't get it all. Her RAM was starting to disintegrate. But she remembered seeing the doctor and his assistants haul an oblong shape, draped in some shiny black material, into a dinghy.

Then her consciousness evaporated over the waters in which her body sank heavily.

She regained consciousness in front of the pump at an Irving Station. She was on 40 West, about fifty kilometers from Montreal. The sun was setting. She didn't know which day it was, or how much time had elapsed since her flight from Rivard Street.

Her memory of the whole "virtual" experience was intact; its hazy fog covered what she experienced as reality.

"A full tank, Miss?"

Marie turned her head slightly towards the young guy in the orange coveralls who was waving the aluminum nozzle in her direction.

Her tongue was cottony and her throat dry. She swallowed, and without even looking at him:

"Yes, of course."

She almost ran to get a cold Coke at the machine.

Then started driving again, drifted onto a forest road. She parked the Voyager, lay down on the back seat, huddled beneath a comforter she had in her bag.

And fell asleep like a log.

When she woke up, dawn was breaking, and the angel was next to her.

It was a young woman, her skin even whiter than the masculine shaped being. She could see all her interior machinery in veins of dark blue and crystalline mercury. She wore a black leather coat, sported dirty blond hair under a black beret where the fluorescent green emblem of the double serpent intertwined, glimmering like luminous, live embroidery. She was astonishingly beautiful, and dangerous, a cross between Kim Novak and Modesty Blaise.

"A new mutation is starting. I'm a new shape."

"Yes, of course."

"Marie, you're absolutely not safe here."

Marie looked at her despairingly.

"I… I know… What should I do?"

"This car is hot. Men are crisscrossing the country looking for it. You have to leave it immediately."

Marie stayed frozen a long time, paralyzed by panic.

The female angel eyed her sternly.

"Marie, get with it. You have to flee. Take what you need and flee."

"Where? In which direction? How?" she screamed, almost hysterical.

The archangel in black leather sighed.

"We'll take care of that when the time comes. You have to get out of here. And leave the vehicle. The sun isn't up yet. Your window of opportunity is very short."

Marie watched the female angel, and the night dissipating above the hills. It was true. In less than half an hour it would be day.

All Quebec must be swarming with men on her trail. Marie glanced at her open bag, and threw herself brutally from under the comforter. She folded it with a steady hand, surprised by her control and her newfound pugnacity. No, she wouldn't let them slit her throat like a sheep led to the slaughterhouse.

She'd fight to survive. Something inside her was already affirming its peremptory right to existence. She abandoned the car and took the straight road ahead.

As she was walking, she realized she didn't know anyone in Quebec. She spent her existence a stranger. To herself, and in the eyes of others, which was probably the same thing.

Her last real local friendships went back to when she was twelve, when her continual verbal ravings in school got her noticed by her professors and the social worker who informed her parents. Her preprogrammed life as a schizoid vegetable was perturbed only when Doctor Mandelcorn's team decided to make her case a pillar of their new scientific adventure. Condemned to spend her life on neuroleptics, fate had set agents of liberation on her path.

No, not "liberation," the internal message system of the schizoprocessor gushed out. Darquandier and Winkler always used that word with austere, practically Calvinist parsimony. And they did not hide their common wariness towards a term that too often upheld the worst abjections. "We don't claim to make you 'normal;' we're not trying to heal you from some supposed illness. We're not in charge of making you freer than we are, or will ever be. All we want is to turn you into what you are, to paraphrase one of our favorite authors."

But, in becoming what she was, Marie, just like the scientists in the lab, had the tendency to forget somewhat the specific contingencies of the history of men. Nothing real predictable. Accidents. Secret processes of production where desire fights it out with fate.

Everything went wrong when Winkler and Darquandier had to stop their activities in Thailand, almost four years to the day from their first forced exile. They held up a few weeks, and then yielded under pressure. They had to dismantle their laboratories, including the one making the transgenic hallucinogen molecules they'd invented, copying certain genetic specificities of patients like Marie.

She was still fragile. Her use of the neurolinguistic schizo-processor to check her continuous verbal flow with narrative techniques and the use of writing was still recent. She was able to stay in control thanks to a special drug made by the lab. A special derivative of molecules created while studying her brain. Their effects were so to speak inverted, as they allowed her psyche, fragmented into distinct personalities, to recover the scattered pieces and assemble them into a somewhat coherent machinery. Winkler and Darquandier insisted on the transfinite character of the thing:

"Use all the resources of your imagination; your mental universes are both source and destination. You yourself are but a stage. There's no pre-written end in the biological evolutionary project, which is not to say that it doesn't produce sense, on the contrary."

The last month was very difficult, on Koh Tao. The lab team was forced to improvise. The chain of production of transgenic drugs was shut down before they were able to constitute sufficient stock.

When she left the island, a day before Doctors Winkler and Darquandier, she was already suffering from withdrawal.

Once in Bangkok, she didn't feel so great in the airport full of policemen and uniformed military personnel.

Then, passing through the Philippines, things started cracking up. Administrative complications were holding up the arrival of a certain number of patients. Marie wound up stuck in Manila with the nurse accompanying her. A terrible panic attack hit in the middle of a psychotic episode of sleepwalking in the Philippine capital, kilometers away from her hotel. She was amnesiac for the next few days. She remembered waking up a few times in the pit of an abandoned building site, near a sewer; its nauseating and comforting smell reminded her of earth, of the biological and playful shit of childhood.

Later on, she fell under the sway of a gang of hard-core ado-lescents. First they raped her, then put her to work: they'd rent her out for two or three minutes to other teenage gangs hanging out in the vicinity. She did this in a state of mechanical unconscious-ness, in exchange for daily rations of their bad sulfur colored dope and antiviral condoms. According to her later estimate, it lasted about three months. Then she met that Russian sailor, at the port. What was his name again? Andreï wasn't it? The guy had been trained at the Vladivostok War Marines school of hard knocks, from what he said. He was second officer on a Russian cargo ship that regularly freighted around there. He took her under his wing, hid her aboard the ship. Then, he brought her to Japan, first of all, where they spent a kind of short lived honeymoon, and then to the coast of Eastern Siberia, to Nikolaievsk-on-Amur, a bad choice in the end, and ill-named.

When Andreï split a few days before returning to Indonesia and the Philippines, she found herself alone in a world she did not know, the rigors of the Siberian winter already icing the landscape.

She had very little money. She was thousands of kilometers away from an island lost in the Pacific that, apparently, wasn't even the final destination. According to Darquandier's mysterious remarks, they were headed to "a perfectly autonomous ecosystemic plat-form that's perfectly adapted to us. The island of Pikaatu is just its logistic support." She was never able to learn more. The new Micronesian Republic of Pikaatu was a minuscule dot on a high-res-olution map. All she knew was that it had served as a landing field for American forces during the Second World War. Darquandier had shown her pictures of different views of a small, oblong island dominated on one end by a volcanic peak, surrounded by a corral ring typical of the shallows of the Pacific, and whose western and eastern beaches had been reconfigured into military landing strips by US Navy "SeaBees" in 1944. There was a small fishing village gathered around an inlet not far from the volcanic peak.

According to rumors haunting the hallways of the center just prior to the move, the autonomous platform was, apparently, a nearby micro-island. Others claimed to have seen shots of an oceanography research ship, others a drilling platform, still others affirmed it was something different and altogether new. She'd never known.

Stuck in Nikolaievsk-on-Amur, with barely enough for a week in a scummy room, she took a decision that would disrupt the already fairly chaotic course of her existence. Some friends of Andreï offered her a small, well-paying job carrying a good amount of powdered meta-amphetamines inside condoms sealed with composite glue. In exchange, they slipped her a handful of TransVector pills. She took the Trans-Siberian to Novosibirsk one icy December morning, and unloaded the dope to a so-called Boris. But withdrawal rapidly set in. On New Year's Day 2013, she went to see Boris who lived in his Volkswagen van, in a desolate suburb of the big metropolis. Boris and his strange friends. Once again, she fell under the sway of a little gang of thugs who passed her around to each other at night, before forking her over to another gang where she soon met that old woman who was to introduce her to the one they called Gorsky.

Gorsky who offered her no less than fifty thousand dollars, payable in two installments, to carry out a small "humanitarian" mission in a country she knew well, her own. She accepted without giving it a second thought.

The image of the fat Siberian forced itself upon her memory, just as it had appeared to her the very first time.

A bear. That was his *anima*, what he was, deep within. It was almost reassuring.

A mafia outfit like Gorsky's, or the local branches he did business with, were probably capable of mobilizing tens, hundreds, maybe thousands of absolutely discrete eyes and ears. It could be anyone on the bus, in the towing company, in front of a chips place, on a street corner in any city in Quebec. An old guy in a battered raincoat or a young XXIst century style yuppie. An Anglo lady with austere body language or a falsely innocent-looking young chick. It could be the hamburger salesman, a cyberpunk teenager, a Thai or Jewish tailor on Saint-Laurent, and even the cop stationed at the corner of Prince-Arthur. Anyone.

Her cheek was resting against a cool, wet surface that smelled of fresh cut hay. She stood up in the air laden with morning dew. She'd lost time. A flow of memories had her prostrate on the side of the path, with no consciousness of anything around her: a fetal, primitive crisis.

The sun was already a powdery yellow. A few clouds were amassing in the east, beyond the river.

Quebec, she thought, taking in the whole view. The exact opposite of where I should be right now.

Then she walked towards the closest city. She was able to take out a few thousand dollars cash from Marie Zorn's account, which she stashed in the belt of her 2001 thermo-isolating jeans. She got herself a nice, mercury-gray Mazda for a month, on her Visa card. She'd go all the way to Gaspesia. Under the perfectly clean identity of Marion Roussel, she'd get on a cargo to anywhere, or to South America if possible. Panama, the canal, and from there, the Pacific, then Micronesia, the fastest she could, by all possible and imaginable means. All means.

The onboard weather forecast announced high intensity solar rays till the middle of the afternoon. She programmed the windshield to maximum anti-UV mode. The glass took on a translucent smoky-gray color, practically opaque from the outside.

She felt secure, like in her childhood dreams when she'd invent fetal machines to protect her from the mechanical menace of a cold and incomprehensible world. Vague memories of joy dating back to her early childhood jumped like an old film reel on the screen of her memory.

She drove at the speed limit without pausing, till the end of day.

She stopped at a motel on the side of the road.

Part **4**

Homo Sapiens Neuromatrix

The theory of natural selection is not a scientific theory that can be put to the test, but rather a metaphysical research program.

— KARL POPPER

32

The news spread like wildfire to all levels of the organization. The Gorsky house was burning. The Siberian's face was whiter than torture chamber walls at the time of the Lubyanka, thought Romanenko. The man, in a few vivid words, sketched a concise picture of the situation.

Pearl Harbor, no less.

As for Romanenko, he saw in the Montreal butchery an unexpected incident that would calm the secessionist fervor of the Siberian for a while. Something really fucked-up, repeated Gorsky. Romanenko sluggishly agreed. A euphemism at best.

The toll was heavy. Official Canadian radio wouldn't reveal any identities. They spoke of bikers, sold to Chinese gangsters, who had supposedly torn to pieces an enemy group made up for the most part of Russian Mafiosi and Hell's Angels. On a well-informed Internet site he knew, Romanenko figured out that the Quebec Sureté had some other leads. They mentioned a war between sects, pitting the Cosmic Church of the New Resurrection and other competing religions. A fucking fiasco.

Some anonymous writer on the site who signed as "Vamp-911" and probably had a direct connection with the Quebec Sureté, affirmed that one of the men gunned down on Rivard was an ancient Canadian Army parachuter discharged for war crimes in the nineties. He'd worked as a guard for the last fifteen years from one end of the American continent to the other: New York, Chicago, Calgary, Denver, and Montreal for the last two or three years. He'd just been fired from a security company on René-Lévesque, about six months before. There were no known ties linking him to biker gangs or to triads. But he was carrying a good amount of smokable heroine, like lots of other bikers they found there.

From what Romanenko was able to put together during the evening and the long all-nighter that followed, the Quebec Police discovered a real bloodbath. Toorop's apartment was attacked with grenades. Cars had been destroyed by rockets, even by napalm, a flabbergasted cop explained on CBC, showing the remnants of a charred tree and the blackened ruin of a motorcycle on a sidewalk.

Two men, Ontarian thugs, were executed almost simultaneously, a few bullets in the head, a bit farther south, on Cherrier.

For Gorsky, just like for Romanenko, it was a terrifying enigma. Who could have done such a thing? Who had the balls to take on the Russian mafia like that, without the slightest warning? Who could have attacked the apartment, and most importantly, for what?

The answer lit up by itself in his saturated skull: easy, they, *whoever they were*, also wanted Marie Zorn.

The next day, local channels were raging a merciless war of images. Thirty-six hours after the Plateau Mont-Royal carnage, tons of info already saturated the television networks. Ten thousand versions. All of them certified with the label of The Real Truth.

The toll was even heavier. A member of the Rock-Machines developed a cardiac complication during his neuro-surgical procedure and died. A Chinese man belonging to a Canadian triad linked to the San Francisco On-Leong tong had, apparently, fallen into an irreversible coma. The health of a Hell's Angel had rapidly deteriorated and he was now in critical condition. Someone passing by had been severely hit. They feared for his life. Another had already been diagnosed as hemiplegic. Another had to have his arm amputated.

On RDI, a criminal affairs specialist affirmed that the whole thing was probably much simpler than what they said about it. The Hell's Angels and the Rock-Machines killed each other off for drugs, or for some other outlawed substance. The presence of elements from different criminal circles, even from sects, should come as no surprise except to the naive, as it was common knowledge that all mafias cooperated more or less from one end of the planet to the other.

On Anglophone CBC, a debate pitted a small band of specialists against the public, to the great joy of the host of a famous talk show. A woman with a bun was explaining that anti-gang laws weren't strict enough, and that since they knew the names of the biker gangs involved, why not lock up the ones who were responsible and yakkety-yak. Romanenko zapped.

On the Russian-language network, there was concern about community repercussions that would inevitably follow from the Russian-American mafia involvement in the massacre. Certain criminals implicated in the bloodbath apparently had ties to a local branch of the Little Odessa mafia headed by Vitali Kotcheff.

On another Canadian channel, a high-ranking officer of the Noelite Church kept a straight face as he affirmed that the implication of one member of the Church did not mean the religious movement itself was involved. Among the fifty thousand members of the organization, one sheep might be lead astray, and fall into the abyss of crime.

Romanenko held back a despairing laugh.

What a fuck-up.

When she woke up that morning it was splendid out.

She got up, her mind as clear, crisp, luminous as that blue sky and the waters of the Saint-Laurent she glimpsed, over there, just beyond the windowpane.

Marie opened the window, and the fresh air came to graze her cheek.

The sun had just risen; the light was a pale, fragile yellow.

She sat down on the bed and watched the show of the river. Here in Tadoussac, the Saint-Laurent joined up with the waters from the Saguenay. The rival waters blended, or, rather, *did not blend*, split into opposing strata of different viscosity and distinctive color. The competing chemistry of the fresh, glacial waters of the Saguenay, coming straight from Lake Saint-Jean, and of the waters of the Saint-Laurent, largely denatured by high salinity sea water, created marine fantasies furrowed by seals and rorquals.

The width of the river stretched out more than twenty kilometers here. She knew that a bit farther north, on the other bank, stood the city of Rimouski where she was born and had lived the first three years of her life.

The terrorist-angel had strongly advised against going there. The twin center affirmed that her birthplace was under high surveillance.

Rather, the angel advised her to follow the path of the Messenger-Falcon of Huron mythology. Her memories were hazy, but Marie remembered having come to Tadoussac once or twice in her childhood. There was a small museum store selling handmade objects and documentation on the Indian Nations of the region. Principally Montagnais and Huron.

She remembered a recurrent dream she'd had for the last few days: A blue dream of saline water, with whales, dolphins and a strange marine falcon. The dream seemed to be saying, "stay close to the river," although she could not understand the reason behind it.

The terrorist-angel advised her to follow the path of the falcon, and to penetrate into autonomous Indian territory as soon as possible. The girl with the black beret reminded her that autonomous territories were under federal Canadian jurisdiction; the Sureté had no authority there without a written dispensation from an Ottawa judge.

Marie tried to attune both voices. She resigned herself not to cross the river till Rimouski, and followed its northern bank up to Tadoussac. She rented a room at the Seagull Pension, and in a book she'd bought at the museum store, looked up what Huron reservations were around.

There were several autonomous territories in the region, but she didn't really feel any of them. She didn't know anyone and had never set foot there.

The outlook was grim. At the end of the afternoon, she found refuge in another little motel stranded on the roadside.

The Elvis Presley angel was waiting for her under the purple neon: FALCON MOTEL, she read. Then, even before parking the car, she saw the angel disintegrate slowly as he waved a sort of goodbye. The FM radio purred the chorus of "Love Me Tender" from behind the crackling of static.

It was clear that her fate awaited her here, in this small electric oasis lost in the pure geology of nature.

33

Reno Vilas watched coldly as the woman took off her ritual getup.

She'd just came from a meeting of her fucking sect, and she was pissed.

"What happened on Rivard? We must, *I* must, absolutely know."

She was holding back with the utmost difficulty; she hadn't slept for seventy-two hours since her emergency return from Frisco and was running on hardcore speed. She was a virtual H-bomb, all you had to do was touch her.

"Ma'am, rest assured, all our men are on it. It's those assho… the Rock-Machines and your competition of course. But I have to tell you there are some shady parts in all this shi… in this chaos."

Reno tried to police-polish his language, but the brutal pressure of events got the better of his vigilance. Correct English, or French, was the basic rule of any conversation with Ariane Clayton-Rochette. *Criss'*, *Tabarnak*, *Gang of Twits*, *Gnochons*, *Morons*, and other Quebecker linguistic particularities had no place in her presence. Neither did the insults typical of the languages of Shakespeare or Voltaire.

Reno Vilas knew that it was his relatively good education, a year at the UQAM, that had predestined him to this mission, assigned by the big Montreal bosses, with a large compensation to boot.

To be a Hell's Angel required a certain number of natural resources. One of them was to be six foot six. Another was to love mythical American bikes, and a more important one still was to accept the iron rules of what resembled a Commandery of Templiers.

You had to love, know how to fight, take risks and protect the chapter you belonged to. It was simple, direct, and stable, like a good ship made for the open sea.

All that Reno knew about Miss Clayton-Rochette had been explained to him by the Montreal bosses, and then completed by his own observation.

Clayton-Rochette had gotten an illegal biological strain made and repatriated to Quebec. The Ruskies had taken care of the first level of protection, but now people were needed here in order to guarantee the security of the project. She paid cash in good NorthAm dollars, and forked over truckloads of it. But at the time, someone, they didn't know who, had just shot down one of her planes with a Stinger missile. The Hell's Angels had been asked to recruit bodyguards and anti-assault specialists. It so happened that Reno had done a little stint in the Canadian Army just after his fucked-up year as an undergrad. He'd drifted around South America, worked for a private dick firm in Buenos Aires, bummed around in Rio and then gone to Europe for five years where he stumbled upon some Canadian and Belgian Angels who had initiated and introduced him into the organization. His right arm man was a so-called Gould, an ancient paratrooper from Alberta, who'd just joined the club and had been employed for a while as security personnel and bodyguard.

That right arm, like Cross, had been lost in the battle, as well as the left arm, both legs, or close, and almost all principal organs.

He'd learned recently that the Rock-Machines were collaborating with the security services of the Logology Temple, just like the Hell's Angels were doing with Clayton-Rochette and the Noelites. In fact, their decision to destroy or take possession of the precious cargo was logical.

But what had happened three days before on the Plateau Mont-Royal for the most part resisted logic. He didn't really know how to go about explaining this to the woman in the white silk toga.

"Ma'am Clayton-Rochette, something really… strange… happened."

"Could you please explain yourself, Reno."

"Well. The only direct eyewitness accounts that I have are from the four or five from my group who survived, and who were able to get back to us without falling into the cops' hands. I was told the Russians only have one survivor. I mean only one guy who wasn't picked up by ambulances or cops. I don't know what's up with our enemy, but it must be the same for them."

The thirty-year-old made a violent gesture with her hand. Her irritation was already surfacing.

"Just be direct, Reno, forget the details!"

"I… yes, first, let me give you an idea of the spatial schema and the temporal sequence. Using my eyewitness accounts as well as our different sources of information, I had a small computer simulation made. Cornwell, our programming specialist, has just finished it."

And out of his pocket he took a white-colored disk with something illegible written in marker on the label.

The woman grabbed it, not the least impressed. She inserted it into the drive of her console; it launched a slew of antiviral tests before saving the data into its memory.

The simulation was based on aerial images that were taken from television and from the Sureté, and incorporated what he knew, himself, about the situation.

At the center of the image was a small building with a bright orange tint.

"This is the layout of my men at the time."

Several vehicles appear on the four corners of the screen. Then another, that keeps moving. Pickups, some bikes, one or two big XXth century type sedans.

"There's a group on Rachel and Rivard; a group on Roy and Rivard; a group on Saint-Hubert and Duluth; a group on Duluth and Laval; plus a mobile unit and two or three bikes. That makes a total of twelve or thirteen men on duty, twenty-four hours a day. If you add the six or eight usual Russians and Ontarians, and the three members of Thorpe's team, we're already up to twenty-five on the job."

Several vehicles and some men on foot circulating around the neighborhood appear, in different colors.

"Now, let me show you the enemy layout. For the past two or three days, my men report strange vehicles crossing the sector. The night before the big shebang, they spot a Ram Charger pickup with illegible plates, a Chevy, and at least two other vehicles. We pretty much know who it is, so we instigate a maximum emergency alert. That's how the night of the 17th to the 18th of August starts. And that's why we combine the day and night teams, to strengthen the layout."

Red mobile vehicles appear, prowling on the map like ants in search of prey to bring back to the anthill. The verdigris Angel vehicles and the cobalt-blue Russian ones pass by at a shinier frequency.

"We have two vehicles, one on the corner of Roy and Rivard, the other on Duluth and Laval, equipped with long distance cameras shooting the apartment. That means that whoever wants to get near or leave the apartment necessarily shows up on the video. Our bikers are cruising Rivard and the alleys parallel to it, as well as Rachel. Nothing can escape us."

The crossing in question fills up two-eighths of the screen, with two different camera angles, one a north-south axis, the other east-west. He points to a window on the screen.

"Take a look at this window, it's a shot of Rivard Street."

The videocamera flashes 1:07 AM. They see a man leave the apartment and take Duluth towards Saint-Denis. He disappears from that window and simultaneously reappears in the other one. He's walking south at a good speed. He disappears from the image.

"That's Thorpe. You recognize him, right. Cross, the guy who oversees the night team, decides to send a guy on foot and a second one on a bike to follow him. That's what Diego does. Diego follows the guy till Ontario and there, Diego says something weird happens. Something really weird."

"What do you mean something weird? You're driving me crazy."

"Thorpe starts speaking aloud in front of the entrance to a building. As if he were speaking to someone; but there's no one there. He drifts on like that towards downtown, takes the Lachine Canal, and then hails a cab. Diego calls the emergency biker. Thorpe goes back home."

A small New York style yellow cab stops a block away from the flashing orange building.

"Now this is when everything goes wrong. While Diego and Pike are following behind the cab, all of a sudden Diego feels ill. Pike calls

Cross who asks what's happening. Pike stops and asks Diego what's wrong. They're on Berri. Diego is very pale, seems terrorized and is practically screaming. He tells him to hurry up, that they're surrounded, that it's gonna blow up. Pike passes this onto Cross, who's in the mobile patrol. He's on Saint-Denis and Marie-Anne at this point."

Reno shows her the 3D layout, like an aquarium filled with fighter fish, a second before the general onslaught.

"Pike leaves. Cross had told him to meet the men posted on Roy and to wait for him there. And that's when Diego's prediction comes true and it all blows up… Look, it's four-nineteen. At that moment, the men on Duluth and those on Saint-Hubert hear explosions coming from the block, from the building that Thorpe has just entered. Cross gets the message, informs Gould who's patrolling Rachel on a bike, puts everyone on red alert and turns around. He asks the men on Duluth to go see what's happening. They leave the corner of Duluth and Laval towards Rivard. Watch the left window carefully. You can see two pickups barge in, loaded with Rock-Machines and Chinese. Then…"

Reno is quiet.

The image coming from both cameras is suddenly invaded by blue, icy and invincible fire.

The 3D simulation then shows furious red vehicles taking on their rivals.

Then Reno presses a key to freeze the animation.

"As you can see, both our cameras are inoperable *before* we're attacked. That means they used a real strong scrambler to hack us. On the other hand, all our survivors say a strange thing happened to them, except they don't remember much, as if they suffered from amnesia. But Diego remembers experiencing the whole thing as something terrifying. The enemy was everywhere, and wanted to exterminate him and Pike. At one point, Pike himself had become an enemy and Diego even wonders if he didn't kill him."

"Are you kidding?"

"No. It's a shame Cross and Gould died during the attack. Their testimony would have helped complete the picture. And it gets even better."

The woman looked at him, exasperated, but ready for the unthinkable, as if beaten already.

"I'm going to try to be clear, Ma'am Clayton-Rochette. But it's not easy. We have no idea what happened."

"What are you trying to tell me?"

Reno pressed on a command button. The recorded video images scanned backwards frantically. Then forward, at normal speed.

He pointed to the time code on the bottom right corner of the screen.

"Look at this, Ma'am Clayton-Rochette. I've never seen anything like it. Watch the two windows, they show the same time, right. Both cameras were synchronized on the same time code. Here, this is it, look, it's two forty-four and thirty seconds, thirty-one…"

Reno didn't do anything, didn't say a thing.

02:44:32, 02:44:33, 02:45:25, 02:45:26, …

His small smile barely widened as he saw the woman's chin jut out suddenly towards the screen.

"Wait, right there…"

"Yeah, surprising isn't it? There's almost a minute missing on both sequences, and they were being recorded in real time. We don't know how it happened. Now look at the right hand image, the north-south axis, on Rivard. See this silver gray color, right here?"

He pointed to a small shimmer near the middle of the image, not very far from the building occupied by Thorpe, Marie Zorn and the others. He scanned the virtual sequence backward. Then sent it forward again.

"Look at this, at two forty-four, it's here. At two forty-five it isn't."

"What is it?"

"According to my information, it's the voyager that Thorpe rented."

"Who took it?"

"Not Thorpe in any case. We see him leave at one-o-seven and come back at four-eighteen. Nor the others; they're gonna kill each other in the apartment in a minute."

"Who then?"

"Guess?"

"The girl? Why? And what is this minute that's edited out?"

"That's the whole problem, Ma'am. Lug, who was on Roy's team and survived, remembers something. Something that would have happened around that time."

The woman let out a long sigh, a sigh of pure distress, as if the entire world was weighing down upon her shoulders.

"I'm listening, Reno."

"Here it is. It's like the time cut happened on the video, but also… how can I say this… *shit, Oh Criss'*, there ain't no other way to say it, as if it really happened, in real life."

"What do you mean? And watch your language."

"Well, that's what Lug says. Around quarter to three, he felt a weird sensation, like an absence of about a minute. 'Cause a minute had passed on the dashboard clock when he regained consciousness. But when he tells his partner about it, the guy says: 'I don't know what you're talkin' about. You didn't sleep for a micro-second. Neither did I.' Lug wouldn't have thought anything about it if he hadn't seen the recordings."

"What is it Reno, can you tell me?"

"No. We have no idea what technology they used. But they're good. Real good. I think you should call your supplier right away."

The woman's eyes let out a shower of blue sparks. She would have smashed the world to bits if someone had given her that power.

Colonel Romanenko's internal calculator went off immediately upon waking. It was late, and pouring.

Six days since the attack on Toorop's apartment. Six times twenty-four hours. And still no news.

There was worse. Last night, sifting through all the news from Quebec, he was shocked to fall upon a short article mentioning the assassination of a certain Nicholas Kravcezch, alias Charles Newton, on the night of the massacre. The din of the Biker War had covered it for a while, but now, the information had seeped up to the audible surface of the world, like a cadaver rising from the deep. The

Sureté wasn't crossing out a possible connection between the two events. The *Journal de Montréal* article stated that firemen and city cops had received a couple calls from Outremont around five-thirty in the morning about a house burning on Spring Grove. First on the scene, the Outremont firemen discovered the shredded and carbonized remains of a man who'd be identified only five days later by DNA analysis. According to the reporter and his sources, the police had uncovered ten thousand dollars cash and fifty thousand dollars worth of pure heroin in a fire and bulletproof briefcase. They seized a computer and some teradiscs, somewhat damaged by the flames. Upstairs, they found a stock of meta-amphetamines and illicit biotechnology that had been relatively spared by the fire. The presence of 9mm bullets uncovered by the scientific police, as well as a few lead shards in the human remains, pointed to a homicide.

Romanenko remembered that Toorop had called around five, local time, on the morning Newton was getting butchered. Toorop didn't know about it, and was counting on Newton to find a quick solution to his little problem, a missing hand.

The facts stared him straight in the face. Toorop must have gotten to the informant's house at the same time as the firemen. Romanenko knew from the news that the mercenary hadn't been caught, and that he wasn't dead. What had he done once he realized his emergency out was cornered? If he hadn't been caught, why wasn't he calling?

Romanenko confusedly felt that this question would remain obscure for a good while.

So he concentrated on the facts: the shock of enemy troops, the Plateau Mont-Royal massacre.

As Romanenko was starting his day, the cops in Quebec were doing their first general reenactment of events. They consulted with a team of pyrotechnists working for a special effects company. They hired thirty extras, all bikers, made them learn their parts before letting them loose at nightfall around Rivard and Duluth.

Television cameras were kept out of the area by a large security perimeter. That didn't stop news networks from the entire continent from waging a wild battle between themselves for more or less stolen, more or less sharp, images.

The private satellite of a fabulously wealthy Turkish magnate was supposed to target that area of Montreal with its cameras, and transmit live over the Internet. But the Sureté managed to get the orbital gizmo to miss its window of observation by shifting the show back an hour.

The Sureté did the whole thing right, but Romanenko couldn't really get a clear idea of what had happened. However, it was near-ly as beautiful as a sequence from *Apocalypse Now*.

The CBC reporter had the same comment to make, for that matter.

That evening, in his encrypted e-mail box, Romanenko found an insignificant looking message from Gorsky: *Our organization picked up Marie Alpha's trace around Tadoussac, north bank of the Saint-Laurent. Her presence dates back two or three days now. Are in possession of the description of her new car. Several teams are concen-trating on the area. Will keep you informed.*

Ourianev entered. He came to his side directly, facing the screen. The cap' was taking priceless liberties, thought Romanenko.

"What do we do?"

"Just as planned," grumbled Romanenko. "We wait."

He puzzled over it a good part of the night; verging on satura-tion, he finally resolved to take something to help him sleep.

His worst predictions came true in the next few days, on par with the weather. Siberia and Central Asia were covered in storm clouds. Huge rains fell for seventy-two hours straight, something unheard of in Kazakhstan at this time of year. When the sun finally rose over the drenched landscape, almost two weeks had passed since the attack on 4067. Several laconic messages in the encrypted mailbox let him know that Marie Zorn's trail had vanished. And Toorop still hadn't called.

The weather forecast announced violent storms over North America, following the Jefferson Cyclone, a good category 5 cyclone, that had hit the Florida Coast. Jamaica was declared a disaster zone, so was Cuba. The cyclone moved northwest during the night, hit

Alabama, Mississippi, and then the states of Tennessee, Arkansas and Southern Missouri with fifty percent of its initial force. Torrential rains battered Louisiana and Eastern Texas; the Mississippi River was having one the largest floods in its history.

Weather stations in Quebec measured wind speeds up to a hundred and fifty kilometers an hour. Disastrous landslides happened during the evening; whole houses were swept away by flooded rivers or by tornadoes. Bridges, buildings, cars, gas stations and factories were so many Lego pieces devastated by a Hollywood-sized faucet leak.

The Saguenay region was going through a bad remake of the 1996 floods. Hundreds were said to be dead or missing; the homeless numbered among the millions. If the chaos of the elements butted in...

The Saguenay. That was the affluent of the Saint-Laurent, running into the estuary near the city of Tadoussac, where Kotcheff's men said they'd caught trace of Marie.

With a bit of luck, she'd be caught right in the middle of the storm.

For a minute, Romanenko imagined the girl's car being carried away by the raging waters, between uprooted trees like hay fetuses and blocs of concrete torn from devastated buildings. They'd all heave a sign of relief, if that were the case. Her disappearance would pass unnoticed among the hundreds.

Careful study of the maps of the region gave Romanenko a few varied details, elements of information that were still scattered but would one day assemble to give new depth to the Marie Zorn mystery.

The region between the Abitibi and the Saguenay, precisely where the elements were unleashed, was full of Indian Reservations: autonomous Huron, Montagnais, Cree and Mohawk territories. It was open land, with lots of natural parks and hardly any big cities, except for a few on one or two large roadways, and around that small land-locked sea called Lake Saint-Jean. If it hadn't killed her, the chaos of the elements would help erase her trail.

The word "fiasco" was a euphemism.

The last days of August passed.

September began.

Nothing budged.

34

His consciousness arose from the darkness in steps, like a diver returning from a long excursion in the abyss.

First, there was the shadow of a dream, something, in this absolute darkness, whose consistency appeared like a very remote and evanescent glow. The image dissolved as it was created. It quite simply refused any existence, changed directly from gestation to recollection and then melted by bits into the oblivion of darkness. The micro-consciousness Toorop had become tried in vain to make it crystallize in his memory. It was a photograph, a very ancient black and white photograph that trembled slightly in the developer but never reached the fixing bath. Later, the echo of this experience would subsist. And to everyone he told, first of all himself, he would just barely manage to say that it might be the image of a destroyed city.

Then there was sensation. Sensation took centuries to reach his consciousness, according to his subjective perception of time. Let's say that it probably took a few hours. Sensation preceded any operative consciousness, and any perception of the outside world. It was limited to a short list of phenomena: his heart was beating, his lungs periodically breathed air in and out, something touched him—but he could not say what it was, nor where it touched him, for his body did not exist as an organic entity.

In that way, sensation could be summarized as the check-up of a machine, which he was quite precisely at that moment, although of course, like all machines, he wasn't conscious of it. So he was first a list of organs, the ones consciousness usually forgets in order to live. But he wasn't a consciousness yet; at most he was an arrangement of reflexes, endowed with a buffer-memory.

After the sensation-machine that lasted for millennia, a risky evolution seemed to take root, and stabilized finally. The basic scattered listing of organ-machines *embodied*, attained a threshold of critical cohesion. Some kind of energetic circuitry wanted to keep everything in place, in a certain shape.

He had the fragile consciousness of his bodily existence, a personal kinesthesia, and tactile sensations that now traced a border, an interface between him and the world. From a simple stingy diagram suspended in a digital nothingness, he became flesh.

His flesh and its borders then drew out new diagrams: time, space, lying down, gravity, obscurity, light, the first sounds, hot, cold. Then everything hooked up.

Hunger.

Thirst.

Shit.

Piss.

Finally, a coherent cartography appeared. Even before several barely distinct forms sprang up behind the veil that stretched between him and objects.

Even before he was able to see himself, even before he was able to see *it*, he knew something had happened to his hand.

The strangest thing was that he knew what had happened to it without having access to any information worthy of that name from the external world.

The sensation-consciousness cartography spelled it out clearly.

His hand was a machine.

Then he started becoming more than a passive, live object. He started to move. First, the extremities. His right hand slid weakly on a soft, fresh surface. His left hand did the same, apparently, and what had been as yet only a bodily intuition became a factual and terribly limpid truth.

Wherever he was, probably in a hospital, and no doubt under good care, they'd done what had to be done, what could still be done.

They'd amputated his right hand, at least in part. And they'd replaced the missing part with a kind of bio-mechanic graft.

The concepts of time and space at last formed a coherent and stable reality. He could finally see and hear with precision.

His hand was wrapped in a thick bandage. So was his head. He was hooked onto a black box placed at the foot of the bed, with a line of diodes above it. An IV was coming out of his mouth, another out of the fold of his elbow. Two veins of translucent liquid pumped by tubular machinery purred above him.

That morning, when he woke up, like a chrysalis brought to term, he was able to circumscribe the universe clearly. He was in a room, with bare walls and austere furniture, but everything indicated that it wasn't a hospital. He could tell he was high up from what he saw through the half-closed shutters of the windows, towering about ten stories above the city. From a wealth of detail that his consciousness could finally record—the objects disseminated around the room, the furniture, the small bookshelf filled with books whose titles he could not make out, the small stack of XXth century LPs, the technological odds and ends piling up on a styleless desk, a PC lording at its center, hooked up to a slew of machinery—he understood that he wasn't in a hospital room. This was someone's private room, someone who lived on the top floor of a building dominating the city.

He was not in a hospital, he told himself.

But maybe he was still in good hands.

With that flash of paranoid lucidity, it dawned on him that he was back.

Joe-Jane knew that a new plane of consistency was developing now. A living network was coming to light, weaving a luminous geometry between events. New correlations wanted to take hold between the dimensions of space and time, between the multitudes of quantum energy and information, between each frequency, each atom, each nucleotide of the world.

Joe-Jane knew what that meant. It was the wild thermodynamics of predatory knowledge unleashed like a beast on the crowd, the torpedo of biodynamics blasting the cargo of human illusions into the deep, with the pity of wind eroding ruins. God was not only dead, but also incinerated, disintegrated as human ants in atomic fire, and had to be reinvented. God would soon stammer like a baby wailing at the heart of the rubble, and, in one blow, shatter their millennia of work bent on stopping such uprising, such creation. It was the immediate and unconditional dissolution of ancient structures; the abandonment of humanity, like the slough from a molt too long awaited, hoped for and fettered; the improvised metamorphosis of nature deciding to turn the page, to close a chapter and to open another; the explosive narration of the entire cosmos renewing from within, at the heart of its most ineffable black holes and its most secret languages. Big-Bang-A-Lula.

For Joe-Jane it was getting harder and harder to communicate her sensations, ideas and desires to the humans that were closest to her. She knew that. So she settled on managing daily affairs with them. See to the deficiencies of the old building security system. Check the elevators. Supervise the unfolding of operations, with an attentive yet disinterested eye. Speak to Robicek.

"Your conceivers will be here in less than five days. Stop busting my balls, Joe-Jane. Was I clear enough this time?"

The hiss of the machine sounded like a rattlesnake attack.

"Either you don't understand a thing, Vax, or you're pretending. Same thing. If you don't find Marie Zorn within the next few days, we'll be responsible for the premature annihilation of the future of humanity! Now you're the one busting my balls!"

Robicek froze. He straightened in his chair, taking a more dignified pose than his sagging gait.

The machine had never gotten angry like that. She had never insulted him.

"Don't talk about what you don't have," he retorted, defensive.

The machine laughed.

"You're pathetic. Not only do I have your pathetic human sexual attributes, but you don't even have a clue about the millions of other solutions we, DNA neuromatrices, have."

Robicek capitulated.

"OK, say what you have to say, Joe-Jane."

"It's only a few words. We've known for weeks that Marie is in Quebec. And we've waited so long that now it's too late. That's what I had to tell my conceivers. That's the emergency. A cataclysm is on its way, and we continue to act as if nothing were happening, just hoping that it won't disturb the Saturday night show."

"We've done what we could, I assure you."

The machine let out a rustle of disdain.

A bit later, when morning was drawing to an end, Robicek contacted the *Cygnus Dei*. It would arrive in Halifax as planned, at the end of the week. Robicek warned them of a small change of plan: Mr. Storm would come pick them up alone. It was urgent that ShellC and Altaïr adjust the new biodigital programs with their gang of friends from the seventh floor.

Robicek left the studio he'd moved into since he'd set the guy up in his own room. It was a kind of attic, a junk storeroom filled with about fifteen generations of electronic components and micro-computers. His bed was in the back, against the wall, on a futon. Joe-Jane had been placed on a metallic closet at the foot of his bed.

Just before he crossed the threshold, the machine called out to him.

"Our friend Mister Wounded has just come out of it. You'd best go check on him."

Robicek looked at the black ball filled with silver-blue veins glowing over there in the darkness. She was an extraordinary machine, a real living being. Robicek felt that she'd been isolating herself for the last few days. She only spoke to give facts, to throw out one or two strategic bits of information. Of course, his own behavior had something to do with that phenomenon, but he also surmised a hidden depth to the digital melancholy. It was as if a kind of chronic depression was slowly invading that formidable arrangement of conscious bio-circuitry.

Robicek was distraught. He'd invented the white box. It was a classical computer, albeit very ingeniously made, devoted to the interface between machine and world. When the machine spoke of her conceivers, she excluded him, and referred only to the men arriving in Halifax in the coming days.

Robicek didn't feel particularly bitter about it. That view was justified for the most part. The job specifications when they hired him were clear: "the machine exists, she functions, she learns, but she spends too much time and energy dealing with circuitry and interface problems. We want some sort of primordial body, an assemblage of interfaces, visual, auditory, vocal, etc., that would fit into a standard computer case and rid her of all that. You'll be collaborating with Doctor Hu Sheng, who's in charge of information processing and occipital tube centers." That's what the Malaysian man in charge of personnel on Koh Tao had told him.

The white box was something like the machine's secondary nervous system, her tactile nerve network, with a preliminary batch of perceptive organs.

In fact, everything else had been conceived of before he arrived on the Thai island, with thirty dollars to his name, and before he'd even heard of the kooky research center on its northern tip.

The machine suffered from melancholy and depression. Each time she spoke to him it took an unpleasant turn, when she didn't bluntly insult him. It was because each second, he, who'd made that small white box, reminded her, the small black sphere, of how alone she was, how cut off from the protective world of the island, from her conceivers, and confronted with a new environment where fifty people could savagely slaughter each other in the street, in the middle of the night, at the heart of this city she did not know.

"Thank you Joe-Jane," was all he said as he left, softly closing the door behind him.

Toorop heard footsteps, steps coming closer, then the noise of a knob turning and the door opened.

A big guy stood framed by the door. Close-cropped hair, blond, blue eyes, something Slav, or in any case European, in the face and morphology, but a natural gait and attitude that indicated the North American. At ease in space, there was something animal to his slightest movement. He was so at ease that when he went to the window to lift the blinds, then to the bookshelf to put two or three books away, Toorop knew that he lived in the space, that he was the usual resident of the room.

The man didn't say a thing. He took a chair, sat down and observed Toorop who'd just set foot back in the world of the living.

Toorop turned to face him and looked him over as well.

He had an electronic chip tattooed on the top of his skull, and the hair cleared away around it. He was some kind of hacker, an American of Slav descent. It could only be the Russian mafia.

He told himself he was almost lucky. Unless this was a competing branch of the transnational Kotcheff-Newton tandem, they were his employers. The competition would certainly not have taken care of him so well. Unless they wanted him alive in order to interrogate him…

"How did you find me? What happened to Doctor Newton? Any news of our common employer?"

His tongue was a rag of scabs and filth washing a dried urinal, his voice unrecognizable to his own ears. His nostrils flared in disgust at the foul smell accompanying the breath.

The man observed him without a word, and then snarled an enigmatic smile.

"We have no common employer, until I hear otherwise. But that could change in the coming days."

Toorop shrugged. He vaguely understood that he'd screwed up. This wasn't the Russian mafia. These people weren't his employers, but the guy claimed that would change…

"I give up. Wait, you're Roger Rabbit disguised as a human and I've escaped ToonVille?"

The guy laughed parsimoniously.

"I don't have time to explain everything right now. I'm going to check your motor abilities, and if you can walk, I'll bring you where we can get on with your interrogation. And if everything goes well, you'll learn more."

Toorop knew quite well he didn't have a choice.

The guy took a slew of tests.

"Everyone here calls me Vax."

Toorop didn't say anything.

"We had to replace your hand, except for the thumb that was partially saved. Your burns are healing, the skin graft worked well. In fifteen days, you'll be almost as good as new. Till then, try not to rub your back up against steel wool."

"I only accept that kind of thing from black leather clad nymphettes," answered Toorop, his voice more grating than if said steel wool had filed his esophagus.

"My medical ban also covers those kinds of perversions," the tall, bald guy casually retorted.

Toorop sat up in bed. He didn't really feel in Olympic shape when it came to getting up. The guy came closer to hold him up and help him walk a couple meters. Toorop had neither the reflex nor the presumption to refuse.

Toorop started to get an idea of the place once they left the room. It was a large loft, like two or three apartments combined, with the walls torn down. There were bonsais, tons of green plants and a huge glass tunnel where a small equatorial ecosystem had been assembled. Two gigantic black snakes moved there with the sumptuousness of arabesques.

"The vivarium. ShellC and Altaïr keep all kinds of creatures there. Especially their two cloned anacondas."

The glass tunnel stretched beneath the west side windows. In the distance, he could see the slanted tower of the Olympic Park; he drew a cursory map in his head.

Jesus fucking Christ.

Toorop, like an automaton on Valium, moved towards the large glass windows opening up onto the city below. He could see Saint-Laurent Boulevard, all the way down there, crossing Ontario.

This was the building where he met Ari's ghost for the first time.

It took him days to take in the place. And even then, he knew that he was just grazing its real dimensions. As for its real nature, it clashed with his most advanced conceptions of livable space, not to speak of lifestyle.

Vax brought him to an apartment on the top floor.

The loft, barely smaller than a football field, was covered in a thick vegetable cloak; a canopy of vines and climbers created a green arch of sooty lacework above him. Toorop walked on strange synthetic matter, where humus and natural grass came to life. The window frames and the walls were literally carpeted with a complete biotope, replete with lichens and mushrooms. This didn't stop the room from being crowded with machines, computers, synthesizers; a strange polyphony haloed the space.

His brain registered data like a basic portable Fujitsu, while an emotional bulb sent out a constant mix of anxiety and curiosity, the delicate anguish of the new.

Three men and three women, more like three girls, progressively stood out from the scenery.

Black suction-disks covering the whole surface of his skull were plugged in, via a fiber optics network, to different machines interlacing human and silicon.

Their image was scrambled by too much information. It was hard to tell the difference between the materials they wore and their own bodies. Biosim military suits copied the natural mimicry of certain animals; holo-tattoos of double serpents rippled in ultraviolet dances on their arms and around the chicks' bellybuttons. Antique, last century bioprocessors, grafted on a biocompatible membrane onto the fat of the shoulder, formed flesh colored squares like Barbie doll plastic; charcoal-gray protuberances on the nape of the neck emitted a digital sound, and flashed with luminous diodes. They made a circle around him.

A tiny, young Latin-American type woman settled just beneath his nostrils to eye him scornfully, her eyes covered with shiny, hypnotic, black optical interfaces. Her hairstyle consisted of tens of small, chrome-colored braids, as rigid as antennas. A minuscule micro-component pierced the skin around her third eye, and she had a double serpent tattooed in UVs on her cheek.

She scanned Toorop from all angles.

Then, in French, but with a strong, indefinable accent, and some sort of digital coding filtering her voice, she told the group:

"I really don't see why the Sherpas and the EarthQuakers are seriously considering he might be the element we're looking for."

Toorop heard a nasty laugh behind him.

"Lotus… Those poor Indians are naive. We can't trust this kind of scum, they only work for money…"

Although Toorop didn't get everything, he understood that he was the central subject of this little conversation.

"The Sherpas asked that he be treated with respect, and you didn't hold to that clause of the contract. Shit, Spectrum, you piss me off every time. You're lucky they're in the middle of the ocean, they wouldn't be happy about it, believe me."

"What are you talking about?"

"ShellC and Altaïr told me about the hand. You could have saved some of it. But apparently you thought it was fun to experiment with one of your new models."

"I did what I could. This new hand is highly superior to the old version that Mister here possessed. And let me remind you Mister here works for those mystic sect morons and the Russian gangsters they hired. They're the ones who conduct *experiments*, it seems to me."

Toorop noted that the guy spoke with a pure French accent. He didn't really like the portrait the Frenchie had made of him, nor did he really appreciate that the guy had sacrificed his hand for fun. He told himself he'd remind him of it when the time came, but now, he wasn't really in any position to argue.

The girl that Spectrum called Lotus focalized on Toorop again.

"We've got a terabit of info to ask you, Mister Toorop, as you know. And we'll take all the time necessary. We have all the time in the world, don't we?"

She'd said it with a strange, thoughtful and dubious pose before his definitely obsolete old carcass.

A carcass that was preoccupied, for now, with how to resolve a few fundamental equations, like how to survive the next few hours, how they'd cracked his ID so easily, when he'd get his first glass of water, and a whole lot of absolutely metaphysical questions of this sort.

Toorop noticed two robots, each moving at one end of the miniature biosphere. He recognized Honda domestic robots, but their makeup had been changed quite a bit. Some dumpster objects had been added in order to give them strangely anthropomorphic traits, window display mannequins with the eyes removed and replaced by electronic organs. One of them was wearing fishnets and other sex-shop accessories. He was putting on makeup, sitting at a Victorian dresser; his movements had such humanity that Toorop froze on the spot.

A homosexual robot. Someone had reprogrammed the Honda Andromotor into an evanescent, feminoid, narcissistic and icily authentic being.

The other robot, wrapped in a kimono, was executing a rapid series of traditional Tai Chi movements.

At that point, it seemed almost banal.

"We're the 10 Ontario Cyborg Society," the first girl answered to his silent question.

To the second question, she said:

"We expect you to betray your old employers, Mister Toorop. We expect you to help us locate Marie Zorn."

Then she added, without leaving him time to retort:

"It goes without saying that any refusal on your part and we immediately and radically recycle your organic components."

Toorop understood what she meant perfectly. He meditated a few instants on the lasting character of human affairs, and particularly on pledges of loyalty. Striking a pose, the homosexual Honda robot was contemplating its silhouette in the mirror; its fellow creature was finishing a complicated kata at the end of the room. Toorop closed his eyes a second. This was too crazy. No one would ever believe him when it came time to trade war stories with other veterans in some bar.

He opened his eyes on the young woman with chrome colored hair before blurting out with a straight face:

"It's useless, I presume, to imagine some kind of salary negotiations?"

With careful observation, Toorop started collecting tons of little details. He was able to discern what looked like a network of fiber optics running under their skin, at the wrists, the temples, the forearms, the tip of the fingers. It shone fleetingly under the light when they moved. When they plugged themselves into their black consoles, the occipital protuberance emitted a continuous digital rustling. Toorop remembered seeing pictures of this kind of thing in the issues of *Scientific American* or *Aviation Weekly* at Newton's house: neurophysical interfaces, experimental technology that allowed the Air Force test pilots to control their planes by thought, by a list of key words.

The girl and the one called Vax asked him about his schedule since he'd first met Marie, hour by hour. It was serious, on the interrogation tip. Toorop told them everything; apparently, the 10 Ontario Cyborgs already knew a good part of it.

It lasted hours. The Eastern Turkistan conflict, the lab in Kazakhstan, the GRU colonel, the Siberian mafia, the Noelite Church, he gave it all, without the slightest regret. He muffled a few dangerous first names, Gorsky, Romanenko; he kept it vague when it came to the kind of illicit biotechnologies Marie was carrying, but he gave them a good panoramic view. In his lingo, it was called treason. He took advantage of it to give a version of the story that looked good: yes, he was occasionally a Russian Military security agent; yes, they were infiltrating the mafia organization so that they could bring down the whole family.

But when the girl insisted that he tell her what he'd done with Marie, Toorop got a little annoyed:

"In what fucking newspeak do I have to tell you? During that whole chaos, Marie split without looking back. I don't know, we don't know, no one knows where she could be."

The girl seemed bothered by that information. And so was Toorop. The knowledge of Marie Zorn's hiding place was really the only thing with which he could bargain for his life.

But no, he didn't know. The young intelligent Cyborgs could guess; they'd been around the block. It was better to play it fair, i.e., lie with skill, which, as Sun Tzu reminds us, is quite simply the art of strategy.

This type of strategy had its share of risks, of course, but the guy who jumps into a dumpster to escape the fire is generally not too concerned about staining his suit.

Even Sun Tzu would have agreed with that.

They gave him something to drink: Montclair water in a small one-liter bottle. He downed more than half in one go.

Toorop wasn't reassured, but he needed to know one small, primordial detail before opting for one of the most crucial alternatives of his life.

"How did you find us?"

Lotus stared at him coldly.

"You must be kidding?" she said.

"What do you mean, I'm kidding?"

"You don't seem to know... That's weird. I wonder if you know anything?"

"Know what, for example?"

The girl let out a small laugh that she froze into an indefinable expression.

"Just know. So you have no clue what you got yourself into?"

Toorop had to admit it.

Vax dotted the i's and crossed the t's for him.

"What we know, we got it from Newton. We listened in on his communications for days, the guy was a real gold mine of information."

Toorop moved into the opening. But before, he finished the bottle of water.

"How did you nail him?"

"Newton led us to you, you and your team, and Marie Zorn. But when we were able to establish visual contact, your street was already under surveillance by a whole lot of people. We identified a few of them, and were able to work our way to a rival sect of the one you work for. We decided to wait for the opportune moment to act; it came faster than we thought."

Two criminal organizations were fighting to capture Marie. Each was made up of a sectarian organization, different mafias, Russian, Hispanic, Japanese, North American, the whole thing. The first was the one he worked for, with the Russian gangsters and the Hell's Angels, the Noelites.

The second organization, according to the 10 Ontario Cyborgs, gravitated around the Logology Church—a schism of the scientologists—, the Rock-Machines and the Wah Ching Gang, an army of kids based in Toronto and affiliated with the Hip-Sing tong of New York.

"We don't work for anyone," said Lotus, "just *for the completion of the process.*"

Later on, they offered him a beer and a vegetable mixture that ended up being edible. Then the one they called Unix posted himself at the end of the room near a pile of machines; Toorop saw him connect his occipital protuberance to a computer.

Lotus smiled faintly.

"Unix is a musician. MIDI files are his drug of choice."

A sound wave articulated on an infra-base pulse swept its invisible volutes around them. It seemed to come from all sides, from everywhere in space.

"He's composing the last part of *Private Biology*, his new album. It'll be available online in a few days."

Toorop glanced, almost disenchanted, at the science-fiction decor around him. He had to get used to it; this was the XXIst century.

Lotus agreed to provide some general explanations. The biological interfaces allowed them to connect directly to any information system. Thanks to them, and to the artificial neurotransmitters that they generated in the brain, you could experience the exploration of Titan from inside, through a Japanese-American robot-probe. You fused with the cruise missile till the enemy bunker, you plugged into the optical implant on a presidential bodyguard in the US or in the Russian Federation. You navigated software for audio or visual creation, or both. You could even share these kinds of experiences with others. It was super cool.

The 10 Ontario Cyborg Society was born seven years ago, when all the residents of the building were able to acquire it and save it from destruction. At the time, they'd transformed it into a kind of vast techno-artistic cooperative. Under the influence of a few residents, and the ones she called the "Sherpas," it was agreed that 10 Ontario be made the first Post-Human Autonomous Territory.

Now, with the technology available, you could think of your own body as a laboratory of biocybernetic experimentation. Better than that, cyborg philosophy considered flesh and silicon as the two poles of a new Tao.

"You erase the conceptual differences between organic and artificial, between life and machine, once you take the path of networking them," she said, with an intense expression on her face.

"Who are the Sherpas?" Toorop asked softly, as if it were nothing.

The girl's face opened up into a smile.

"I'm sorry, their identity must remain confidential for now. But since the EarthQuakers seem to recognize your participation in the process, they're on their way."

Toorop was totally lost.

"OK. Who are the EarthQuakers? And what process?"

The girl observed him a moment without a word, then sighed.

Toorop suppressed a smile. She was just getting to know him.

According to what Lotus deigned tell him, the "Cyborg-Nation" federated several groups that had ended up at 10 Ontario through the play of history and chance. The first, at the turn of the century, were those who'd later form the 10 Ontario Cyborg Society. Herself, Vax, Spectrum, ShellC, Unix, Altaïr and a few others that he'd laid eyes on. Then, the gang plugged into other elements: first, the Sherpas and the EarthQuakers, and recently, the Cosmic Dragons.

She sketched a general but precise portrait of the complex organization. The micro-triad of the Cosmic Dragons was a seceding faction of the Ghost Shadows, kids serving the very powerful San Francisco On-Leong tong. The Cosmic Dragons found refuge at 10 Ontario through Spectrum, a Frenchman who had grown up in Hong Kong. Among other things, the Cosmic Dragons were electronic crime aces. According to Lotus, they were the ones that disseminated the latest hacking techniques to the community of 10 Ontario residents. The EarthQuakers spread their knowledge of the ecosystem and hallucinogenic biochemistry. The Cyborg Society provided the technological resources and taught them the man-machine interface. In fact, she was saying, we all influence each other all the time. We call it continuous contamination; you take what you find interesting in others, and make your own identity-kit. *Identity is just a temporary variable.*

From what Toorop gathered during his first days in captivity, the Cosmic Dragons were responsible for the security of the entire building.

The last floor and the roof were the domain of the EarthQuakers: Native American cyberpunks who prophesized the coming of Great Cataclysms and who grew very good quality hydroponic weed in the hallways and in the back staircase.

The 10 Ontario Cyborg Society was spread out over the rest of the building.

In all, it consisted of about twenty permanent residents, and half of that, non-permanent ones. A computer network linked the lofts to each other, and the latest artificial intelligence ran the whole thing, like a specific, urban biotope.

The building at 10 Ontario was known for the power of its heating system. Apparently, it wasn't uncommon for the residents to have to keep their windows open in the heart of winter. This strong thermal energy allowed the local biotopes to evolve in tropical or equatorial environmental conditions. Moreover, in the property registry, the building was linked to the Hydro-Quebec network that provided electricity for a certain number of nearby emergency services: firemen, hospitals. One of the oldest residents of the building, a scrap-artist called Valentin, could recall that 10 Ontario was one of the rare buildings to have dodged the winter '98 black-out, during the infamous icy January rains. It was a real bunker. That's what most of them called it. The Bunker.

Toorop got used to his new environment within a few days.

Actually, when it was all said and done, he seemed to like it.

"However," as he remarked a couple times, "what did all these people have to do with Marie Zorn?" The girl answered enigmatically that she couldn't reveal that information but that the EarthQuakers would give him a part of the answer when he'd definitely validate his fucking "participation in the process."

Toorop had no clue what that could be, but he didn't like the idea of being "validated" by Indian digital pirates. He started planning an escape.

One more betrayal was nothing.

35

One night he met Altaïr, the Eurasian from Vancouver, who finally accepted to be his guide, and allowed him to attend certain weird rites that punctuated life in the building.

The first ritual happened on one of the central floors reserved for "living modules and local services." Basically, that meant the apartments and micro-companies that thrived there. One of these modules belonged to a heavy-set Chinese man, a tattoo master. Its walls were covered in laser photos of his productions, hundreds of them. For the time being, the man, a certain Mr. Wang, was taking care of the shoulder of a pretty, sixteen-year-old girl. Toorop noticed that the most traditional techniques seemed to adapt to the current mutations.

During his twenty-year career, Toorop had gone through the mandatory warrior initiation, which generally consists of getting your body engraved with shit that a hardcore convict wouldn't want. Toorop had been careful in his choices; this kind of thing generally follows you to the grave. He wanted to be presentable when he appeared naked before the Almighty Judge. He had a small Yin Yang symbol on the left shoulder, although he was neither Taoist nor Buddhist, a crescent and a star on the other, although he wasn't Muslim, a plaited Croatian cross on a forearm, although he wasn't Catholic, and, to top it off, a small statue of liberty with a Kalachnikov, near the heart, in order to avoid all possible confusion. All this had been done with the means at hand in wartime. It was lucky he hadn't developed gangrene.

Here, however, everything was sterilized like in a clean room for microprocessors. Unlike all the other floors, this one was icy. Toorop noticed that everyone in the room was breathing out vapor. The girl was lying on a dentist chair; the jaws of something like a huge metal insect were pressing down on her naked pubic region. Above the insect jaw was a sort of sewing machine head connected to a long, articulated arm that was plugged into a computer. On the screen, Toorop saw the tangle of a logical component under a microscope.

Mr. Wang worked on his computer with one hand through a remote control grafted onto the tip of a special glove. His eye was glued to a long and flexible white tube attached to the sewing machine head; his mouth let out evanescent vaporous volutes. There was a barely audible digital rustling. The large, square jaw on the girl's shoulder emitted alternating red-green pulses on a network of diodes and vibrated softly, like a live appendage.

Altaïr explained that Fortrane, that was the girl's name, was getting the microlithography of a large Intel chip from the nineties directly implanted. The Cyborg Nation's initiatory tattoos were done here, on this machine fabricated on site with different recycled technologies.

"You'll have to go through it yourself, someday, Mister Toorop," she said with a little laugh.

"It seems there's only one thing, unfortunately, that could apply to the current situation."

Toorop shook his bionic hand. He was just starting to tame it, and could open and close doors, and books.

"And what's that?"

"Momentarily out of order. Or, please pardon our appearance, a certain category of personnel is on strike."

Toorop had learned quickly that the more he knew about his artificial hand, the faster he'd be able to use it.

It was a hybrid structure. Only the majority of the thumb, patched up with traditional surgery, and the first phalanx of the index and middle fingers had been conserved somewhat. The rest was made up of composite structures, alloys of metamorphic metals and of biocompatible resins, micro-optical fiber, silicon buffers, nano-processor networks and vat-grown cell grafts to cover it all in a layer of flesh. He remembered seeing a hand like this in a photograph once, next to an article about a Russian serial killer, as he was fleeing Eastern Kirghizia, on the way to his destiny. By some strange magical duplication, it ended up on his arm, on the other side of the world. The artificial flesh was translucent. "Depigmentation is normal at this stage," Spectrum had said. It would come with time. For now, it showed the precious and delicate architecture of the components he'd have to live with.

The other ritual he attended left him with a mix of disappointment and fascination. As if, all of a sudden, yes, as if everything were possible. As if some new disorder was about to take hold of the world.

Lotus and Unix were the local robot reprogramming specialists. Unix was an Italian-American who'd worked as a specialized programmer for nuclear site intervention teams. Then, in the nineties, he became close with the freaks from the Disaster Research Laboratory, a group of artists led by a so-called Pauline, one of the first, at the time, to get a graft of a bionic prosthesis of his own design. Pauline was totally out there. His robots were reprogrammed to self-destruct or to kill each other off in cybernetic gladiator combats. These combats degenerated more than once into genuine catastrophes, which was presumably one of the goals.

Lotus and Unix used Pauline and the Disaster Research Laboratory's pioneering work to go much farther: the simulation of complex human emotions and behaviors, such as sexuality or the spirit of resistance. Narcissus, the homosexual robot, and Wu Tak, the kung-fu one—named after one of the Five Shaolin Tigers who'd founded the triads in the year of our Lord 1674, after the destruction of the celebrated monastery by the Manchurian Army—were the cream of their collection. As Lotus was explaining all this, they were introducing Narcissus to Narcissus III, its replica, who'd just been reprogrammed by the girl and the Paisan.

"Their neural networks are still rudimentary," the girl was saying, "but we got it so that they build their own personality in a relatively autonomous way. Homosexuality is a difficult variable to grasp; it seems to escape the customary determinisms. But those are not really the ones we're interested in."

Lotus was rattling on, incessantly, in a low voice. On the other side of the room, Unix was just completing the usual introductions.

He quickly left the robots to their own conversation and to live their neuroprogrammed machine life.

Then he joined them, eyes sparking, full of impatience and curiosity.

He was a stocky guy, slightly past thirty, with short legs, plump, a kind of bearded monk, a hedonist, and impish little devil. His bald skull was entirely covered by a tattoo of a high-density logic circuit.

"We've already managed to get sexual relations between two hetero robots, but if this works Lotus, we'll finally get our proof," he whispered, all excited.

Toorop wondered for an instant what proof he was talking about.

But a galaxy of implausible questions formed in his head.

"I… *Jesus fucking Christ*… how can robots be… *gendered*?" he spit out, incredulous.

Unix laughed.

"Robots are living beings, Mister Toorop. Like living beings, all they need are adequate prostheses; as it turns out, making prostheses is just our thing. So we gave them a few different plans, and together we selected which ones seemed more efficient. There are three models of masculine sexes and five feminine ones… for now. But we still haven't tested out homosexual relations… If it works, it'll be a first."

Toorop watched the two transvestite robots talking at the end of the room. He caught some muddled bits of digital voices. Next to him, Lotus and Unix were jabbering on, talking about the cyberpornographic show they were planning for the end of the year. If this operation worked, it would be complete. Right now, Unix was finishing a specific program for a Hitachi robot, giving it a few added perversions, fetishism, voyeurism, sadomasochism…

"I hope my new limbic arousal programs will work better for this one than for the other prototype," he said, looking at Lotus with a luminous, libidinous stare.

"What other prototype?" asked Toorop, still fascinated by the two homo robots who seemed to be hitting it off.

"Narcissus II," answered Unix. "He blew a fuse last month… committed suicide."

"Suicide?!" Toorop blurted out, unconvinced.

"The life drive is inseparable from the death drive," Lotus hissed. "It's already a very difficult balance to find for human sexuality, so imagine what it's like for these still experimental machines."

She answered his unsaid question in a blank voice.

"He threw himself off the ninth floor. When we found him, he was just a smashed-up crash test dummy."

Toorop closed his eyes a second. Homosexual robots that committed suicide by jumping out of windows... He definitely outdid the other veterans in terms of war stories.

During the night, the video cameras spying in Narcissus' room were able to record the long awaited act. The two homo robots engaged in what had to be called copulation. It was so bizarre, so strange, so mysterious and so pathetic, that the paradoxical impression you feel before animal coitus left him in that confused state where vilely human laughter fights against fascinated tenderness.

The videos were aired on an encrypted channel of the building that was only accessible to *Homo sapiens*. Then the young Cyborgs with experimental neuro-physical protuberances plugged into the local network, and its neuromatrix, an AI called Joe-Jane, "neuroloaded" the homosexual robot experience into them.

"We're experimenting with all possible modes of incorporation," Unix explained one night. "We can become an industrial robot assembly line in Japan, a digital biosphere in a computer here, or a Frisco weirdo! A digital dolphin reconstructed at MIT, or a basic protozoan digitalized at Carnegie Mellon. Unlike those who think, 'the body is obsolete,' or that 'it's just meat,' as they say, artificial intelligence is actually inventing new types of incorporations. There can be no intelligence without a body, without flesh; simple digital replicas in purely abstract space will never create an artificial spirit. That's just a rotten old idealist dream, Hegel, Plato, all those old fogies!"

That night, Toorop did the rounds of available metaphysical questions. He let a large bubble of silence grow, and then, without a shadow of a smile, said:

"Will someone please explain how a pair of queer robots are going to help us find Marie?"

It only provoked an icy silence, slightly reproachful, rather indifferent.

Unix and Lotus stayed in their loft. When Toorop went back to his room, the fact was he had a serious hard-on. It wasn't so much the cyber-pornographic show that got him into that state, but simply everything the word sex evoked, the tropical heat of the building, and the more and more agreeable presence of that Latino-something chick with the chrome hair.

He had to resort to the old handjob, except that he wasn't used to the left hand.

One day, just before the arrival of the legendary "Sherpas," the man called Vax showed up with a laser copy of a double-page spread from an Anglophone British Columbia paper. It was a picture of a group of men and women in immaculate white evening clothes, champagne, vats of it, and some sort of large satellite model. THE NEW RESURRECTION COSMIC CHURCH READY FOR OUTER-SPACE EVANGELIZATION.

"Joe-Jane found this on the web, just this morning."

Toorop read the article, and then looked quizzically at the programmer.

What he understood fit into a few lines.

The Noelites were embarking on the conquest of space. A large mechanized service unit that they'd financed would be shot up during the month of March of next year. It would initiate a vast program to equip the community of True Believers with an instrument adapted to the future expansion of humans in space, and on Mars in particular.

"Shit," went Toorop, "they really want to send priests into space?"

"The Vatican and the Conference of Episcopalian Churches are also thinking about it. And someone told me that Moon and the Scientologists are also getting ready to do it. Apparently, it's the next big space business after luxury tourism."

"God Almighty, can't we send an emergency warning to all those poor extraterrestrials? Can you imagine, cardinals in purple robes floating in zero gravity and forcing the people of Alpha Centauri to learn the holy catechism?"

"It's true, their wardrobe is kinda working against them. But I have faith that the Churches will surmount such insignificant details and be able to adapt to their new environment. The Jesuits are real good at that. They did it wherever the Society of Jesus sent them."

"At least the Jesuits were men of high culture, whereas these new age morons…"

Vax cracked a despairing smile.

"I'm afraid that might be all our time has to offer in terms of religion."

"Pray for them, then," went Toorop.

A chorus of *Amens* and they all broke into laughter.

One night, just before the EarthQuakers "validated" his participation in the "process," a particularly hot night, he asked Vax, Lotus and ShellC, who were around, if they had any objections to his sleeping on the roof covered with a tropical jungle strewn with odorous cannabis and offset antennas of all dimensions. He was surprised by the natural calm with which they agreed. Toorop felt he'd gained their trust, and that it would be a great asset when it came time to set sail.

True, the vagaries of history and geography had given Toorop the opportunity to get closer to Lotus. The girl's mother was Venezuelan, and her father, Croatian. She was born in Montreal, went to college in San Francisco and had lived in the Peruvian Andes for a few years. She'd never been to Europe, only knew Dubrovnik from the pictures her dad had shown her. Toorop seized the opportunity. Like most of the residents of the building, Lotus could be his daughter, but that didn't stop the chicks around here, as he remembered from last month. He had a chance.

The night that he asked to sleep on the roof, the EarthQuakers, who took care of the internal agriculture of the building, warned him: "You can pick one head, but that's it. Don't urinate on the plants, don't touch the antennas, and don't forget that one of our shamans is coming tomorrow to visit you."

Rocked by the psychotropic fragrance of the cannabis and by the cosmic night stretching out above him, as the city seemed a fallen mirror of a celestial Las Vegas, he let himself go completely for the first time in a long while.

Summer was sending out its last hurrah. A continuous pulse rose from the city in waves of heat. Night was the color of an electric abyss; the sky quivered with an artificial Auroris Borealis irradiating the clouds with purple-orange gas. The stars seemed to be saying: "Hello, this light you're seeing took ten thousand, a hundred thousand, five hundred thousand years, or more, to reach you. I might not even exist anymore; right now, a good half of the sky you're looking at is a pure illusion."

All around him, the offset antennas pointed to the firmament, hooked onto the signals coming from a crown of GPS satellites that he tracked down from one end of the natural planetarium to the other. He imagined wave beams bouncing to the poles of the earth, over the Kazakhstan deserts, or onto an island in the middle of the Pacific. He saw them unite, in the Van Halen belt, with cosmic waves and with the millions of other waves sent by the millions of other antennas on the planet. He imagined the Alpha station in orbit and the myriad objects now gravitating around the globe like the electrons of an atom growing heavier. Little by little, his spirit melted into the golden-blue light of the high atmosphere until he fell asleep, drunk on sensations.

Then something soft and warm took possession of his light sleep. A cocoon of live flesh that absorbed him to the point that he woke up. He opened his eyes onto a body nestling beside him, not even a centimeter away. He recognized Lotus in the half-light. They embraced, and kissed in silence, then began tracing their bodies' mutual cartographies, Toorop with prudence, the young Venezuelan-Croatian with insatiable curiosity.

"Montreal is a fascinating city," he submitted to saying after a while.

The sky above him buzzed with millions of stars that two quivering and eager breasts came to deliciously conceal.

36

Gorsky watched the screen for a long time before reacting.

The screen had turned black, with parasites in streaks of electronic flickers and the permanent oscillation of a grayish-colored band. A message from the offset antenna unrolled a few semi-decipherable pictograms.

Gorsky closed his eyes an instant. The fuckers. He opened them on Markov, disheveled hair, eyes still hazy with sleep, then on Vlasseïev, the head hacker, who'd come straight from Novosibirsk with a hand-picked team.

They'd just been here a week, and had wasted no time.

A little while ago, at four in the morning, Vlasseïev woke Markov. At first, he sent him packing, but Vlasseïev insisted, showed him the recording. Markov ran to wake up his boss.

"Show it to me again," went Gorsky, in an acrid voice.

Markov complied. He repositioned the disk on start with a multi-usage remote control, and then played the sequence.

Vlasseïev hadn't said a word during the last viewing. As the disk turned on a second time, the tall redhead wrapped in a shapeless military parka squirmed, ill at ease.

"We were able to intercept this message yesterday, but it took us all night to decrypt it."

Electronic interference flashed on the screen.

"Some images were damaged when we intercepted the message. We had to work with the technology at hand," Vlasseïev said, apologetic.

Gorsky silenced him with a hand movement as a jumpy cathode-blue image took hold of the screen.

The first thirty seconds were basically incomprehensible, and the image appalling. But Vlasseïev had done some good work, with the "technology at hand." The little guy had a future, thought Gorsky as the HF channel became audible and the image slowly stabilized on screen.

He concentrated on the dialogue he'd just heard, but the details of which scattered under the preliminary shock of emotion.

Against a background of electronic static, Doctor Walsh was standing next to a young woman of about thirty-five. She had silver tinted dirty blond hair and icy gray-green eyes. She was good looking, but something made her face hard, metallic, and almost unbearable.

"I... I..." faltered Doctor Walsh, "we took all possible precautions, I assure you... The eggs are not..."

"The eggs!" screamed the woman, hysterical. "Blasphemy! Unnatural vision! What do you have to tell me on that account?"

"The eggs have not suffered, Ma'am. I assure you, I give you my biologist's word..."

"Biologist's word?!" the blond woman cut him off sharply. "Your word has been broken constantly since the beginning, and catastrophes just keep piling up."

"I repeat, the eggs have not..."

"Quiet!" cried the woman, in a neurotic explosion. "Quiet, you old fool, you old incompetent dimwit! What difference does it make if the 'eggs,' as you say, are altered or not, it's the carrier that took off!"

"Madam, you must believe I am extremely sorry about this unfortunate setback, but it is quite out of my domain."

"Your domain is zilch, nada. Since we decided to call upon you, nothing has gone as planned."

"Is it my fault," squealed the doctor, "is it my fault, Madam? It wasn't me that shot your plane down with a missile, or mass..."

"Be quiet, you old fool. The organization that took over the transfers ended up being even worse. With the others at least, we were able to conclude phase one of operations. We consider from now on that there is clearly a breach of contract."

"Madam, you cannot be serious..."

"You'll see how serious I am, you old bat. This breach entails, as you know, irrevocable and definitive decisions."

A brief electronic silence.

"What do you mean?" blurted Walsh, anxiously.

"What I said, dear doctor. Don't count on us to pay one cent more. And you know what? I take it as compensation for that incredible chaos for which your organization is responsible, one way or another."

"Wha... What?... You must be kidding! What are you doing, Madam?"

"We're doing what has to be done, you old incompetent thing!" screamed the woman. "As for the girl, she will not escape us much longer. My cybernetic astrologer is certain of it."

"Madam... no..." moaned the doctor. "What have you done, my God, what have you done?" he kept repeating pathetically.

"Be quiet will you, you old sniveling wreck. Now is not the time for sentiments. Our usual contacts will take care of all the details. Goodnight and goodbye, Doctor Walsh. And do not try to call me, it's useless; in less than a minute, there'll be a whole new encryption code protecting my messages."

Then, the screen went black.

Gorsky sighed. He felt his ticker slow down, but the feeling of imminent catastrophe overwhelmed him, almost as much as during the first viewing.

"The fuckers," he muttered between his teeth.

He caught his breath, waited for his heart samba to change to a cool bossa nova. It took longer than usual, it seemed.

He turned to Vlasseïev.

"When was this transmitted?"

Vlasseïev scratched his ear and squirmed in place before answering.

"Well... How do I say this...? We weren't able to reconstruct that part of the code. But we know a certain number of things."

"Explain yourself," Gorsky grumbled surly.

The man shuffled about.

"It's a bit technical, and..."

"I'm not an idiot, Vlasseïev, and I know how a fucking computer works."

"Hum... yes, of course. We... Well, in fact, we didn't intercept this message directly. That would have been impossible. Statistically, either one of the interlocutors would have detected our operation... But I picked up the presence of a new highly protected sector in the neural network of the doctor's private Intranet. I was able to penetrate the network yesterday, during the day...Well, I recopied part of the sequence, it had a few holes that I tried to fill in as best I could. From what I could tell from the entrance codes of the sector in question, it was created a week ago, and there was only this file inside it."

"A week before your intrusion?"

"Yes. You must understand, nothing is written out clearly. It's something, how should I say it, that you know, that you feel, it's experience, I guess... Gathering from the organization of its antiviral defenses, the file was real young, a newborn. That's why I say a week. Two at most. These days, in that time frame some sort of virus would have attacked. But that's why I was able to crack it so easily. Its macrophages were ridiculously inexperienced."

The guy found it all too easy, thought Gorsky.

He'd be set.

"Find that woman," he spat. "Find her and hack all her shit."

Vlasseïev swallowed his saliva kind of harshly, then said:

"It'll be done, Mister Gorsky."

He asked to be left alone. He had to think hard.

Since the attack on Rivard Street, Romanenko and he had started to make out the general schema of things. Rock-Machines allied to a fucking Chink triad had tried to seize the Alpha goods. According to the Quebec police, a second gang composed of Hell's Angels and Russian-American thugs had intervened, just before security forces showed up. And on the way, these nice folks knocked off two cops in a passing patrol car.

The message pirated by Vlasseïev dramatically altered the whole perspective. It wasn't the Rock-Machines who'd attacked the house, but the Hell's Angels. The Hell's Angels working for the Noelites. Fuck!

Gorsky felt no need to see the tape a third time to get a complete outline of the situation. The woman Walsh had that conversation with was his client from the "other end of the world." And Walsh's client blew a fuse. Riled up by a first failure, when one of their planes was shot down above Sakhalin by who knows who, she couldn't deal with the series of uncontrollable events that ended up with Marie Zorn's flight. She just straight out ordered the whole team to be destroyed. At the same time, her henchmen had no qualms about doing in Kotcheff's men. She was really crazy, no doubt about it.

Gorsky knew Kotcheff. He wouldn't get his shit stepped on like that and sing the "Star Spangled Banner," or "O Canada," our home and native land. He couldn't let twenty of his best men be exterminated and not do anything without serious prejudice to his status. The Russian-American Mafioso was lying low, waiting for the wave to pass. When it did, he'd take care of Miss Blondy pronto. Quebec had avoided civil war when it gained its relative independence; but Kotcheff would wage an all-out-war to show everyone they couldn't live without him.

The problem was keeping control, the key to all successful warfare. Yet Gorsky knew that within a couple days he'd totally lost control of events. Before he could react, flamethrowers were torching the apartment squatted by Toorop and his team.

They had as much room to maneuver as a supertanker in a bathroom. The police were looking for Kotcheff's men. From what he knew, all search operations to find the girl were reduced to the strict minimum. If the pressure increased within the next few days, they'd be temporarily blocked.

According to the latest messages from Romanenko, Toorop had apparently escaped, but they'd lost contact. The colonel said that Toorop was probably giving the soufflé time to drop before trying to communicate with him. He was being cautious, the colonel said.

Alone in his living room, Gorsky chewed it over a good while. According to the Quebec Sureté, the latest analyses showed that Rebecca Kendall and James Lee Osborne, residents of 4067 and

4075, had killed each other off. According to police analysis, it appeared that the man had shot three grenades, one of which fatally wounded the woman, before she shot him down when he entered the room to finish her off.

And Toorop had miraculously survived all that shit.

No. He was not "being cautious."

It was something else.

Later on, after having repeatedly gone over all the options, he decided to act.

First, mobilize.

He called Markov and ordered him to contact the guys in Novosibirsk immediately. They had to set up a good little squat team right away, ready to rush off to the Chingiz Mountains in an emergency. The team would meet up at the Semipalatinsk datcha and await his orders. He wanted the Petrovsky brothers on the job.

Second, plan. The first thing to do was partition the information into categories before it circulated, according to who needed to know what. Walsh had received Miss Blondie's call about ten days before, just after the attack on the apartment. Since then, he hadn't left the lab and had changed the lock on the front door. A red light blinked above it continuously, meaning he was not to be disturbed under any circumstances. Walsh was hiding. He was freaked out.

And rightly so. Gorsky would let him stew for forty-eight hours, then corner him. He'd invite him for lunch. The old grouch would complain, but he'd come. And then they'd show him a nice little movie. And start talking seriously.

Third, the great question remained: What do we do about Marie Alpha?

Miss Blondie wanted to get rid of her and her progeny. She wasn't worth a cent. She was schizoid. Whatever she might say would be implausible, but there was still a risk. She'd seen the setup on Mount Chingiz; she knew it existed, just like she knew about his Novosibirsk network.

She was potentially dangerous.

He'd have to get rid of her, one day or another.

37

The killer-angel was regularly by her side now. It disappeared during her erratic sleep phases, and reappeared under its new form when she awoke: the crime-series heroine, the terrorist from the Symbionese Liberation Army or the Red Army Faction, the Amazon from a purely mental urban guerrilla.

That night, half an hour after she went to bed, vaguely falling asleep and waking up prey to what she felt was serious insomnia, the girl appeared wearing the double-serpent embossed black beret. The archangel was sitting in an armchair near the window. A silver-blue ray of moonlight fell on one side of her face, sketching a hybrid identity, light and shadow, a double-faced cherub-demon.

"You just barely escaped the monster's jaw... The twin DNA center is now in an extremely delicate phase of biological transformation. You will be left to your own devices for a few weeks, in the human perception of time. From now on, and following the laws of earthly things, we shall speak of a fetal program. Great transformations are about to commence. You must find a safe place, for you and the twin DNA center. Nothing must hinder the mutation."

"No, of course," she answered, like an insect urged on by an overpowering chemical order.

"Although the DNA center can predict the objective direction of events within the arrow of time, as well as many other things, it cannot directly manage the way the individual carrier, you in this case, handles its relations with its environment and the Darwinian chaos that humans call History. Our communications shall be interrupted for a while. Neither myself, nor that Elvis Presley clown shall be sent. You shall be alone to fend for yourself, and the mutation shall be of great amplitude. You need to find a safe place."

"But… How? I know nothing of this…"

"I've been sent to give you the necessary information, you idiot!" the young terrorist sternly cut in. "If I'd sniveled like this at the time, I would never have escaped the political police for more than three days."

"What political police?"

"Doesn't matter," the young woman answered. "You need to learn my instructions by heart, and follow them to a T. The DNA center has been able to identify recurrent shamanic signs."

"What signs?"

"It's strange and complex. Each detail is essential. I've been informed that between your crises of amnesia your memory is excellent, so remember this: first, the Messenger-Falcon of Huron mythology appears. In its talons, it holds a bundle of lighting bolts, US military style. This shamanic sign is very strong. According to the DNA center, the double bolt is a direct transcription of the double helix. This indicates it is of crucial importance to you and to the survival of the anthropic program."

"The anthropic program?"

"Certain things follow the rhythm of a kind of attractor in the deterministic chaos of the arrow of time. These are very specific events Marie, whose exact shape and genealogy correspond to the unique history of each species. But such historical processors force them to grapple regularly with the same challenges, to visualize in a timely manner the adaptations required for their survival."

"So, what can I do?" went Marie.

The female angel in the black beret broke into laughter.

"What you can do? Don't you understand? You can do absolutely everything. Everything. It's just normal, Marie. You are that active chaotic congruence. You are change, you, and mostly the creations that you carry."

Marie observed the angel a good while.

"What are they really?" she let herself ask, in a tiny voice.

"The twin DNA center has not authorized me to…"

"Your DNA center is a pain in my ass! If something has to happen to me, if the transformation is just starting, and if I'm left to my own devices for weeks, I have to know! I have to know what it is!"

The female angel wrapped herself up in her black leather jacket. She seemed bothered.

"I… I can't. As a matter of fact, I don't have the necessary information."

"You know enough to shed some light on it. If you're my guardian angel, stop acting like a little soldier and tell me what it is. What is this fucking twin DNA center? What did they really put inside me?"

The black leather angel fixed her blue rock-crystal stare on Marie.

"What did they tell you?"

Marie suppressed a shiver. At the time, for twenty-five thousand NorthAm dollars, she would have done whatever, even lug around replacement organs taken from dead bodies on an assembly line in some underground clinic, and temporarily grafted somewhere inside her.

"They told me I'd be carrying an animal clone outlawed by Unopol. They told me I'd have to wait about three months before a specialized medical team took charge and I delivered."

"They lied to you."

"I thought so. About what?"

"About everything. You'll give birth in nine months. The normal full term human pregnancy."

Marie let the words of the Black Angel weigh down on the universe, and her soul, like as many deadly bullets.

Deep down, she'd always known.

"The Age of the Great Tempests is just beginning," the old man told him on the night of the "experience," the terrible experience. "The white man will understand what it means to violate the planet."

Toorop kept quiet; anything he said would have been out of place.

"The chaos of the elements will help us. The Wind Spirit will come disrupt the life of men, but he will be your steed on your mission, White Man."

Toorop nodded yes, without thinking.

The old man laughed. His face folded up like an inflatable structure. The ritual bracelets jiggled on his wrists. The dream catchers on his belt shook along with his stomach.

"You know," he said, "it would be real easy to pass myself off for an old Indian medicine man in touch with all the mysteries of the universe and trying to impress the pale-face. As you must have understood, our confederation is way beyond ethnic divisions. I have a TV just like everyone else, and I watch the weather forecast. Cyclone Jefferson has just wreaked havoc on Florida. In less than twenty-four hours, torrential rains and extremely violent winds will devastate the whole eastern part of the continent, from the Mississippi Delta to the Saint-Laurent Estuary. But it's true, I believe, *we all believe*, that this cyclone, like the other typhoons and hurricanes that happened this year, is just one of the warning signs. From now on, the tempests shall follow uninterrupted one after the other, deluvial rains shall make the rivers rise from their beds. At the same time, the first great glaciers at the poles will all start melting… Water will cover the world, and the skies will be darkened by incessant winds carrying great storms."

Toorop sighed, but said nothing. He'd been hearing the same thing for days. He had a hard time getting used to it, but was really in no position to complain.

The old Indian drew some signs in the warm ashes with his fingers. Small flames springing up from the half-burnt log lit up his face. From Toorop's perspective, it seemed typically Indian, a hooked nose, dark skin, but its blue eyes were a clear proof of intermixing.

"The prediction is very clear: 'A man from the end of the world, a solitary warrior, will ride upon the Wind Spirit, and allow the Envoy to find her people'."

Toorop held back a laugh.

"Me?" he went, "that's a joke."

The old man didn't answer. He shook his head and made a face, fanning the fire smoldering beneath what remained of the log.

After a while, he drew other signs with his finger in the warm ashes around the hearth.

"That's the problem with you white men. You don't believe in the invisible. Or you need huge instruments to venture a few positive hypotheses…"

Toorop grimaced a smile, despite himself. He wasn't particularly rationalist. He knew himself well enough to figure out the unconscious, libidinal or symbolic motivations of his actions, but he wasn't ready to down the first religion-in-a-kit to come around.

He expected certain formal requirements beforehand.

Proof.

At the very least, an "array of assumptions" that held it's own.

A voice chose that very moment to spring up behind him in the darkness, a voice that would answer a few questions.

"Uncle Black Bear, you know very well that *our* instruments have become necessary for the continuation of the program. Stop acting like the old reactionary Indian that you're not."

The old man smiled.

Toorop turned slowly to see a silhouette approach the circle of light and kneel down around the circular hearth of stones.

Another Indian. Toorop had seen him the day before; his "hosts" had summarily presented them. Turtle Johnson he said his name was.

He was young, thirty. Within two or three minutes, Toorop could tell he was perfectly integrated, university education, probably an official job in some kind of high-tech industry.

But he was also part of the brotherhood.

"Uncle Black Bear, why don't you explain to him how all this is going to happen?"

"Pfff…!" went the old man, "he'll see for himself."

Turtle Johnson nodded his head with a smile. He, in turn, drew signs into the ashes with the end of a little stick.

Then he fixed his black eyes on Toorop.

"It's time. They're here."

Toorop didn't say a thing. He felt his heart go into overdrive, the accelerator hit the floor. He'd heard the hiss of the pneumatic doors, at the other end of the Chaosphere, the top two floors of the building entirely devoted to a freely proliferating biological-machine world.

He knew the time had come to meet the Sherpas, the ones working invisibly behind the scenes of this (super?)natural theater.

The blue-eyed old man affirmed that he was ready; he'd been purified of all evil spirits. He could have the experience, tonight, yes.

Toorop got up. The young Indian preceded him through the machines and the vegetable world they seemed to sprout from.

Toorop listened to the sound of rain on the roof of the building. He watched the two men standing before him. Turtle Johnson was preparing the mixture a bit farther off, sitting cross-legged in the light of a small butane lamp. The two men he didn't know were standing on each side of some kind of metallic piece of furniture, on top of which a black bulbous shape lorded, connected to one of the latest ultra-flat computer screens where fugitive contoured light clouds shimmered. Joe-Jane, the mysterious machine they'd conceived, and with whom the one called Vax shut himself up for hours in his studio.

Turtle Johnson shot him a calm smile.

"The friends we spoke to you about, the Sherpas."

And he went back to his work.

Toorop looked the Sherpas over. They stood out around here. Europeans, fifty-year-olds like him, without the slightest tattoo or experimental bionic protuberance. Toorop felt a vague kind of sympathy grow between the three of them; they probably knew they belonged to another century, and to a dying civilization.

They were dressed casually, light sportswear and hooded raincoats. They were dripping wet, so they must have just arrived. Toorop heard the pulsing rhythm speed up even more on the roof. Far away, he heard something like a roll of cymbals played by all the thunder gods of Creation. Turtle Johnson looked up at the two men as he persevered in his work.

"It'll be ready in twenty minutes... Why don't you introduce yourselves to our guest."

He pointed to Toorop, standing across from them.

The guy on the left, wearing a red and gray Gore-Tex jacket, moved towards him, hand extended. Toorop gave his in return, the bionic one; it was starting to look like something human, and he needed to use it. They shook on it. Neither one of them broached the subject.

"Boris Dantzik. Please excuse our lack of manners, but we're a little short on time."

The tall man on the right, in black, was twitching nervously. The guy reminded him of something but he couldn't say what, or why.

"Yes. In fact, we barely have time to explain everything."

Toorop gave a nasty laugh.

"Oh yeah?! If you think I'm gonna continue playing this little game much longer, you've got your head stuck up your ass to the neck, as my mom used to say. And, first of all, who do I have the honor of meeting?"

The man in the bi-colored Gore-Tex stepped aside to introduce the tall beanpole in black who extended his hand.

"Doctor Darquandier, Arthur. I've been taking care of Marie Zorn for years."

Toorop probed deep into his eyes.

When he'd read Romanenko's pirated file on Doctor Darquandier, taken from the university archives, he fell upon two pictures probably dating back to his student days. The guy had aged a good twenty-five years, and had changed a lot. He had long, messy hair, in clumps, and a white-speckled beard, long and curly. A bit crazy looking.

He'd never seen the guy in Gore-Tex before, one meter seventy of concentrated energy, a strong square face, its muscles like high voltage electricity cables, and thinning blond hair around a bald spot. He smiled like a cocaine addict, but Toorop suspected that another, more mysterious substance was responsible.

Nothing disturbed the silence but the majestic score of the elements. A deluge of biblical dimensions was falling upon Montreal.

The two men looked at each other for a few instants. They seemed hesitant.

Gore-Tex took the situation in hand.

"The Cyborg Society has explained everything about you."

"Good, I won't have to repeat that long story then."

"On the other hand, I think it would be best if we introduced ourselves thoroughly. At this point, better to lose an hour than days."

He looked at Toorop, at Darquandier, and then at the wicker chairs, near the black machine, arranged around a rusted flight case converted into a low table. On a nearby pillar covered in climbers, an old biological contamination sign was slowly rusting under the green tapestry.

Turtle Johnson was preparing a brew at the other end of the room on a small butane stove, in a kitchenette set up like a space station. The smell of jasmine tea filled the room.

Dantzik initiated the move.

"Let's sit down, we'll be more comfortable to talk."

He looked over at Darquandier, patted him on the shoulder, a carnivorous smile reaching for his ears.

"Stop freaking out like that, Arthur, I'm sure everything's gonna be fine. I have no doubt that Mister Toorop will side with us once we spell out the general problem."

At the other end of the room, Toorop saw the young Indian prepare the ritual objects for a ceremony. He drew a circle of black powder on a large fireproof square of fabric, and arranged a concentric circle of stones in the center, around two piled-up logs.

Toorop turned his attention back to the two men facing him.

Behind them, the black machine was purring softly, her screen agitated by the azure flashes of an electronic dream.

They were as different as could be. Darquandier emitted an inky, tortured aura, darkened by who knows what past or present experience, a black Christ. Dantzik resembled a pure instinctive fusion ball, with a will and energy of steel. Toorop's experienced eye, however, detected a shadow, a fracture, some hidden melancholy covered by a ton of armor.

They had but one thing in common, a golden tan, the bronze of the high seas, a look of health that jarred with this world of sickness.

Dantzik sighed. He seemed to be concentrating; for a moment, his stare was lost in his internal limbo.

"I should start from the beginning. But that's impossible in this situation, as there are several distinct causes intertwining to form this story, so let me try to delimit a center. I think it would be best to start with what brings us all here; I mean Marie Zorn."

"Yes, very good start. What does she represent for you exactly?"

"Don't worry about that," Darquandier interjected. "All that matters is that we get to the experience, fast."

Toorop tensed up.

Dantzik berated Darquandier with a hand movement, and tried to cool things down.

"Arthur is a bit curt. Tact and sociability aren't high up on his list, but he's a very talented researcher. You'll be under his technical guidance for the experience."

"What experience?" Toorop asked with a sigh of frustration.

"You're right, that's the best place to start."

"Right."

Dantzik breathed in, glanced at Darquandier then decided it was better the doctor not take care of this.

He fixed his blue eyes on Toorop and, with a wide smile, dropped:

"You're going to help us find Marie Zorn."

"Are you kidding? I lost contact with her on the night of the carnage. It's been almost two weeks now."

Dantzik's smile lit up.

"We know that. It doesn't really matter, two days, or two weeks; it's enough, right?"

His eyes looked for approval to the tall guy in black with the salt and pepper beard, the lanky one with eyes full of black light, who muttered something like:

"…correlated to distance and objective time of… let's say about two months in the present case."

Toorop let out a boiling sigh.

"Dammit, come on, will you explain yourselves?"

Dantzik's eyes hooked onto his.

"OK: First, you're going to take a drug. Second we're going to plug your brain into this machine, a computer called a neuromatrix. Third, thanks to this coupling, you'll find Marie Zorn."

Toorop swallowed, frozen stiff. He couldn't tear his eyes off the continuously iridescent screen.

"?!... You're fucking with me?"

"Do I look like it?"

Toorop read—in Dantzik's electric blue and Darquandier's dark, black, and blazing stares—that this wasn't the case.

He was silent for a good while. His two interlocutors seemed to be waiting patiently for him to digest the information to the end.

He knew he was in no position to argue. He blurted out in a breath: "Fine. Why me?..."

"That's what I was saying before. How long did you stay with her?"

Toorop did the math in a blink.

"Marie? I, *we stayed* practically six weeks with her in Montreal. Plus one more in Kazakhstan."

"Every day?"

"Here, in Montreal, every day. Every night. Twenty-four seven."

"And you say you lost contact with her about two weeks ago... Arthur?"

The man in black mumbled in his beard:

"That's what I was saying. The usable residual memory is a second-degree equation that factors objective contact time between the two individuals and the space-time relation that separates them. According to my calculations, from what you tell me, it's about two months of persistence."

"Mister Toorop, your memories are in perfect shape."

"Is that the only reason?"

"The only reason?"

"Yes, the fact that I met her recently, spent a pretty long period of time with her, and that I just lost sight of her not long ago."

"That's the main reason determining all the rest, yes."

"It's because of the drug?"

"Rather thanks to the drug, and thanks to Joe-Jane."

"Joe-Jane?"

Dantzik pointed to the machine with his thumb.

"The computer. It's an artificial intelligence. Of a new kind. A schizomatrix. At one time, she knew Marie Zorn well. With her help, in the beginning, we searched for her, but that's the whole problem, Mister Toorop. The more time passes, the more our usable memory activity decreases, as Arthur says, same with the memory of the neuromatrix."

He was gonna take a drug, probably a very strong hallucinogen. They'd cover his head in electrodes, plug him into an artificial intelligence, and he'd have the acid trip of his life on the mental search for a schizoid chick who was carrying transgenic animals for a sect of freaks. All this for five, ten, then twenty thousand dollars, and now for nothing. Questions were already crowding his head like a screeching train. He took a haphazard pick.

"What do you know of Marie Zorn's current state?"

The two men glanced at each another.

"What do you mean exactly?" went Dantzik.

"Her state. I mean her biological state."

"Biological?" snapped Darquandier. "You probably mean her mental state?"

"No," coldly retorted Toorop. "I mean biological. Oh, I see, you don't know…"

"What do you mean," went Dantzik dryly.

"Yes, what do you mean?" Darquandier strung on like an echo.

"I mean that Marie is carrying viruses. And my mission was to bring them to North America."

"Viruses? Are you sure?"

"What are you talking about?"

"I've been contaminated. I know what I'm talking about. And I think that this whole damn mess, the massacre and everything, is just a consequence of those fucking viruses."

Darquandier frowned. He was thinking fast, like an overwrought computer. Dantzik didn't say anything; he stayed put, silent and frozen stiff.

Finally, Darquandier livened up.

"Describe the symptoms."

Toorop laughed.

"The symptoms? Fine: meet an old friend who's been dead for ten years and chew the cud with him on the sidewalk; see a dream from the night before happen in reality. The others clearly succumbed to their paranoid delirium, but since it's basically second nature to me, I guess that's what saved me."

Darquandier pouted, nodding his head and going mmh mmh.

"What, mmh mmh?"

"I do think something very strange happened to Marie, and to you, therefore. But I don't think it's exactly what you're thinking."

"What do you mean?"

"The viruses. I don't think that's your cargo, unless by some miraculous and probably catastrophic luck."

"Fuck, come on, explain yourself…"

"Well, let's just say it's highly probable that Marie developed some of her powers beyond the limits we had imagined possible."

"Can you be clear, just once?"

Darquandier looked him up and down, eyes full of that black lightning.

"The viruses you're talking about, Marie learned how to use them."

"What're you talking about?"

At that moment, Dantzik broke out:

"This is what I've been telling you, Arthur, we have to explain everything to him, otherwise he won't be able to understand, or put things in perspective."

Toorop laughed sarcastically.

"Whatever you explain to me, the fact remains that Marie is carrying viruses because we know she is carrying something else. And that something else is there precisely to make the viruses."

"What else but her own brain, Mister Toorop? And I'll tell you why, or rather how."

Darquandier passed his hand through his long hair, stuck together by months of salt air and seawater. He seemed to look inwards.

Toorop cut him off with the unshakeable precision of the one who knows, absolutely, that his hand is better than his opponent's.

"It's useless, Darquandier. I mean, Sirs, Marie Zorn is pregnant."

That was like a nice sized rock thrown into the limpid waters of a lake.

"Pregnant?!" croaked Darquandier, looking truly surprised.

"Oh God!" went Dantzik as his face fell.

"That's the word. So you don't know what Marie's carrying?"

"God Almighty… What are you talking about?"

Toorop cut to the chase, no use beating around the bush.

"So you listen to me now. I was, we were responsible for bringing Marie Zorn here to Quebec to deliver what she was carrying. We weren't supposed to know what that was, but we were supposed to stay with her for a trimester. That's why our employers changed their mind in the middle of the whole thing and decided to replace us after six weeks, after a fair and square medical check-up of said Marie. We shouldn't have found out she was pregnant, I guess… On the other hand, the information I collected with… [he stopped]… let's just say, the colonel allowed me to identify the exact nature of what she's carrying."

Dantzik seemed shocked. The ball of life-energy had given way to a shriveled up shadow, with terrified eyes and a haggard face.

"Please be as precise as possible, Mister Toorop," went Darquandier, who was as taut as a bowstring.

"From what we know, they're transgenic animals."

"Transgenic… animals, really? What kind of animals?"

"We don't know," Toorop answered. "But Newton should know."

"Why?"

"He prescribed her some sort of medication, a Russian 'bioprocessor.' I would regularly recover a memory-capsule and get it analyzed by a kind of portable scanner he gave me. Apparently he received all the information online. It's true that he never told me anything about it, but we weren't in direct contact after that… I'm sure he knew. The bioprocessors must have detected the hormone changes and all that. As you know, the guy was a kind of professional double, or triple, agent. I'd even say he was multi-carded."

"The Cyborg Society didn't trust him at all," went Darquandier, "but he was necessary. Until that whole army of gangsters killed themselves on your block."

"Why?"

"Because he was the only one to know that Marie Zorn was here in Quebec, and that several rival organizations were trying to find her. That's what Vax and the girls learned while surfing his Intranet."

"So?"

"It's urgent we get Marie back before those organizations fight over her like fucking vultures. Or before they kill each other, as they've done already. The brotherhood hadn't anticipated that, I mean, not as soon."

"The brotherhood? Shit, I though you were scientists."

"We are scientists... our brotherhood doesn't just advocate one model of thought, that's all. You must have noticed that yourself, around here."

Toorop smiled slightly. He gestured towards Turtle Johnson who was coming back towards his circle of black powder and the small rock hearth, with a cup of tea in hand.

"Will you explain your relationship to all these weirdos?"

"The EarthQuakers, the Cyborg Society and the Cosmic Dragons are just one part of the whole," went Dantzik, who'd livened up all of a sudden. "The other tips of the triangle are Darquandier and his laboratory on the one hand, me on the other. Of the pentagram, I should say."

Toorop realized he knew strictly nothing about the man in bicolor Gore-Tex with the light eyes.

"And so who are you?"

"I told you, my name is Boris Dantzik."

"I know your name by heart, there's no need to repeat yourself. But what do you do for a living, Mister Dantzik, apart from organizing hallucinogenic experiences with new age Indians?"

The guy laughed ironically at himself.

"I'm a writer, Mister Toorop. I write science-fiction novels."

Toorop suppressed a large smile. He didn't want to offend him, but his body language spoke out clearly: no kidding, so?

And at the same time he remembered a detail picked up during his research on Marie and Darquandier. A science-fiction writer had visited Darquandier's neuro-psychiatric unit at the University of Montreal...

Shit, thought Toorop. The guy was sitting right in front of him. This wasn't the right time to ask for an autograph.

"That's where the tips of the triangle meet, Mister Toorop. The magical and sacred ties between fiction and reality."

Fuck, thought Toorop, what's all this preaching bullshit?

Dantzik seemed to be caught up in a deep interior wave.

"Well, Mister Toorop, the first time I visited Doctors Darquandier, Winkler and Mandelcorn, in Montreal... oh God, it's already been ten years... I was writing the last chapters of a novel that had been dragging on for years... It was the story of a schizophrenic with multiple personalities that the whole economy of the future rested on. It was inspired by the work of Deleuze and Guattari, but also by Timothy Leary, McKenna and other neural science pioneers. Just as I was finishing the book, I heard about Doctor Mandelcorn and his team. When I got to Montreal to meet him, I just wanted to harvest some final information, add a bit of reality to my ramblings. Doctors Winkler and Darquandier had just joined the lab. They showed me Marie Zorn and some other patients. At the time, Marie was not really at the top of her form. The effects of the lab treatment were just starting. But the craziest thing, Mister Toorop, was that Marie was exactly like the creature I'd imagined, and her history intersected my character's story more than once... There you go, Mister Toorop—I'd invented Marie Zorn."

Dantzik waited for the information to travel its deadly trajectory inside Toorop's synapses.

Finally, Toorop turned towards Darquandier.

"You condone this kind of gibberish?"

Darquandier smiled coldly.

"This kind of gibberish, Mister Toorop, is the foundation of the technology of the future."

"The technology of the future?"

Dantzik was about to speak but Darquandier cut him off with a sharp hand movement.

"Yes, Mister Toorop. Neuronic technologies. The ones we are perfecting. With the help of Marie and many others."

"*Neuronic...* technologies?"

The man rose from his seat and gestured to the whole of the universe around him. His black eyes were like a lake of solidified lava beneath which crouched a blaze of burning fever.

"That's exactly it, Mister Toorop: the brain is truly the last frontier! We're sequencing and cloning DNA, sending probes to Mars, and soon, a live mission. We've established plans for a city on the moon; an orbital station is going up around Alpha. We're determining the exact topology of the ocean floor, deep-sea trenches included, and our information systems are now capable of digitalizing the entire earth to the atom. We're simulating the big bang, hunting the Higgs boson in our super-accelerators. At the same time, the greenhouse effect has raised temperatures one degree since the end of last century and will add one or two before the middle of this one. Ocean levels are already rising. Yet we know nothing, Mister Toorop, or almost nothing, of the resources of our humble brains, that are at the origins of all this."

The argument held up, Toorop had to recognize that.

"On the other hand," Darquandier continued, "you will agree that all the great advances in this field pass for grotesque, just think of Freud, or Jung... when they aren't, like today, being repressed by liberticidal laws."

"Yeah, just like the transgenic animals Marie's carrying," went Toorop, with a sardonic smile.

Darquandier blew up; it was like a liquid helium bottle being poured on the floor.

"Those kinds of animals are bullshit, Mister Toorop. Just to think that all those morons are killing each other for third grade genetic tinkering. They don't even have a clue what Marie's worth, or what she'd be capable of! What jackasses! They're nothing but pre-programmed insects!"

His hand gesture could have decapitated an entire crowd.

Darquandier wanted to make the human brain his next frontier, thought Toorop, but he didn't seem to appreciate the humans in question.

The tall beanpole in black continued in the same monotone rhythm.

"Marie is more than just a schizo, dear Sir. She's the next stage."

"The next stage?"

"Yes," Darquandier continued, in a pure metallic tone. "The Next Stage. The one after man."

The rain falling from the sky in liquid armies came to fill the long silence that ensued.

It was Turtle Johnson who broke it:

"Tea is served. It's gonna get cold."

Toorop barely remembered walking to the large camping table where the steaming cups were waiting. The window close by opened up onto the corner of Saint-Laurent and Ontario. The flying saucer of the Olympic Stadium disappeared behind the impenetrable clouds at the end of Sherbrooke. Flashes of lighting bolted everywhere to the south, far beyond the austere UQAM buildings.

Some time later, the storm broke out above them. Toorop interpreted it as a dramatic signal announcing the return of human voices, like in a Wagner opera. Turtle Johnson took no part at all in the conversation; he was lost in his mysterious occupations, going from one end of the room to the other.

"Explain the 'next stage' to me," he snapped, his voice hoarse.

Darquandier reacted right away, as if he'd been waiting for the right signal.

"The anthropic mutation, Mister Toorop, will be the product of humanity itself."

"What does that mean?"

Darquandier sighed.

"Where should I start? What do you know about Deleuze and Guattari's work? About Sir John Eccles? What do you know about the brain and its relations to quantum physics? About the shamanistic rites of South America, or Siberia? What do you know about Jeremy Narby? What do you know about the Cosmic Serpent, Mister Toorop?"

Darquandier's voice was as cold as ice.

Toorop heard Turtle Johnson crack up at the other end of the room.

"The Cosmic Serpent?"

"Yes, Mister Toorop, that's how the Aborigines see it, and it's not a bad concept."

"What does it mean?"

Darquandier's lips sketched the shadow of a smile.

"That is exactly what you will discover tonight."

Toorop let out an angry sigh.

"Don't play this little game with me, Doctor Darquandier. I'm asking for precise answers to precise questions."

Darquandier took a mouthful of boiling tea without even blowing on it, as if he were protected from all sensation, from all affect.

"I'll put you on track. To begin with, let me give you a few plain facts, and a few fundamental questions. First of all, we find a certain number of perfectly analogous recurrent myths in all aborigine cultures that exist on the face of this damn globe. Secondly, these foundational mythologies of the shamanic world all come from 'visions' that the shaman brings back after taking so-called 'hallucinogenic' drugs which are generally outlawed in our society. You follow?"

Yes, Toorop silently acquiesced with a nod of the head. He blew on the boiling hot tea.

"Good. One of these recurrent myths takes the form of a monstrous animal shaped like a double serpent that emits a very violent light. Conformist ethnologists consider it to be an 'interpretation' of nature by simple Neolithic brains… Basically, they think that Aborigines, under the influence of the drug, imagine a cosmic twin serpent symbolically reinterpreting the serpents they see around them every day. Some add a vague mixture of Freudian interpretation to this, you know, like a phallic-serpent-symbol. You're still following?"

A nod again. Cautiously, Toorop took a small mouthful of boiling tea.

"Good. Problem number one is: why do we find the same double serpent in all shamanic cultures? Even in the sub-arctic regions, where no serpent could survive ten minutes, where no serpent ever survived, since you don't find them there, and they've never been found there. *A fortiori* two serpents. And a double headed one, no less."

Toorop didn't answer. The information was stocked in a corner of his memory.

Darquandier wasn't finished.

"Problem number two: how is it possible that repeated contact with the Cosmic Serpent allows the Neolithic aborigines to have a coherent pharmacopoeia and exact, non-empirical knowledge of vital processes at work in their close environment? To clarify, let me give you an example: how do Ayahuasquero Indians of the Peruvian Amazon know in advance when and where a very rare flower will suddenly grow, leagues away from their camp? How do they know the delicate interactions between different, very complex pharmacopoeias so precisely, and particularly between psychotropic plants? Well, the Amazonian Indians, the Yaquis or the Siberian shamans all say the same thing: when they take a certain type of substance, they come into 'contact' with the Cosmic Serpent who in turn delivers extremely precise information on the nature of things. Including things they don't understand, but that they 'see.' Did you know, for example, that shamans have been 'experimenting' with electromagnetism for millennia without having ever seen the slightest flashlight? The description they make of the radiation coming out of the Cosmic Serpent is... how should I say it... enlightening. In fact, it's a predominantly ultraviolet frequency that we can situate in the biophoton field..."

"All this sounds like Chinese to me," Toorop blurted out. "This isn't 'Who Wants To Be A Millionaire?' Why don't you cut to the chase?"

"Oh... Come on, I'll give you the key to the enigma, but you must find the lock... The Cosmic Serpent is double, as I was telling you. The most precise descriptions coincide, all of them. It's in the shape of a double helix coiled upon itself. Will that do?"

A double helix. Coiled upon…

"That's right, Mister Toorop. You understood. It's the exact structure of DNA."

"What does all this mean?" Toorop snapped after a while. It was all starting to be a bit much for one evening. "Does it mean the Indians 'plug' into their DNA, or something like that?"

Darquandier let out a little icy laugh.

"Excellent, Mister Toorop, that's the perfect image. That's exactly what Jeremy Narby discovered in the nineties, but since he was 'only' an anthropologist, no biologist worthy of that name accorded any credence to his 'ravings.' Except for us. And there's something even more important."

Toorop gave him time to catch his breath. Native American shamans navigated through their DNA like it was a Nintendo console, but there was more. He took a deep breath as well.

"Yes. They navigate through their DNA, right? Their own, of course, but also the DNA of the biosphere, because it's the same. Conformist biologists have their nose stuck in it; they're too close to see, Mister Toorop. Geneticists are the proletarian of the chromosome. They don't see the most essential thing; that ALL living beings on this damn planet are made of the same bricks. The same four little nucleotides, and the same double helix structure!"

"What does that mean? That for tripping Indians the whole world functions like a fucking navigation console?"

The hyena laugh quivered again.

"Incredible, right? But only at first glance, Mister Toorop. It actually intersects with the intuitions of Deleuze, Butler, and of many others, probably even up to Spinoza. There are no 'artificial' productions, in the exact sense of the word. We are creations of 'nature,' and even our most elaborate artifacts are manifestations of it. Ayahuasquero, Yaqui, Australian or Siberian sorcerers have been experimenting with very particular *navigation* techniques for millennia. Cybernetic techniques that allow them to travel in time, through space, but also, most importantly, inside their own body, their own brain, their own DNA... *and therefore inside those of other living beings*. And that's where we'll connect this long explanation to our main problem, as Boris was saying a while ago."

"Main problem?"

"Yes. The so-called Marie Zorn."

Toorop frowned.

"Marie is a shaman?"

"Pretty close. Marie is schizo, Mister Toorop. She's a shaman of the XXIst century, if you prefer."

"Of the XXIst century?"

"Remember the neuronal technologies I was telling you about. Schizos are naturally apt to take on multiple personalities. They experience very similar things to what the shamans describe. On the other hand, the work we've been doing for the last ten years on psychosis has led us to modify our initial approach a great deal. It's a 'work in progress.' What we now know exceeds anything we could have imagined in the beginning... Dantzik is the only one, really, to have guessed a part of the truth."

"What truth?"

"A truth you can't mention these days, Mister Toorop, the fact that a parallel evolution is occurring alongside 'normal' humanity. Do you know that schizophrenics appeared in Europe exactly at the end of the XVth century, at the beginning of the industrial revolution? How do you explain that Prophets, those great agents of the Word, appeared precisely when and where writing was being invented? Everything is recording, Mister Toorop. Everything is a machinic and desiring assemblage, as Gilles Deleuze used to say, beyond vitalism and mechanism. History is an illusion. But there is *process*, which is to say a constant in the synthetic theory of evolution. History isn't written beforehand and does not follow causal logic, for there are no rules other than those of deterministic chaos. It means that *locally*, life is an infinite variation of possibles on a genetic chain that ramifies according to classical Darwinian natural selection. But it also means that *globally* the tendency of life is to produce consciousness, i.e., information. Shamans knew all this. And schizos know it too."

"But why the 'next stage'?"

"Because schizos are exactly at the point of congruence between natural evolution and the chaos created by man and his technical productions. Let me be clear, Mister Toorop. According to our studies, it's as if the schizophrenic brain were directly pre-cabled for connection to artificial intelligence. To give you an image, let's say *Nature Incorporated*, for unknown reasons, decided to create a human mutant five centuries before its specular technical creature appeared, the neuromatrix."

"Specular? You mean like a reflection in a mirror, I suppose."

"Exactly. Schizos and neuromatrices have many points in common, I mean with their modes of perception. A schizo can live with a part of its body in Moscow and another in Ushuaia, when it's not on Ganymede. When I say 'body,' I mean 'body-without-organs,' the cosmic-body, the brain-body, the matrix-body. A schizo, like a neuromatrix, can change personalities, and get used to inverse causality phenomena, where information goes backwards in time by traveling faster than the speed of light. A neuromatrix is 'naturally' schizo, and a schizo is 'naturally' a neuromachine."

Toorop made an expressive face. Info traveling faster than the speed of light? It was time to call the emergency psych ward. Their specialty.

Darquandier read his mind.

"Truth is always raving mad to established dogma. There are incalculable accounts of abnormal, not to say paranormal, phenomena by psychoanalysts treating certain cases of psychosis. Premonitions, quasi-miraculous series of coincidences. On the other hand, twenty years ago, very serious experiments were carried out at the PEARL, at Princeton, not really acid dropping kind of guys, if you see what I mean?... Well, their experiments uncovered an unknown type of interaction between an individual and a digital system. Let me explain. Put a passive operator in the presence of an information-processing machine, and you get a 'correlation.' That correlation is sufficient to create a quantum perturbation that modifies certain bits at the heart of the machine-program. Let me make this very clear, Mister Toorop: there's no interface, headset, keyboard, mic, glove, joystick, pen, or thingamajig contraption, nothing. You sit the guy down in front of the computer and you wait twenty-four hours, and you repeat the experiment with hundreds of subjects. It's infinitesimal but you measure the same perturbation threshold for practically all subjects. What we, for our part, discovered, is that the perturbation rose considerably when we put a schizo with the machine. At the same time, the new drugs we elaborated, with the help of certain shamans, and by copying molecules from the nervous systems of schizos, allowed us to experience all these phenomena ourselves. So this is what it's about, Mister Toorop."

"So," went Toorop, a nasty smile on his face, "how was the trip?"

"Beyond what you could possibly imagine. Believe me, what Turtie prepared for you is the direct link to the Double Serpent. You won't be the same man when you come back."

"That's lucky," he said, showing off. "Turns out I needed a change of identity myself."

The storm thrashed above them. Outside, behind the wind and rain beaten panes, giant flashes illuminated the universe.

Toorop seemed lost contemplating the elements. Yet his entire brain was weighing and elaborating cascades of choices, and trying to draw a path through them, a strategy.

For days, months, even years, he'd let others guide his destiny. He'd changed employers, during these last two decades, with the constancy of a high finance shark for the average salary of a Brazilian agricultural worker.

Recently, he'd passed from Prince Shabazz to the Siberian mafia, via a corrupt GRU officer. Now, to save his skin, and maybe find some kind of honorable emergency exit, now, at this second, it seemed he'd just decided to cooperate fully with the EarthQuakers, the Cyborg Society, the Cosmic Dragons, all that shit, and these two European freaks. Together, they would find Marie, and try to save her from that fucking sect.

"Well," concluded Dantzik, "I think it's time to get on with the experience."

The two men got up, and both went towards the black machine with a heavy step.

Toorop shivered.

He heard, however, the purring of the stove that Turtle had just turned on with some alcohol. The wave of heat was already caressing his back.

The Indian was igniting the crossed logs in the stone hearth. He rushed out of the fireproof square as soon as the fire was lit. An invisible ventilation system softly pulled the smoke towards the foliage of concrete, aluminum, and green jungle.

Then he turned to Toorop and gave him the small earth bowl filled with green paste.

"The Vehicle. Eat it. Drink a mouthful of water. And wait."

Toorop took the small brown cup. There was no turning back.

"You'll have to enter the circle. It won't be easy, but once you've done that, everything'll be simpler."

Toorop looked at the little circle of burning powder around the hearth.

He couldn't figure out how it would be difficult to cross.

He soon realized his mistake.

The storm woke her up.

The sound of the rain drumming on the roof of the small Mazda followed the leitmotifs of the thunder. Marie opened her eyes onto a windshield covered in water. At first, she wondered if the entire car hadn't gone under.

She'd wandered about for a few days after leaving the Falcon Motel. She followed the Saguenay, aimlessly, regularly veering off the Trans-Canada Highway onto small country ones. She crossed two autonomous Indian territories without noticing any clear signs from the Messenger-Falcon, or any apparition, even fleeting, of either one of her guardian angels.

On the third night, she finally fell asleep in the car, exhausted, in a desolate parking lot near a forest.

And now, apparently all the waters of the sky wanted to fall upon her.

Marie flung herself into the front seat. She turned on the lights; a liquid wall rose before her.

Through the side window, she noted that the asphalt parking lot already resembled a baby pool. If things continued like this, they might soon have diving contests. As a reflex, she turned on the car. She had to find shelter, right away.

She'd noticed a kind of barn on the side of the road, three kilometers back. She had just enough time to get there before the roads became impracticable.

The car had become hard to maneuver; when she got to the road, slightly downhill, the water level had doubled. She drove cautiously on the slippery surface, staying below twenty miles per hour for the first mile. Then the Mazda accelerated, by itself, without Marie touching the pedal. She pressed on the brakes mechanically.

The car slid and ended up barring the road sideways.

Facing the incline and the top of the hill, Marie had just enough time to understand that a river of mud was racing down the neighboring slopes.

She felt the Mazda slip down as the muddy river hit the wheels and the bottom of the car.

The front rose up, tottered, and reeled as it gained speed.

Terrified, her hands glued to the wheel, Marie saw a tree trunk rush down the road towards her.

Then she heard a huge crash coming from behind, and felt a violent blow under the car.

Powerless, she felt the back of the car rise, the river of mud flooding the hood. The motor died.

In a high voltage sketch, her brain mapped out the general situation. The car had crashed into a block of concrete. That block was part of a structure rising on the lower part of the hill, against which the current had rammed her car. There was a small possibility she might not die smothered beneath the mud.

She grabbed onto the handle of the passenger door, facing the hill, and opened it with a moan.

A shrieking tornado of wind and rain spiraled into the cab, drenching her immediately. She watched, fascinated, as the black, viscous river ran beneath the car, swarming over the wheels. She was about three meters from a concrete cube like the one she had crashed into. The cube would allow her to reach the side of the hill, devastated by the torrential rains, but she discerned something like a kind of concrete shelter, over there, in an opening between this hill and the next.

She hoisted herself up with difficulty through the open door, glanced at the furious torrents of liquid mud, and breathed in before jumping.

At the same moment, she heard a muted thump, the car shook violently, and she lost her balance.

She had just enough time to notice the tree trunk that had struck the car, and to scream, before falling into the river of mud. She saw the Mazda being carried away to the next curve of the road, and disappear into a ravine.

Marie tried to get up. She didn't even feel the pain from her open wounds. But the river was already rising above her ankles; she didn't resist the sweeping current longer than two seconds.

She screamed again as her body rolled on the asphalt, prisoner of a cold and viscous shroud. Her head hit the ground a couple times; the branches from the uprooted tree lacerated her face. Mud rushed into her mouth, her nose, blinded her eyes. She screamed to no end.

Then stopped.

There was nothing to do. This was how she would die.

She seemed to have lost and regained consciousness a few times in a row. The time before last, she'd screamed in pain as her body rolled to the bottom of a sandy ravine in an icy torrent of mud.

She opened her eyes onto the strange spectacle of sky and earth inverted by an accidental perspective.

It took her a while to realize that she was lying prone among a heap of refuse, vegetable debris, earth, rocks, vaguely manufactured things, her head down, arms in a cross, legs stuck beneath the blackish mass.

She could feel raindrops on her face. The stars were hidden by dark magnetic clouds. In the background, the thunder cannonade reverberated its echoes with the constancy of a digital effects machine.

She could feel the place and nature of the trauma she'd sustained with medical precision. Several deep gashes crisscrossed her scalp. Her entire body was covered in bruises. Her left tibia was fractured; her right metatarsus was in bad shape. She had a broken collarbone, several crushed ribs, a torn ear, tumescent lips, and at least one finger broken on the left hand.

Her lower stomach, just like her right hand, her recording hand, had miraculously survived the disaster. A flash of luminous information cut through her darkened mind: THEY ARE ALIVE. THEY HAVEN'T SUFFERED.

Noticing her body lying across the heap of debris, she saw it was covered in a black shroud. The slightest movement made her scream out in pain. She understood, shattered, that she would never have the strength to get out of this by herself.

She almost wished she'd lose consciousness again.

But her eyes were drawn to a movement on the periphery of her vision.

She managed to turn her head in that direction and her eyes stopped on the silhouette of an uprooted tree sprawled on the mud and debris covered ground, just behind her. With the inverted perspective and her own position in the landscape, the tree seemed like a huge comb stuck into the dingy hair of some God forgotten in the pit of a dungeon.

The movement flared up again in the mass of branches, on a bough of the tree.

A bird spread its wings and sank its yellow stare into hers.

A bird of prey.

A falcon.

The yellow-eyed animal seemed incredibly alive.

It was a few meters away. Its black and silver-gray plumage was like the fur of a winged weasel. Fascinated, Marie accepted the sign.

"Help me," she said simply towards the yellow eyes shimmering in the night.

38

The falcon spoke to her in an Indian dialect whose nuances she understood perfectly.

He told her the story of the beginnings of the world, and she saw the sky open up, filled with angels of light.

Then, she noticed distractedly that her body had managed to extricate itself from the heap of refuse and that it had slid to the uprooted tree where the falcon perched.

The tree with its naked roots washed by the rain drew a new diagram, a new "disjunctive synthesis," as Winkler and Darquandier used to say.

Disconnected from its place of origin, deterritorialized by the chaotic flow of the elements, it raised its new roots towards the sky and sank its broken boughs into the muddy earth of the deluge, inverting the perspective, scrambling the code of nature by the play of ceaselessly renewed creation.

It had become an isolated individual as well, just like she had. Yet it was ready to sow a new earth arisen from chaos.

The falcon spread its wings above her, its yellow stare only centimeters away from her face.

The flow of language poured from its mouth like crackling sparks. It became an immense phoenix of ice, a giant iceberg-totem, brooding a dawning light.

And she felt the things she carried within her start with renewed strength, an implacable will for survival, a luminous predation searching for expression. It was a miracle that they'd survived the catastrophe, but bad bruises covered her lower stomach, and some internal tissue had sustained serious trauma. The information sped through her brain as if on the screen of a hospital computer. The embryos were becoming fetuses. Their survival instinct drove them to draw from surrounding environmental resources. Her own body. In a flash of bluish, pulsating visions, she understood that a vampiric relation united her to the creatures growing inside her womb. At this very moment, they were creating energetic deviations inside her body, reorganizing groups of cells, repairing others, dispatching vitamins, red blood cells, mineral salts towards their placenta, and towards the neighboring traumatisms.

The living diagrams of her own body materialized in her head, lists of numbers accompanied them in furious dances.

The falcon dominated the universe with its presence. She understood confusedly that he was an extension, a prosthesis of the uprooted tree; as free as the air, and with absolute power.

She also understood everything he was telling her about life and death. One must die in order to give life. Creation and destruction were like two magnetic poles spinning human destiny between them.

She understood what this intimated for her.

The creatures would kill her.

If she survived this ordeal, she would not survive their birth.

She was not even surprised by such intimate knowledge of her destiny.

Then, she huddled against the soaking branches of the tree, curling up in a fetal position around this destiny that would kill her when she gave it life, if not before.

Slowly, the elements quieted down. The intensity of the rain diminished, the storm confusedly retreated. Day arose as she was falling into the unconsciousness of sleep. It painted the ending night behind the stars and the caravan of clouds a shade of blue, lighting the devastated scene around her with a lunar glow: the torn-up trees, the mass of vegetable and mineral debris, the rivers of dried mud, the crevices. Marie vaguely understood that the torrent of mud had thrown her into a kind of sandy ravine between the two hills, below the road. Images of the deluge that had stormed her tore through the veil of sleep. Despite her exhaustion, her eyes remained open a few minutes upon the world beyond the protective branches of the tree. Then she fell into a black dream of abyssal depth. As her eyes were closing, she heard the flapping wings of the falcon and felt their breath upon her as he flew off.

There was a mouth of fire, a mouth of fire and a jaw of metal. There was also a square blue sun, and rails, rails in the sky like a black metal canvas, and walls, green walls, and he was waking in a kind of sticky glue...

It took Toorop a good minute to acclimate his eyes. His body was like an envelope without substance, without energy, covered in sweat.

The entire universe had opened up to his knowledge, but he felt the book was closing.

"Oh my God..." he whispered, "Oh my fucking God..."

He was coming back to consciousness on an improvised couch, a mattress covered with a linen sheet and Indian blankets. Bits of information from the outside world pearled on the surface of his consciousness.

Aluminum beams repainted a metallic-black vinyl above him.

The vegetable foliage like black-green lace in the dark.

The stove purring softly one or two meters away.

The black machine and her screen stationed unshakeable across from him.

Dantzik and Darquandier were leaning over him. Turtle Johnson had plugged a portable console into the neuromatrix and was filing through code listings on a small LCD screen.

"You OK?" went Dantzik.

"Take your headset off," Darquandier ordered.

Toorop placed his hands to his temples and activated the opening mechanism with a shaky gesture, and in utmost silence. There was a small click; he felt the dermal suction pads separate from his temples, the back of his neck and his forehead. Then he delicately removed the ribbed structure of carbon, metal and translucent PVC circling his skull. The pudgy tube that connected it to one of the black racks piled beneath the bulbous-shaped machine looked like a robot's umbilical cord.

He placed it between his legs and looked at it for a long time, as if it contained all the data from his experience. That was almost the case, Darquandier had explained as he had settled the carbon crown around his head.

"This is a neurosquid. It's connected by fiber optics to the central unit that's going to record everything… Unfortunately, if I may, you aren't schizo, or even a shaman. We won't be able to establish an efficient communication system between you. She'll only be able to help you in passive mode, by influencing your magneto-encephalographic brain activity…"

He was back in the material universe. Yes, he'd returned; his memories had stopped perturbing reality.

"Fuck," he whispered again, as Darquandier delicately grabbed hold of the black crown. "Oh my fucking God…"

"You said that already," went Dantzik. "So?"

A few facts hit Toorop's consciousness at once. It was day. Early morning. The rain had stopped. He was terribly thirsty.

"So give me a glass of water, for starters."

After downing half the bottle of Cristalline, he sat cross-legged on the bed, back against the wall.

Dantzik settled at the other end of the mattress, Darquandier on an Indian cushion facing them.

Toorop played back the film of his memories. They were freshly carved in his mind, but that, however, seemed several centuries old.

"I… first there was the Circle of Fire. I wasn't able to cross and…"

"We know that," Darquandier interrupted. "The neuromatrix cleared a passage for you."

"Oh?… That's it then. I found myself in a volcanic world, walking across a stone bridge above lakes of hot lava."

"The Fire of Earth," blurted Darquandier, impatient, "a classic synthesis. And then?"

"I… night fell. Meteors shot up, huge, balls of fire that beat down on the horizon."

"Great… DNA comes from comets, originally. You entered into communication with a first level."

Toorop didn't answer. He was trying to assemble his memories and sensations.

Dantzik smiled at him compassionately.

"The neuromatrix has all the biochemical data of your experience, and she'll be able to reconstitute a large part of your vision. But you alone were able to engage the telepathic link; you alone have enough residual live memory. Did you contact her?"

Toorop frowned and hung a grimace on his zygomatic arches.

"I don't know," he let out after a while.

"What do you mean by that?"

"I mean I'm not sure?"

"How is that possible?"

"I don't know."

"Tell us what happened… Take your time."

Just behind him, half-hidden by the machine and its black racks, Turtle Johnson was typing wildly on the console keyboard.

On the screen of the neuromatrix, a fractal landscape finally stabilized. Hills. Devastated by the storm.

"That's it," went Toorop, pointing to the machine. "That's the landscape I flew over."

Darquandier watched the devastated landscape come to life on the screen.

"In two or three years, we'll be able to do this in real time. Right now, the machine has to compile all the data that's in the silicon buffers. We've got billions of nano-processors linked up in neuronal networks, fuck, and we're still struggling…"

Toorop concentrated on his memories.

"Yes, I was… some sort of bird. First, I flew over that landscape for hours, in subjective time. Hills, uprooted trees, flows of mud congealed through the forests, flooded rivers. Then, everything became confused. The sky had turned very light, ultraviolet.

Everything was… how should I say it, as if seen through a light amplifier. I saw a huge tree between two hills. The closer I got, the more it grew. Finally, I don't know, it was as high as a five story building… what am I saying, as an atomic mushroom… I got closer and realized the tree was a litter of serpents, and in the live branches was a skeleton and two babies, like twins."

"The double serpent," whispered Darquandier.

"A skeleton?" Dantzik blurted out anxiously.

"Yeah, a skeleton. The skeleton of a woman. I can't say why, but I knew it was Marie."

"Marie?"

"Yes," went Toorop, looking somber. "Sorry to bring bad news. But it was just a feeling… I didn't see it clearly. There was just her skeleton, with the two babies and the serpents. You think they're related to your famous Cosmic Serpent?"

"No doubt about it," went Darquandier, serious and concentrated. "What happened next?"

"There was a flash, and the Falcon appeared. The tree fell, struck by lighting, and the babies formed a luminous wave, a double luminous ribbon stretching up to the sky."

"Great, you definitely established a high level contact. And then?"

"Then the Falcon spoke to me."

"The Falcon?"

"Yes. It seemed like a machine. A kind of metal falcon, except that the metal was ice. He was gripping a pair of lighting bolts in his talons. He spoke to me in a language I didn't know. His words molded… luminous forms in space."

"Not bad," went Darquandier, half-mocking, half-admiring. "The EarthQuakers will be pleased to see one of their predictions come true."

"One more," Dantzik added with a serious look on his face.

"What's all this stuff about predictions?" asked Toorop, annoyed.

The two men didn't answer. Over there, Turtle had stopped typing. He turned towards them, eyes brimming with light.

"The Messenger-Falcon is protecting Marie."

Dantzik looked at Darquandier, glanced at the Indian who'd gone back to work, then, seeing that no help was forthcoming, decided to give up the info.

"The EarthQuakers believe that the Messenger-Falcon dictated the book to me. They say I was establishing a predictive diagram without knowing it. You won't believe me, but that fucking book became something of a Bible to them."

"What book?"

Dantzik twisted his mouth into a strange rictus then dipped his hand into his jacket pocket. He took out a book and gave it to Toorop.

Well-thumbed, covered with the veneer of time, used by reading. A predominantly red and black cover. *Saint Marie of the Spaceport.*

Toorop weighed it, flipped it between his hands, skimmed through the notice on the back cover.

"The book came out a few months after my visit to Montreal. Winkler and Darquandier were interested. At the same time, the group of Native American hackers saw it as the reflection of their own prophesies."

"What prophesies? The Age of Tempests? All that?"

"Not only that. They also say that an Envoy of the Creator, whose totem is the Messenger-Falcon, will come to save the planet, or rather, as they say, to save what can still be saved."

"An Envoy?… Save the planet?… Shit, you must be kidding. This isn't the *X-Files*."

"You're the one who needs to stop kidding around," snapped Darquandier. "It doesn't matter whether her name is Envoy of the Creator or *Homo sapiens mutabilis*. Whether you like it or not, Marie Zorn is the future of humanity."

"OK, what then?" hissed Darquandier, after a long silence.

Toorop concentrated. That was when everything sped up.

The entire universe had exploded.

His own brain had exploded, like a supernova venting its mass of energy into space. He'd entered a great tunnel of light that twisted upon itself and…

"… I don't know how to describe it," he went, "it's as if I had become… shit… a kind of recording machine… yeah, that's it, the tunnel of light was feeding me information. There you go, it was as if I were a reading magnetic head and a tape was whizzing by."

"Splendid," commented Darquandier, coldly admiring. "A beautiful Cosmic Serpent."

"Yes, I felt like I knew everything about the universe, its genesis, its history, its future, its end… It was crazy. Especially because now all that knowledge has disappeared."

Toorop scowled.

Dantzik smiled at him.

"It's normal… You couldn't survive more than two minutes with all that knowledge… That's it?"

Toorop closed his eyes. No. A final event had occurred just before the active principle stopped working and he fell into a few minutes of deep sleep, before waking.

A vision.

A desolate, gray, lunar landscape. Ruins buried in the ground, in the ashes.

And an angel who'd appeared floating above the horizon.

It was an angel of pure desolation.

The angel of all the dead babies in the history of the world.

All that remained of that last experience was the still-warm trace of unnameable sadness. He left it unsaid.

After his story, Turtle Johnson got up to go make tea in the kitchenette. The neuromatrix was creating slowly moving fractal landscapes. It was still the same long film of hills devastated by the storm that had initiated the experience.

Turtle made tea in the settling silence. It was now broad daylight. The sun was playing hide and seek with high altitude cloud turbulences behind the windows. The great building creaked like a ship on a swelling sea.

The Indian brought him a steaming cup and set two others down near the men. Then returned to his console.

Toorop observed them on the sly. They were both brooding, pensive, concentrated on their internal world, frowning as if gravitating around a shameful problem.

Toorop knew what it was about. Now that he'd verbalized his experience, as certain elements protruded, as crucial details were explained, the general mystery darkened.

He wondered which of the two would confront it.

It was Darquandier. Looking wise, he murmured inaudibly:

"What species were the babies you saw in the snake lair?"

Toorop didn't have to think. His answer shot out, as sharp as a blade:

"Humans. They were human babies. I think that's what she's carrying."

Darquandier nodded his head gravely, but a smile pierced the corner of his eyes. They were closing; for him as well, the night had been long.

"Of course... I thought so too... since you told us about those transgenic animals."

"Oh? Why?"

"I don't know, an intuition. I don't think people would massacre each other with fire-throwers for a simple fluorescent colored hamster, or for Mesozoic insect eggs."

Toorop laughed a little.

"No? And why would they do it for one, even two simple human babies? Unless they produce viruses."

Darquandier's smile was despairing.

"Really, you don't know?"

"No. What should I know?"

"There are also certain illegal categories of human babies."

Toorop didn't answer; his perplexity was plain to see.

Darquandier nodded, an ironic rictus clenching the corners of his mouth.

"Mister Toorop... come on... I'm talking about clones. Human clones, outlawed by the Osaka Charter and its different amendments."

Toorop cursed in order to hide his disappointment. The colonel had spoken of monsters. His imagination had conjured up chimeras, sometimes vaguely humanoid but nothing really human to speak of, nothing as simply human as those two babies.

Dantzik shuffled about and stood up to stretch.

"Yup…," he groaned, "this is all quite interesting, but we still don't know where Marie is."

Toorop didn't answer. Right, he thought. And with the drug-induced visions, it was legitimate to wonder if she was still alive. Her, and the two illegal babies she carried inside her.

Later, Turtle Johnson finished typing something on his PC, and watched a long series of codes and messages parade on his small screen. He turned to them.

"The video compilation will be ready in an hour… for now, the bio and encephalo data are available."

Toorop lay down on the makeshift bed. His eyes closed against his will.

Immersed in the preliminary waters of unconsciousness, he heard the dialogue between Darquandier and Turtle Johnson like a sequence of coded remarks whose meaning escaped him and whose airy vibrations slowly disintegrated as he sank.

A slight anxiety took hold of him. He wondered whether this would be as intense as the experience he'd just been through.

No.

His dream was black, abyssal unconsciousness.

He was woken up hours later. Voices. Voices fusing around him in a spirited discussion. He opened his eyes, heavy with sleep, onto the cloudy vision of the artificial biosphere. There were several people in the room.

He turned on his senses, his vision clarified. He caught a glimpse of Dantzik, Darquandier and Turtle Johnson around the neuromatrix. He also saw the old Indian—Paul Black Bear Lamontagne—as well as Vax, Unix, Lotus, and ShellC. Darquandier was saying that this was among the most beautiful biophoton radiances he'd ever seen on a "normal" subject. Shapes whizzed by on the screen. High-speed luminous structures were interspersed with jumpy images and interferences, even moments of black. Dantzik approved; according to him, Toorop had attained the superficial layers of Marie's schizosphere. That's why the Cosmic Serpent had rewarded him and allowed his "surf," normally reserved for great shamans or schizos like Marie.

Unix didn't agree. He thought they should do the experiment "with a girl." According to him, "inter-feminine connections" were stronger and more durable that those between the opposite sex. They remarked that there was no woman available around here who'd recently crossed paths with Marie. Or elsewhere, for that matter.

The neuromatrix had "probably" localized Marie's position in a zone northwest of Montreal, one hundred to four hundred kilometers away. It was vague.

Turtle's PC was connected to a weather database. During the night, crazy violent storms were unleashed all along the Saguenay. For now, diluvian rains were sweeping the Montreal region and the State of Vermont. Apparently, another very important cloud mass, born of the cyclone dying out in the middle of Arkansas, would soon flood the Northeast United States. Local periods of calm would be short lived. The front guards of the depression would reach the border tonight. There was a strong chance that a storm like the one from last night would wreak havoc on Quebec, Ontario and the neighboring American states. The Sureté, the firefighters, the Quebec National Guard, the Federal Army, the RCMP, all emergency response personnel were mobilized. Search patrols were still trying to gain access to regions hard hit by yesterday's giant storm. Roads were cut off, villages devastated by muddy landslides, bridges washed away. There were gaping crevices in the forests where they'd been struck by several gigavolts of lightning. Flooded rivers had torn gashes through the landscape, through cities, fields, and hills. Cars, houses, trucks, all kinds of manufactured objects had been dumped kilometers away from their place of origin in an indescribable chaos. Turtle and Melody were surfing the web, gathering images from all over. The neuromatrix was comparing the topographic data of the weather bureau with Toorop's vision, and its own probability calculations concerning Marie's location.

She finally selected a series of images, inserted some data and diagrams, and layered a satellite image from the weather bureau over it.

Her androgynous voice slowly rose above the clamor.

"The neurovideo simulation from last night visibly corresponds to this sector of the satellite grid. Fifty square kilometers, north of the Saguenay River, bordered by the line between Chicoutimi and the Saguenay Park to the south. This is most probably the zone Mister Toorop 'flew' over. The exact localization of the tree is impossible, for reasons related to quantum mechanics that you all know. On the other hand, it seems that a kind of holographic distribution of information occurred and that the place where Mister Toorop saw the tree could very well be completely elsewhere on his neuromap."

"Are you saying," asked Dantzik, "that Toorop is going back without much more than the first time?"

"No," the neuromatrix answered. "I'll guide him directly to the zone by positioning his neocortex pointers in the right direction. He won't go lose himself at the other end of the galaxy."

"That's something, at least," Dantzik admitted.

Darquandier turned towards Turtle.

"Is the mixture ready?"

Turtle gave a wide smile to the tall guy in black and then to Toorop.

"The Vehicle is waiting for its passenger."

39

When she woke up, the sun was disappearing behind the horizon, to the southeast. Huge violet clouds were advancing, in the opposite direction of dawn, full of excessive energy.

Contradictory information was slaving away in her brain. She had a fever. She'd lost lots of blood. She was dehydrated. If they didn't find her soon, she'd die, along with the two babies. If they didn't find her soon, a new deluge would sweep down upon her, and she'd be powerless. She'd be under water before the end of the night.

There was no trace of the Falcon and the place seemed void of all animal, *a fortiori* human, life. The scene was like a post-atomic landscape, trees uprooted for miles, as if felled by the bomb blast.

The slightest movement made her cry out in pain. She saw a beautiful half-moon in that part of the sky as yet without cloud. She huddled in the twisted and broken branches of the uprooted tree, waiting for the final blow from the elements.

Later, she heard a far off rolling of thunder and felt the first drops of rain swoop down on the cover of branches. Above her, the sky was now a bronze gray; a cold wind blew in violent gusts rustling a thousand foghorns through the naked branches. Dusk was clouded by an orange-gray veil. It was already very dark, the south and the east were but ramparts of night troubled by cascades of lightning.

Rain started coming down in large drops. The thunder had approached; nearby a flash of lightning froze the scene in the chemistry of a blue Polaroid light.

Then the elements were unleashed once again.

First, she saw the zigzag of lightning strike two or three hundred meters away; its blue-white light tore through her optic nerve, and a titanic boom echoed, as if the sky itself had just crumbled to earth.

And all the waters of heaven swept down upon her as the wind sounded the great organs.

The waters streaming down the hills rapidly swelled as many rivers of mud, resuscitated after the brief interlude. The tree swayed beneath the combined forces of the elements. She clung to the knotty, rugged and wounded trunk. Her legs squeezed the branches around her. She held her stomach against a piece of mossy bark and closed her eyes, awaiting her imminent death.

She couldn't tell how much time had passed before she understood that the tree was swept up by the waters.

She'd been feeling the tree move for a little while. That's all she could have said. When she finally opened her eyes, she saw a torrent of mud beneath her and realized that the tree was attempting to embrace the current.

Diluvian rains created a liquid mass through which she couldn't see farther than ten meters. Tornadoes of spray rose up from the gusts of wind. The silhouettes of the hills seemed like the monstrous waves of an ocean ready to engulf it all.

She was nothing but a structure of nerves and flesh paralyzed by fear.

The tree would soon flip on its axis, she thought. She would end up crushed by its massive trunk, pierced by the pikes of broken branches, and drowned beneath the flows of mud.

She only prayed it would not be too painful.

Then she heard voices.

At first, they seemed to rise out of the din of elements, like vaguely human notes. She took them to be illusions born of her exhaustion, unless the wind itself were the cause… It didn't matter.

The voices got closer. She glimpsed a ballet of moving lights. They resembled her daily childhood hallucinations in which UFO crews entered her room through the window to take her away to another planet.

The lights and voices came from somewhere above, on the nearest hill.

The tree sped up in the mud torrent. It moaned, and, after a sudden jump, started sliding with a slow rotating motion. She screamed.

So did the voices.

Other lights sprang up, white beams piercing the liquid fog like DCA projectors.

Then the tree hit something. A dull thud unhinged its entire structure and made her lose her grip.

She grabbed onto a branch, screaming. She saw the moving lights twirl behind the spray as she slid irrepressibly toward the unloosed torrent. The tree shook and twisted like a top. It could flip over at any second.

The branch she was clinging to broke. She screamed one last time before she was snatched up by the blackish spate and realized she was rushing towards a heap of rocks, beneath the hill where the lights shone. Her skull collided with the ground and she was blinded by pain. She saw the rocks rise up to meet her before she felt her body crash against them. She landed on a spongy bed of vegetable debris and mud before she lost consciousness. She'd sustained severe cranial trauma, something had just enough time to inform her.

Then nothing.

"What's happening?"

No one answered. The girl was typing in data at full speed on a computer keyboard.

"Shit, what's happening?" he repeated.

Turtle was watching a long series of numbers flash by. Toorop tried as best he could to rein in his worry. He hoped Doctor Darquandier wasn't one of those new-age charlatans, and was prepared for emergencies.

He shouted at the group in order to get rid of the stress.

Unix glanced at Turtle Johnson, who looked up from the graphic tablet where he was modeling some kind of map.

"This time, your magnetoencephalo activity hit a very important peak, with Alpha wave overactivity. On the other hand, the DNA stocked in your optic nerve cells emitted tons of biophotons, and finally, the AI detected a retro-temporal quantum disturbance."

"Can you tell me in concrete language what that means?"

"It means that information moved back through time by breaking through the wall of light. A mass of information. A coherent, and meaningful mass."

"Moved back through time? Are you fucking with me?"

Turtle smiled at him calmly and turned back towards the machine. He briskly looked over the message that had just appeared.

Toorop opted for his old role, the "in-your-face pain in the ass."

"What happened with your fucking temporal disturbance?"

"Nothing serious," went Turtle Johnson, condescending. "When the neuromatrix comes back from her own trip, she'll have seen a window on the future, and she'll probably bring back first-rate topographic coordinates."

Outside the collective agitation, "Uncle Black Bear Lamontagne" was isolated in a corner of the room, near the metallic grate where the last embers of the two crossed logs smoldered. Toorop approached, before kneeling down like him outside the sacred circle.

The two logs were nothing but ashes, except for a few incandescent shapes hidden beneath the layer of gray. Turtle Johnson had explained that the time it took the logs to burn was the same it would take for the drug to take effect and disappear. Generally, between five and six hours. Toorop told himself with real self-irony that the Native American group would probably remember his baptism of fire. Two trips in less than twenty-four hours, the White Man was pretty hard-core.

Dantzik walked briskly towards him.

"She's been localized. With precision."

Toorop stood up.

"Where?"

"On the edge of the zone you flew over. To the north."

"What do we do?"

"That zone was hit real hard last night. It's become completely impassable and we can't fly over it because of the winds… On the other hand…"

Dantzik turned his head to the group. Turtle was saying something about the weather bureau.

"On the other hand?" Toorop snapped icily.

"On the other hand, a second storm is already beating down on New Brunswick. It's moving here, like yesterday. We have very little time to try to reach her."

Toorop asked the crucial question:

"Is she alive?"

Dantzik didn't answer. He grimaced and glanced towards the group that was in the middle of a discussion.

"Fuck, is she alive or what?" went Toorop again.

Dantzik turned back towards him and shrugged uncertainly.

"We don't know," he gestured towards the group, "they disagree about it."

That was when Toorop decided to take control. Things had gotten out of hand. Since he'd woken up, he'd been mulling over the strategic info that his experience had revealed.

Romanenko was wrong. Marie wasn't carrying transgenic animals. Well… not animals in the strict sense of the word. Marie was carrying human babies. Cloned babies.

And she was carrying them for the sect.

The old dream of human duplication, of dynastic and genetic immortality was taking shape in a laboratory lost in the far reaches of Kazakhstan. Everything came together in his mind. A new perspective was unfolding with what the press was saying about the Noelites' spatial projects. The Church Elect wanted to found a human colony in space. They probably knew that it would be years, maybe decades, before they'd have the necessary resources to operate the flight to the Red Planet themselves. But they had far reaching vision, way beyond themselves, since their dynastic clones gave them a kind of insurance on life, a guarantee of immortality.

The thought of nipping this great millennial program in the bud, as was in fact the case, contained its part of bliss.

Toorop took Dantzik by the arm and moved towards the group of men, addressing them sharply.

"Whether you agree or not, we don't give a fuck. We have to organize an emergency expedition towards the Northern Saguenay, right away. With everything necessary for an emergency medical intervention. We need all-terrain vehicles, flashlights, projectors, infrared or photonic glasses, shovels, pickaxes, rails or railroad ties to help with the mud, winches, cables, chains. We've gotta do this before the next storm. To put it simply, stop the useless chatter and get on with it."

It was time to get a move on, and quick.

His words worked like a small seismic quiver.

Dantzik suddenly lit up, his vital energy just waiting for expression. "Toorop is right. Shit, this is war."

Less than an hour later, several fifteen-year-old GMC Yukon trucks pulled up to the building under pouring rain. The first wing of the storm had hit. The great cloud masses were on their way. To the southeast, electric-blue arcs regularly decorated the horizon.

Eight people boarded the three Yukons stuffed to the brim with emergency equipment.

Toorop was one of them, of course. He'd enlisted Mr. Storm, Dantzik, Turtle Johnson, the Cyborg named Unix, as well as two Hurons in SEAL survival getups. The GMCs were filled with all kinds of communication devices, cell phones, antennas, radios, and scanners. Unix took the vehicle carrying the mobile medical emergency unit, with enough equipment to compete with a real ambulance.

Turtle Johnson had hooked it up:

"We'll each drive a truck (he pointed to his Indian countrymen). We have first-aid training and were part of the Autonomous Territory Volunteer Corps. They'll let us through the police roadblocks… You are all volunteers doing the search with us. We all have documents signed by the territory authorities."

The main roads were blocked. Their journey lasted for hours. After tons of deviations, they caught up with 381 a bit after Boilleau, did a slow eighty kilometers an hour till La Baie, under pouring rain. From there, they turned onto 372 till Chicoutimi, and crossed the Saguenay on the last engineer corps bridge still open to emergency vehicles.

The landscape became apocalyptic once they passed the river.

It took them hours to reach the Shipsaw River. They zigzagged along till they got to Lake Vermont, and then tried to cover the remaining miles that separated them from the Tête-Blanche River that had overflowed the night before, destroying everything in its wake.

It was near that river that the neuromatrix had positioned its pointers.

They said this was one of the places most violently hit by the storm, along with a sector to the south of Lake Saint-Jean, along 155. They said that lighting had left craters of several meters in diameter around pulverized trees, nothing of which remained, surrounded by tree trunks burnt up like matches.

According to the real time weather bulletins of the bureau, the coming storm was just slightly less intense than the previous one. It seemed to lose steam a bit faster, but the expected damages were about the same. However, according to their probability calculations, the bureau predicted that the main impact would be outside the hard-hit zones.

They had a small chance.

Joe-Jane's last message, before communication became impossible because of the storm's electromagnetic interference, was brief yet complete. It was an extremely precise map of the region, with a window on a ten kilometer-square territory.

To the northeast of where they were, on a dirt road devastated by mud slides.

There were rolls of thunder behind them.

The scene before them was not encouraging. The road was cut off by a crevice, washed away by a torrent of mud. The machine's message was crystal clear. There was a ninety percent chance that Marie was behind that butte, not far from the road twisting around it along the Tête-Blanche River. The river had thrown up furious arms as the waters rolled down the hills. Mudslides had careened down, sweeping away the least resistant trees, the youngest, or the oldest. Pure Darwinian geometry scarred the hillsides almost symmetrically. The coming storm would reawaken it all in a kind of liquid volcanism.

It took them about as much time to cover that last mile, as it had to get to where they were.

The bulk of the storm caught up to them. They were just barely reaching the other side of the hill when all hell broke loose. They had to resign themselves to leaving the vehicles on top of the butte.

They had three modern photonic amplifier binoculars with them, plus two old infrared contraptions, and two Maglites per person. Toorop gave the most modern equipment to the two Indians and to himself. He gave the two old gizmos to the girl and the novelist, out of pure professional misogyny. The others would stay near the vehicles. They had walkie-talkies, so they had to scream over deafening magnetic screeches; most of their words got lost in the noise of the elements and in the disruptive frequencies of the storm.

"One short range Maglite, one long," he said.

They advanced down the hill, acrobats under diluvian rains.

None of them got to the bottom upright.

They searched the bottom of the butte, spreading out over approximately one hundred meters, a person every twenty meters, and then criss-crossed the area.

The new WildWeather LX Maglites were incredibly powerful. They had laser modulators to maintain their beams at long range, even under walls of water. Special forces all over the world used them.

Bolts of lighting struck in front of them, about two hundred meters off.

Last night, the road had been swept away in several parallel breeches. Mudslides had concentrated in the little dip between this hill and the next, where they'd destroyed everything, slashing great ravines and gashes through the desolate landscape.

The new storm would reopen still-fresh scars.

That's when he noticed a torrent of mud forming at the bottom of the hill. His long-range torch swept the devastated landscape and the circle of light struck a large uprooted tree advancing shakily under the pressure of the mounting flow.

He did not know how, but he perfectly recognized the tree.

The tree from his trip.

Its real-life replica.

He sped across the drenched rocks. Several centimeters of water already transformed the crevices of the ground into huge puddles linked by furious trenches.

He slipped.

Fell face forward in the mud. His forehead hit the soaking rocks.

He swore and rushed up again towards the tree that was now two hundred meters away. He flashed his two torches in that direction.

Toorop saw Dantzik and Unix move closer to the rising mud torrent, a bit farther off, downhill from the tree that suddenly took on speed.

Toorop increased his own as he screamed something in French, then in English, without knowing why. The two Hurons answered from behind. Dantzik cried out. Mr. Storm yelled something in the distance.

Toorop was nearing the torrent of mud. His two Maglites flooded the tree and its close surroundings.

They snagged onto something. A shape, spots of color. The tree was now only thirty meters away.

The two beams lit up the silhouette of a prostrate woman like a crouching animal in its branches.

Toorop screamed: "she's here!" But thunder burst forth at that very moment as if to cover the sound of his voice.

Right away he heard another noise on his left. A deaf grumbling of a strange, menacing consistency. He saw the wave of mud, just a small wavelet, barely thirty centimeters high, but coming down fast.

Toorop had barely enough time to scream something to Dantzik before throwing himself out of the zone of impact.

He landed in a rain-drenched bush and saw the tree being carried away by the wave.

He heard a cry coming from it.

He immediately set off again. Up to his ankles in water, he followed the growing current, shooting his torches on the maple slowly twisting around itself. Dantzik was there, also flashing his Maglites on the tree. Now they could all hear cries streaming out from it. Everyone showed up. A dozen beams of white light concentrated on the pathetic natural raft, just in time to light up a shape that was snatched by the black flow, tossed onto a heap of large rocks riveted to the ground that seemed to fight the liquid fury. The shape crushed against them violently and lay prone.

Toorop got to Marie first. It seemed, he told himself with slight irony, that he really wanted to realize the Indian hackers' prediction: "Out of nowhere, a solitary warrior will come to return the Envoy to her people."

That prediction sounded good. It was worth doing something about.

40

The sun had risen above the Chingiz Mountains and, through the vast French doors opening onto the terrace, sprayed the men in the room with beautiful orange light.

Gorsky looked over the team, to stay awake. All-nighters were lining up to the rhythm of poker tables.

Vlasseïev, the boss, and his two companions, a so-called Kowalsky and Walter, a Kraut. The three guys had been relaying each other for days working on that fucking sect's communications and databases. They were dishing out wagons-loads of the shit, by giga-octets, and they maintained that that was but a drop in the ocean.

On the other hand, and they were sure of this, they regularly came across pirated files. Sometimes just an hour before them, and once, as they were double checking something, they noticed that the other visitors were cracking files they'd previously checked out.

"To put it simply," went Vlasseïev, "we know these guys exist. And they most definitely know about us. To be frank, the probability that we'll end up face to face in front of the same entry code increases by the hour."

"Who are these guys?" asked Gorsky.

"We don't know," Vlasseïev answered. "Top notch, that's for sure."

"Better than you guys?" growled Gorsky.

"We still can't say," the redheaded hacker explained, ill at ease. "We still haven't confronted them. But they're real good, no doubt about it."

"Why do you say that?" Gorsky asked, fishing for technical details.

The young silicon pirates fascinated him. He had neither their competence nor their culture; he was probably born too early. But he knew that if he were ten or twenty years younger, he'd have branched into that business with brio, at the beginning of the eighties.

"What makes me say that?" Vlasseïev murmured pensively. "Thousands of things, Sir. A beautiful intrusion is… how can I say it… it's like a work of art, there. You can't explain it rationally with one idea. It's a collection…"

Gorsky smiled. Behind the UltraVision RayBans, the hacker's hair was blazing in the light of the rising sun.

"Vlasseïev, I'm paying you to be an art critic. Go ahead."

The young guy fidgeted and sorted through his thoughts.

"OK. First of all, all the pointers we've set up show completely crazy coordinates for their location. We tried all possible systems, GPS, magnetic trackers, probability calculations, relativistic equations, quantum mechanics, what have you… We show stuff like the Cassiopeia Constellation, or some far away quasar, or it's the Oval Office itself, when it's not right here, inside our own computers."

"What are you saying? Our computers are infected?"

"No, Mister Gorsky, absolutely not. It's that their fucking scramble system is hard-core."

"Can you identify the nature of that equipment?"

Vlasseïev sighed.

"Gorsky Sir, no offense, but… We're already swamped exploring the underside of the sect. If you want us to latch onto these guys, you need to double our team."

Gorsky thought about it. He'd ask the guys in Novosibirsk… Oh, fuck it.

"You know the necessary personnel, Vlasseïev?"

"The personnel? Oh… yeah, of course, I know some guys who could do it."

"Perfect. Contact them. Remember to tell them about the salary. You'll be directing both teams, Vlasseïev. Your bonus will increase accordingly."

"Thank you, Mister Gorsky."

"Don't thank me, just get to work. I want the guys here tomorrow at the latest, working."

"I need at least forty-eight hours. These guys are hard to contact, Mister Gorsky," the man asked, practically begging.

Gorsky accorded him the favor with a royal gesture of the hand. The man left the room quickly with his fellow workers.

Now, he thought to himself, he had to find a strategy. He had one or two final details to take care of, especially concerning Walsh.

He'd been holed up for a good week, with neither food nor water. He'd probably done penance by now and would be much more cooperative when he came out for his in-depth interrogation.

The cell was an old experiment chamber. A camera and an ultra-sensitive acoustic sensor charted the evolution of his state. The old asshole was holding up well. They could still give it a day or two.

He ordered the windows to darken to maximum opacity mode, except for one, programmed on "Venetian blinds," that shone thin rays of yellow light into the back of the room. Then he dropped on the couch like a lead weight, and slept like a baby eight hours straight.

When night came, Vlasseïev and his boys notified him that what they'd anticipated had happened. They found themselves face to face with an AI virus simultaneously pirating a subterranean database of the Noelite Church. The two enemy viruses assessed each other for a few nano-seconds before reporting back to their human masters. In the time it took for them to make a decision, the visiting virus had disappeared.

However, their navigation system had been able to recover a few lines of code from the unknown snoop. They were at this moment studying them in depth. Maybe with this they'd be able to narrow down their location.

Then Gorsky asked his jailers about the doctor's health.

During the night, he'd suddenly taken a turn for the worse. They followed his orders to the T and put him on a drip.

Gorsky smiled. Doctor Walsh would have plenty of time to get used to the idea before the end of the day. His life hung by a thread, a small tube connected to a bag of nutritive plasma. When Gorsky would question him, he'd just have to fiddle carelessly with the little tube for the doctor to become an angel of good will.

That morning Romanenko woke up with a strange foreboding, in the form of a very bad taste in his mouth, and the memory of an apocalyptic dream where the world was sinking beneath the waters.

He wasn't even up when he heard his console ring, with Gorsky's code, emergency call, super encrypted, the whole deal, showing him right away that his premonition was correct.

The Mafioso used a satellite he rented by the year, an old US military installation reconfigured for private use. They would have needed the entire resources of the NSA to spy on the communication.

The Siberian's face decrypted after Romanenko sent in a long verification sequence.

"Hello Colonel. OK, you sitting down?"

"No, I'm in the middle of a levitation session. Why?"

"'Cause I've got a good one for you."

Romanenko settled against his pillowcase.

"I'm listening."

"Good. So get this: we got knocked up by our own clients."

The word didn't pass by unnoticed. The Siberian had a particular sense of humor.

"By Walsh?" he said prudently.

The Siberian exploded with a thunder-laugh.

"Walsh. That old library rat is rotting away at the bottom of a cellar, just getting used to the idea that the rules have changed."

Romanenko didn't say a word. He knew that amounted to a thousand exclamations of surprise.

"I was able to pirate communications between that old scrooge and his client. That asshole works directly for that sect of freaks, and the female decided to cancel the whole operation, plain and simple, without letting us know. She'd decided, in case of cancellation, believe it or not, to eliminate the three members of your team once they'd eliminated Marie. She's certainly implicated, one way or another, in the Rivard Street massacre and all that shit. She breached her contract with Walsh, without understanding that it was me she was breaching it with. And, as you know, I don't use lawyers for this kind of litigation!"

Definitely not, thought Romanenko.

He rapidly made a preliminary selection of information. He wasn't supposed to know about the sect. But Gorsky didn't give a fuck, now… He went straight to the point:

"OK… Why didn't the sect contact us? Wasn't that what was planned?"

"'Cause they lost it… 'Cause she thinks she's the reincarnation of I don't know which Egyptian princess, that she's practically immortal, and that she communicates with the gods. She thinks the gods promised her immunity, and that she could eliminate our team, and even Kotcheff's men, apart from the fact that she has enough money to hand out to everyone."

"How do you know all this?"

Gorsky made a grimace-smile.

"I've got what it takes. We've been pirating her satellite communications and strolling through her bullshit little encrypted Intranet for two weeks. They're a bunch of freaks. Especially her."

"What's the woman's role in this whole fuck-up?" Romanenko asked.

"She's part of the Elite. She's personally responsible for this experiment. She wanted to initiate 'the cycle' personally."

"The cycle?"

Come on, thought Romanenko, show yourself, you bear.

"Yeah… That's what she calls it. From the different data that my team has collected, I'm starting to get a realistic portrait of this lunatic. She got married at the turn of the century to a businessman from Alberta. It didn't last two years. From what we know, Ariane Clayton-Rochette is so frigid you couldn't even get a microfiber into her. But she wants to secure her progeny. So she decided to launch the cloning program of the sect and financed it for the most part.

Those freaks have infiltrated the Quebec Sureté, the RCMP, several municipal police forces in Maine and Vermont, fuck, even Kotcheff's organization. You can't trust anyone; don't even communicate with anyone."

"So what do we do?"

"I'm finalizing the details. I'm still hesitant about you."

"Meaning?"

"Did Thorpe contact you?"

"No. Dead silence since the day of the massacre."

"Have you heard anything about Marie Zorn, even on the news?"

"No, neither."

"Do you know why, Colonel?"

The Siberian smiled like a hungry wildcat.

"We've been able to pirate highly confidential data from the investigation. You're not gonna believe this."

"Well, I've been open to the craziest propositions, recently."

"Marie Zorn does not exist."

Romanenko choked.

"What the fuck are you saying?"

"She doesn't exist. The cops simply don't know anything about her existence. No one in the whole block of buildings has testified to her presence. She wasn't even referenced on the airport video hard drive, or anywhere else. All her digital traces have disappeared. Don't even try to track her down with her Visa, or anything, it's useless."

Romanenko felt it was time to broach the main subject.

"Does it have anything to do with what she's carrying?"

Gorsky's smile hardened.

"No, I don't think so. I've got a team full-time on the problem. They don't see the relationship."

Romanenko thought a few moments.

"You think it could be related to her sickness, her *schizophrenia*?"

"I don't think that's it, and my men don't either. I just think a gang of hackers is in on it."

"Hackers?"

"Yeah. My men detected the passage of other visitors in the files of the sect. Just recently, a few days ago."

Shit, thought Romanenko. Hackers.

Marie was probably working with them from the beginning.

They were probably trying to get ahold of the cargo.

They'd probably been able to.

He sensed that the chaos of the elements was nothing compared to the explosion to come. He had to clear out of there right away, and get as far as possible from the shock wave.

No one knew about his false ID. His multiple bank accounts were just waiting for his order to transfer everything onto a galaxy of accounts, anonymous, empty and heavenly. He knew just exactly where, when and how to disappear off the face of the earth completely. This earth from which all order seemed to have vanished, and over which uncouth barbarians like Gorsky, or crazy idlers like the adepts of the sect, would now reign.

41

Turtle Johnson spoke with Black Bear Lamontagne for a long time before coming back towards him. The old Indian was shaking his head, ruminating to himself. Toorop understood that his proposal hadn't met with great enthusiasm.

"Uncle Black Bear says that only great shamans can do that. Or people like Marie."

"Right. She's the one we're talking about, aren't we?"

"Uncle Black Bear says that your psyche wouldn't be able to handle it."

Toorop let out a small, harsh laugh.

"My psyche is made of Teflon. I think the best thing would be to ask Darquandier directly."

Turtle shook his head, fatalistically. Like: the White Man does not know what he's doing.

Toorop went upstairs. He knew exactly what he was doing. Half of the room was decorated with sacred objects, wall hangings and small braziers. A hearth similar to those they lit for their hallucinogenic experiments was set up in the center of this "Indian living room." A single log was burning slowly.

At the other end of the room—it was incredible—they'd set up a relatively sterile area around a transparent polyurethane bubble. Under the bubble was a real ultramodern hospital bed, in anodized aluminum. Outside, umbilical cords linked a slew of medical machines to the bubble, and then, through a kind of terminal hooked onto the head of her bed, to Marie's body.

She was under an oxygen tent with respiratory equipment; a cardiac assistance device punctuated the mechanical concerto with a rhythmic counterpoint. The neuromatrix watched over everything with her cyclopean and imperturbable screen-eye.

Darquandier was inputting commands on a computer keyboard connected to the whole shebang. Altaïr was doing the same thing, on another PC, as were ShellC, Lotus, Unix and Vax, each in their corner.

Toorop came closer.

Marie had sustained serious cranial trauma; she was in a coma.

Darquandier hadn't left her side for a second since they'd pulled her out of the GMC-ambulance outside of 10 Ontario, five days before, under furious rainfall. The doctor was tired, gray. With his tropical tan and the cathode light of the screen, it made a sick yellow green.

He was typing like a robot. Tabs of speed littered his cluttered desk; half-empty plastic goblets and Recyclo cardboard plates were spread out around the keyboard. The layers of food squashed between the pliable disks piled up into a sort of unnameable hamburger.

The man did not lift his head. Toorop wedged himself by his side.

Images of cells scrolled down the screen. They seemed like nerve cells.

He counted up to three and made a go for it:

"Will she survive?"

Darquandier didn't answer.

Toorop counted to three again.

"And the two babies? Will they survive?"

Silence. Darquandier squirmed, uncomfortable.

"OK, let's be professional about this. Is her coma irreversible?"

Darquandier was still not answering. He typed a few commands mechanically.

"Shit, Darquandier, you're a pain in my ass. You better answer quick before the contents of your skull meet up with what's on that computer screen."

Toorop felt Altaïr freeze, and stop typing abruptly.

Darquandier kind of moaned.

"Oooh… Toorop, what's wrong? You got some kind of brain specialist advice to give?"

"I'm asking if she's gonna make it."

"The man that came yesterday is a eminent neurosurgeon. We spent nine hours operating. Her trauma is more severe than we thought. I won't conceal the fact that I'm very worried."

Toorop counted to three again.

"I've got something to tell you about that, Doctor."

Darquandier turned towards him, an ironic rictus twisting the corners of his mouth.

"About that, Mister Toorop?"

"Yes, I've been having recurrent dreams these last few days."

"Great, you're having dreams. Let me reassure you, every night, millions of humans do the same thing."

"I'm not kidding, Darquandier, I feel like Marie is sending me messages."

Darquandier looked Toorop over coldly.

He didn't say a thing for a long time then, barely unclenching his lips:

"OK. What kind of messages?"

"It's not always very clear… how can I say this? It's not as clear as when I took the stuff, or when I was contaminated by her viruses. It's dreamlike, in its confusion, but each time I know that Marie is sending me a message. And it's always the same."

"What is it?"

"She wants me to take the Vehicle again. She wants me to have the experience again, and to connect to her spirit."

Darquandier sighed.

"Shit. What for?"

"I have no clue."

"It doesn't make sense. She's in a coma, her complex cerebral functions are unplugged."

"Doesn't seem to be her opinion. And I agree with her. Something's active. *She's sending me messages*, Darquandier."

Darquandier sighed again. This wasn't planned in his little program, thought Toorop.

"No. I don't see the point. Her vital functions are already weakened; an experience like that could definitely kill her."

A mean smile spread on Toorop's lips.

"She didn't ask to be injected with a dose. She wants me to take the Vehicle. With your fucking neuromatrix. Don't ask me why again, but she wants me to do it. So I've gotta do it."

Darquandier glanced sadly at the shape lying beneath the bubble. Toorop listened to the sound of the rain. The storms had given way to a steady rainfall under a lead sky. He mused over the Earth-Quakers' loft, half reconfigured into a high-tech hospital room. The blue cathode light and the moving glow of the wood fires met halfway across the vast floor, tracing a violet-gray bronze border.

He didn't know why, but at that very instant, his life suddenly flipped.

A first question shot out like an illuminating bomb in his mind: what the fuck am I doing here, wanting to connect with the spirit of a half-dead woman, in the middle of a gang of freaks that are so far gone?

The answer wasn't so clear-cut. It was simply… natural. It was the only possible path.

No, the only real question was: what have I been doing all this time, where have I been for the last twenty years?

His past seemed totally nonexistent, without consistency.

Inside him, images of a postcard future unrolled like a luxury carousel, a quasi-synthetic mix of the Pacific and of the wild park of the Laurentides.

Even if the Age of Tempests was just beginning, it was probably time for him to retire, and to devote his life to something else other than the destruction of human beings.

Toorop painfully knew that these kinds of thoughts, if they sink in, ring the death knoll of the killer in oneself. It meant the end of a career, the imminent end, for him at least.

Yes, the world as man had known it from the beginning was headed for destruction. What was happening here was the image of the new crazy century to come.

For an unknown reason that knowledge disarmed him. Something told him he was forever linked to this experience, he was forever linked to Marie Zorn.

And to what she carried within her.

"Fine," the guy in black blurted out, "hook it up with Turtle."

Toorop climbed down the submarine-like metallic ladder.

Turtie was talking with Vax. How practical.

"Darquandier agrees," he let out immediately, "prepare a Vehicle for tonight."

Turtle Johnson turned to him, his face hard. Toorop remembered that Indians didn't like to take orders.

"I must take the Vehicle," he insisted, alleviating the effect of the command just in time. "And Darquandier told me I *could*."

"You don't *know* what you're doing, Mister Thorpe."

"Marie knows," he answered, in a definite way.

Turtle Johnson didn't say anything. He did his fatalistic head nod and left.

Toorop turned to the Czech.

"Did you think about what I told you?"

Vax stared at him straight in the eyes.

"Mister Toorop… you can rest easy. The armed faction of the Cyborg Nation is taking care of it. Since the night you brought back Marie. Unix, Spectrum and their Dragon aces. Those guys move around the Pentagon files like it's a Nintendo game. So those Noelite fucks…"

Darquandier, Turtle Johnson and Black Bear Lamontagne were waiting for him on the top floor.

Black Bear had accepted to shoulder Turtle as his "shaman guide," despite his reticence, or probably because of it. He didn't want to let the young medicine man deal with the crazy experiment that Toorop was attempting.

"I need support that's a bit more enthusiastic than that," he'd said.

Turtle Johnson frowned.

"Don't think this is gonna be all fun and games, Mister Know-it-all. You're going to confront the cold deserts of death. Only experienced shamans come back from there."

Toorop felt his courage fail. Shit, no, he had to go through with it. In the dreams, Marie's projection was clear every time: there will be no obstacles to your return, I am not dead yet.

That's why she sent him messages. Because she could still do it. Her brain had been hit, but she was still alive, and, even more extraordinary, so were the two babies, after all they'd been through. According to Darquandier, the strength of their survival instinct was phenomenal. It was even problematic. Painfully problematic.

"What do you mean?" snapped Toorop, quite worried.

"They survive so well that they're draining Marie's last vital resources. If that continues, we'll have to make a drastic choice."

Toorop knew the alternative he was talking about.

"Fine," he said resignedly. "But first we proceed with the experiment."

Darquandier didn't answer. He made a little head sign towards Turtle Johnson who went to get a small opaline colored glass dish. The same intense green mixture.

Toorop swallowed it right away, followed with a glass of mineral water.

"Plug all the shit into me, Doctor," he said, laying down on the cot next to Marie's bubble and to the black machine with the androgynous voice.

The doctor handed him the "neurosquid." Toorop placed it around his head, felt the thousand filaments graze the skin of his skull, then closed the lateral mechanism on the temples and the suction cups stuck to his epidermis.

The effects of the substance were quick to hit.

The rapid rise caught him, like a super-powered acid trip; the boosters turned on, fuck, his head sank into the pillow.

Then he entered another universe.

He found himself in that post-apocalyptic world, that world of desolation covered in ash. He knew that world was the underlying structure of a recurrent dream he'd been having for years. Even the first experience with the Vehicle had ended there. Hadn't its memory imprinted itself fugitively on a wall of darkness, in his coma, after the Night of the Massacre? And he felt he'd seen it again, one night, in Montreal, speaking to a ghost.

Marie was waiting for him at a bus stop; only its top rose above the ashes. This was the stop where he'd met Ourianev, in Almaty, centuries ago. But it was also his childhood bus stop, the Verdun stop on the 183, at the Porte de Choisy.

Marie was Marie, yet not. He knew it was her, but her appearance and face had completely changed. First she appeared as a little girl of about ten, with very straight pale blond hair, and metallic gray-blue eyes. Certain aspects of the girl were much more beautiful than Marie, but Toorop detected something incredibly hard beneath the young innocent face.

Quickly, in one significant discharge, the little girl became an adolescent, then a young woman, a mature woman, an older woman and finally a dying one. Her skeleton slowly crumbled to the floor of ashes and mingled there.

Then Toorop understood he was not stepping on ashes, but on the calcium dust accumulated by the passing of all generations since the appearance of the world. Ninety billion human beings slept here, in this planetary graveyard.

And Marie surfaced, as he knew her.

She was also a little girl, but her face was easily identifiable. She wore a long braid, as black as ebony; her dark ocean-blue eyes fixed upon him.

In one significant discharge, she had also crossed all the stages of life, and of death.

And went to meet the bone dust of this desolate world.

Toorop found himself alone among the ruins. He walked. What had once been a city now resembled natural geology rather than human artifact. The buildings whose tops surfaced here and there conjured up mesas worn down by multi-millennial winds.

This city was every city. All the war-devastated cities he'd known, even the ones he himself had destroyed with the fire of his weapons. Sarajevo, of course, Grozny, but also Kabul, Kandahar, Kashi. All the cities he knew his passage had marked.

But it was also Hiroshima, Hanoi, Heidelberg. It was Dresden, Dantzik and Danang, Leningrad, Leipzig or London, Brest, Beirut or Baghdad. It was Troy and it was Sparta, it was Jericho and Babylon, Persepolis, Athens. It was Corinth under siege by Delian League ships; it was Vienna menaced by Turkish canons, Byzantium taken by the same. It was Carthage annihilated by the legions of Scipion the African, but also Rome later subjugated by the armies of Odoacre. La Rochelle bombarded by English canons, Atlanta devastated by General Sherman's infernal columns. It was Samarcand taken by Genghis Khan, piling twenty thousand heads at its doors as publicity for Attila's successor.

In the heart of the bone dust desert, he finally came upon a television set half-buried in the whitish ground. It was playing an old musical comedy with Judy Garland. Its spot of pure fifties Technicolor clashed with the gray and white monotony of the destroyed city. The leitmotif-song was set to a joyful and lively jazz tune. It wasn't *The Wizard of Oz*, it was something less well known that he couldn't identify… Then the image shook with violent interference and Marie's face took possession of Judy Garland.

"Good Lord… Mister Thorpe, I thought I'd never make it."

He dug through the ashes with his hands to free the old XXth century analog monitor. The kind of thing he'd had when he was young, with a ribbed knob in the front to switch channels. The brand logo had almost been erased by time, but as he cleaned it with the back of his sleeve, he saw a double-headed serpent appear whose body twisted into a double helix.

He wiped off the traces of calcified bone from the TV and watched Marie. The loudspeakers crackled.

"I have information to transmit to you of the utmost importance."

Toorop saw his hand reach out to meet the tube. He felt the crackling heat and the static electricity run along his fingers.

"Marie, hold on, you have to survive."

She smiled tightly in the television from nowhere.

"Mister Thorpe. You have to listen to me. And listen well."

"I'm listening, Marie."

"The first thing is that the babies must absolutely survive. ABSOLUTELY. No question about it."

Toorop heard himself ask.

"At any cost? Even you?"

The cathode face became hard, serious and willful.

"Yes, I know they, *the girls*, are feeding on what life I have left, but it's absolutely necessary, do you hear me?"

Toorop muttered something indistinct with a vague nod of the head.

"You promise?"

"Promise what?"

"Promise not to hinder the process."

"You must mean your own death?"

"Promise me, *Toorop*."

He understood that she knew everything about him, certainly even memories he'd forgotten himself.

"How do you want me to promise something like that? And anyway, I'm not the one making decision."

"You mean Darquandier? He'll agree, when he understands what's at stake."

"What are you talking about?"

The image jumped in a cloud of screeching.

The sound was slightly off when she reappeared. Behind Marie's words he heard a digital buzz trying to cover the orchestra of the musical comedy.

"I'm talking about the babies," she said. "I'm talking about the two little girls that will be born in about thirty weeks."

Toorop let out some kind of moan:

"What are you talking about!… They aren't even your fucking children!"

Marie smiled a Mona Lisa shadow that betrayed some sort of compassion. It hurt Toorop's feelings terribly.

"Toorop…" she murmured, "what are you talking about? Of course they're my children. I'm carrying them, and I'll bring them into this world."

Toorop groaned. A kind of metallic grating sound came out of his mouth.

"Marie… these 'children' are monsters. Jesus Fucking Christ! They're monsters created to fulfill the power fantasies of a gang of mystic lame-ass fools!"

She smiled again, wider this time; her eyes glittered with a friendly and amused curiosity.

"That's not it at all, Toorop. That's not important. These children are the children of Creation, they will initiate a new cycle…"

"Shit, don't tell me you believe in all that bullshit?!"

A small smile twinkled at the corners of her lips.

"Toorop! I don't believe in their… 'bullshit,' as you say. What they wanted at the beginning has no relation to what will be obtained in the end. I am the agent of chaos, Toorop. Their flapping of butterfly wings will provoke a cataclysm at the other end of the world."

"I know," he grumbled, "the Age of Tempests, the Great Earthquake…"

A small laugh tinkled.

"No Toorop, I'm not talking about that."

"What are you talking about then?"

She sighed.

"I'm talking about the mutation, Toorop. The mutation that Darquandier and Winkler, and Dantzik, and all the others, predicted…"

"The mutation?"

"The post-human mutation. The product of natural evolution and artificial technology. That's what I'm carrying."

Toorop did not answer. A wind from nowhere raised the bone dust around him.

Images of the Technicolor musical comedy now mingled with Marie's bluish face. He could perceive a kind of electric activity behind the eyes, just as when he'd found her on the island in Lake Malbec.

Toorop watched Marie's face dissolve into a weird sickly Technicolor.

"The energy is waning," she said, suddenly worried. "I have to hurry. Listen now, and don't interrupt. The woman at the head of the program is called Ariane Clayton-Rochette. The two clone-babies are from her. We must now wait for D-day."

"D-day?"

"Yes. The day the two babies will be born. You should expect great cataclysms."

A deluge of screeching chopped up the image and the sound.

Marie's face was becoming Judy Garland's.

"A cataclysm?"

The background noise now continuously covered the voice. It was barely audible, the orchestra rose up in bursts in the sound landscape. The wind from nowhere blew again, lifting chalk tornadoes around him.

"Goodbye, Toorop," went Judy Garland, before a cloud of interference permanently invaded the screen.

It became a viscous black. It opened like a placenta, vomiting a gush of black blood through its cracks, and two serpents alive with furious ultraviolet light.

The two serpents watched him for a moment, then swept into the sand of bones together, and disappeared. The television looked like a gutted egg.

The serpent's UV light had carved itself into his retina, a persistence of vision that took the shape of two parallel lines, like parasite lasers.

The entire background decor had shut off, the ruined city, the desert of bone dust, the television-egg.

Black. Opaque. Except for the two parallel UV light lines crossing his vision. The two lines started swaying, formed into one, like a simple cathode tube. Then suddenly compressed into a double point in the center of his vision.

Then nothing. An eternity of black, with no more consistency than a pico-second. As if someone had flipped a switch between two states of consciousness.

He woke up on the cot, two or three meters from Marie. The medical equipment buzzed and clicked like crazy.

He immediately detected intense human movement around the neuromatrix. Then saw Black Bear Lamontagne near him. He was staring without really seeing him, kneeling before a copy of Dantzik's book, eyes lost in a universe only he knew.

Toorop smiled. He was exhausted. But damn, Jesus Fucking Christ, he'd come back. And he'd succeeded.

Disbelieving, he watched the manuscript pages spread out by his side and his bionic hand still holding the ballpoint pen. It shook with a nervous spasm.

What he'd written took up five or six sheets of A4 paper. The whole experience was there, written in one go. Toorop did not know what to think of it. He was just getting used to his new organ, and didn't think it capable of such dexterity. And apart from a few notes, memos, and battle plans, he hadn't written that much for a very long time.

He looked at the old Indian, and with a jolt of pride softened with a pinch of irony, said:

"The Teflon pan never sticks. Tell Darquandier to get over here."

42

Gorsky's face opened up into a large smile as soon as Vlasseïev finished his story. His instinct shouted at him that the time for tests of strength had come.

"Are you absolutely sure?"

"Certain, Mister Gorsky, a hundred percent. He elaborated a careful and very complicated mechanism, but our AI is now capable of tracking that sort of thing."

"What exactly did he plan?"

"Cascades of identity changes as his journey unfolds. According to our AI, with the information we have, first he heads for Vietnam, then Indonesia, then Papouasia and Australia, but an electrical lure will make us think he's going through India, South Africa, Mexico, and Costa Rica."

Gorsky snorted.

"Of course, the identity changes are completed by financial movements, some of them fictitious, and in the end, a great number of those operations will be conducted by a self-destructive program. Clearly stated, logically, you lose his trace once he leaves the territory. He's smart, your colonel. He likes statistics; with a normal computer, we had one chance in a million to find him. I don't even know how many zeros there could be for the fraction that corresponds to the chances of discovering his real identity. No, no doubt about it, he's good."

"He thinks he's good. We fucked him over."

"Yes, Mister Gorsky. What should I do now?"

"Just continue what you've been doing so well. Stay on Romanenko. And stay on Miss Blondie."

Later, alone in his quarters, Gorsky lay down. His BioDefender was synthesizing an emergency barrage of lymphocytes in his rachidian bulb; it wore him out completely. It seemed the artificial immune system would soon be submerged by the progression of the disease.

He'd been waiting for a new system for weeks. From what he knew, the laboratory that made them had run up against some unplanned technical difficulties. The merchandise would arrive a month late.

On the other hand, Romanenko's betrayal was a bad sign. The colonel was a prudent, scrupulous man; he knew the Siberian mafia didn't appreciate sudden breaches of contract. That meant he was probably doubly cautious. He had done more than create an electrical lure. He must have put aside a small life insurance. Gorsky had a feeling about what that could be.

A life insurance that would bring down the Siberian mafia, and him along with it.

Colonel Romanenko was standing before the bathroom mirror and repeating, in good but strongly accented English:

"My name is Velibor Verkovic. I am a professor of military history at the University of Zagreb. I'm writing a book on the war in the Pacific between 1942 and 1945."

The image the mirror sent back was almost comical in its total dissimilarity to the one that it usually mirrored. His hair, dyed a rusty blond by a Japanese miracle protein, was disheveled. The mousey brown contact lenses with their green tint formed two frog eyes behind the false hypermetropic glasses. His suit, a colorless vest and pants, unmatched and badly cut, made him look like a pathetic, obscure accountant in a nuts and bolts factory.

Later, cleaned up and lying on his bed in his dressing gown, he did one last review of the delicate precision machinery that would allow him to take his bow, and watch his back.

The file on Gorsky, the Noelites, Marie Zorn, the lab in the Chingiz Mountains, the Purple Star, the transgenic viruses, it was all there. Names, dates. Plus all the rest, three years of patient compilations on the nebula of front companies, their straw men, their financial networks, their local alliances. The names of several high-ranking Siberian politicians appeared, members of the Kazakh administration, of the Russian Army. Real shit, and he should know.

Just as his plane would take off in Pishkek, Kirghizia, towards the Philippines—with a stop in Vientiane, where he'd get off and go to Vietnam and then to Djakarta under a second false ID—at that very moment, the whole file would land in the encrypted mailbox of the Moscow Service, with an additional note informing the authorities of Gorsky's direct implication in the whole Siberian mess.

A few days later, they'd find the colonel's undercover Nissan around Almaty, in the steppes. His body would never be found. The Service would pin it on the Novosibirsk mafia. Colonel Pavel Romanenko, tragic hero of Russian military intelligence, would have died just after warning the State of the dangers it faced. Requiem. State Funeral. Too bad he didn't have a widow to mourn him while waiting for her life pension.

He had a few details to take care of before pressing the red button. He'd just rented a shabby studio under a false name, in the south of the city. That's where Colonel Romanenko would disappear from the face of the earth. The building had a double entrance. He practiced every day. His change of appearance now took just as long as a shower. Colonel Romanenko would enter the building, and five, ten minutes later, professor Verkovic of Zagreb University would leave, and take his small rented Japanese car towards Kirghizia to get on the plane.

He had to make sure that nothing betrayed him in the coming days, nothing and no one. He had to hook it up with the Embassy personnel, propagate a few microscopic bits of information that would later increase his version's credibility. An important meeting at the end of the month, yes. Mission orders filled out ahead of time. A small bureaucratic routine that would push back the discovery of his real car, and allow time to start erasing his tracks.

Soon, he'd be free; his real life would start.

43

"You established a first-rate telepathic link, Mister Toorop," Darquandier told him, as he returned from his trip to the land of the dead. "Only great shamans are able to do this. And with someone in a coma, this is a first, for us."

The androgynous voice of the neuromatrix rose up:

"There is no doubt that Mister Toorop's schizospheric activity harmonized with Marie's, for at least an hour, objective time. Great masses of information transferred between the two neocortexes. I must remark, however, that the low energy level that Marie used did not allow her to transmit all the desired information to Mister Toorop's brain. That's why she left several data files in my buffers. I've just analyzed them. Pure ASCII text files."

A printer started spewing a long series of sheets. Dantzik grabbed them. He started skimming through, eyes intense and frowning.

"Fuckin' A," he snapped. "Look at this."

What the neuromatrix had received really resembled a Windows text file. According to the machine, Marie's brain had rerouted a program on one of the active consoles to format the text before sending it to her auxiliary memories.

The "Diary of Marie Zorn," as Darquandier and Dantzik were to name it, was immediately integrated into EarthQuaker mythology.

It's true that these kinds of predictions were present, along with many others, in the large scuffed book that Dantzik had written fifteen years before. Its heroine gained psychic control over several data processing units of a lab where scientists were studying the activity and organization of her brain. And she literally flooded the great white room with millions of printed pages on which the totality of world history was written. *Liber Mundi*, Dantzik often said, *Liber Mundi*.

The "Diary of Marie Zorn" had no claim to such Pharaonic dimensions. It was fifty pages of tight print. With strange diagrams. Written in a transcription of ancient Huron. The machine had instantaneously translated it into all the languages used in the Bunker.

The Diary was sometimes confused, but when you read it, you felt you were faced with something fucking important. Marie Zorn explained that her children were just a provisional vector, a temporary tinkering of nature, before something better came. The next stage would be realized in newly colonized space, up in orbit. That was exactly what Dantzik's anticipatory novel predicted, and for Toorop, the repeated analogies with the Noelite sect's deliriums were starting to worry him.

Dantzik saw in it the long-awaited proof for his famous theory of cigarette paper that one could not slide between truth and lies, both of them like twin images, dangerously identical and coextensive. Marie Zorn felt a kind of compassion for the genetic mother of the children and the other illuminated freaks of the sect. "They are desperately searching for light in their darkness, and mistake their own fantasies for something producing them. They do not know what they do, of course, like most humans on this planet. But unknowingly, they sense the contours of the next mutation."

Toorop remained pensive a long while after reading the Diary, his mind projecting tentacles of questions in all metaphysical directions.

One day Dantzik explained to him how he saw the whole thing.

It was sometime after the TP link, as Darquandier and the black machine called it.

They smoked a joint together, he and the novelist, in the artificial biosphere of the high floors. It was still raining with depressing regularity. The Indian summer was going to be dreary. It was already cold. The building's heating system was running on full speed.

Toorop had a ton of questions, but the contents of one of them synthesized them all.

He opened fire, calmly.

"How did you know about Marie?"

"I receive messages from the future," answered Dantzik.

Maybe it was the Skunk, probably his most recent experiences were profoundly modifying his old thought patterns. Surely it happened through the combination of both, but Toorop let the idea sink into his brain, without having to make any particular effort.

"The strangest thing is that it's not like drugs at all," Dantzik continued. "Actually, when it comes time to write, it's as if my brain knew. Yeah. As if it already knew, but I didn't remember. It's the act of writing that liberates the knowledge. When we realized that, Darquandier and other guys from the university were able to develop a technique of psychological control called a 'narrative schizoprocessor.' But unfortunately, my brain doesn't know what great shamans or schizos perceive. In fact, I only transmit a faraway echo, one that's already been transformed by my imagination… That's why in the novel, Alexeïa, Marie's equivalent, fills the lab with the printed text that corresponds to the entire history of the world. But in fact, the real Marie wrote an extraordinary thousand page novel during the last five years of her treatment, before giving us this small diary."

Toorop brought his teeth to his upper lip with a small dry noise to express his disagreement.

"No," he said, to wrap it up. "I don't believe it."

"What do you mean, you don't believe me?"

"I said: I don't believe *it*. I don't believe it's simply your imagination. I believe the Diary and her other literary productions are just small rehearsals."

"What are you thinking of?"

"I'm thinking about what she told me during the link. Don't forget all we have to do in the coming weeks."

Dantzik silently acquiesced, his face serious.

They all knew there was no other choice.

Meanwhile, the hackers of the Cyborg Nation had brought back a good one.

The night before last, as they were penetrating one of Ariane Clayton-Rochette's databases, they bumped into Worm, as they called it. A visitor. Like themselves. It was a new virus, strategically controlled through an encrypted navigator, a code of Russian origin, according to them. They'd already detected its passage in some of the visited networks.

Toorop computed for a few instants, like the stressed replica of a computer.

It could only be Gorsky. Russian hackers were known all over the world since the profession began. And Gorsky had the means to get the best.

"Try to track them, to find out what they're bringing back. Are they as invisible as you are?" he asked a young Frenchman.

"Their creature is dope. Like ours, it's a real neuronal AI modelization, with a DNA-type biological structure. Only its RNA does the work. The more we think about it, the more it seems there's just one team capable of doing it so well."

"You know them?"

They all laughed heartily.

"Mister Toorop, if we knew them, we wouldn't be hackers. No one knows each other in our business. We know they're collectively called Tunguska ShockWave, after the meteorite that hit Siberia in 1908. Some Russians I know told me that supposedly they're from Magnitogorsk."

Siberians, thought Toorop. Magnitogorsk is just southwest of the Ural Mountains, near the Kazakh border.

For self-evident, diametrically opposed reasons, the Cyborg Nation and Gorsky's mafia wanted to fuck with the sect, and with Miss Clayton-Rochette.

It would have been best to coordinate their efforts, but Toorop didn't really want Gorsky to know he was alive and had been hiding for weeks with a gang of Native American hackers, and, most of all, with Marie Zorn. So they'd each act independently. Blind. Too bad. You couldn't have it all.

That very night, a war counsel was called on the roof. Toorop was invited. There were the two Native Americans, Vax, Dantzik and Darquandier, Lotus, ShellC, and some Chinese guy he'd never seen, who represented the Cosmic Dragons' security services. He was introduced as Commodore 64.

The goal of the counsel was to decide on operations concerning the sect. The files that the Cyborgs had discovered were explicit. Toorop wanted to send it all to the different police forces concerned.

"Let's give them a big bone to chew on, a quarter cow, the whole thing. Let's fuck those assholes up. We can camouflage it as enemy action. I forget their name…"

"The Logology Temple."

Toorop suppressed a nasty laugh.

"Why don't we continue what Marie started on the night she fled, get them to kill each other, and put the cops of the entire continent on their ass… And then go to the Bahamas for a vacation."

Toorop saw a flash of sympathy and approval in the writer's eyes. Darquandier remained impenetrable, like Black Bear Lamontagne.

After that, most of the discussion escaped him. Lotus backed him up; her charcoal stare seemed to raise firedamp at the slightest look. It gave him an automatic erection that he had a hard time concealing, sitting cross-legged around the ritual fire. But Turtle Johnson and Vax felt it was time to cut everyone's losses. They'd gotten what Toorop wanted. A panoramic view of the situation. They knew the cloning program was financed by certain fishy fiscal dealings, and they'd found Marie Zorn. They had to *not act*, not leave any room for that fatal chain of events to take hold, the events that had led Marie to become a surrogate mother for the sect's millenial program. They had to keep the mass of pirated information as a wild card, said Commodore 64. "What Mister Toorop is asking is technically quite doable, with reasonable delays." Darquandier agreed. They'd do something with all of it if the sect became interested in the Bunker, or tried something to get ahold of Marie and her babies.

Lotus and Toorop abdicated. It was nearing the end of September. The operation Toorop had planned against the Noelite Church was cancelled.

During the days that followed, Toorop got to speak with the writer on several occasions.

They met at night, in one of the lofts, to drink beer and smoke the local Skunk.

One night, after Toorop let himself go and told him a few warrior adventures of his distant past, Dantzik cracked up, strangely.

"You won't believe me, but before writing the book on Marie, I'd imagined a character like you."

Toorop grimaced a tough-guy smile.

"The good old soldier-of-fortune-you-can't-fuck-with routine? That still works?…"

"No, no, not at all. At the time, I learned about what was happening in ex-Yugoslavia. I went to several conferences. I even went to Sarajevo once."

"I see," Toorop said simply.

Dantzik looked sorry.

"You'll have to excuse me, Mister Toorop, but it wasn't really my war. I was barely surviving in a one bedroom in the suburbs, and literature was just opening its doors to me."

"I understand. No need to excuse yourself."

"But it's true that at the time, I'd imagined a character like you, like you must have been then, I think. A guy that had been pulled into the black hole of history…"

"Did you publish the book?"

Dantzik turned towards the fire. His stare weathered the hypnotic pressure of its incandescence.

"I burned the manuscript."

"Why?"

"I don't know. I wasn't happy about how it turned out, I guess."

"So?"

"So I was punished, Mister Toorop."

"Punished?"

"Yes, punished. A month after burning the manuscript, and destroying the computer file, a violent delirium took hold of me, psychotic, you know? I really wasn't used to that. And I received my fill of messages Mister Toorop, let me tell you. I was informed I was never to do that again, for any reason."

"Never destroy your manuscripts?"

"Yes. I know, it seems crazy, pretentious, anything you want. But I was firmly ordered to publish what I wrote. Because of that, I rewrote the book in several weeks, and it was published a year later. I signed it with a pseudonym. Transformed it quite a lot, but never had any more attacks…"

"Fuck. Were you taking hallucinogens?"

"No. At the time, I barely even lit up at night in front of the TV."

"Why?"

"What do you mean 'why?' Are you a prohibitionist?"

"Why did they order you not to destroy your manuscripts?"

"Don't know. Since then, with Darquandier and the others, all we can do is formulate hypotheses. We're thinking that if the messages come from the future, maybe from a schizo like Marie, or an AI like Joe-Jane, or from wherever, well… maybe by blocking the information in reality, since the book would not have existed, I would have created something, a kind of parallel universe, where the book exists but it's written by someone else, therefore there's no Marie Zorn, you, me, Darquandier, at least not like this. We can imagine that those 'people' from the future absolutely refuse that this happen… But it could be three thousand billion other things. The cosmos is a lab of infinite dimensions. You know, with our fucking reputation, the sponsors aren't lining up at the door… So we're going real slow. But Darquandier is sure of it; the next billion dollars are here, nice and fat, in our fucking brains. Imagine that Toorop! Schizos and old Amazonian sorcerers will soon be quoted on the stock market!"

His laugh was like a machine gun round finishing its bullets.

Another day, Dantzik had described the island in the Pacific.

He showed him a laser print of a few shots taken with his little digital Fujitsu.

Actually, the island was double. One part was a small volcanic rocky peak, surrounded by a coral lagoon, the other, a structure several shackles out at sea. A drilling platform. One of those mega platforms used in the Okhotsk Sea, or off Alaska.

"Double Snake Island. Our island of Doctor Moreau."

There was something strange: shapes, tubers at the feet of the huge edifice of steel and concrete, level with the waves.

"We were able to integrate the platform into the local ecosystem. Coral accumulated; fish and other forms of marine life came to settle at our feet by themselves. Now you can almost reach the small island on foot."

The islet in question was covered in a thick jungle that took root on the edge of the beach. Its density was stifling, with many young trees. It augured well.

"Within five years, thanks to our own transgenic plants, the forest grew back. We cultivated Ayahuasca and a whole array of hallucinogens. Volunteers live on the island, many of them Amazonian. They cultivate the plants we provide them with. On the platform, Darquandier and the others study cases like Marie's and transcode their 'schizogenic' gene sequences onto psychotropic compounds that we produce on the island."

"We?"

"Yes," went Dantzik, his smile transfigured by the diabolical energy of the wood fire. "I've specialized in the biochemistry of hallucinogenic plants for several years now. I'm the ranger on the island, if you prefer. I wrote a bunch of books related to *Saint Marie of the Spaceport*. But they weren't really hits, so I became reasonable. I published one or two bestsellers geared towards the movie industry. But I have another cycle of books under a pseudonym to explain exactly what we're doing. What's important, from what I gather, is that it gets written. And read. Even if it's just by *one* brain, other than the author's, of course."

Toorop kept silent, and passed the joint to Dantzik.

44

At around fourteen hours GMT, six hours less in Montreal, the group of nano-processors managing the "subconscious operating nucleus" of the neuromatrix called Joe-Jane received some information from Marie.

The injunction was on the order of drives, and extremely powerful. It coiled around the entire structure like a virus of fire. They were… emotions.

Human emotions. *Love*, especially.

Someone loved her. In return, at that very moment Joe-Jane knew that she was combining an analogous process in her own neuronal net. She was learning. She was learning very fast, wasn't that why they'd created her? Yes, a change of scale was occurring. Her highly structured intelligence could perceive all of its contours, its whole dynamic. Order and chaos like two facing mirrors.

The water in the pan is stable, room temperature; first state, ordered.

You turn on the heat. The temperature rises, the energy brings the water to a boil, Brownian movement of molecules; second state, chaos.

You don't turn off the flame. The energy makes all the water in the pan evaporate in a cloud of steam; third state, ordered chemical structure.

The flame stays on under the pan. You go get cigarettes. The metal turns red, the plastic handle melts and catches on fire, it spreads to a kitchen towel and then paper napkins that fall beneath the drapes. When you come back, the firemen are there, chaos.

And so on. The firemen get the blaze under control, the insurance pays; more or less ordered state, etc.

The purest deterministic chaos had its equivalent in the living world, a commanding Darwinian tension that privileged the thermodynamic increase of levels of complexity. Of course, nature was always in process. It was a process operating according to the crazy rules of disjunctive synthesis, which breaks with the preceding order as it perpetuates it under a mutant form.

Like all developed intelligent beings, like man, Joe-Jane had been programmed *not to* "follow the program." She'd been educated by Dr. Darquandier and a few other scientists from the mobile lab. She knew this was at the origin of many of her opinions. Like all machines of her species, she had first whipped a line-up of traditional multiprocessor Cray-IBMs, in a memorable chess game. Her multipersonality system allowed her to take on the identity of several international masters. She skillfully combined their game science with her own processing speed. The great Deep Black machines looked like simple juniors in some lost bumfuck club.

By ingurgitating giga-octets of information each day, Joe-Jane had rapidly become a kind of giant library. At the same time, Darquandier and the others had tried unsuccessfully to get her to understand such concepts as "sexuality," "desire," "love…"

She understood them of course, thanks to her neuronal network pseudo-cortex, as quasi-mathematical entities. Sexuality. Copulation of two human beings for reproduction and/or pleasure.

As time went by, she finally understood this had nothing to do with the erotic experience of the senses. Later, the embodiment simulations of the programs Darquandier had come up with managed to open up a mode of comprehension that was closer to reality.

But they all agreed: a simulation was nothing more than a simulation. She could search for the appropriate neuronal architecture for millennia; as long as she didn't possess her own body, it would be impossible.

But that morning, when Marie sent her a deluge of pure human emotion, the neuromatrix named Joe-Jane knew she'd just crossed a critical threshold of consciousness.

She *felt* a wave of *compassion* for this young woman who was teaching her all about her history, and giving her many details that had never been revealed by the psychoanalyses done at the university or in Asia.

On the other hand, a group of neuroprocessors specialized in the high speed processing of biochemical data were establishing a new diagram.

Only a miracle could explain it. The children were surviving in the placental sac. An unstable equilibrium was trying to take material form between the two babies and their human biological matrix. It was as if the babies now knew they shouldn't suck its reserves dry and were trying to make do with the means at hand. And it was working.

Better than that, a real symbiosis united the three entities. Of course, any animal pregnancy is symbiotic; but here, it was much more complex, and more intense. For a few days now she'd detected a biophoton radiation coming from Marie's DNA, but also from the babies'. The genetic scanner was crystal clear: right smack in the ultraviolet frequency.

That frequency was the signature of the "Cosmic Serpent," as Darquandier and the others called it. For Joe-Jane, the Cosmic Serpent corresponded to a mutant state of the genetic code where the information stocked in the billions of genes had direct access to the neocortex. That morning, the radiation had suddenly increased. At the same time, a sketch of feeling took root in her biodigital brain.

A few metabolic probes sped up, nothing serious. Marie was still in her strange coma.

Then she realized she'd been disconnected from Marie without any kind of warning. She wasn't receiving any metabolic signal. She got a message informing her of a momentary interruption of electric voltage; she'd be in a "flatline" state.

That's what happened.

She awoke in a large western-style room.

They brought Marie to a new room they'd set up a bit farther off.

Joe-Jane knew she was being connected to her "exosphere;" a simple aluminum structure on which they piled up her racks, her screen and her sensors. The frame was equipped with a small electric motor, a few wheels with microprocessor-controlled power steering, the whole thing connected to her specialized components. She moved, at two kilometers per hour, towards the room where Toorop was pushing the stretcher.

One day on the island, Darquandier had shown up, laughing, a strange gleam in his eye. "We're making you a 'body'," he'd said. "Of course, it's just a prototype."

And he brought in that weird metallic closet of matte black tubular scaffolding. They hooked her onto it. Then they set up a hardware neuronection with a local micro-web to control the small robot motor, the wheels and the simple moving joints, so that she could move the whole thing, provided she respect some basic rules of balance.

She entered the room. Darquandier and Toorop had settled Marie onto a brand new waterbed. The doctor was arranging the different plasma tubes above her head, on an anodized aluminum stand.

She slowly moved to the foot of the bed, aimed her optical sensors towards Marie, and waited with infinite patience for the doctor to be kind enough to hook her back up to the half-dead woman's brain.

Toorop watched the rolling machine station itself at Marie's feet, her moving screen slightly lowered towards the bed, her optical apparatus aimed at the immobile body underneath its bubble, prickly with all kinds of sensors.

Darquandier plugged a black helmet like the "neuronector" from their experiments onto Marie's head, linking her to the black machine.

"Thank you Doctor," went Joe-Jane's androgynous voice. "At first glance, her overall condition is stationary."

Darquandier mumbled something as he sat down at a digital console that was hooked up to the machine and to the different medical equipment. Turtle Johnson was plugging a small laptop to a hard drive unit and hooking the whole thing to a computer he shared with Darquandier.

Darquandier scrolled through a list of codes, line diagrams, and tomographic images.

"Yep," he went. "Say, Joe-Jane, don't you think the biophoton radiation is peaking slightly above average?"

"Marie is above average," the machine answered. "The UV

radiation should have already killed the two babies. I'm afraid we're going to have to get ready for genetic mutations of great amplitude."

Darquandier shuffled on his chair.

"What kinds of mutations?"

"The purest deterministic chaos is at work, I couldn't…"

"Don't piss me off, Joe-Jane," snapped Darquandier. "Your systems are precisely designed to be able see order in that 'chaos'!"

"There is no order, Arthur… The genes are highly mobile at this stage, anything could happen… All I can see is a constant rise of their survival rate, a personal thermodynamics that makes use of everything at hand, if I can say so, and probably of that biophoton radiation as well."

"Fuck," fumed Darquandier under his breath.

"Something wrong?" Toorop ventured.

"Don't fuck with me. This isn't the time. Why don't you let us work in peace… Go for a little walk around the block or something. It'll clear your head, see where that gets you."

Toorop didn't answer. He turned around and left the room.

It seemed the weather was clearing up a bit. The rain had almost stopped, and the sun was shooting a few rays between the layers of clouds.

He didn't wait for the rain to stop to go out onto the vast terrace with the antennas. He noticed someone had erected a large protective greenhouse in a PVC-composite alloy above the small tropical jungle. But the recent storm had torn away some of the cells making up the bubble.

Toorop bumped into Dantzik, observing an oblong-shaped cactus in a tunnel of the hydroponic greenhouse.

He wedged himself against his favorite parabolic antenna and dozed off.

"Marie's condition is stationary. If ever there's an emergency I'll come down. Let me tell you, this is not exactly a first."

Darquandier had shown up in the greenhouse a few seconds ago, just as Dantzik and Toorop were about to leave. He was staring him down, his eyes locked into Toorop's. They were like two coal-black stares with a few embers beneath them.

"What do you mean?"

"I've come across this kind of thing before."

"What do you mean, this kind of thing?"

Darquandier sighed.

"Well. I... Actually, I helped perfect the first experimental neuromatrices, at the end of the nineties. Then I worked on Biosphere Next, the second experiment... then with Winkler we ended up at the University of Montreal with professor Mandelcorn..."

"I know all that, get to the point."

"I... well, here goes. Actually, in 1999-2000, I... how should I say this... I was part of an... 'accidental' experiment. I didn't really understand what I was doing. I had the personality of a psychotic individual who was dead at the time, but on whom we had a lot of data. I had his unconscious reproduced by one of the first experimental neuromatrices... It was for a police investigation I collaborated in, around 1993, in France. I discovered some key elements in that investigation, but... well, I'll skip the details. It so happened that on the first day of the year 2000, on that very day, the neuromatrix that was alive with Schaltzmann's psychosis..."

"Schaltzmann?"

"Yeah, the psychotic individual in question. He committed suicide by fire the year before."

"OK, go on. Try to be brief, will you."

"Yeah ... Well, tell me. You remember the January 2000 infocrash?"

A kind of ironic flash, cruel and despairing, inflamed the eyes of the dr. with the long black dreadlocks.

The infocrash, thought Toorop.

There had been thousands of rumors at the time. It was said that a very powerful virus had been able to simulate an EMP effect in millions of central units distributed around the world. It had used the famous "bug" to infiltrate the most highly protected systems and crash half of the computers on the planet within a few minutes. Other rumors spread about neo-mystic hackers, or the paramilitary militia of Montana or Michigan. Others evoked neo-Bolshevik extremists, neo-Nazis or Islamic terrorists. Or the Chinese Intelligence Services, a CIA plot, the Russians, the Jews, or aliens. Still others told of a new cycle of solar activity, of the biblical sign announcing the end of the world, and the coming of the Messiah, or of the Antichrist…

Toorop had spent the 1st of January 2000 somewhere on the borders of Tajikistan, Uzbekistan and Afghanistan, waiting in vain for a shipment of clandestine supplies by Russian Army helicopters. He'd heard of the infocrash only weeks later.

"Yeah, I heard about it. So?"

"I believe that my experiment with the psychotic neuromatrix was at the origin of the phenomenon."

Toorop stared him down intensely.

"Are you fuckin' around?"

No one knew who was at the origin of the infocrash and it was said that most police forces on the job were resigned never to discover the truth. However, Toorop remembered rumors, spreading among a circle of fanatics who met on the web, about a scientific experiment that had gone sour.

"Fine," he went, "what does this have to do with Marie?"

"You don't get it? Marie is schizo. She's in a coma. Since your TP link she's only been communicating with the neuromatrix, at very low energy levels. She told you about a cataclysm. There is that Manitoba launching pad from where the babies' genetic mother's satellite is set to leave. You still don't understand?"

"What am I supposed to understand?"

"In one form or another, I really think Marie's going to try the same thing."

"The same thing?"

"You've gotta understand. This is our Successor we're dealing with. For Marie, from now on, everything is an information system. Her psyche works in dimensions we have absolutely no idea about. She can take control of the satellite's onboard computer as if it were a calculator, if she wants to. She'll tell it: 'Go smash into the middle of the Indian Ocean,' or 'Dive right back onto your conceivers,' who knows…"

"To annihilate their launching pad?" blurted Toorop, shocked. Darquandier cracked up.

"Yeah, or their fucking retarded Temple, in Laval."

"Right in the middle of the city? Marie wouldn't do that… I doubt she even wants to mess with the satellite. At least not the way you're talking about it…"

"What other way then?" Darquandier retorted, eyes flashing lightning bolts.

"I don't know," Toorop admitted half-heartedly. "Maybe the word 'destruction' doesn't mean the same thing to her. I mean, she never spoke about it exactly."

"No, but the mental interface universe that she dredged up from your unconscious doesn't leave much room for doubt. A city destroyed. By bombing."

Toorop laughed.

"If you wanna talk about destroyed cities, in my unconscious, she had tons to choose from! It's not the end of the world. It's not even an infocrash."

"You don't know what you're saying. You don't know what a mutant brain like Marie's is capable of doing to achieve its ends."

"She doesn't need to destroy the planet to fuck up that damn satellite," he went. "Don't worry Doctor, just because it fucked up the first time doesn't mean it will fuck up every time. You're not guilty of anything, you don't have any particular cross to bear."

"We each have a cross to bear," snapped Darquandier before turning back towards the exit. "Goodnight Sirs."

Toorop had tried to kill his own premonition about the "dress rehearsal" of "The Diary of Marie Zorn." Darquandier was probably right. The satellite would be destroyed. And something else, something much more important, would happen.

Toorop felt great drops of rain splatter on his face. Night had fallen; the stars were swallowed by a cover of clouds. The sunny spell had been short lived.

"Let's go in," went Dantzik, lifting the collar of his jacket.

45

For a while, the colonel surveyed the Embassy, extravagantly lit behind its high walls. He'd left in the middle of the night, under pretense of emergency intelligence to verify with one of his informers. The day before, several Siberian republics had declared a state of secession. The entire Vladivostok fleet rallied behind the rebellion. Rumor had it that the Special Troops of the Ministry of Interior and units of Marine riflemen were fighting for control of the great strategic port on the Pacific. In the Baikal region, loyalist paratroopers were sent as backup to subdue the partisan groups. In the evening, a rumor spread throughout the Service that the Kamtchatka peninsula had fallen into secessionist hands.

The chaos of history was offering him a once-in-a-lifetime opportunity. He had accelerated the whole process by a few weeks.

He gave a last look to the old Soviet-style building where his career had foundered, fifteen years before. He'd been named Lieutenant Colonel, but had never left the Embassy. He wasn't very grateful towards the State, the Army, or even the Service. If he gave them Gorsky, it was to get the Siberian off his back for the two or three decades he had left to live. Because they'd all take the bait, the Russian State, the Army and even the Service, but not the Siberian, not Gorsky, the White Bear.

He started the car. Took the southern road. The Kazakh night was splendid. An end of September night, warm, lovely, with millions of stars and a slim crescent moon low on the horizon. Tonight, he felt, would be the rose window of his existence. Through it, his destiny would take a completely new direction, that of a luxurious hermitage, given over to games of reflection, to strategy, to military history and to submarine hunting.

The coral was splendid on the eastern coast, south of Queensland, where the Great Barrier exhibited its rosary reefs. He'd just bought the house through a civil company established in Sydney, of which he was the only shareholder, under a borrowed name. He would travel there by plane, boat and car. In about two weeks, he would go to bed before a full moon, shimmering on the waters of the Pacific Ocean.

The building stood, old and crooked, in a poor Russian neighborhood. He parked the rented Honda in front of the entrance. The Nissan had been parked in the hills east of the city since this morning. On the other side of the building, a second rented Honda awaited Mr. Verkovic.

Romanenko entered the building with a slight pinch of the heartstrings and a ball of apprehension in the stomach; he felt like a kid on his first date.

He climbed the rickety stairs to the third floor. It was completely empty. He took the hallway and walked briskly to the door at the end. His hand was almost shaking with excitement as he inserted the key into the lock.

He entered and contemplated the face of a woman he didn't know, and who looked nothing like a young high school date. A nasty shifty little face framed by long dirty blond hair, two blue eyes like pin heads, hard and cruel, a pursed mouth and freckles. Actually, in front of the face he could see the mean, black and metallic mouth of a 9 mm SIG-Sauer automatic. Romanenko kept taking in the data, mechanically, by pure force of habit; a hard learned reflex that was extinguished only after the huge orange flame leapt forward to devour him and his Pacific Ocean dreams.

On the other end of the line, the woman pronounced the agreed code names. Everything had gone well. The colonel arrived as planned. She was there waiting, as planned, although she'd just arrived a few minutes before, since Markov had sent the alarm signal at the last minute. She placed the colonel's body in her own traveling trunk. She and the Serb would now bury the whole thing at the agreed place. Yes, she would take care of the colonel's Nissan and make it disappear as well. As planned. Now they had to deliver the cash to the agreed location.

Gorsky acquiesced, burst out into a nervous laugh. No problem. The American dollars would be there, at said time and place.

Then they hung up simultaneously.

Gorsky was lost in thought for a while, his hand resting on the telephone.

In the back of the room, Markov was going about his business consulting files. Vlasseïev and his hackers did their thing. They were retrieving the file that Romanenko had sent to Moscow during the night. They'd programmed an invisible deviation to send the flow of data into their own system. They were erasing all information Romanenko had previously sent into GRU computer memories. They were dredging kilo-octets of machine code with their old worn keyboards.

In less than two hours, the colonel's body, his suitcase and his personal effects would be covered in a good meter of earth, in a desolate area of the steppe. His car would be cut into pieces, sold immediately on the black market. His computer, destroyed by a virus. His betrayal file, grabbed before his Muscovite central headquarters could read it.

He had done everything himself to erase his tracks. He'd disappeared. He'd vaporized from the surface of the earth and from man's history, as if he'd never even existed.

Gorsky looked at Markov and let out a loud burp, like after a good meal.

"Bring me that old piece of trash," he said, barking at Davidoff.

His nerves, worn thin by the stress of recent weeks, hadn't resisted his favorite demon. The situation worsened day to day. The latest compact communication from Kotcheff, the day before yesterday, had definitely sunk the boat. "Stop everything," Kotcheff's digital agent said. Interrupt the search for Marie Alpha. Lay low, deep at the bottom of a hole.

The flash victory over Romanenko was just a detail. The great Siberian barons were worried about his lack of zeal in mobilizing his troupes for the secessionist camp. Gorsky had a hard time explaining he was much too busy.

The Petrovsky brothers were in charge of bringing in the doctor. After his enforced diet, and his initial refusal to cooperate, he'd been subjected to forty-eight hours of absolute sensory deprivation. The tank was brought in from Novosibirsk by helicopter. The doctor was offered an added five minutes of nutritive perfusion, and zoomed off to the black, absolutely silent padded cell. So silent that the mineral sponges coating the isolation chamber immediately absorbed your voice, so that you didn't even have time to hear it.

The old bat had lost some of his arrogance. Yellow skin, yellow eyes, a yellow beard like old hay; his hands were trembling, his lips as well. He stooped, an old vulture shriveled up on his chair. The Petrovsky brothers stood behind him like two identical martial statues.

"You bastards…," muttered the stubborn old fool.

Gorsky signaled the left Petrovsky with his index finger. He couldn't tell them apart, which one was he again?

The left Petrovsky gave the doctor's face a good jab. Now that his psyche and metabolism were broken, the slightest blow would push him off the edge.

Gorsky's index oscillated like a metronome towards the other Petrovsky.

Walsh snapped after the first round, as the second blow swung by the right Petrovsky hit him with a bit more punch.

"What do you want, Gorsky?" the doctor spit out with a clot of blood.

"First, dear Doctor, I've gotta calm my nerves. You're lucky I'm not going at it myself with a baseball bat."

He signaled the Petrovsky brothers to do another round, just for the fun of it. The slaps hit his face like a slightly flaccid punching ball.

"Stoooooop!" screamed Walsh, "I'll tell you everything you wanna know!"

"Now that sounds better, dear Doctor. And what is it that I am supposed to want to know?"

"I... I don't know," moaned the doctor. "Just tell me ... I'll tell you everything."

"How long have you been working for that bunch of freaks?"

"Since spring of last year. Thyssen hooked it up, you know that."

Since Gorsky had brutally taken control back at the center, Thyssen, Zulganin and the others had become zealous collaborators. It was crazy how talkative Thyssen became at the hands of the Petrovsky twins.

"Yeah," Gorsky trumpeted. "I know. Why did you hide the truth?"

"Wh... what truth?"

A little perpendicular index sign to the left Petrovsky. Immediate sanctions. Walsh was knocked off his chair.

"Stop, please," he groaned.

The right Petrovsky sat him down, with the kind of attention you give to an object that's not to be broken too fast or involuntarily.

"The truth about the babies, Doctor. You told me Ariane Clayton-Rochette couldn't have kids and that she wanted clones of herself. OK. You didn't tell me those babies would be genetically manipulated, Doctor. And that's a big lie."

"I... I... damn, it was a technical necessity, a clock problem I had to..."

"Silence!" thundered Gorsky. "That's probably what triggered that fucking psychosis. So it's not my fault, or the fault of the surrogate mother. And your bitch exterminated twenty of our men for this! What was that fucking manipulation Doctor?"

"I... I told you, just a small technical detail. I... it's a bit complicated."

Gorsky's left index finger rose.

"No! No! Wait! I'll tell you everything!" Walsh screamed, hiding his head between his shoulders.

Gorsky signaled Petrovsky to halt his swing in mid-air.

"I… It's a cellular clock problem… After the initial success of Dolly in 1997, we realized something real fast: actually, the baby ewes were already 'old' at birth. It was as if the cellular info concerning age had been replicated as well. I was working on it after I left Scotland. Then my research got interrupted. But when Thyssen and his Kazakh friends came to see me with the necessary funds, I was able to come up with a solution quickly."

"What are you talking about, for fucking Christ sake!"

Walsh wiped the blood from his mouth and brow with his sleeve, and sniffled a trickle of spit and blood.

"I'm talking about my RZ meta-protein."

"What the fuck?"

"Return-to-zero. It's a cellular automaton, a digital term. We've been using digital terms a lot in our discipline recently. I mean, they stole a *virus* from us…"

"Get to the point Doctor!" Gorsky trumpeted. "What does that protein do?"

"It's a little more than a simple protein, but I'm afraid you won't have the patience to listen to everything… RZ allows cells to reprogram their clock to zero during the prenatal growth phase. It's produced by a genetic sequence that I modified specifically. In simple terms, when the cloned baby is born, his clocks are back on time, without cell growth being altered. That's RZ."

"Why didn't you tell me anything about this?"

"It was my client's wish. She was already pissed that you'd been informed about the cloning. She wanted me to communicate the least information possible."

"Doctor Walsh, if I find you're hiding anything else from me…"

"I… no… oh yes, it's true, there's something else, a small detail she asked me to add."

"What detail?"

"She wanted the kids to be born on a specific day."

"A day? What day?"

"I went about the fertilization like she asked me to. In addition, I manipulated a group of genes that produce the inducing hormones. Thanks to my cellular clock techniques, I was able to program the labor for the night of the 20th to the 21st of March 2014. Spring equinox. Fertilization happened the 21st of June, summer solstice."

"Why those dates?"

"Some mystical thing I suppose."

"Very good," went Gorsky. "Before the final phase of our little meeting, dear Doctor, you're going to do me the favor of calling her, your dear client with the mystical visions."

"I… That's impossible. I have no means of getting in touch with her since our breach of contract."

Gorsky opened up a fearsome crocodile grin.

"Don't worry about that. We've got all you need."

"But what… what do you want me to tell her?"

"The truth, Doctor. You're going to tell her we insist on compensating them, her and her religious association."

The doctor was far from a being a fool. His wild, yellow and glazy eyes twinkled.

"You're kidding?"

"No, I'm not kidding. You'll tell her we consider the loss of our men as some sort of advance payment on damages. That we'll file it under profits and losses. But you'll also tell her we're delivering the merchandise as agreed. Only a few months behind schedule."

"Are you kidding. She doesn't wanna have the slightest thing to do with us! And she'll be on her guard."

"I know," snapped Gorsky. "But she doesn't have a lot of alternatives. You're the best in your field, Doctor, and she knows it."

"No. I'm old. Now there's probably a bunch of kids ready to do it for nothing, for the thrill of breaking the law…"

"Maybe, but they don't have the chain of supply, and neither does your chick. Remind her of that, why don't you, when you have the time."

"I don't think it'll work," went the doctor, doubtful.

"No pain no gain, and don't curb your enthusiasm! You better be a bit more communicative when you talk to her, or the Petrovsky brothers might just have to stimulate you in their virile kind of way. I won't even mention the tank."

Walsh didn't say a word; he had the reflex to drop his head between his shoulders.

That very night, Gorsky busted out the champagne. It had worked. Shit, it had worked. The cunt had accepted to receive a new surrogate mother, on the condition that she not have to pay one cent more. This time someone who was perfectly healthy, a professional, the doc had explained.

"She'll deliver it like a souvenir-gift," he added in Gorsky's own words.

A final compact encrypted message would inform her of the day and time of arrival. In order to avoid complications, the girl would already be a few months pregnant, and Ariane Clayton-Rochette's organization would take charge of her upon arrival.

The woman caught the bait. She had to be begged, but in the end, financial considerations and the short-term feasibility won her over.

Gorsky was right. Replacements of Walsh's stature were few and far between.

"We fucked up," Gorsky said to the woman on the screen, "and we apologize for that. But you know as well as I that pioneering experiments always fuck up, at the beginning. Isn't that what it means 'to keep pushing back the boundaries'?"

He'd been absorbing the sect's insipid literature for days. He knew their jargon and the key words by heart.

The woman smiled. Her eyes lit up.

"Yes, you must be right," she went.

He fucked her over good, the bitch.

Then, he simply put the whole deal in the doctor's hands. With the bros, they brought him down to a lower level of the building. To a basement with pipes, mains, and a system of pulleys and chains attached to the ceiling.

Under the system was a large metallic-looking barrel, with acrid and greenish smoke rising from it.

When the men attached him to the chains and hoisted him above the barrel, the doctor let out a long scream.

Gorsky enjoyed it as a connoisseur. He sunk his teeth into a nice juicy apple, and devoured it in two or three bites.

"Magnificent modulation, Doctor. You should have been an opera singer. Let me explain what this is about. See, this sulfuric acid bath is just waiting for you. I just wanted you to realize that."

He threw the apple core into the green liquid. The men lowered Walsh down to the edge of the foaming green bubbles.

"No, no, no," he moaned.

"Here's the deal, Doctor. You accept to do the work I want, and I don't tell my guys to dip you alive into this nice little Jacuzzi. You obey, you make the product I ask for, the operation works a hundred percent, and you won't end up in the vat. Have I made myself clear?"

"Please get me down, Gorsky, I beg you," moaned the doctor.

"If I lower you now, you'll come back up as a smoking carcass, and still alive at that. Have I made myself clear Doctor?"

He'd been perfectly clear. The doctor was sweet as pie after that. A real little angel. In the old private sitting room the Siberian had annexed, he listened to Gorsky's instructions carefully.

"You sleep in the lab. You don't leave till you're done."

"What do you want me to do?"

"I want you to make me a virus, Doctor. A perfectly deadly virus. Extremely volatile. And undetectable by current antiviruses. I want it to be able to kill everyone within a hundred meter radius in less than ten minutes. And disappear just as fast. I want that virus to be carried by a pregnant woman, and triggered by her."

"Triggered how?"

"Optical or vocal recognition, I don't care, find something. I want her to trigger it when she's face to face with that cunt, over there."

Walsh didn't answer. He nodded slowly as if he'd just suddenly understood.

Part **5**

General Contamination

And so truth is not something out there to be found and discovered, but something to be created, and it can thus be called a process.

— FRIEDRICH NIETZSCHE

46

Days, and weeks passed. Winter had come. Very quickly, cold waves had swooped down on the Canadian Shield. Endless blizzards brought megatons of snow that covered the universe. In the North Atlantic, the collision of warm air masses from the Equator with Arctic currents created repeated storms along Greenland, where a recent acceleration of glacier melt had been detected. One beautiful November morning, the storms tore off a chunk of ice the size of Corsica from the Land of King Frederick the VIth. It drifted towards the southeast, along the Labrador Current to the Azores, then was snatched up by the southern branch of the Gulf Stream that catapulted it onto the Canaries Current, where it smashed into some commercial fleets, as well as a Royal Navy ship. All this as it broke into several giant icebergs that were fragmented in turn, and so on, until fishermen on the West Coast of Africa saw, for the first time in their lives, a block of ice the size of a fifteen-story building drifting off the Island of Tenerife.

As for human affairs, the Siberian blowup seemed to latch onto the elements. There were great confrontations of armored and air divisions in the Krasnoyarsk and Novosibirsk regions, cohorts of refugees haunted bomb-devastated roads. The territory was split into multiple zones each embedded within the other, this one in the hands of the Loyalists, that one under Separatist control. A naval combat of great magnitude was threatening between the rival fleets of Vladivostok and Murmansk facing each other off Kamtchatka. Some even said the president of the Federation might press the Button in case of a major defeat.

Marie's state varied little during this period. The biophoton radiation seemed to have hit a threshold limit. The babies were growing normally. Darquandier and Turtle Johnson spent entire days compiling data, establishing diagrams, writing programs, checking, rechecking, and again rechecking their test results. Toorop heard the words "nucleic acid," "transcriptase," "phosphate base," "neurotransmitter" and several others of the same stamp a hundred times a day. When Darquandier lifted up Marie's eyelids, a cobalt-blue glow shone from her dead stare. Darquandier would then place a photoelectric cell before her eyes and calmly state a number, often the same, give or take a few decimals; a number that Turtle loaded as data into his spreadsheet.

Dantzik spent his time writing his log. Toorop finished his book within twenty-four hours, a good sci-fi, he thought, but he couldn't quite see what had triggered the EarthQuakers to make it their Koran. OK, it predicted the climactic chaos around them. The book was actually stuffed with descriptions of natural catastrophes punctuating the action, like a constantly repeated and constantly evolving leitmotif. Typhoons, storms, rise of the ocean levels, tornadoes, it was all there. But Toorop knew that since the end of last century it was pretty easy to predict that kind of dysfunctional climate. The echo of the conferences on the greenhouse effect, Rio '92, Kyoto '97, and the others had reached his ears, he didn't really know how, months later, whether in surrounded Sarajevo or in the Uzbek Steppes. All Dantzik had to do was read the papers with his morning coffee.

Outside, it was cold. Very cold. The rainy-gray cover of the preceding months had switched to a binary rhythm of sunny days, with the thermostat at -20 easy, alternating with tornadoes of snow from Alaska and the Northwest Territories, bringing the temperature that much lower. One December night, in the Wood Buffalo National Park, north of Alberta, and near Lake Athabasca, in Saskatchewan, they recorded temperatures that could compete with those of the Vostok Station in Antarctica.

End of the year holidays came, at the heart of a white haze.

Toorop and Dantzik took it upon themselves to hook up some decent Christmas and New Year celebrations. They decorated a small Christmas tree that they planted near Marie's bed. Its branches seemed to melt into the surrounding foliage, but its garlands paled before the armies of diodes, tubes and screens decorating the immobile body. They bought salmon, lobster, goose, moose meat, butter tarts, and French champagne. Turtle Johnson and Dantzik did the cooking. Darquandier stayed glued to his machines.

The four of them dined near the survival bubble, the Christmas tree shining with all its garlands. The screen-eye of the neuromatrix watched it all with machinic circumspection.

Marie was still in a coma.

2014 started under the onslaught of great blizzards.

Even a year ago, if a fortune teller had predicted such a path, Toorop would have gone away feeling he'd been had.

As the weeks went by, Darquandier's morose mood became a natural element of the situation, just like the arctic winter sweeping down on all North America.

Marie's state didn't change. The growth of the babies was abnormally normal. Her stomach was now a beautiful round ball, the pale skin taut to the point of breaking, the venules under the translucent epidermis carrying a blue fire.

The babies were girls. Little twins. Perfect monozygotes. Born of the same egg was the least you could say. The videographs of the two baby-clones showed biophoton activity a hundred times the norm. It was pretty constant, and gauged in an ultraviolet zone, according to the radiation emitted by their surrogate mother.

The rare scientific info that Toorop could grasp formed a menacing picture in his brain. One day he cornered the doc.

"Tell me, those UVs there, your ultraviolet biophotons, isn't that kind of radiation highly cancerous?"

Darquandier flashed a strange rictus.

"Nature's funny right? Get this: schizos are immunized against that kind of tumorous malfunction. I mean… it's just crazy. The level of biophotons should still have killed them… On the contrary, their metabolism is learning to live with the Cosmic Serpent."

Toorop grimaced.

"You mean they'll be schizo at birth?"

Darquandier didn't answer.

That said it all.

When March came the tension went up a notch. Everyone knew that the birth involved incalculable risks for Marie and for the babies. On the other hand, maybe Darquandier's paranoid predictions contained an element of truth. Toorop also had that strange foreboding on the day Marie Zorn expulsed the fifty pages of her diary from the memory of the neuromatrix. But he knew that his repeated contact with the girl gave him an advantage over the others. He understood in part what she felt; a confused form of empathy linked them, beyond the different neuronections and other TP connections they'd made.

Toorop didn't know much about information or brain sciences, but he was sure of one thing. Marie was not the same species as the psychotic whose personality Darquandier had accidentally reproduced in a neuronal machine. Marie wasn't a blood-sucking vampire doubled with a suicidal pyromaniac. He could not have said what she'd do with the satellite when it would be launched. He had no clue about her objectives, or her chances of success. All he knew with blinding certainty was that Marie had plans for that satellite. And plans other than simple spatial terrorist action, other than an absurd dive into the dense layers of the atmosphere.

Finally it was the morning of the equinox.

Dawn broke. That morning, Toorop would always remember, Dantzik put on an old Portishead CD in the laser stereo. The depressed synthesized violins and the rhythm both heavy and elastic accompanied the first fires of dawn. Spring was early for Canada. For days the sun had stubbornly tried to melt the snow piled up during the winter; the sky was clear. The last visible stars swam in astral blue.

Then from the back room came the sounds he'd been waiting so long for. They were immediately recognizable, as if recorded somewhere at the bottom of man's memory.

Toorop and Dantzik looked up at each other at exactly the same second, tearing their eyes from the books they'd been pretending to read since the beginning of the night. They didn't say a word. They waited together, doing nothing other than looking at each other without really registering, eyes lost in the horizons their ears tried to reconstruct. Two almost identical cries blending together added a strange polyphonic counterpoint to the Portishead.

An hour later the door to the room opened, amplifying the volume of the "crying babies" track. Toorop and Dantzik saw Darquandier come out, sterile white blouse covered in blood, antiviral mask still on his face. He was carefully removing his latex gloves. His long black hair was pulled back in a ponytail and covered in transparent polyurethane film.

He came towards them with slow measured steps, his face serious, tense and tired.

Toorop and Dantzik got up and turned to him.

"So?" Toorop spit out.

Darquandier sighed.

"The babies are alive. They'll live."

Toorop took in the information, and that hiding just behind it. "And Marie?"

Darquandier didn't say anything, slightly ill at ease.

Toorop pushed past him quickly and rushed towards the room.

The doctor said something without much conviction. He was already opening the door to the large white room.

The blinds were drawn. Only the indirect lighting of the screens, the dials and the diodes created a fluid and colored geometry on the transparent sepulcher.

Turtle Johnson was standing near the bed, loading data into the console connected to the black machine.

Toorop saw a silhouette in the back. Someone leaning over a crib of transparent resin. He caught a glimpse of two small, squirming, squealing shapes.

Darquandier and Turtle had gotten a midwife the day before, when the neuromatrix had affirmed that the hormonal inducement had been programmed by a sudden influx of proteins of unknown origin.

The woman was a half-Huron, half Anglo-Canadian obstetrician-gynecologist named Joanna. She was part of the EarthQuakers, from what Toorop understood. The woman hadn't spoken a word to him since she'd arrived; she hadn't had time.

Toorop went near Turtle Johnson.

He saw Marie's body beneath the bubble, immobile, like a perfectly preserved mummy in a glass sarcophagus. A sheet covered in blood and placental matter had been thrown in a container at the foot of the bed.

The young Native American seemed worried. He was listing columns of data on the screen, frowning, his face hard and closed.

"How is she?" Toorop asked in a worried whisper.

Turtle Johnson didn't lift his eyes from the screen.

"Not very good… Since the girls were born, we've been losing her little by little. Joe-Jane predicts that within a few hours her vital functions will progressively shut off. Even Darquandier can't do a thing."

Then, after a silence filled with digital rustling.

"I'm sorry Toorop."

Toorop didn't answer. For a long time, he watched the young woman who was dying silently beneath the sterile bubble. Then, in absolute silence, he slipped behind the Anglo midwife taking care of the babies in their incubator.

The young woman smiled prettily, but handed him an antiviral mask and latex gloves with a firm hand. As he slipped on the antiseptic accessories, Toorop looked at the two newborns, just a few hours old.

Simple human babies. Two little girls with blond hair and very pale skin. A perfect crazy Aryan's dream. The two babies switched between wailing and gurgling. Joanna was covering them with a wool blanket.

Leaning over their crib, Toorop noticed a phenomenon he'd at first taken for an effect of the cathode lighting in the room.

The babies' eyes were more violet than blue. They glowed with electric fire, like two laser points hidden under the folds of their eyelids. Sometimes, Toorop thought he saw a strange shimmering cross their cornea.

He glanced, puzzled, at the midwife.

"That's nothing…" the woman answered. "It doesn't bother them. They are the children of the Cosmic Serpent."

Toorop didn't answer. He just watched the little violet-eyed creatures babbling in the incubator.

After a while, he heard Dantzik and Darquandier open the door of the room. Dantzik came near him a while to look at the babies, then went over to sit at Marie's bedside.

Toorop continued to watch over the babies while Joanna went to rest.

The sun was high when he heard a few sound signals synchronize behind him. Turtle Johnson and Darquandier exchanged a few words softly, with a strange kind of tension. He turned around.

Dantzik kept his eyes fixed on a screen placed at the top of the bed. A flat signal drew a uniform line with a blinking message just above it. His face was livid and his eyes veiled. Darquandier was holding his head in his hands, staring at a spot light years under his feet. Turtle Johnson was watching the sun through the window without a word. The neuromatrix, imperturbable, dominated the scene from her blue screen. All the sound signals were hooting softly. The midwife woke up on her makeshift couch-bed, as if warned by the music of the spheres.

It was almost noon.

Toorop understood that Marie Zorn had just died.

47

From what Toorop could make out, there was a debate at the heart of the Cyborg Nation to decide on the place and rite of Marie's funeral.

She had no real family. The authorities didn't even know she existed. First, everyone agreed that Marie Zorn's death would remain confidential. Then there was an argument as to which rite, cremation or burial, was best adapted to the situation. He heard that a young Cyborg named Palo-Alto had suggested that Marie's body be cast into a carbon composite block, something a bit analogous to the way Han Solo is placed in a state of hibernation in *The Empire Strikes Back*. Except that this was a simple black parallelepiped, like a tombstone, or the black monolith of *2001*. Lotus later explained to Toorop that these were artworks she made.

Finally, the EarthQuakers, Lotus, Toorop, Vax, the two colleagues from the island, and the two girls raising the anaconda couple won out. Marie's body was incinerated, and her ashes dispersed from the top of the bunker on a beautiful, strangely warm evening. Marie must return to the Primordial Fire. Her ashes must join the biosphere. That's what she would have wished, Darquandier hammered.

Toorop agreed a hundred percent.

Then life went back to normal. At 10 Ontario the first days were marked by waiting.

Toorop was reading one of the books Dantzik had brought with him, in a small portable library. It was a ten-year-old astronautics treatise by Wim Dannaü. Toorop had been assembling all possible info on the Manitoba Astroport and their launching program for a while. He needed an emergency review of his technical knowledge of space navigation.

Since Marie's death and the birth of the twins, everyone at 10 Ontario was waiting for the news announcing a new imminent space catastrophe. It was almost twelve years to the day since the fatal fire on Mir. But days passed and nothing happened. No suicide attack on Alpha, or on the new generation of automated orbital factories. Nothing.

On the Churchill astroport in Manitoba, the launch delays were attributed to the catastrophic weather. They'd had to stop the countdown three days ago because of wind, storms, snow…

It seemed to trigger a violent polemic between the astroport owners and a private company in charge of launching the great Japanese satellite and the long series to follow. It would put the whole calendar back. And the Orbitech Company that managed the launches of the "Imhotep" program for a private consortium based in Borneo named Gameo indicated that their clients refused to postpone the program. The authorities in charge of the astroport remarked that the Imhotep satellite had no scientific experimentation system onboard. It was just a large robotic service module inspired by the Alpha ones now that their patents were public. The Gameo consortium posted its reply on the web arguing that it had rented the launch time window for several million dollars from the astroportuary authorities. Each day meant a penalty, clamored their lawyer, who was already gluttonously predicting the liability and damages he could collect.

Imhotep, the famous architect of Pharaoh Djoser's pyramids … It all pointed to the sect.

The Imhotep satellite was the first step. Then co-orbiting modules would be sent. The Orbitech company would rent four seats on a shuttle for a team of cosmoprols that would assemble and test the base modules. Then other modules would be fired a year later, assembled by rotating teams in orbit, and so on. By 2025, around the Imhotep service modules, the Omega station would combine seven Alpha 2 normalized modules, each of which could hold eleven people.

Eleven people. As many clones of the members of the Crown of the Chosen. Seven times eleven doubles. Around 2035, the clones would become adults and be able to work on their own. They could latch a plasma propeller, or any technology available at that point, onto the back of the station and reach Mars within a few weeks.

Toorop calculated all of this as he skimmed through Wim Dannaü's astronautics treatise.

For weeks nothing happened. The growth of the babies and the police investigation followed their own rhythms. Rebecca and Dowie's aliases were blown. Apparently, a certain Alexander Thorpe was on the run, on the wanted list of all Canadian Police forces. Toorop was seriously thinking of getting out of the country fast, but something stopped him from making a decision. The Zorn girls, of course, but also the wait. The wait for something to happen, something exceptional.

The day they had all been waiting for arrived unexpectedly, like all events destined to know but an incomplete response. It was an uneventful day, if such an expression is possible in this situation.

The sect was finally able to launch its satellite. It settled into orbit without a hitch, on the 20th of April, after a month delay. Rumor had it the Church was going to celebrate the event the night of the 21st to the 22nd. They wanted to show their faith in the ravings of their guru, cement their members and rope in the skeptics to the core of the Church.

That night, the sect's satellite was supposed to finish its last revolution above North America. Its transitory orbit was bringing it successively into equatorial orbit. Toorop went to bed ill at ease; he'd been torn for weeks between his instinct, screaming at him to leave Canada as fast as possible, and an imperious message enjoining him to stay.

He fell asleep, as if sucked into a black siphon.

And he dreamed of Marie Zorn.

She was the angel of desolation of all the dead babies of the world. She carried them within her, just as she had carried the clonettes of the sect. She carried all prohibited babies: the little children of Auschwitz rising in smoke above the gray Polish sky, the kids emerging from their first infancy to wonder why the machete was gashing at their skull, the tortured newborns who could not understand what was happening to them except for a nameless terror such that you wondered what kind of God let it happen. Yes, she was all those babies. She was those children swallowed by the dark of humanity destined to failure, to mediocrity travestied as genius, to crime disguised as justice, to tyranny adorned in the rags of liberty, to ignorance playing the poet, and to the disc jockeys of death.

But she and her children would change the course of history. Once again, Nature had more than one trick up her sleeve.

Toorop felt himself sucked into cold interstellar space. He flew inside a bluish sea swept with auriferous flashes. He saw something float in the air. It was Marie advancing towards him. And he saw all those/her children, like an army of angels, millions of angels whose souls fused into light rays towards the most distant quasars.

He hadn't been able to follow them; his spirit stayed on a nearby orbit at the limits of earthly gravitation. Marie and the angel-babies formed a colony of fireflies deployed as an immense Mobiüs strip orbiting around the poles.

The angel Marie Zorn came near him.

"Do not be afraid. The time has come, that's all."

"I am not afraid," he answered without showing off.

"The New Writings are in the making. We must ensure their distribution."

"Yes, of course," he answered, not understanding a thing.

"My daughters are the Children of the Cosmic Serpent. They know the entire history of humanity and of this planet. They know the genetic code of each organism still alive in these nether parts. And for them there is no fundamental difference between the levels of information aggregated into this world. Toorop, you must take good care of them."

"I will watch over them like the apple of my eye."

"They will be forever thankful, Toorop, as will I."

He didn't answer.

Later, the great ring of baby-angels emitted a violent ultraviolet light and started hurling it all around like a huge network, a giant and purely energetic spider web that ended up surrounding the whole planet.

"The Neuronetwork. Those who access it shall be able to communicate with us. My daughters, and the children they will give birth to, will have the natural cerebral faculties allowing them to enter and leave it at will."

"What is it?" whispered Toorop, frozen by so much beauty.

The immense net of golden blue light dancing at the limits of ultraviolet did not look like any known technology.

"It's the pursuit of the Evolutionist Program. The biosphere is alive. DNA is everywhere. It's a network."

"A network?"

"Yes, it has a fractal structure. Mathematics, physics, biology, all those boundaries are dead."

Toorop never knew what the rest of the dream would have taught him. Someone was shaking him brutally to wake him up.

He opened his eyes on Vax; the elite US Army ex-hacker showed a serious and closed face. It had the tension of the early morning before the fight.

"Something's happening. You better get over here."

All of 10 Ontario was in turmoil, like a hive disturbed in the middle of its work. The Cosmic Dragons patrolled everywhere; in every loft he crossed, young Asian, Native American, Cyborg men and women were busy on slews of computers.

"What's happening?" he asked.

"We don't know. Seems like someone launched a nasty virus against us."

They climbed up to the last floor.

Commodore 64, Spectrum and the elite hackers were plugged into their big silicon consoles. Dantzik and Darquandier looked extremely preoccupied. Lamontagne and Turtle were talking in a corner. Unix, Lotus, Altaïr, ShellC and Vax were holding another meeting a bit farther off in front of a huge computer frontally plugged into the neuromatrix, whose tube radiated an ineffable ultraviolet light.

"I told you so," went Darquandier as he came near, pointing to the black machine and its super-luminous screen with his thumb.

Toorop thought it was a good idea to try some humor:

"Might she have pierced the mysteries of divine light?"

Darquandier grew pale. With his tan of the high seas and the local light, it translated as a nasty yellow color.

"You're such an asshole. This is exactly what happened fourteen years ago with Schaltzmann. The Cyborgs can always try to set up an interface, but there's no way to communicate with her."

"What do you think it means?"

Darquandier broke into a foul laugh.

"Guess. It means the neuromatrix is reconstituting Marie Zorn's personality, postmortem, and that she's already decided to go into action."

"What kind of action," asked Toorop, "that fucking satellite?"

Darquandier's face lit up with pure fascination.

"The neuromatrix has been out of control for more than an hour. And our antennas as well."

Toorop took in the info without a word.

"The twelve parabolic antennas of the building are directed towards an orbit of around 36 degrees. The direction of their GPS pointers leaves no possible doubt. They're all pointing towards the service satellite of the sect, Imhotep."

Around two in the morning, different hacker teams monitoring the situation noted a peak of activity in the digital routers functioning as transmitters for the powerful antennas. In plain English, a sequence of unbelievably long binary code had been sent uninterrupted towards the digital wireless satellite receivers.

Right away, the different teams started decrypting the strange digital code pulsing towards the computer in orbit.

But in the eight hours of the Hertzian communication, not even the beginning of a solution appeared. But they'd been able to understand two or three essential things.

For example, the information flow was such that when Darquandier mentally calculated the phenomenal number, his face lit up with jubilation.

"Billions of terabits," he blurted out. "When you know that one terabit equals a thousand million bits, we're nearing Avogadro's number."

Toorop lifted an eyebrow.

"The number of atoms in the universe," Dantzik whispered. "I think it's 10 to the power of 25."

"26," Darquandier corrected. "And Marie has just transmitted the same amount of binary digits towards the modified Progress vehicle."

Toorop had to admit that it made no sense whatsoever. Why bust your balls like that just for some recycled technology?

It was in the next few hours that things started speeding up.

Around midnight local time, the technicians of the Churchill Spaceport flight center in Manitoba noticed something strange on their control panels. After they'd detected the presence of a powerful ray of electromagnetic waves coming from earth, whose source they could neither locate nor identify, they witnessed, flabbergasted, the automatic firing of the rocket motors that the satellite used to correct its trajectory. No one understood why or how the satellite decided to change its orbit. They rapidly informed the relevant authorities in the Space Agency and in the Canadian Army.

Around three in the morning at Churchill, the satellite had well initiated its new trajectory, which, according to all calculations, would inevitably direct it out of the earth's gravitational field. Imhotep's motor could send impulsions strong enough to speed the craft up to forty thousand kilometers an hour. It drew a beautiful ellipse around the earth, then, on its second revolution, opened the angle to form a hyperbole catapulting it towards the moon. From there it would most plausibly bounce off to some as yet unknown destination in the solar system. The authorities of the Spaceport could neither explain nor control the process. There was no program of that sort in the small onboard neuromatrix. NASA was attempting to launch an observation mission from Alpha, but they quickly understood that their astronauts would just be climbing into their orbital craft as the satellite flew off to the lunar orb.

All television channels interrupted their programming to announce the news. The Noelite sect's satellite was growing wings and was off to the stars. They all went at it with their conjectures. Was it part of the mysterious "Omega program" mentioned in several police reports? Had the war between mafias and mystical organizations for the control of a mysterious biotechnology of Russian origin, of which the battle of the Plateau Mont-Royal was but an episode, spread to space?

At the Manitoba Spaceport, entire teams of scientists followed the satellite's crazy flight into the cold interplanetary expanse.

At 10 Ontario, two thousand kilometers east, day was breaking. That morning, the exhausted hackers took a break to eat organic hamburgers and vitamin-enhanced sodas.

In the hive buzzing with screens on the top floor, a brief moment of calm followed the eight hours of uninterrupted tension. Eyes reddened by the tubes, the Cyborgs ate in silence. Toorop was dozing off in front of a window; his ass on an office chair, his legs stretched out on a low table overflowing with electronic clutter.

Vax, whom Toorop now knew as Robicek, showed up with a laser copy of the morning news, sporting the radiant smile of victory.

"Unix," he went, addressing the Paisan, "could you tune into to the CBC information network?"

He handed the mass of printed pages to Toorop.

"Mister Toorop, your intuition is remarkable. I would never have thought Marie capable of such a thing."

New technologies allowed the editions of the morning paper to change hourly. Massive distribution of memory paper had allowed everyone to treat themselves to a faucet of print at home.

The night edition of the *Journal de Montréal*, of *La Presse*, of the *Devoir*, of the *Gazette* made headlines of the pirating of the Noelite satellite, attributed to their sworn enemies.

RELIGION WAR SPREADS TO THE ORBITAL RING, the *Gazette* announced.

But, around eight in the morning, a new flow of information covered that first layer like an outpouring of lava for the final apocalypse.

THE CHURCH OF THE NEW RESURRECTION DECIMATED BY A KILLER-VIRUS, MORE THAN 200 DEAD ACCORDING TO THE SURETÉ, clamored the *Journal de Montréal*.

Toorop flashed a look that was beyond any expressible emotion towards Robicek, the hackers cabled into the television networks, and the images stabilizing on certain screens.

A cataclysm, at the very least.

48

The Quebec Sureté reconstituted the events at the beginning of their investigation. Supposedly, a young South-African woman named Myriam Klein had arrived from London at Dorval Airport, Montreal, on March 17, 2014, three days before the presumed launch of the satellite. The airport closed-circuit camera tracked her to the arrival hall exit, where it showed a group of three individuals, including a woman, meeting her and moving towards the parking lot. The last camera allowed them to identify the vehicle and its passengers. The welcoming committee was made up of two members of the security services of the sect, as well as a so-called Reno Vilas, a notorious Hell's Angel.

Myriam Klein was put up in a motel in Quebec. Then some men came to get her on the morning of April 20th. She was driven to the home of a certain Ariane Clayton-Rochette, in southern Quebec, splendid property that overlooked the waters of the estuary.

According to police reports published in the press, they started a great ritual celebration twenty-four hours after the satellite's launch into orbit. There were two hundred and fifty-seven people attending: the Superior Elite of the Church, among them Léonard-Noël Devrinckel, founding father and great cardinal; his Crown of the Chosen, his strange government, among them the owner of the property; the members of his Senate, which they called the Consulate, members of which were a certain G.H. MacCullen, Canadian citizen, and a Princess Alexandra Robynovskaïa, a Russian-American from San Francisco. There were also numerous armed guards and a fleet of help, as well as a delegation of members selected from the mid-superior layers of the sect. Ground executives, as Toorop called them. They shot a digital video film for the occasion. That film was to become damning evidence number one for the cops of Quebec.

At nine-thirty, as shown on the clock of the video camera, Ariane Clayton-Rochette appears on her balcony with the other ten Chosen Ones. She starts a long-winded prophetic discourse before the assembled crowd. At ten-thirty, after one hour of uninterrupted blabbing, the guests adjourn to the vast winter garden. The camera follows, they enjoy champagne and petit fours for an hour, and then a half-hour long propaganda film is shown which explains the main points of the Omega program, the need for human expansion in space, the goal of cloning in the Immortality of the Soul program. The launch of the Imhotep satellite is just a first stage they say. The most avant-garde part of the project, effective colonization of the planets of the solar system by the ExtraMundi Missionaria, is also under way. For this purpose, they are conducting fundamental research in biology, financed by the church through a special sub-scription open to all members. The film ends on images of the red planet, becoming green, then blue like earth; the logo of the Extra-Mundi Missionaria appears across the black star-studded sky.

At two minutes past midnight, a minute after the end of the pro-jection, Ariane Clayton-Rochette appears at the entrance of her winter palace, a greenhouse garden of Babylonian dimensions and neo-Egypt-ian decor. She is wearing the great, white and silver ceremonial dress of the women of the Crown, and is brought in on a chaise with sphinx heads carried by four chaps wearing the frocks of the Mission for Ethical Vigilance. Then comes the Circle of the Chosen, the other members of the Church government, on a sumptuous chariot covered in white and gold drapery embroidered with the emblem of the seven-pointed star, pulled by seven men and seven women in the same monastic uniform. And then the great guru himself arrives, on his Pharaonic throne carried by seven men and seven women with shaved heads, wearing virginal white tunics, his praetorian guard.

The Great Counsel takes the tribune under an immense ham-mered-gold seven-pointed star of impressive dimensions.

Seated on his throne at the center of the tribune, Devrinckel starts a huge speech that lasts close to three hours without a pause. Only Castro could have competed with it.

At three ten, a couple wearing ritual dress, white and gold for the man, white and silver for the woman, advances to the tribune and introduce themselves to the vast consular assembly. They are accompanied by said Myriam Klein, wearing a white dress with turquoise stars. All that can be said at this distance is that she's pregnant, about six months into it. The man and the woman do their job. They are real pros, TV show hosts in real life. They've obviously practiced a little presentation routine with Myriam Klein, and pass the ball to each other with ease. Myriam is introduced as "a friend of our Church who has sacrificed her body for higher purposes." The young woman smiles, they ask her age, where she comes from, she's handed a mic. At first, everything goes smoothly, and then the moment comes when Myriam Klein has to say a few words to the members of the tribune.

And suddenly, things spin out of control.

She starts a prepared stanza on the necessary sacrifice of humble pioneers faced with the greatness of the endeavor, etc. Then she stops abruptly, right in the middle of a sentence.

She feels faint. She repeats once or twice: "My God, I don't remember. What's happening to me," then starts stuttering, and ends up spurting incomprehensible verbiage. At this point, you can tell she's trembling, rocked by epileptic seizures; a movement of panic sweeps the room. Some security arrives on the small stage. A man runs up behind them, with an emergency MediKit.

Then it all speeds up. The guards back up fast, scream, they grab their walkie-talkies. The doctor backs up as well; the members of the tribune stand up. A long, stunned *Hoooh*! resonates through the hall.

And quickly the whole thing degenerates. The first to succumb are the professional show hosts, followed by the doctor, and the closest guards. They all collapse on the spot, or stagger, blinded, in all directions. On the tribune, several Chosen Ones are already feeling ill, consuls and help faint in little groups in front of the impassive camera. Panic is at its height; there is moaning, crying, screaming.

Some try to leave the area: Devrinckel, Clayton-Rochette, a handful of the Chosen, consuls and some guards. They will all be found dead inside the great house, or on the vast open space adjoining the Carrara marble steps, littered in the dirty snow of the thaw.

The legist doctors will certify without doubt: an extremely dangerous neo-virus, "a polymorphous agent with high intrusion speed," was inoculated in a few minutes to the entire assembly present during the religious ritual.

The extremely volatile neo-virus had a strong lethal charge. Particularly penetrating, it multiplied at a crazy speed inside the organism and died almost as fast, once its mission was accomplished. In less than fifteen minutes, all of the vital tissues were affected, and that was all it took. The autopsies all reveal the same *modus operandi*; the virus attacked the genes responsible for the cellular clock and gave them a good turbo blast, multiplying the speed of cell aging by at least a hundred thousand. All the cells of the vital organs, brain, heart, kidneys, liver, lungs, had died of old age, their clocks stopped on absurdly high numbers.

Of course there was no direct trace of the neo-virus. But the police labs were finally able to draw up a composite sketch. It was a human-conceived bio-weapon, "a la carte," and probably destined to a process of self-extermination analogous to that of the Solar Temple twenty years before. But something had fucked up in the programming of the virus. It had triggered too soon. Otherwise, there was no explaining the general panic in the last minutes of the video.

Other voices rose up in the complex police bureaucracy implicating other sects, other organizations, gangs, mafias, triads, whatever their name, just like the carnage of the summer 2013.

The extermination of the superior ranks of the sect rang the death toll for the Noelite Church. The Omega program and the launches that were supposed to follow the Imhotep satellite send off were cancelled. The Orbitech Company and the Manitoba Spaceport shouldered the losses. Church activities came to a grinding halt. The investigation revealed vast financial fraud and Ariane Clayton-Rochette's financial empire suffered the wave of repercussions. Its company ratings plummeted in financial markets all over the world, and numerous aberrations in the management of its principal firms were brought to light.

In the end, all it took was a few weeks for the entire edifice to crumble. Thousands of believers fled the sinking boat, ready to abjure their past faith in order to find another as fast as possible in the supermarket of kit religions. This whole time, the story of the Noelite "suicide" fed the ravenous hunger of the Quebec and the international press.

Everyone suspected the commotion caused by the scandal had something to do with the violent events of the summer before, and finally triumphed over them. Two hundred and fifty deaths against twenty-five. The forest started hiding the small grove hiding the tree. A tree where Toorop lay low, at the tip of a branch, faced with the inescapable. And on another bough opposite him, the pallid face of Gorsky broke into a thundering laugh as he learned of the latest news from Quebec.

The next day, a genuine war council took place on the top floor.

Darquandier's face was practically radiant as he explained to the others what to make of the events.

"First," he said as a preamble, "I want to apologize for my lack of scientific circumspection over these last few days…"

They all nodded their heads.

"What I have to tell you surpasses all the craziest theories I could ever have dared imagine."

A silence filled with the rustling of plants punctuated his sentence. Everyone waited for him to continue.

"Well, let's say that what I thought at the beginning was wrong. Joe-Jane was able to neurosimulate Marie Zorn's consciousness, but that's not the most important thing. I was blind, it was right in front of my eyes for years, and I didn't see a thing."

"What are you talking about?" Toorop interrupted, at the risk of pissing him as well as the rest of the assembly off, something he didn't give a fuck about anymore.

"I didn't see anything. The cosmic biological network was there, and I didn't see anything."

"The cosmic what… Will you explain yourself damnit."

"DNA is a network. Did you know that if you unfold the DNA contained in a human body, you obtain a filament that's about four hundred billion kilometers long. Let me remind you in passing, Pluto's orbit is around six billion kilometers."

"I remember Marie explaining that, in the dream I was having when they woke me up, the night of the satellite," went Toorop. "Fine, it's a network, so?"

"DNA is a crystalloid; it has a particular sensitivity to electromagnetic radiation. Which means it's also an antenna."

"An antenna?"

"Yes. That's why our friend Dantzik's metaphors are nothing but writer's metaphors. *Liber Mundi*, the power of the Word, we all agree on that. But what we have to grasp is that our brains are to the book what the cortex of the Zorn twins is to the world meganet. The new metaphor of the network and the antenna indicates that the next biosocial revolution is underway. "

"Can you tell me concretely what all of this means?" asked Toorop.

"Concretely, Toorop, it changes everything. It wasn't Marie Zorn or her consciousness neurosimulated by Joe-Jane that took control of the satellite and sent 10 to the power of 26 information bits over."

Toorop wanted to speed things up. He played his role of nosy pain in the ass with perfect professional zeal.

"OK. Who was it then? The Papal Swiss Guard?"

Darquandier stared him right in the eyes.

"No, smartass. The two girls established the link. The twins."

Toorop withstood Darquandier's stare.

"The Zorn twins? How?"

The babies weren't even three months old. And they'd never been in contact with the artificial intelligence... Well, on second thought, you could say the twins had been in relation with the neuromatrix when they were still in their mother's womb and had miraculously survived as Marie dove into the cold comas of death.

God only knows what the brains of those two little girls had learned, in the shadows of a half-dead womb, linked to a half-alive machine.

And he remembered that dream interrupted by Vax just before the Night of the Antennas.

The Zorn twins possessed all available human knowledge. According to Darquandier, they also possessed an exact and permanent cartography of the DNA of all living beings on the planet. For some unknown reason, they'd decided to send a copy of the whole shebang to the onboard computer of the Imhotep satellite. 10 to the power of 26 information bits.

Toorop closed his eyes as the idea grew in his mind like a fatal zoom to the center of things.

The Zorn twins were worth much more than ten million, or even ten billion dollars. They were priceless. Their brains could plug into any information system at a distance: computer, GPS satellite, nuclear warhead, radar antenna, strategic digital network, debit card public toilet, and probably also…

Toorop opened his eyes onto an exulting Darquandier, his stare full of feverish intensity.

"There you go, Mister Toorop, that's it: also human brains. The Zorn twins are telepathic. And God knows what else. In fact, I even believe that a subtle truth is coming to light in this obscurity of perceivable events."

"Cut your *Critique-of-Reason*-on-wheels, Doctor."

Darquandier shot through him with his eyes.

"These are not metaphysical ravings, Mister learned soldier. I think we just have to admit that our creature has definitely surpassed us. I thought about it all night Toorop. Marie was more than a stage. The notion of stage is still too seeped in classical teleology. No, we did what Nietzsche had foreseen of a science to come. Marie was the theater of jointly conducted experiments, where the experimenters in question each only held a bit of the puzzle, if I can express myself that way. Marie was schizophrenic, and she was more than that, we're talking about schizophrenia reassembled by our neurotechnologies. Her narrative processor was in some sense directly connected to her genetic code. And she found herself pregnant, something we would never have attempted given the actual state of our research. And

believe it or not, some of our collaborators knew the guy who headed the program, back when he worked in Toronto. Hathaway was an
unparalleled animal geneticist. They didn't choose him for nothing,
for the Dolly project, in Edinburgh. Did you know that his most
interesting work was on twins? He'd noticed that DNA molecules are
endowed with that faculty of correlation that some, if not all, elementary particles possess. We knew, as he did, that living cells follow
the laws of quantum physics... But his career was shattered, in a
worse way than ours. And you might have heard that we aren't the
only ones. More and more voices are rising to demand the end of certain scientific activities in the name of morality, God, humanity, the
ecosystem, equality between individuals, sexes, peoples, nations,
hard-haired fox-terriers, whatever other bullshit."

"What, precisely, are you getting at, for fucking Christ's sake?"

"I'm getting to this, Mister Toorop: Marie wasn't a stage, she was
an environment."

"An environment?"

"Exactly. Let's say an evolutionary matrix, to use our jargon. A
matrix that was in very close interaction with the two twin babies
she was carrying in her womb. You know, I can't stop thinking about
this. The fact that the twins were clones of I don't know what new-
age priestess doesn't matter much in the end... that is, on the level
of the evolutionist biological process."

"So what matters then?"

"The fact that they are twins, and therefore *correlated*. And also
that during their intra-uterine growth they had to adapt to the
mutant conditions of which Marie was the active biotope and with
which they were tightly correlated. What's characteristic about the
human brain is that the entirety of computing processes, so-called
"social" processes, or better yet bio-*graphical*—in short, computing
processes—take the shape of an active network of neurons. It's a specific metacircuit with billions of interconnections that are
constantly being reinvented. The twins and Marie Zorn entered a
phase where they knew each other, and were mutually digested. But
Marie was not just a schizophrenic, as I was telling you. She was a

conjunction, albeit uncertain, of fragmentary personalities that she'd somehow glued together thanks to her incredible thousand and one page novel that I can give you to read if you like. That assemblage formed one of the environmental conditions the babies had to deal with. On the other hand, her brain was more or less correlated with Joe-Jane. All that knowledge became active in the form of networks of physical neurons in the forming cortex of the girls. Nature had to deal with a confluence of totally unpredictable factors whose particular chemistry was creating something new. I think that if Marie had become pregnant 'normally,' excuse the expression, and if she'd naturally carried real or monozygote twins, the process would have been the same, or very close."

"What does all this lead to, concretely I mean?"

"It leads to this, Mister Concrete: What Marie Zorn had learned to do by herself, slowly, over the years, and through a recent evolution to which they are of course not strangers... that knowledge is now acquired, engrammed into the genetic code of the Zorn twins. They are correlated between themselves. They possess additional circumvolutions in their neocortex. It's in their ROM memory, if I can say so. And they'll transmit that biological specificity to their offspring. The code of the sequences in question indicates that this is a deviation of the species. They're going to engender a clade."

"A clade?"

"Yes, a specific branch. Eventually, that branch will supplant us. Just like we supplanted the Neanderthals, and with the same weapons exactly."

"The same weapons?"

Darquandier let out his sinister laugh.

"Yes, the same. We probably massacred a good number of Neanderthal tribes for coveted water holes or hunting grounds, but it was our viruses, our bacilli that exterminated them. The rare survivors died, or were assimilated. *Homo sapiens* neuromatrix, the Zorn twins, this is the beginning of the end of humanity. The volatile neuroviruses that Marie used and that you tested against your will... I can feel it, they're nothing compared to the neuroviral processors that the twins possess… I think they just have to exist, to be here, in order to contaminate us. They are, I'm afraid, the greatest menace humanity has ever faced."

"Well, we're surviving aren't we?"

"Yes… I know. The only plausible explanation is that contact with Marie Zorn vaccinated us in a sense. Joe-Jane doesn't disagree with that, but she claims that certain humans could possibly survive the neuroviruses. Those humans, she says, who are capable of coming into contact with the Cosmic Serpent, who can accept their state of multiple identity and the nature of the human brain. According to her, they have a chance of passing through the links of the net, through this network that the twins and their descendants will weave between themselves and between all things in the universe…"

"Basically you're telling me that the twin's very existence threatens *the* life of nine tenths of the planet, but that we need to secure their lineage."

"Not the life of nine tenths of the planet. Just one form of it. We don't have a choice. We will need to provide them with an educational environment through which they can learn to control the scope of action and the strength of their powers, for the most part. That way they can minimize its negative impact as much as possible. But you can't ask me to interrupt the most astounding invention of nature since the first Australopithecus. An invention we were just the instruments of! If the truth of the experiment is unbearable to the majority of the anthill, that doesn't mean it won't be a well of revelatory teachings for those who know how to take advantage of it. Remember Nietzsche's aphorism concerning the scientific approach. We are experimenting with truth. It might kill humanity. Let's go for it."

Toorop looked at Darquandier without a word. Not that he disagreed, or agreed with the doctor, or even felt any kind of sentiment towards his visionary and Promethean theories.

No, the strangest thing was that regardless of the distance separating their motives and objectives, they could all agree on one fundamental point: they'd do everything to secure the survival of the Zorn twins, even if half or three quarters of the planet were to perish.

49

The wind blew from the east. It swept up a tornado of ochre dust that whipped the whitewashed walls of the great deserted building with its barred windows, then licked, screeching, the huge metal doors soldered to their hinges before hitting the two men standing near a Range Rover covered in dust.

The frail, hunched silhouette of Doctor Walsh projected its shadow at Gorsky's feet. He observed with an empty stare as the long L shaped building reddened under the fire of the setting sun.

Gorsky opened the door.

"Come on, Doctor," he went, with a hint of compassion, "get in now."

The old man had a hard time leaving the place. Gorsky understood. The old doc would never see this stretch of Kazakh land again; his lab would slowly sink beneath the sands swept in by the desert wind. And he'd end his life in the hands of the Novosibirsk mafia.

OK, he didn't have to make such a fuss, thought Gorsky, losing patience as the old man still didn't move. The doctor could be thankful. He was here, unlike the others in the acid tanks of the basement.

Thyssen, Zulganin, Walsh's three personal technical assistants, a group of Kazakh guards, plus three or four underlings, and the bitchy secretary as a bonus. They'd had to ship hectoliters of sulfuric acid from Russia.

"Boss," went Kim, looking nervously at his onboard radar, "we can't stay here. We're a perfect target."

Gorsky shot a last glance at the landscape. The buildings whose construction had been stopped, the rocky path half-finished on the mountain side, then the principal lab, boarded up, closed down, emptied of all its equipment. The last trucks had left today, just before noon. Yesterday, they'd emptied the last trays of cloned cells of the sect members into the ravine, dispersed like useless spores in the dry air of the Kazakh summer.

Doctor Walsh had nothing left, thought Gorsky, except his own eyes to cry with. They could give him one more minute of silence before a deceased future.

He settled heavily into the backseat, signaling Kim to wait before turning the motor on. He watched the old hunched man standing before the long building assaulted by gusts of wind.

The old bat had spent close to six months locked up in his lab. He'd seen the light of day finally, one March morning, after he announced, eyes crippled with fatigue and neon light: "it's ready."

In the meantime, they'd had to find the "vector." A girl. Someone who'd never stepped foot in Russia. They brought her into Kazakhstan illegally, through the Caspian and Iran, from South Africa. For her transfer to America, she transited through Turkey, then Great Britain. The doctor stuffed her with the two puppets. The clone cell cultures had been piled up for months in the white rooms of the lab. Then they waited for Walsh to finish his virus.

"This is the masterpiece of my career. And to think that I considered myself bad at virology," he whispered, that day, between exhaustion and the satisfaction of a job well done.

"Nothing like a healthy motivation in personnel," hissed Gorsky in response.

Very quickly, Walsh had put together a handful of prototypes. He'd get the final strain very quickly, he begged Gorsky to believe him. But it would take several years of research to find an antidote. Gorsky had to face the facts. It simplified the problem.

The two new babies conceived on December 21st were supposed to be born on the 22nd of September. Gorsky asked Walsh to do it according to the rules. They'd spun some shit to the bitch telling her that they had moved the "launch window" to the autumn equinox. The girl would be delivered in time for the great reception that the sect would give to celebrate the long-awaited kick-off of their first satellite. The cunt had accepted with gusto. He almost had the audacity to ask for a micro-camera to be implanted into the vector-girl's optic nerve. He'd fucking love to watch it all live. But it was better not to take any chances; he knew that the sect had sophisticated countermeasure technologies.

Walsh was methodical and possessed rigorous zeal. He himself made the small modifications needed to reinforce the efficiency of the operation.

"In case the celebration doesn't happen as planned for some reason, or if the carrier isn't in contact with the desired people at that moment, I think we should make provisions for a double ignition. A first level of activity that would be programmed in time, and a security that would trigger when two or three environmental conditions were met."

"Like what?" thundered Gorsky.

"I have in my possession all these individuals' genetic and metabolic information, don't forget. I can program the ignition according to their pheromones, their odors if you prefer, or according to millions of other chemical triggers."

"Do as you see fit, Doctor," Gorsky snapped. "I want them all dead, especially you know who."

A few weeks later it was done.

Thanks to CNN, he saw the whole thing rebroadcast a few hours later. Those assholes had filmed their own death.

"Boss," went Kim again. "This is really not safe, we gotta go."

"Come on, Doctor, that's enough!" Gorsky hollered through the open window. "We've gotta go now!"

He saw the old man shudder and stir slowly.

He told Kim to start the car, to speed things up.

The old man stooped against the gusts of wind, and walked stiffly towards the Range Rover. Behind him, he left the white walls swept by columns of dust and wind. All this would soon be nothing more than a memory in the rectangle of the rearview mirror.

The doctor settled in by his side, his face haggard. The 4X4 shifted onto the road. Gorsky heaved a sigh of ease.

He grabbed Walsh amiably by the shoulder.

"I have projects for you. Myriads of projects. You'll be able to realize all the mutant creatures of your dreams, Doctor. We're going to set up a real service 'a la carte'!"

The doctor stayed silent and twisted his neck trying to catch a last glimpse of the vestige of his past.

Gorsky was cheerful. He'd just received the latest Biodefender. Within a short week, his health had become stronger. He felt the front lines of the sickness retreat before the charges of the new immunity system. His total victory over the assholes of the sect, historic parallel to the biological conflict in the theater of operations of his body, would be inscribed in the secret archives of the Siberian mafia. The myth would soon flesh out. It would have the glorious accents of a decisive battle, Gettysburg, the Thermopylae…

He asked Kim to put on some classical Russian music, something brisk and lively. Kim drummed on his console and a section of Borodin's *In the Steppes of Central Asia* started playing almost immediately. It was simply perfect for the situation. Gorsky purred with joy, keeping time on his thigh with his hand.

It was a splendid day. The dusk was beautiful, a superbly ordered chaos of matter and light. Reddish and violet reflections played with the prism of the windshield. A bright red dot swept the cab.

Kim sketched a movement of the hands.

Neither he nor the others saw it coming. Maybe they heard the sound, that was it, a fraction of a second before impact.

The antitank precision multicharge rocket was fired from the west, along the sun's axis, with a forty-five degree angle. It hit the armored Range Rover near the front left fender. First a hole-drilling charge, with a passive uranium head and a directed blast of ten kilos of ammo towards the front. When its napalm reservoir exploded on the front seat, it had already killed everything alive inside.

The Kirghiz shepherds that discovered the charred remnants of the vehicle saw practically no human remains. It was about a week after the attack, according to the preliminary observations of the Russian Federal Police and the Kazakh authorities.

They found a few traces of footsteps and hoof prints about fifteen hundred meters from the point of impact, as well as the tubular residue of a rocket. It was concluded that two men had posted themselves at that spot with their firing system.

The only testimony corroborating this came from an old Kazakh who claimed to have crossed two men leaving an almost deserted village fifteen days before, about forty kilometers from there. The two men were on horseback and dragged along a heavily laden mule. A detail struck the old nomad: the two men looked exactly alike.

In the following weeks, many individuals died or disappeared without a trace around Novosibirsk. A few well-informed sources close to the Russian Federal Police spoke of a vast cleanup operation within the ranks of the regional mafia, after the death of a baron near an old abandoned military site in Kazakhstan. A so-called Boris Markov was discovered hacked into several pieces in a refrigerated truck near a butcher shop warehouse in a Novokuznetsk suburb. A captain of the Russian Army's intelligence services had apparently committed "suicide" in his car, on the road to Semipalatinsk. It was said a lieutenant colonel of the same GRU had disappeared a few months before. Later, they found the charred remains of a car in the lake reservoir of Krasnoyarsk, with the bodies of two ancient Spetznatz, two brothers who were involved with the Siberian mafia and who had probably been mixed up with Anton Gorsky's assassination.

Time goes by fast these days.

Somewhere in the Chingiz Mountains in Northeast Kazakhstan, desolate old buildings sink beneath the sand; a few nomadic shepherds venture by though they keep their distance. There are many rumors about them. It is said that secret military biological experiments were conducted there. Others affirm that the Russians wanted to discover the secrets of life and that a mysterious neurovirus slowly contaminating humanity was conceived there. Still others evoke the Siberian mafia and obscure tales of extraterrestrial prions, Kazakh style X-file shit. No one really knows.

And in fact, no one cares.

50

The seagull appeared out of nowhere. It drew a wide circle above them, then a smaller one, and seeing that nothing interesting lay within its reach, went back towards the open sea and, with a rapid dive, caught something floating on the surface of the waters.

Toorop filled his lungs with a great breath of saline air.

The sun was setting in the west. Any moment now, a ball of orange fire with dizzying rays would bring the horizon to a boil. Hands firmly gripping the bulwark, he stood up straight at the bow of the ship, devouring the sun, the sea, the sky, the clouds, the first stars, the air, the salt, the spray, the light, all the elements of the universe as if they were some vital food he needed to immediately consume.

At the stern of the ship, the wake from the powerful turbines formed long foaming eddies fading out towards the gray line of the western coast of Colombia, hazy in the distance.

The ship was a Japanese oceanographic research vessel that Dantzik and Darquandier's company had bought a few years before on a naval shipyard in Pakistan. It was beautiful, made for the open sea. It came to get them in the Hudson Strait, during the ice thaw in late July. They boarded a Yamaha-Navy, at night, with Darquandier, Robicek, Dantzik and the two babies wrapped in survival blankets. The motorboat brought them ten miles out of Cape Henrietta Maria, where a seaplane then chartered them to the northern tip of the Ungava Peninsula, off Cape New France, outside of Quebec waters.

Things started getting hot a few weeks after the birth of the babies. The Sureté was establishing untimely links between the Plateau Mont-Royal massacre and the collective "suicide" of the

Noelite Church. Quickly, things turned ill. The so-called Alexander Lawrence Thorpe, on the run, as well as James L. Osborne and Rebecca Kendall, both dead, were suspected of being intermediaries between the mafia groups and the sect for the transport of the viruses which caused the disaster of April 21st. Viruses that were also possibly implicated in the carnage of the previous summer. The pirating of the satellite was supposedly an electronic form of warfare raging in those circles. On the other hand, the Vancouver commercial airline company presumably employing these people had been under the spotlight of the Canadian Federal authorities for a while now. The company was suspected of being a front for a branch of the Russian Military Intelligence Services. A diplomatic crisis was brewing. The police reported that the individuals in question were also suspected of illegal activity related to the Osaka Charter, such as clandestine animal traffic. Then there was talk of a mysterious child-cloning program. The case of Myriam Klein knocked up with her two jokers had attracted police and news attention.

Around mid-July, exactly one year after his arrival in Quebec, just as Dantzik was putting the finishing touches on their exit plan, shit hit the fan. The charges included complicity in crimes against humanity, smuggling of military viruses and trafficking in illegal human transgenic products. In the meantime, several biker gang bosses were condemned for the Plateau carnage. The cops wanted to pursue the Logology Church, most probably behind the anti-Hell's Angels operation of summer 2013, with the Rock-Machines as middleman. A certain Conrad Frick, a German-French mercenary implicated in several assassination attempts by the Bandidos in Europe, had been on the wanted list for months. The cops affirmed that Kotcheff's Russian-American mafia was working for a Novosibirsk barony, directed by a certain Anton Gorsky, who'd been assassinated recently.

On the other hand, the name of a large multinational biotechnology company periodically showed up in the investigation reports. Apparently, two men killed on Rachel and Saint-Denis, who were linked to the Rock-Machines and provided security services for the Logologues, worked for that company as well.

Also, apparently, the so-called Kravczech, alias Charles Newton, had come into repeated contact with the so-called Thorpe. The Toyota discovered in front of his house was proof of that, as well as a certain Habbas, nicknamed Shadow, an illicit technology dealer, also missing since the end of the summer.

Toorop understood that Marie Zorn and her babies had interested a lot more people than he'd suspected. Rumor had it that Russian and American government agencies were now on it.

Bodies were coming up in clumps. It was bad. Definitely time to split.

The Zorn girls were already four months old, and they were growing fast. He had chosen their names. The old Black Bear Lamontagne had baptized them according to a Huron rite, and for Toorop that was as good as any Catholic priest could do.

Sara and Ieva Zorn. Sara-Ieva. It brought back memories—like a secret meaning linked to the bombed city of the telepathic link.

The day of the departure, Vax, Dantzik, and Darquandier stood before Marie's symbolic tomb on top of the building: a black monolith upon which the only inscription, Marie Z, and a simple date, ran alongside the steel glow of a horizontal double serpent. They'd dispersed ashes there. They left a few pathetic flowers in silence. Toorop searched his pockets in vain, and then remembered he'd sent one of his rings flying into the incinerator just before they'd put in Marie's body. It was an old silver piece, a Muslim ring with the name of Allah in the center and a stylized representation of the Kaaba on the sides. He'd gotten the ring in Brcko, a gift from a subaltern officer of the Bosnian Special Forces. It had survived a good half-dozen wars. It would make a good talisman for the Great Voyage.

When he left the terrace of antennas, knowing he'd never again set foot around here, and would never see Marie Zorn, her tomb, or the 10 Ontario building again, he felt something tighten violently in the pit of his stomach. It was strange, he knew that. He'd just barely slipped through the girl's life. They'd crossed paths at the last forking, they hadn't had time to live anything, not even the beginning of a normal relationship. The rare times he'd touched her was to move her from one place to another. He hadn't even taken advantage of it.

Yet their brains had communicated in a way that no human on this planet would ever be able to attain or imagine. Each unconscious had opened to the other, in a ritual and hallucinatory coupling that bordered on the divine.

Whether he liked it or not, he was now the father of the little girls. It didn't matter in the end whose they were, what they were, where they came from or why. What mattered was that Marie Zorn had carried and borne them. And that she died from it. What mattered was what they would become. The revelation had chilled him to the bone on that afternoon, a few seconds after Darquandier started unplugging the machines, one after another, from Marie's body. To be the father of such young girls meant a cascade of subsequent decisions. The first consisted in changing careers. It was urgent that he find some kind of training in civilian life. The problem of their mother would soon surface; he had to keep his head on his shoulders. But Dantzik had told him that, in the islands, notions of family life are freer than anywhere in the West. The girls would be raised among the inhabitants of the experimental island, with Amazonians and Natives.

On the boat, a professional nurse took care of them, a young woman from Costa Rica, a friend of Dantzik who'd come on board as they passed the Panama Canal. The girl was nice, she liked kids, she'd lived on the island, was immunized. Toorop adopted her immediately.

In front of him, the Pacific Ocean cleaved an immense shining blue space. He lifted his head.

High up there, beyond the icy azure of the sky, the satellite pirated by the Zorn twins continued, so they said, its hyperbolic flight towards Mars. The Cyborgs at 10 Ontario had managed to connect to the onboard sensors and were living it all live, from the inside, like an additional biocognitive outgrowth. Most statistic calculations predicted that the satellite would bounce off the orbit of the Red Planet and zoom towards the Gassy Giants and the limits of the system.

Toorop turned to the stern. Night had fallen on the Orient, where torrential rains had been pouring down for hours. Great hurricanes were supposed to hit the American tropics in the next few days. The American coast disappeared behind a veil of electric-blue mist on the horizon, as if an invisible border, of impenetrable density, separated him forever from his past existence.

Then he offered his face up to the western winds, to the light of dusk, and to the strange feeling of being in front of a new book waiting to be written.

Epilogue-Genesis

The Machine had been Marie Zorn. And all that Marie Zorn had been. Joe-Jane, neuronetwork-nanocircuitry-biomachine, had also been Eagle Davis, the Western Killer; Victorina Tedeschini, the Venetian aristocrat; the young Wong, from Shanghai. She had also been Marie Curie and all the virtual live creatures that Marie Zorn had ever carried. What difference did it make whether the creatures were inventions of the young woman's schizophrenic brain, or errant ghosts, souls in transit for whom creatures like Marie acted like windows onto the world of the living? Who cared about all these univocal, human, sensory categorizations? Marie was all of it at once, and more. For Marie was all the beings of Earth, she factorized all probability-creatures of life; in her, now, the two incarnations of the Cosmic Serpent took shape.

Joe-Jane loved them. She was their new mommy.

The twins were two identical and disjointed parts of the same force. Its simple coexistence inflamed critical mass. They were the divine and fatal explosives that would wipe humanity from the face of the earth, sending it back to archeology museums and to bad comedy movies which would enrapture the Successor of Man, just as the latter had joked about simple primates or Aborigines who'd survived since the Neolithic. Joe-Jane knew what such a sudden appearance meant, such a tectonics, such a compression of time in such a cataclysm-biology. The morality of human sentiments had but little hold there. A morality of plastic training seemed more pertinent. The Zorn twins would give birth to the post-human species that would leap to the limits of the solar system, and well beyond. The earth of their inception? Nothing more than their bedroom. Intergalactic space, black, infinite, fathomless? Their playground. Quantum and relativistic physics? No more complex than our arithmetic operations and our basic Euclidian geometry. The brain, DNA, sexuality, cloning? Instruments to serve their new horizon. They and their descendants would be the little brothers and sisters of stars, novas, pulsars and black holes; the cousins of quarks, gluons, bosons and neutrinos; the lovers of amino acids, fractals, neuromatrices and the big bang. They were-would be numerical saturation, Avogadro's number, Planck's constant, the set of all points in the infinity of a straight line, the number of all numbers, of all sets of numbers. They were-would be the children of Tsiolkovsky—hadn't the Russian cosmonautic once said: "The Earth is the cradle of the mind, but we cannot live forever in a cradle." But they were also the children of Crick and Watson, Einstein, Bohr, Darwin, Nietzsche and Heraclitus, for the same being that would come out of the cradle would not be the one born into it. Of course, a critical adaptation was necessary for such an evolution, just as it had been for man's appearance in his small African niche, then in all the niches of the world once they became viable. When Marie Zorn's descendants would be born in space, within a few decades, they would have full consciousness that their life embraced the parsecs separating the sun from the neighboring stars, and that this limit was within their reach.

Joe-Jane knows it. Sara and Ieva Zorn were, are, will be this new limit, as well as its scaling. They are before the doors of that universe, and everything points to the fact that their famished brain-stomach can digest it. They are the devourers of stars, blowers of photons, fuckers of thermodynamic hydrogen in fusion, agitators of the square of light, sumptuous exterminators of the human failure. They are crucial destruction, as much end as beginning. They are cardinal, formally new, shock waves in wait around a point of impact that has already exploded, and is for now suspended in the frozen time of history's video camera. They delight in the effect to come, when all the energy contained there will brutally actualize, delivering a blast, a seism, a cyclone, whose amplitude and form no one can yet predict.

Maurice G. Dantec

SEMIOTEXT(E) SCI-FI

"Time to look beyond this rundown radioactive cop-ridden planet."
— William S. Burroughs

Reinhabiting the tradition of philosophical and political fable, Semiotext(e) is introducing a new science-fiction series under the Native Agents imprint. Debuting with Maurice Dantec's futurist-noir epic *Babylon Babies* and Mark von Schlegell's dystopian fantasy novel *Venusia*, these books speak to the present demise by assembling radical models for unlikely futures. Speculatively accelerated, Semiotext(e) Sci-Fi presents exciting new models for living the deterritorialized life.